Acclaim for *The Single Mum's Wish List*

'What fabulous, confident writing! One of the freshest, funniest, most exciting new voices I've read for a long time.' Jane Fallon

'A warm and insightful debut with a clever, funny and totally relatable heroine.' *Sunday Express*

'Very funny and delightfully relatable – this was a real treat.' Trisha Ashley

'We've all been a "Martha Ross" at some point, so we loved this hilarious and moving novel about starting afresh.' *Take a Break*

'Fresh and funny and REAL . . . Martha really spoke to me. She will steal everyone's heart!' Veronica Henry

'Beautifully written and emotionally intelligent. I rooted for Martha from the start.' Sara Lawrence, *Daily Mail*

Also by Charlene Allcott

THE SINGLE MUM'S WISH LIST

and published by Corgi Books

More THAN A Mum

Charlene Allcott

CORGI BOOKS

TRANSWORLD PUBLISHERS
61–63 Uxbridge Road, London W5 5SA
www.penguin.co.uk

Transworld is part of the Penguin Random House group of companies
whose addresses can be found at global.penguinrandomhouse.com

First published in Great Britain in 2020 by Corgi Books
an imprint of Transworld Publishers

A CIP catalogue record for this book
is available from the British Library.

ISBN 9780552175807

Typeset in 10.75/13.5pt Sabon LT Std by Jouve (UK), Milton Keynes.
Printed and bound in Great Britain by Clays Ltd, Elcograf S.p.A.

Penguin Random House is committed to a sustainable
future for our business, our readers and our planet. This book
is made from Forest Stewardship Council® certified paper.

1 3 5 7 9 10 8 6 4 2

For all the mums, especially mine.

1

THERE WAS A time when I blamed Dylan. For quite a
while actually; a month or so, certainly. It's easier
than you would think to decide that everything is someone else's fault. And it was particularly satisfying to pass
the mantle of blame to Dylan, because my husband did
everything with an enviable ease. Almost all situations he
met with a stoic presentation of calm. At first I found this
trait appealing, but I grew to hate it like a kitten that's
initially such a delight and then pisses all over your favourite rug.

I grew so adept at the blame game that I believed I was
able to pinpoint the very sentence that sent our lives hurt-
ling at full pelt towards Shitsville. Dylan said, 'I think I'll
take Mickey up on his offer.' As he spoke, his eyes were
trained on the crossword on his lap, and in that moment it
occurred to me how self-indulgent crosswords are. They
require so much time and isolation; if you're in a room
with a person but that person is also doing a crossword,
you're barely with them at all.

'You really want to go fishing on Saturday?' I asked. I
can recall the effort I made to keep my tone even. I didn't
want him to hear an admonishment but an opportunity.

'Not especially, but Mick has been having a bad time

of late.' Mickey was Dylan's best mate – not really a friend, if assessed by the normal requirements of the role; more of a relic from childhood. A thin, wiry man with greasy hair never quite covered by a tweed cap, Mickey was harmless really, or at least the only harm he ever did was to himself. He was always entering or leaving another toxic relationship, or losing what little money he had in an ill-advised business 'opportunity'. He had a skittish energy that made it draining to be around him for extended periods, and a propensity to cry with little to no warning. One Christmas he had nowhere to go and we let him join our family celebration. He started weeping as the pudding was lit, and when we cleared the kitchen later in the evening, my mother asked, 'Is he one of those crack heads, Ally?' Mickey was the kind of person I would have let drift from my life a long time ago. Dylan didn't let things drift; it was one of the reasons I loved him. I'd like to think that at any other time I would have respected his commitment and his willingness to give his free time to someone so intent on wasting their own, but the Saturday in question was *the* Saturday, the first in a month of Saturdays that we would all be together – no work, no parties or play dates. Nothing but us. It was on the calendar next to the fridge: 'Family Day' in red biro.

I wanted to say, 'Do you know who else is having a bad time? The woman you snore contentedly next to every night, the one who caught your thirteen-year-old daughter studying a wet-T-shirt competition on YouTube and who is ignoring the mould she found in the cupboard under the stairs – even though Google told her it might well be toxic – and who supports this family with a job she blagged her way into and could be unceremoniously sacked from at any moment.' I didn't say that. I didn't say any of that.

2

What I said was, 'If that's what you want to do, babe.' And even though I didn't mean a word of it, I can only assume that's what he heard, because a few minutes later he put down his crossword and went down to the shed to seek out his waterproof trousers.

Dylan and the kids had got me a gadget that measures your sleep. When I opened it on my birthday, our youngest, Chloe, shouted, 'We knew you'd love it, coz you're always too tired!' The device lived on my wrist and would dutifully tell me how much sleep I'd had each night and, through the magic of technology, the quality of said sleep. The morning after Dylan abandoned our family day, after Chloe had forced me from slumber, screaming my name, I took a moment to look at it. I had had three hours and twenty-four minutes of 'good quality sleep'. I wasn't even sure I believed that. I shoved it into the bed-side drawer.

'What?' I called out. Chloe burst into the room. I made a mental note to advise her later that 'what?' is not an invitation. Her usually pale face was a vibrant pink; she was breathing heavily and, seeing her distress, my motherly instinct kicked in. I scrambled out of bed and pulled my dressing gown on. Chloe began shaking her head. I grabbed hold of her shoulders in order to gain her attention. 'What's wrong, darling?'

'I need a mask,' she cried, and started sobbing. I let my hands fall.

'For fuck's sake,' I muttered. Chloe stopped crying and her eyebrows shot up towards her hairline. 'I mean, why?' I said. I pressed my fingers against my temples. 'Why do you need a mask? Now?' Chloe began to hop from foot to foot. I noticed her pyjama bottoms only reached the middle of her shins.

'It's a cooompetition!' she wailed.

'Dylan,' I hissed. My husband sat up slowly and rubbed his palm over his face a couple of times.

'What's going on, sweetheart?' Chloe leapt into the space I had vacated and nestled her head against her father's chest. He gently ran his fingers through her hair as she outlined her crisis. Her class was studying the Egyptians and each child was supposed to make an Egyptian burial mask. The winner would get a big book about the pyramids, and she wanted the book, and also Ms Khavari was really, really mean and she would definitely be made to miss playtime for her indiscretion.

'It's OK,' whispered Dylan. 'We'll fix it.' Chloe sighed happily.

'How?' I enquired sharply. 'How exactly will we fix it?' Dylan untangled himself from Chloe and shrugged.

'I'll buy her one on the way to school.' Dylan gave Our daughter a quick kiss before lying back down and pulling the duvet up to his neck. I resisted the urge to drag it from his body.

'Where, pray tell, do you plan to find an Egyptian burial mask at eight in the morning? The petrol station?' Dylan grunted in response. 'It's fine! I'll sort it.' I retied my dressing gown and searched its pockets for a hair band. Finding nothing, I resorted to pulling my fine auburn hair into a knot. As soon as I had done so, I felt it unravel. 'I'll sort it like I sort everything.' Chloe and Dylan glanced at each other. I hated it when they did that and they did it often, it made me feel like an outsider in my own home.

On the way to the kitchen I thumped on the door of our eldest, Ruby.

'I don't have to be awake for twenty minutes!' she screamed.

'Good morning! I love you!' I called back.

Ruby wandered into the kitchen after me, and rested her chin on her hands as she watched me pull the contents from a packet of cornflakes and cut a ragged oval from the box.

'What are you doing?' she asked.

'I'm making an Egyptian burial mask,' I answered, as I stabbed eyeholes into the cardboard.

'Why?'

I sighed.

'I thought it might be a fun way to start the day.' Ruby didn't respond. 'It's for your sister,' I added.

'Bet you wouldn't make a burial mask for me,' she said, before yawning without covering her mouth. I looked at her; her face was impassive. At some point between dinner the previous evening and that moment, she had acquired a streak of blue in her hair. I thought, I carried you around inside me; I fed you from my own breasts, wilfully destroying them in the process, and this is what I get?

I had hated pregnancy, every single second of it. The physical strain was bad but the emotional toll was worse. When I got a positive test I cried, not happy tears but from the shock of the sudden realization that my life as I knew it was about to be stolen from me. I was waiting by the door when Dylan got in from work that evening, and as soon as he saw my face he knew. He picked me up and spun me around in circles, and then he wouldn't stop apologizing, stroking my still-flat stomach protectively.

'It's fine,' I told him. 'Nothing's changed.' But I was wrong.

'I *would* make you a burial mask. Do you want a burial mask?' Ruby took my effort and held it up to her face. She could only look through one of the eyeholes at a time.

'No, thank you,' she said, and placed it on the counter. 'Can I have some coffee?' she asked, as she dragged a bowl from the cupboard and poured the abandoned cereal into it. Flakes littered the counter top in the process. She left them there as she carried the bowl to the fridge.

'No. Why is your hair blue?' Ruby left the fridge door open as she poured milk on to her breakfast.

'It's not blue, it has a blue highlight. Megan does it.' Ruby returned to the counter to eat. I retraced her steps to close the fridge door before cleaning up the cereal and cardboard.

'Who's Megan?' I asked. 'Is she in your year at school?' I used to know everything. I knew how long she slept, when and what she ate, and she'd give me a running commentary of every thought that crossed her mind. Now whatever was on her mind was hidden behind a curtain of sneers and eye rolls.

Ruby carefully finished her mouthful before saying, 'She's not a kid. She's a guru.' Panic broke through my exhaustion and I felt my breathing become shallow.

'Sweetie, what have you been watching? Is it some sort of religious sect?' Ruby crossed her eyes. I could only assume this was a reaction to my lack of education.

'It's nothing to do with sex. She's a beauty guru on You-Tube.' She said this last word forcefully, as if challenging me to reveal my complete ignorance by asking her what this was. Of course, I knew what YouTube was. I was a marketing manager. She should really be asking me about YouTube, and I would direct her to a series of videos on motherless children and perhaps spark the merest flicker of gratitude within her.

Dylan walked in with Chloe on his back. He was wearing black tracksuit bottoms and a grey T-shirt, ready for

6

his daily run after dropping Chloe at school. As he helped her to the floor, I watched the muscles in his shoulders move against the thin material of his top. He still had a great body, but then he hadn't birthed two children, and had time to himself to use for exercise.

'Did you do my mask?' Chloe asked me giddily. I handed her my cornflake-box creation. 'Thank you?' she said slowly.

Oh, I'm sorry, I thought, do my artistic efforts not meet your exacting standards? I pulled open the drawer that holds all the unclassifiable items in the kitchen, pulled out a few felt tips and handed them to her.

'Decorate it in the car,' I said. She considered my suggestion and, clearly having no other options, gave me a quick hug before throwing both the pen and the mask on the kitchen table and asking her dad for something to eat.

'You wanna lift or you walking?' Dylan asked Ruby, as he fed bread into the toaster.

'Thanks, Dad, but I think I'll walk.' Just like that – no faces, no character assassination.

'I'm going for a shower,' I said to no one in particular.

'All right, babe,' Dylan said, with his eyes trained on the toaster. 'We'll probably be gone by the time you get out.'

'Have a good day,' I said. I waited for him to look up, to smile, maybe to kiss me. His toast popped up and I left the room.

I always have the shower as hot as I can take it. I enjoy dancing the line between pleasure and pain. As I smooshed shampoo into my scalp, I focused on erasing the irritation that had grown within me. I pictured it flowing down the drain with the suds. I clenched my teeth as I heard the faint thud of the front door being slammed, and knew it hadn't been successful.

The morning might not have unfolded precisely like that. The blue streak was definitely there around that time, and it may have been the morning of the Victorian costume and not the death mask, but there was no kiss – that much I know is true.

2

'MORNING, BETTY,' I SAID, before getting myself positioned at my desk. It's important to greet your colleagues in the morning. People judge you by how you are and not what you do.

Bettina looked up from her monitor and let her eyes return to the screen before saying, 'You have jam on your top.' I pushed my chin into my chest; a splodge of red was sliding down my pale-blue shirt. Breakfast had been a doughnut, hastily consumed whilst wedged between fellow commuters on the Northern line.

'Shit!' I clawed through my bag for a tissue and found only one that had been minimally used. I swiped at the jam, only succeeding at expanding the circumference of the stain. 'Shit!' I said again.

'You need club soda,' Bettina said in a matter of fact tone. I threw the tissue back into the wasteland of my handbag.

'Where am I supposed to get that?' Bettina shrugged. I covered my face with my hands and contemplated hiding like that for the remainder of the day.

'Here,' said Bettina, the faintest hint of a sigh in her voice. 'You can wear my jacket.' I drew my hands away to see her thrusting the navy-blue blazer in my direction. To the uninitiated, Bettina can come across as a bit of a bitch, but she simply favours plain delivery. She puts this down to her Italian parentage. Italians, she says, don't smother things in unnecessary extras – food, clothes, advice – it's all about the best-quality essentials, without fuss. She may be harsh but she's honest and, as she had at that moment, she comes through. For me, one generous act is worth a thousand platitudes.

I stood up and slipped the jacket on. It was far too big. I'm small, five foot one (I would guess, but I've made no effort to confirm it) and a size eight (although nothing is firm any more). In my younger days, my size made me feel petite and girlish, but by my thirties, I just felt short. Bettina is about five foot nine, more in heels, which she almost always wears. She's all curves, so shapely she makes any item – the chunkiest polo neck and the baggiest cardigan – look outlandishly sexy. Bettina is what the internet calls a 'real woman', making me some sort of woman in training. She walked round to my desk, readjusted the shoulders of the blazer, and rolled up each sleeve a couple of turns.

'Oh no, I can't,' I said, cringing as she creased the beautiful material.

'You don't have a choice,' she said. Bettina stood back and surveyed her work before nodding in satisfaction. 'You look cool.' She wouldn't have said it if it wasn't true. 'You can't stand in front of everyone looking like you've been stabbed.'

'Stand in front of everyone?'

'You're presenting the Emerge conference plan at team catch-up,' she said, one immaculate eyebrow raised.

'Yes, of course,' I said, scrambling back into my seat. 'Just got to print a few things off.' I switched on my computer and opened the Emerge file. It was empty. It's not that I didn't work hard – I worked extremely hard. I just worked hard at the wrong things.

Pepperpot Communications provided marketing and social media strategies to businesses. It was a young company. Young in that it had only been formed a few years ago by Carter, the introverted but iron-willed director, but also young in that the office was populated by children. Most of the team were in their twenties; the women had high spirits and low necklines, and the guys injected a boisterous competitiveness into every act. I didn't resent their youth, but I was intimidated by it. Their brains were so malleable, they seemed to absorb information without even trying, and they weren't afraid of making stupid suggestions because they were supposed to be making stupid suggestions.

I had experience – experience of printing a thousand flyers at short notice and coming up with the best wording for a mailshot – but experience that had become invalidated by time and Apple. I spent most of my evenings desperately trying to get up to speed on the latest digital innovations, only to see the self-satisfied smirks of my colleagues when I pronounced 'meme' as two words. The sad thing is, I think my age was in part why Carter hired me. I remember coming for the interview – I'd been out of work for three months and we were living off the dying embers of my redundancy cheque. The fact that he'd only called me in as a favour to his mother, who took the same life drawing class as my aunt, was heavy on my mind. I researched the company with greater diligence than I had my university thesis, so I knew that the environment would be vibrant and youthful, but I was unprepared for the air hockey in the foyer and the green juice the receptionist brought to me before wandering off, leaving me staring helplessly at her denim-clad bottom.

Carter came out to collect me himself. He was the only person in the building wearing a suit, a suit so exquisite I had to resist the temptation to stroke it rather than shake his extended hand. He looked tired but handsome; his skin still bore the trace of a recent stint in a warmer climate, and his dark hair was so well cut that the handful of grey strands looked intentional.

'Thanks for coming,' he said, before leading me to his office – a glass-walled cube in a corner of the building which immediately made me feel like a guppy in an aquarium.

'Thanks for having me,' I said as we sat. 'I mean, thanks for seeing me.'

'That's fine,' he said. He opened a leather-bound notebook and studied me briefly, as if weighing up whether I was worth sullying the soft, cream pages, before picking up his pen. 'Tell me what you're about.'

I launched into my prepared speech, outlining general marketing strategies and what I hoped were innovative plans to engage with customers. Carter looked stylishly bored. Sensing I was losing him, I ceased my monologue. In that moment I became tired of pretending. I had spent weeks maintaining an I've-got-everything-in-order front to friends, family and ex-colleagues – even I wasn't buying it any more.

'I can see you've got a lot of young staff in here, and I'm sure they're full of fire and all that good stuff, but what do they know about drive? Drive is when you've got a mortgage to pay and kids needing a constant stream of shit. And the people you're selling to – company owners – they're me, they're my peers. I'm sure your team is full of bright ideas, but I'll have the ideas that speak to your clients because I *am* them.' Carter put his pen down.

'Sorry about saying "shit".' He cleared his throat before speaking.

'Where did you buy?'

'Hackney.'

'A good investment,' he said with a brisk nod.

'I hope so,' I whispered. Carter glanced down at my CV before looking at me with his eyes narrowed. I believe that in that moment he decided I was a decent fixer-upper.

The problem with gratitude is that it makes you vulnerable. From the moment Carter called to offer me the role, I lived with the sense that I owed him, and part of that meant not revealing where I was failing. I could postpone the presentation, ask for more time, and Carter would probably be cool with it, but I'd still feel like I was letting him down. I did a quick search on social media marketing for conferences and printed off a few pages. I stuck those on to a clipboard I found in my desk drawer.

'How's it going?' asked Annie. Annie was my assistant, officially. When Carter asked me if I needed help, I had answered emphatically that I was fine. Eventually he presented her like a new puppy one morning. He sent me a follow-up email explaining that I should offer her the benefit of my expertise and that she might be able to help me out with my workload. Annie even had the energy of a puppy, albeit a frighteningly ambitious one. On her first day, I told her to read through the client folders, and a few hours later she had reorganized the entire filing system. At five she came to me to ask for feedback. Annie has delicate features and curly blonde hair, and as she stood before me, her blue-grey eyes wide, she looked angelic. I told her honestly that she had been brilliant, really helpful and full of good ideas. I told her to let me know if there were any of my projects she particularly wanted to work on. She beamed.

As she left the room I heard Bettina mutter, 'Big mistake.'

'*Pretty Woman*?' I said with a laugh.

'I don't know what you're talking about,' said Bettina, in a way that made clear she had no interest to.

'The film. Are you quoting *Pretty Woman*?'

'Oh yeah,' said Bettina, 'that one about a woman who fails to recognize a conniving little witch after her job?' I made myself laugh. It went against everything I tried to believe in to buy into the competitive-woman stereotype. Still, when Bettina spoke I listened, and it wasn't long before I started to reflect differently on my words of encouragement. As the weeks went on, I felt Annie wasn't so much watching me as examining me; not learning from me but learning about me, so that she might know my weaknesses. Her eyes flitted over my desk as she asked me how things were going.

'All good, thanks. Just having a minute to myself to prep for the meeting.' Annie glanced at my computer screen, still open to Google.

'Anything I can help with?' she asked with a sweet smile.

'I'd love a cup of tea,' I said, and watched her smile fade momentarily. It hadn't occurred to me before then that she probably hated me a little bit. I remember being young and ambitious and thinking I knew more than my superiors, only in my case, I was probably wrong. By the time Annie had brought me my drink, the meeting was due to start. I thanked her and took a couple of mouthfuls, despite the fact it was still scalding hot.

'Do you need me to carry anything for you?' Annie asked. I stood up purposefully.

'Thanks, I have everything I need.' I patted my clipboard. Annie gave a little frown.

'OK then. I've done a bit of research if you want it later. Emerge is a complex one. I'm sure you'll be great.' She turned on her heel and marched off to the meeting room. She liked to arrive promptly, get a seat at the front. Bettina shook her head.

'Don't say anything,' I warned her.

'I haven't and I won't, but if I did I'd say bring your A game, Ally.'

Carter was sharing some company news as I settled at the back of the room.

'We'll probably switch to a new client-management system in July.' There were a few murmurs of approval. I slid down my chair; I had only just got my head around the last one. When the room was full, he announced the morning's agenda: I was up first.

'So, Emerge,' I said carefully, 'as in arrive, turn up, show up, spurt.' There was a snort from the back of the room. I probably should have edited the list I printed from the online thesaurus. I flipped the page. 'Anyway, the plans for launching this conference are to –' I glanced down at my printed sheet – 'create an online buzz using quality advertisements focused on the conference's main objectives.' I paused to let my words sink in.

'Which are?' asked a guy called Tom. Tom's brawny, six-foot-something frame seemed to contradict his thin, plummy voice. He always had over-gelled hair and his face, when at rest, formed a scowl. He was in charge of video production for the organization, so his question may have been a valid desire to understand the tone of his future work, but I couldn't shake the feeling that it was an attempt to trip me up and enjoy the fall. I waved my hand around, hoping to convey that I was leading up to something important, but I was trying to buy myself

15

time because I could not for the life of me remember the brief.

'Do you know the feeling you have when you're creating something, when you start to gain momentum and there's a point when you feel like you've taken off and after that you're flying? This conference wants to sum that up.' I reeled off some vague and completely fabricated statistics about the effect of community on personal growth and the significance of leadership. As I spoke, I heard some murmurs within the group, but my discomfort didn't offer me the headspace to assess the tone of the reaction I was receiving. I decided the important thing was that I had said something; I could iron out the details later.

'Thanks, Alison,' said Carter, when I was silent for long enough to indicate I had finished. 'Elle, do you want to update us on the financials?' Elle, a kind-faced, quiet woman, stood up and smoothed down her short black dress. She walked purposefully to the front of the room, and gently but firmly pushed me aside so she could take my space. She pressed a button on a small remote in her hand and a large projector behind us came alive, displaying a colourful pie chart.

'This is an overview of this quarter's spend,' said Elle. I took my seat and focused on looking engaged for the rest of the hour.

'It was good,' said Annie as I shredded the papers from my clipboard, 'absolutely fine.'

'Thanks, Annie,' I said, although I was not particularly grateful for her answer to a question I hadn't asked.

'But I was thinking that maybe I could send out an email, with an overview of the aims and how we can support the conference. You know – for clarity.'

'Sure. That might be helpful.'

I returned to my desk and scoured my inbox for the original brief. My throat grew tighter as I read it – Emerge was an event for orthodontists and not, as I had assumed, some form of spiritual-growth seminar.

'What was that?' asked Bettina from behind her monitor.

'What do you mean?'

'In the meeting – you were just rambling.' I rubbed the back of my neck to try and ease out the tension that had been growing there throughout the morning.

'It wasn't that bad, was it?'

'It was that bad,' said Bettina bluntly. 'What's going on? Trouble at home?'

'No, nothing like that.'

'Problems with the kids?'

'No. I mean, no more than usual.'

'Dylan then?'

'No, of course not. Everything's fine,' I said, and I had no idea why that made me feel so nervous.

3

EVERYTHING *WAS* FINE. My children were healthy and, whilst not always happy, they had no real reason to be unhappy. Dylan was the same affable, easy-going guy I had met fifteen years before. The person I was at that time is unrecognizable to me now, but in all those years, Dylan had hardly changed. A few grey hairs around his temples, one or two fewer beers of an evening, but he was more or less the same man who'd pulled up to my house in a Corsa to collect a frightened twenty-two-year-old girl. Dylan had been my driving instructor. I'd just graduated and was working in a pub whilst trying to secure a job in PR. Nothing seemed to be panning out as I had been promised. I had believed that if I worked hard and tried not to stuff up too much, I would leave university with the door to a sparkling career wide open, and maybe a soon-to-be fiancé as a bonus. The reality was that my on/off (but more off than on) boyfriend David had dumped me in the middle of my final exams. The rejection resulted in more time spent crying than revising, and three years of study ending in an academic whimper. With no experience, I was having difficulty convincing an employer to look past my uninspiring grades. I lived in the box room of a shared house in North London. My housemates' only ambitions were to out-party each other. The eldest was a thirty-six-year-old man who scraped together a living writing pornography – I was very keen to find a new tribe.

I decided that learning to drive might be my ticket out of there. My own transport would allow me to move somewhere cheaper and look for jobs further afield; and more than that, it would give me a sense that I was taking control of my life. I needed my foot on the accelerator. I had next to no money. I kept a weekly food budget of eleven pounds, which I managed to achieve by exclusively buying food in plain white packaging. My transport budget was even more meagre, which meant walking miles across the city every week. I chose Dylan as an instructor for no other reason than he was very, very cheap.

When I opened my door to find him there in ripped jeans and a T-shirt, the sleeves rolled up over his firm biceps, I admit I took a second out of my nervousness to note that there was an attractive man before me. Everything, from the deep tone of his greeting to his handshake, so strong I could feel the throb a few minutes later, shouted 'man'. Everything except his smile, which was that of a mischievous little boy, and remained on his face the entire time I told him my fears about the open road. When I had finished relaying the various ways in which I could very possibly die, he grabbed my hand. I remember thinking it wasn't the most professional move but I didn't want him to let go.

Dylan spent the entire hour trying to fill me with reassurance. He was largely unsuccessful. At the end of the lesson I pulled up a few metres from the house and I could almost smell the relief that filled the car.

'You did well,' said Dylan.

'I did not,' I said, and then started to cry. It may have

been an overspill of adrenaline but it felt like more than that. Looking back, I think I was weeping from the recognition that it might never be easy to get what I wanted.

'Let's get a pint,' said Dylan. I nodded my head.

Set up in the shady boozer round the corner from my house, I was able to focus on the man before me. He had a way of cocking his head when I was talking that made it feel as if he was really listening, trying to hear something beyond the words. He encouraged me to tell him about the messy unravelling of my relationship. I asked him about his own romantic history.

'I got divorced last year,' he said. I felt ashamed. This was a real-world, grown-up problem; I was still playing around in the sandpit of life. 'Yeah, it was hard but necessary. Some people are only meant to be in our lives for a limited time.' I laughed.

'Like you,' I said. 'After I get my licence, we'll never see each other again.'

'That's why I like my job,' said Dylan. 'I get to come into people's lives and help give them this . . . gift. And then never see them again.' I raised my glass.

'I look forward to never seeing you again,' I said. Dylan knocked his pint against my wine glass.

'To never seeing you again.'

Of course, it didn't work out like that. The day I passed my test, I ran across the centre car park waving my certificate in the air. When I reached Dylan, waiting anxiously in the doorway, he grabbed the paper from me and without pausing to look at it, he kissed me. I don't know if he had been waiting until the end of our professional partnership or was just caught up in the moment, but I know that it was welcome and did not feel unexpected.

Following that, we were largely inseparable. When Dylan

20

was at lessons I'd wait in his bed, eager to return to snack-based meals and action films. Dylan educated me on the finer points of Arnold Schwarzenegger movies and, despite a hatred of guns, car chases and very unsubtle good-versus-evil plotlines, I found myself falling for them. He made everything, even the mundane, better. When I worked my shifts in the pub, Dylan would sit in a corner, nursing an ale and completing his crosswords. He told me he wanted to keep an eye on the (primarily geriatric) regulars and he would wait until I had cashed up, wiped down all the tables, and swept the cigarette-butt-strewn floors before walking home with me. As I remember it, when we weren't sleeping, we were laughing. That's what I remember, nothing but laughter. Dylan knew all the bouncers in London and, when it seemed necessary to expose ourselves to the potentially dangerous influence of those outside our gang of two, we would head out for a dance. He was never the best mover; I was always slightly nervous for the unfortunate souls who found themselves beside him, but he did it because I liked it, and seeing him jam along with live bands and drunkenly chat to students from Barcelona felt like I was getting a glimpse at a completely different side to him. And I liked that side to him, but I also liked the quiet, steady, patient parts of him. Despite having been burned by marriage before, Dylan wasn't bitter. If anything, he seemed determined to do it again and do it properly. He asked me to marry him after we had been dating for six months; I laughed and told him to ask me again in a year and he did, to the day.

Dylan supported me through my first marketing internship, boiling pasta and running baths, ensuring that I didn't have to worry too much about how to stretch the pittance a multi-million-pound company was offering each week.

I think it was the ease with which he cared for me that inspired the idea that he could be a good father; one who would be present and proactive, the kind my mother told me would be impossible to find. But ideas are only sketches, scribbled quickly and lacking in detail. The theory became practice and it didn't match up to the picture I'd had in my head. Everyone told us that children change things; I hadn't realized they meant *everything*. We didn't make a childcare plan because I'd assumed it would be obvious – he'd help when help is needed and perhaps occasionally when it's not.

I cried when we found a childminder for Ruby. She was five months old. Dylan held me and allowed my nose to run on to his T-shirt but offered nothing else, not to work less and have the baby or to work harder so that I could be at home. When I collected her at the end of the day and she would fall asleep in the back, sated by care that I should have been giving, I would cry again in the dark of the parked car, careful to recompose my face before carrying her into the house. So, to some degree the deceit started long ago.

Everyone said it would get easier as they got older, but by then I knew better than to listen to everyone. There was even more to organize – parties, play dates and school places – and it seemed like I had even less help to get it done. Dylan didn't change other than to become a slightly opaque version of the man I had met. His tendency towards introversion blossomed into a personality trait, and the drive I thought he might develop was nowhere to be seen. Even the girls knew that I was the general and Dylan my lieutenant, and every working day offered a window of peace until half past three, when the missives would roll in: 'WHERE IS MY SWIMMING COSTUME???' 'WHAT DID WE SAY ABOUT PIERCINGS?' 'CAN WE GET A GERBIL.

PLEASE. PLEASE. PLEASE.' I rarely complained because it wasn't exactly a hardship. There were no helplines for married mothers with two well-rounded children, but when I was made redundant I picked up a newspaper for the first time in years and read a piece about emotional labour, how it was not the doing that was exhausting but the being – being all things to everyone. But even after I knew it, I couldn't stop, because you can't change course without something to push you from the path.

I decided to call Dylan and pre-empt any afternoon interruptions, but as I reached for the phone Carter tapped my desk.

'I wanted to ask you to attend an event tonight.' That was unexpected. He'd just watched me crash and burn in the team meeting and yet he was offering me extra responsibilities. 'It's a book launch – personal development meets business meets hipster aspirations. I'm not really interested, but from what you were saying you seem to have caught the bug. I want you to network with the attendees, see if there's any potential new clients.'

'Tonight . . . I'm not sure I can.' It's not that I had anything on, it's that I didn't want anything on. There was a mint Aero with my name on it in the fridge. It literally had my name on it: a hot-pink Post-it with 'MUM' in block capital letters.

'I'll send you the details,' said Carter, appearing uninterested in my indecisiveness. 'Think about it.' Something about the way he said this made me take the words as both an offering and a warning. I opened my emails so that I could be ready when he sent through the information.

'Don't go,' said Bettina. Not advice: an instruction.

'I should take the opportuni—'

'It's not an opportunity,' she interrupted. 'It's a chore.

Don't you think if there was anyone worth meeting, he would go himself? You wouldn't catch me there.' I didn't think that was relevant – Bettina did copy and would have no reason to go. 'Come for a drink with the OAPs.' The OAPs were myself, Bettina, Marcus who managed IT, and occasionally Dee the part-time bookkeeper. Dee was in her fifties; Marcus was thirty-seven and loved any opportunity to seek dating advice from the female side; Bettina's age was officially classified, but her in-depth knowledge of nineties pop music suggested to me that she was safely past thirty. I liked our evenings together. Having a drink with them after a day with the kids at work felt like slipping off tight shoes. I could be myself; I didn't have to feel anxious about not knowing the hidden or explicit meaning behind Jay-Z's latest album. As I weighed up the options in my mind, I received two new emails. The first was an overview from Annie, the second the details from Carter with a postscript that he would be offering Emerge to Annie, to create space for me to pick up a new client.

'I'll go for a drink next week. I should go to this thing.'

'Ask Annie to go with you.'

'Why would I do that?' I was flummoxed; Bettina constantly counselled me to try and keep Annie reined in, and here she was suggesting I hand over an advantage like a piece of gum.

'She definitely won't go, and maybe that fact will get it into your head what a waste of time it is.' Although spending more of my day with Annie than necessary was a hideous concept, I wanted to prove Bettina wrong.

'Annie!' I called.

'Yep,' she said from behind me. I turned to face her desk and watched her type for another minute before stacking some papers and coming over.

'Was the brief OK?' she asked as she approached.

'It was fine. It was good.' I had wanted to tell her she should have sent it to me for review first, but I wasn't sure how to frame it. My boss at my first position after interning, Reginald Peterson, a loquacious man with a habit of taking long lunches with female, junior staff members, had taught me about the shit sandwich – negative feedback should be delivered with two bread slices of praise. The concept was really brought home when he later handed me a couple of stale compliments with a deep filling of firing. In that moment I couldn't think of two nice things to say to Annie, so I made a mental note to come back to it.

'I wanted to invite you to an event tonight. It's the book launch for a bestselling author – it looks like there might be a significant opportunity to engage some new clientele.' Annie hesitated, a very unusual occurrence.

'Hmmmm,' she said.

'Hmmmm, as in yes?' Annie became very interested in the cuff of her shirtsleeve.

'I'm doing a thing, actually.'

'A thing?'

'Yeah, been planned for a while. Sorry.' I turned away from her.

'No problem.' I listened to Annie walk away.

'My point,' said Bettina, 'is if it were an opportunity, she'd be on it like a rat on a carcass.'

'Point taken,' I said. I was drafting a response to Carter in my head when my line rang and, as though I had summoned him, he was on the other end.

'Annie's accepted Emerge. You might be able to pick something up tonight. Something you can be more invested in.'

'Thanks,' I said, although I wasn't entirely sure what I was thanking him for. I turned to look for Annie but she had scarpered. Carter hung up; he didn't really have time for goodbyes. I called home without dropping the receiver.

'Yup?' I heard Ruby say.

'That's not how we answer the phone,' I said.

'It is how we answer the phone, I just did it a few seconds ago.' Ruby began to laugh energetically. I could picture her throwing herself back against the sofa, her long dark curls tumbling around her face.

'Where's your dad?' I asked.

'Gone. I killed him.' I closed my eyes.

'Get your dad.' Ruby screamed for her father several times. I heard the muffled sound of a negotiation before he came on.

'Babe,' he said cheerily.

'What's she getting you to do?' I asked sharply.

'Rubes? Nothing. She wants to download some app.'

'Don't let her get any social networking, she's on a break.'

'Yeah . . . OK,' said Dylan. 'Wait, why were you calling?'

'What did you let her download?'

'Shall we deal with it later?' Dylan's voice dropped a level as he said this, speaking in a tone that he clearly hoped might placate me, as one would with a vicious animal. I tried to push images of my daughter being groomed by Romanian people smugglers out of my mind.

'Fine. I have to stay late tonight – something came up. Is that OK?' Say no, I thought. Say no, say no.

'Yeah,' said Dylan, 'that's fine.'

'Are you sure?' I asked. Bettina waved to get my attention; she was standing, holding her bag, and mimed throwing back a drink. I shook my head at her, and she shrugged and blew me a kiss before walking away.

'Course, babe,' said Dylan, 'work's your thing.' I felt annoyed. Work was not my thing; work had to be my thing so that everybody else had money to fund their things.

'Sure, thanks,' I said.

Maybe he smelled a whiff of insincerity because he said, 'Did you want me to order a takeaway?'

'No, there'll probably be food. It's sort of a party, really.' Who was I saying that for? My husband, who thought that parties were a punishment? 'What about your lesson?' Dylan's schedule was in green pen on the calendar. He had a double lesson in Shenfield that evening.

'Ruby can hold the fort. She's old enough.' I thought of all the destruction my eldest daughter could be capable of in a few hours.

'Do you want me to call my mum?' I asked.

'Of course not,' said Dylan. 'We can cope without you for one night.' I told Dylan that I'd be as quick as I could and to try and get the girls to do some homework. I wanted to avoid another morning panic.

4

THANKFULLY THERE WAS booze, although served in those child-sized plastic wine cups, meaning I had to have three before I felt any effect. The room was crowded and hot, and I could feel sweat patches forming under my arms. I would have to get Bettina's jacket cleaned, which meant dry cleaned, which meant time and expense. Dry cleaning is a luxury only the child-free can afford. The book launch was held in an East London hotel; it looked derelict from the outside, but the inside was stylishly kitted out to offer 1940s boudoir vibes.

Everyone seemed to have arrived in small groups, using the event as a social activity. I wandered over to a table holding a stack of books. Each had a stark white cover with the words 'INVESTING IN YOUR FUTURE SELF' in bold black. A bored-looking brunette in her twenties sat behind the table, scrolling lazily through her phone.

'Will the author be signing?' I asked.

'After,' she said, without looking up. I was tempted to give her a piece of my mind, warn her that she could be missing out on amazing things and life-changing introductions if she didn't look up from her screen, even occasionally. I thought of Annie then and felt a little guilty for judging her eagerness so harshly; she already understood that she wouldn't be young and beautiful for ever. I bought a book, perhaps only to force the woman to engage, which she did very grudgingly, and then stood in a corner flicking through its pages. A sentence caught my eye.

Life is as real as you make it. Make it so real it hurts.

I looked up at the people milling around – I saw terrifying strangers, not new clients. A plump, red-cheeked woman wearing a dress covered in a ladybird print walked towards me, smiling broadly. 'Solo flyer?' she asked. I nodded.

'Me too, I don't miss anything Frank does. I use all his tools. This one is much more personal, don't you think?' When I failed to respond in the appropriate manner – that is to say I didn't respond at all – she nodded towards the book in my hand.

'Oh, this. I haven't read it.' The woman looked disappointed in me, so I added, 'I've been saving it until after tonight.' She grabbed my arm.

'What a great plan. I wish I had done that now, although I don't think I could have waited. You're very strong.' I raised my fist to my head, as if to display my bicep, and instantly regretted it.

'Do you use the . . . um . . . tools at work?'

'Yes. Definitely. I mean, he started writing business books, but of course business is life and life is business.' The woman laughed and a beat too late I joined her. When she had composed herself, I extended my hand.

'Alison,' I said.

'Beatrice,' she said gaily, before accepting my handshake. I focused on applying what I considered the right amount of pressure; Beatrice responded by gripping my hand in a vice-like hold.

'I'm here for my work. I'm in marketing,' I said. Beatrice

nodded enthusiastically. 'Is there any marketing involved in your work?'

'Sort of. I mean, I'm a librarian so the council take care of it, I suppose.'

'Fabulous. Must run.' I strode across the room, powered by a sense of having wasted precious time. I couldn't mess around with small talk – it was time for life to get real.

'I'm Alison,' I said to two men in tailored suits. 'I'm a marketing strategist and I'm here to build connections.' The men looked at me and then back to each other.

'This one's for you, Wes,' said the shorter of the two, before moving away in the direction of the drinks table.

'Thanks for coming over. What is it that you're offering?' asked my new potential client.

'A full-scale service – rebranding, bespoke social media development packages, the works. Do you think that would be of use to you?' Wes licked his lips.

'Everything can be of use. We can't talk now. Too distracting. Let's reconnect after the event and think business.' I wasn't sure what I was agreeing to and it seemed impolite to ask. I suddenly felt nervous and very aware of the potential for malice in the world. I excused myself with promises to find him later, and stood in a corner to call my mother, a finger pressing my free ear closed to drown out the background.

'Yello!' she sang.

'How many gins in are you?'

'One,' she said firmly, 'and it was tiny.'

'Can you call round mine and check on the girls? I'm out and Dylan's at a lesson out of town.' I heard a clatter and the sound of breaking glass. Mum swore but I didn't want to ask her what was happening. 'Look, if you're pissed don't worry about it.'

'I'm not even nearly pissed, Ally, chance would be a fine thing. I've literally just stepped in from Eddie's and you know how he can go on.' Eddie is my stepfather – ex-stepfather technically, since he and my mother divorced many years ago, but I don't know if it's a title one is required to relinquish. 'He called me over to help him with something – I get there and he wants me to tell him his mother's maiden name! I thought it was for a password at the bank or something, you know they're always asking these ridiculous questions, but no: he just wanted to make sure he had remembered it. For what reason? She's dead, and I for one am not sorry about it.'

'Mum! What if someone said that about you after you were gone?'

'What would I care? I'd be dead. Wish I'd had a few drinks, he'd be far more tolerable and might look a little better.'

'He's sick, Mum. I don't know if it's fair to have a go at his looks.' Mum snorted loudly.

'He's sick because he's so hateful and greedy. You know I asked him for two hundred pounds for my charity? He probably has that under his mattress. He said no, and do you know why?'

'No,' I hissed, 'obviously I don't, and I don't have time to know now. Can we park it? I'll come and have a cuppa soon, I promise, but can you just pop up to mine and check on the girls?' Mum was silent for a few seconds and I thought perhaps she was angry at my dismissal of her. Eddie might be the closest thing I had to a father figure, but he was still her ex and everyone deserves a bit of time to bitch about their ex. I made a mental note to make time to chat to her and another mental note to write down all my mental notes. I heard Mum swallow and realized she

31

wasn't angry but topping up her gin levels, and it was my turn to feel angry; often I longed for a grandparent who would make fairy cakes and slip warm fifty-pence pieces to my children before leaving for home. 'If you're going to go, you shouldn't drink, Mum.'

'I'm thirsty,' said Mum defiantly. 'Anyway, isn't Ruby old enough to stay in with her sister? You were making the dinner at her age.' I briefly wondered why everyone felt the need to tell me how old my daughter was, and inform me of her capabilities. Was I the only one who remembered when she got the bus home from the shopping centre in the wrong direction and we had to collect her from the end of line, where she had been sitting on a bench sobbing for thirty minutes?

'I made dinner because if I didn't, I wouldn't eat,' I said very calmly.

'And what a wonderful lesson to learn at such a young age,' my mother chirped. I noticed Wes move towards the hall. I wanted to try and find a space near him.

'Just go if you're sober enough,' I said, and ended the call. Some silent signal had caused everyone to mobilize at the same time, and I could no longer see Wes through the crowd. I pushed past a few people, who looked at me either critically or with amusement, and gave up when I found myself in the centre of the anonymous crowd.

'This could be the first day you live as your true self,' a voice echoed around the room. Floodlights lit the stage. The man standing there was handsome and poised. His dark hair was cut close to his head and his clothes were sleek and unobtrusive. He wasn't the sort of person you could pin down – I would have believed he was royalty as readily as head of an underworld criminal gang – but he was definitely something, whatever he was. 'If you decide you want it to be,' he continued, after an unnatural pause.

'Of course, you could continue living exactly the same way you have been and producing precisely the same results; it's no skin off my nose.' He smiled to let us know this was a joke and I heard laughter around me, but I knew he had made everyone feel as nervous as I did. If he could say anything that would stop tomorrow feeling like part of a prison sentence, I would be sold. Frank Molony started to pace the stage, striding quickly as though warming up for an athletic event. 'I've been where you are,' he said. 'Exactly where you are, standing listening to someone, hoping that doing so will lead me to the life I want. My sincerest apologies, folks – it won't. You've got to promise to take action outside of this room. If you're honest, you know who you want to be – make a commitment today. If you can't make it to yourself, make it to me. Commit to getting up tomorrow and being that person.'

Frank went on to explain how we operate in the world, as a construct of other people's ideas about us, with our true selves hiding or fighting to be seen. He promised that if we stopped pretending, success would follow. 'The world will accept you as you are. Trust me,' he advised at the end of his talk. 'Any questions?' Dozens of hands flew into the air. Frank looked around the room and pointed to a woman behind me. 'The lady in the electrifying top,' he said. She flushed and picked up the hem of her blue jumper; her body language said 'this old thing'. Frank nodded, urging her to ask her question.

I watched her take a couple of seconds to compose herself before asking, 'How do you maintain such a positive attitude?'

Frank gave her an inviting smile. 'What's your name?'

'Caroline,' she said.

'Well, Caroline, maintenance does take work. You should

33

see me in the morning.' He chuckled and we laughed with him. 'But the key for me is elimination. You see, I think a lot of people focus on adding to their lives, but to my mind the first step is to start cutting stuff out. Rip out the toxic people and the job that's holding you back. Get rid of what you don't need, Caroline. You need to make space.' I couldn't help but think about what I would do if I had more space – sleep, think, get a bikini wax – it would be a dream.

A man near the front asked a question about how to improve relationships. Frank appeared unruffled by the potential breadth of the subject. 'In all relationships, whether it be with your colleagues, your mate or your children, you have to ask for what you need. When your own needs are met you can engage with others as a whole person.' Half a dozen more hands flew into the air; Frank removed his suit jacket and placed it carefully on the back of a chair in the centre of the stage. 'Don't worry,' he said. 'I'm ready for you.' He walked to the edge of his platform and surveyed the crowd before choosing a young, swarthy-faced man to my left. He sweated and stuttered through a question hiding within it a potted life history, and Frank listened. Throughout the ramblings he remained inhumanly still, as if quietening all other senses in order to fully absorb the question. Yet I couldn't help but notice that all the time it was being asked, Frank was looking at me.

I left the room feeling light headed. I'm not sure if it was the wine or the words or simply being in his presence for the first time, but I needed air and made a beeline for the door. The temperature had dropped dramatically and I pulled Bettina's blazer around me protectively. I tried to give myself a pep talk, similar to the kind I would give my daughters when I saw signs of caving in – 'the water's not that cold', I would say, or 'do this and we can have ice cream'. The temptation to run down the steps and hail a cab felt physical, and I had to close my eyes and whisper, 'I am worthy,' several times before I could scrape together just enough confidence from the dregs within me to turn back towards the building. I walked straight into a chest; it was firm and smelled faintly of vanilla. I took a step backwards, too quickly; large hands grabbed my arms to steady me and stayed there long after I was. I didn't do the thing, the shrug we do when we want to politely disengage from someone, because I was happy looking into his eyes – deep, smiling and questioning. Questions that made my face turn hot.

'Steady there, girl,' he said. The sort of comment that would usually make me roll my eyes and dismiss the man, except perhaps to refer to whilst drunkenly exalting my husband in comparison to other men. I didn't roll my eyes; I kept them fixed. Fixed enough, I hoped, that they didn't betray my thoughts. Frank removed his hands and placed them in his pockets. 'Frank,' he said. I giggled. He pulled a packet of cigarettes from his trouser pocket and a slim, silver lighter from within the packet. 'I'm funny to you?' he asked. If he was offended, he didn't show it.

'No,' I said, 'it's just, of course I know who you are.' I gestured towards the building, as though it stood there only for him.

'I never presume,' Frank said. He held the cigarettes out towards me and I shook my head.

'No, I mean, I don't smoke. I did for a minute at college but I was never very good at it, and then my stepdad got emphysema and, you know, it didn't seem right. I don't mind if you do, though, I quite like the smell actually.' In my head I screamed, 'Stop talking, Alison. Just stop.'

He smiled and said, 'Maybe you should,' before balancing a cigarette between his lips and lighting it. As he inhaled, he watched me, and then he turned his head to allow a plume of smoke to float off into the evening. I examined his profile, which was strong and a little unforgiving. In fact, the only soft thing about him was his eyes, which made me want to climb in and take a nap.

'What do you think?' he said, and I swallowed. I was taken aback by his directness and offended that he would think it appropriate to proposition me, but only mildly – more because I knew I should be than out of genuine affront. 'Of the book,' he added when I failed to reply, and then I felt ashamed that I had thought he was coming on to me, and also that in the moment I realized he wasn't, I felt a sharp prick of disappointment. The book was tucked in my bag; I glanced at it as if somehow, through the leather and detritus, it would telepathically inspire me to say something clever or at least witty.

'You think it's all bullshit, don't you?'

'No, not at all!' I cried. I wanted to tell him how he had made me feel when I heard him speak, but I wasn't sure myself. 'I think it's very profound, the things you write . . . well, think about . . . I think—'

'I think you haven't read it,' he said. He narrowed his eyes, perhaps because of the smoke from his cigarette, perhaps attempting to peer into my disingenuous soul, and I shook my head guiltily.

'No, I haven't, and I probably won't because I really don't have the time to read; I probably haven't read a whole book in eight years, and to be fair I usually think this sort of thing is really wanky, but you were not wanky, not even a little bit wanky, I promise.' I gasped in horror at myself. He laughed then, deep and full. As soon as he was finished,

I wanted to hear it again. I cursed myself for not being able to think of anything to say that might provoke it.

'You're pretty fucking authentic,' he said, and I thought at first it might be a backhanded compliment or that he might have been mocking me in a way I felt men often did. As if my small stature reminded them of the power imbalance and inspired them to exploit it. 'I could see it, even in there.' He indicated to the hall. 'You don't hide who you are.' This made me feel a little sick, because if I couldn't hide it that meant the effect he was having on me would be clear. I wanted to distract him but also continue to intrigue him. I tried to think of something witty and charming, something that would market me as the woman he was suggesting that I was.

All I could muster was, 'I try.' I cringed that my communication skills, the skills that were supposed to be the basis for my career, had failed me. I tried to tell myself that it didn't matter because I didn't even know this man and, of course, I was married.

'No, you don't try, it's who you are, and let me tell you it's a breath of fresh air,' he said. 'Let's get out of here.' And I felt my spirits rise because he was suggesting the very thing I had wanted to do, but also because he was suggesting that he wanted to spend more time with me and I wanted him to want that, I wanted him to approve of me.

'But your thing?' I asked, gesturing at the building.

'It's good to play a little hard to get,' he said, and then flicked his cigarette into the gutter.

'I can't,' I said, with far more conviction than I felt. 'I'm supposed to be meeting someone.' He raised his eyebrow. 'Not like that – a networking thing. I met someone who might be a potential client.' Frank placed his hands back in his pockets.

'Let's make a deal. If you come for a drink with me, I'll introduce you to someone who will be more use to you than whatever prick was trying it on with you tonight.'

'But you don't even know what I do.'

'I know someone for everyone.' And with that I was able to construct a reality in which going for a drink with Frank was good for my job, and what was good for my job was good for my family. Frank stepped down to the pavement without waiting for me to confirm I was coming, and when he turned back I thought for a second he was unsure. But then he said, 'What's your name?'

'Alison,' I said, and he nodded once as if confirming that this was acceptable. I watched him walk for a couple of seconds before running to catch up.

5

FRANK HAD BARELY extended his arm before a black-cab driver made a sharp U-turn and pulled up beside him. I hung back on the pavement, still unsure about taking that last step. Then he held the car door open, without that self-deprecating flourish men sometimes do; it was clearly just what he did. I wondered if he still had a mother? Sisters? A daughter? And I forgot about my hesitation.

I love taking black cabs; it reminds me of one summer holiday when Mum and I took them everywhere. We would walk up to the high street and get a car all the way to Regent Street. Mum would take me to Hamleys for a new addition to my increasingly vast Barbie collection, before treating me to an overpriced burger in Covent Garden. Sometimes I'd ask for a Happy Meal, but Mum would shut this down firmly, saying, 'Lunch is the most exciting meal of the day – breakfast is too early and after lunch there's still time for some mischief.' I didn't know until later that Mum had uncovered Eddie's affair with the 'homely spinster' next door earlier that summer; a few months draining the savings account was her ill-thought-out revenge. By autumn we were struggling for bus fare, and Mum and Eddie's marriage disintegrated within a tornado of screaming and broken crockery, but none of that had diminished the thrill of a black-cab ride through the city.

The cabbie was one of the jovial, chatty types. Perhaps one of the last of his kind, all elongated East End vowels and enlightening local facts.

'What you been doin' at Regency 'all then? You know the Krays used to go to the cabaret there?' Frank and I turned to each other and smiled. He slid his arm around my shoulders and, though I was still smiling, I felt my jaw tense. Frank turned to look at the driver in the rear-view mirror.

'We just got married,' he said. I tried and failed to mask my laughter with my hand. Frank retained his beatific expression.

'Yeah?' said the driver. I saw his eyes flit over me doubtfully.

'It was very quick,' said Frank, giving my arm a squeeze. 'Between us, my new wife needs a visa, but that's secondary to the fact that we are completely and utterly in love.' At this Frank turned back towards me and kissed the top of my head gently. If you could take that kiss in isolation, I would have completely believed that he loved me. It seemed the cab driver did because he accepted Bettina's blazer as my big-day outfit.

'*Mazel tov!*' he shouted. Frank gave me another squeeze and I laughed again, but tried to make it seem like excitable giggles – which it was, to a degree. My days had become so predictable – work, homework, dinner, squabbles, Netflix – all fine, all the makings of a perfectly acceptable life, but don't we all have moments, if not months, when we hope we could do better than acceptable? Rushing through the dark streets, the fabric of Frank's expensive suit grazing my cheek, I felt like I was getting a glimpse into another world, a world that with one different turn in the road could have been mine.

The road we pulled up on was not what I was expecting; it looked more like the setting for a violent crime than a London hotspot. I had been anticipating a chic hotel bar and received a back alley. The driver was nonplussed and waved away Frank's attempt to pay; 'Thank me by living well,' he said. I hugged my new husband around the waist as he pulled away – the driver's generosity made me feel the need to offer him a believable portrayal of wedded bliss, and I couldn't pretend it felt uncomfortable. As soon as the car was out of sight, Frank untangled himself from me and placed his hands in his pockets. I felt embarrassed by this for some reason, and tried to cover it with chatter.

'That was mad! I can't believe he bought it. As if we just got married and the visa thing!' Frank shrugged. This wasn't crazy for him; it was Friday. He knocked on what looked to be an abandoned shop front, and it was opened by a giant of a man with a severe haircut. It seemed to take him a moment to recognize Frank, but when he did his mouth moved into a wide grin. Despite his size it made him look childlike, particularly as he was missing one of his front teeth.

'Frankie!' he said, and pulled Frank towards him for a hug. Frank let himself be smothered before stepping aside to let me enter.

'Alison, this is Carlos. Carlos, Alison.'

Carlos nodded his head and said, 'Welcome to the club.'

At the end of the shabby hallway was another door, and going through it was like stepping into Narnia. The room beyond was in such sharp contrast to where we had come from, I had to check behind me to be sure. The tired hallway was still there, Carlos waving from the other end. It wasn't a trick but it felt like magic.

'This is where I come to find solace,' said Frank, which made me feel that I could be part of bringing him comfort. Gentle house music murmured out of invisible speakers. Glass tables, brimming with champagne bottles, sat in front of glossy leather banquettes on which sat equally glossy patrons. As we moved across the room I saw a popular television actor in conversation with an infamously chaotic model and, forgetting I wasn't there with one of my girlfriends, I grabbed Frank's sleeve in excitement. He looked at me questioningly.

'I-I have to go to the toilet.'

'It's next to the bar,' he said. 'I'll be over there.' Frank gestured to a dark corner of the room. I let go of him and scurried away. I berated myself for saying 'toilet'; it was too descriptive but I wasn't sure what alternative to use – 'bathroom' was very American, 'loo' a bit old lady. I settled on 'ladies'. I decided the next time I needed to excuse myself, I would say that, and I knew then I would need to stay for an hour to allow the opportunity to arise.

The toilets were bigger than my living room and so clean it looked like they hadn't been used all night, if ever. Just when I thought I couldn't conceive of any more decadence I sat on the toilet and felt warmth spread through my thighs. It was heated! The seat was fucking heated! I was so shocked I almost forgot to pee. That moment was one I returned to again and again. I didn't recognize it then but it was when I decided that Frank made the ordinary amazing.

As I washed my hands, my reflection brought me back down to earth. The line of gold-framed mirrors revealed a woman very much out of place with her surroundings. My face carried a sheen that was definitely more sweaty than the dewy I had been aiming for, and Bettina's jacket was too proper for the rock-star vibe of the establishment. As I was trying to encourage some volume into my hair with my fingers, the model came out of one of the stalls.

'Y'all right?' she slurred. I smiled. I should not have felt star-stuck; I was a working woman and this was a girl who, in unfortunate circumstances, was young enough to be my daughter. Still, seeing her beside me and not on the pages of a Sunday supplement was jarring. I had to fight the urge to touch her minuscule bum.

'You not hot?' The model sniffed a few times after she spoke, drawing my attention to her nose, on the right nostril of which was a stark white globule. I indicated to the area by gesturing to my own, and she turned to the mirror and dragged the back of her hand across her face before giggling and thanking me. As she did, she eyed my jacket suspiciously. 'You *must* be hot,' she said, pulling at one of the lapels. It shifted to reveal some of my jam attack from earlier in the day. 'Oh fuck,' she said. I was grateful she appreciated the severity of the situation. 'I know.' She grabbed at the hem of the camisole she was wearing and pulled it off over her head. She held it towards me and, when my face failed to register understanding, she said, 'Have it. You're a six, right?' If I could bottle a moment, it would be that one.

'I can't,' I spluttered.

'You have to – what is that, blood?'

'Jam.' Her frown told me it didn't make a difference.

'Come on,' she said, growing impatient with me, 'get over yourself.' And I wanted to. I wanted to rise above myself and reveal a much stronger, more powerful version of me – why not start with a vest? 'Anyway,' she continued,

43

'I look good in this.' She adjusted her black lacy bralet and ran a palm across her exposed stomach. She would look good wearing faecal matter, so that seemed beside the point. I took the camisole and placed it next to the sink. I thought for a second about retreating to a stall and then decided, what the hell? Nothing about the night was going to be normal. I stripped down to my bra, swallowed the self-consciousness I felt about revealing my scarred mum-tum, and wiggled into the top. It was close-fitting but looked sexy rather than restrictive. The model instigated a high five and I slapped my hand against hers. She left and I threw the jammy shirt in the bin.

At the table, Frank had a bottle of cognac and two glasses in front of him.

'I thought you'd done a runner,' he said, and for the first time that evening I saw a glimpse of vulnerability in him. It was nice; it made him seem more youthful and helped me relax. 'You changed.'

'I got a bit hot,' I said.

'That you did,' said Frank. He said it coolly, without any indication through his tone or expression that he was saying something improper, and I sometimes wonder if my biggest mistake was my reaction to this. I could have squashed the moment with a joke or a question, batted back any suggestion of sex with a comment about my dear husband, but I chose not to. I held his gaze – two, three seconds longer than would be natural. Those few seconds were a choice.

'You know who you remind me of?' asked Frank, after he had poured us both drinks.

'Jessica Chastain? I sometimes get that, although I can't see it myself.'

'I don't know who that is,' said Frank.

'She was in *The Help*, but you might not have seen that one. It's a bit of a chick flick, and she's blonde in that and I think it's the hair mainly, why people say—'

'No, not her, whoever she is,' interrupted Frank. 'Holly Collins.'

'What was she in?' I asked, cringing at my ignorance.

'She's not an actress. Not that I know of anyway. We went to school together.' He was leaning in, the scent of his aftershave muddled with the alcohol. 'She was my first proper girlfriend. We didn't move in the same circles – it was obvious she would be better suited to someone more academic – but I couldn't get her out of my mind. She's probably the reason I didn't get any GCSEs. I basically hunted her down. It was her smile, like she was hiding something. That's why you remind me of her.' I took a sip of my drink in an attempt to hide said smile. I rarely have neat spirits – only at Christmas time and in dire emergencies – but rather than the burning sensation I usually experienced, I tasted something sweet and earthy that slipped down my throat and sent warmth racing through my chest.

'You don't strike me as someone who chases,' I said. This was my honest assessment: that things and people came to him.

'I do, when I think they're worth it.' That beat again, a silence to allow his audience to feast on all the hidden meanings. I took another sip and the action felt slow, my awareness of his scrutiny impeding natural movement.

'So, she was worth it?'

'In some ways. She taught me the power of a beautiful woman.'

'What happened?' I asked, eager to move on from that topic.

'Not a lot. We went to Laser Quest, I think. After we

had sex, I lost interest. Boys will be boys.' Imagining him as a callous, horny teenager made me think of my girls and the little I could do to protect them from the sinister motives of some men. I excused myself to make a call.

'Why have you sent Nan to babysit me like I'm a baby?' said Ruby when she answered the landline.

'I didn't.'

'Don't lie. She told us you think we need looking after. She's drunk, yunno. She's dancing.'

I held my breath for a few seconds. The real world was knocking and I wasn't ready to let it in.

'Where's your father?'

'Stuck in traffic.'

'Get her some blankets so she can sleep in the living room, and get on with your homework.'

'God, you're doing distance nagging now.' She yawned and I heard the thump of her landing heavily on sofa cushions.

'Just get your dad to call me when he gets in.'

'When will you be back?' I looked at my watch and readjusted my plan for the evening again.

'An hour, two tops.' That gave me time for one more drink. I returned to the table. Frank asked me if everything was OK and I told him everything was wonderful, because as I watched him top up my glass, it was.

6

A NY GUILT I FELT HAD been replaced by frustration –
could I not have two hours to myself? Two hours to
be someone other than housekeeper and secretary to two
children and one overgrown one? I considered the battle I
would have with Ruby, forcing her to delete whatever soul-
less void under the guise of social connection Dylan had
let her have access to, and added another measure to my
glass. Frank raised an eyebrow as I drank down a large
slug.

'Do you know what you need?' he asked. I shook my
head. Frank removed his jacket. I watched as the muscles in
his arms pushed against his sleeves. 'A dance.' I hadn't been
conscious of it but the music had increased in tempo and
volume, and a few people were congregated on a space
between the tables. Frank stood and walked to the centre
of the room. He began to move without waiting for me to
join him. He looked completely at ease and didn't hold
himself in that awkward, self-aware way so many men do
when they dance. I could have been content watching but I
knew I'd be happier beside him. I took another sip of cognac
and walked over; as I approached, Frank slowed the pace
of his movements, giving me a chance to fall in with his
rhythm. The song playing had a sultry Spanish undertone

and it seemed completely appropriate for him to grab my hand and pull me in. I twisted towards him and landed with my back resting against his body. He led our movements so that we swayed in unison as the song soared. It had been so long since I had danced, properly danced. I had jumped around with the girls in the living room and stood in drunken circles shouting lyrics at weddings, but danced? Succumbed to the will of a man and the music? Not for a century at least.

The next track was wild, impossibly fast African beats under vibrant jazz sounds. Frank turned me until I felt dizzy, and then we held hands and did a makeshift salsa round the floor. When that track ended a slow song came on, and I became aware of the individuals around me merging into pairs. I took a step back from Frank and it was like taking a step back from everything. I could feel sweat plastering the silk of the camisole to my back; I knew I was red-faced. This wasn't the kind of place I came to; the man looking at me questioningly wasn't mine; none of it was real. I half ran back to the table, slung on Bettina's blazer and gathered my bag. I returned to Frank on the dance floor and took his hands in mine.

'Thank you,' I said, and he nodded graciously. As I moved to the exit, I was trying to work out the best route home and determined that I would need to know where I was first. Stepping back into the ruinous hallway was sobering. I was acutely conscious of how much I had drunk and how the evening was running away from me. Before I reached the heavy outer door, Carlos blocked my way.

'No one's going anywhere for a while,' he said sternly. I panicked. It occurred to me, far too late, that there was no one around me I could trust. I barely knew Frank; any affinity I felt for him could well be booze or hormones. I hit Carlos on the chest. He was solid, like a wall; he didn't even flinch. He held my wrists and smirked as I wriggled maniacally like a fish on a line.

'Wanna control your bird?' I followed my captor's gaze to Frank, now a few feet behind me.

'I'm not his bird!' I screeched, anxiety and feminist indignation overcoming me. 'And I do not need to be controlled! I need to go home. You can't stop me. This is kidnapping.' I wasn't sure if it was kidnapping, given that I had entered of my own volition, but I knew it was wrong. Carlos still had a hold of me. I remembered, when I was a girl, my mother telling me to 'bite first and think later'. As I launched my head towards him, I felt Frank reach round and pull me backwards. I relaxed against his chest, too tired to do anything more.

'What's the problem?' Frank said. His voice was commanding; not threatening but with the promise of threat if the correct response was not obtained.

'The squat are kicking off again.' I twisted my head to look at Frank, who was nodding in understanding. He turned me round to face him.

'Next door aren't the most reliable of neighbours. The street will be cordoned off for a while. Is there anyone you need to call?' I didn't know why I felt like crying.

'Excuse me,' I said, and went to the ladies'. Dylan answered immediately.

'They're working you hard, babe,' he said.

'It's over,' I said, 'we went for a drink.'

'Well, it's Friday.' I heard him shift in a chair or perhaps our bed.

'I'm sorry.' I wanted to say more but the words caught in my throat.

'You OK, baby?'

'Yeah, course. There's something kicking off here, traffic accident I think, and the road is closed.'

'I'll come get you,' Dylan said. I could hear him moving, preparing to leave; his lack of hesitation caused my guilt to expand.

'The girls,' I said.

'Your mum's here. She's asleep but she's here.'

'Seriously, Dylan, you've been driving all evening – stay where you are. I'm with Betty and she's close by; I'll stay at hers if it gets too late.'

'You sure? I've got my shoes on?' He would have had them on. Dylan didn't lie.

'It's fine. Thank you. I'll be fine.' My husband chuckled.

'My strong, independent woman,' he said softly.

'You sound tired,' I said.

'I'm a bit drained. That woman shouldn't be allowed on the roads.' I forced a laugh. I had been hearing the same joke for fifteen years. I stayed in the toilet for a minute or two after we hung up. I felt frightened, but I was no longer frightened of Carlos or whatever was unfolding on the street outside; I was scared of myself.

Frank was waiting for me near the toilets.

'Everything good?' he asked.

'Sorry about earlier, everything's fine.' He handed me another drink. He didn't ask me any more questions and I wondered briefly if he wasn't interested or didn't want to know the answers. The table we had been sitting at had become occupied, so we took seats on stools at the bar. The waiter was a man who looked to be in his fifties, a weathered kind of handsome, the kind that you suspect looks better now than before.

'What's Frank got you on?' he asked, nodding towards my glass. I looked at it.

'I'm not sure actually.' He laughed and leaned in, pretending to speak only to me.

'Don't let this one boss you about,' he said. 'He needs to be put in his place from time to time.' I smiled at Frank, who moved his stool closer.

'Is that so?' I asked. He shrugged. The barman laughed again. For some reason it made me feel proud that Frank was so well known and so clearly liked by the staff there. Of course, I could take no credit for him, but perhaps the fact that they had chosen him and he in turn had chosen me made me feel validated in some way. The barman slid my glass a few inches away from me.

'Let me make you something – if it doesn't knock your socks off it's on the house. What do you like?'

'Rum,' I said, my earlier fear and frustration already distant. The barman whistled as he upended bottles of liquor and squeezed limes into a mixer. I rested my chin on my hands and watched him work. I always enjoyed seeing people do things with passion. I could feel Frank beside me, but I didn't feel the need to engage him and he didn't do anything to gain my attention. The barman placed his creation in front of me and stood with his arms folded expectantly. I took my time, holding the glass towards the light and examining it before sipping. The barman tapped his foot expectantly.

'It's not bad,' I said. He looked crestfallen. I laughed and he wagged his finger at me. 'Fine. I'm lying – it's the best thing I've ever tasted.' He did a little tap dance before walking up the bar to serve someone else. Frank dragged his stool even closer.

'Calmer now?' I couldn't meet his eye.

'I'm sorry,' I said. 'I'm having a bit of a moment.'

'Yeah?'

'It's lasted about two years.'

'Wanna talk about it?' he said. And I found that I did.

Three years ago, things were sort of coming together. The girls were both in school and I knew it was time to elbow my way back into the rat race. I'd had nine years of trying and failing not to let motherhood curtail my career, but largely it had been unsuccessful. Projects and promotions went to younger, less encumbered colleagues; my requests for feedback were largely dismissed. My employers treated me like an ugly ornament from a relative after a holiday – useless but not acceptable to throw away.

As soon as the girls were settled in their new classes, I applied for an internal managerial position. Two of us went for it: Caris and me. Caris had been my friend since the day I started. She had big brown curls and an even bigger laugh. I gravitated towards her immediately. We often took lunch together, and shared problems from both inside and outside the office. Caris and her husband had completed several rounds of IVF, and more than once I'd had to cover for her when another failed attempt had resulted in several tearful trips to the ladies'.

When, over Pret sandwiches, we learned we were both applying for the role, she went uncharacteristically quiet. Caris suggested it was best that we didn't talk about it, and that agreement seemed to extend to offering me congratulations after I was given the job. Technically, I became my friend's superior, but I trusted Caris and I never made a point of highlighting my seniority. The trust, it seemed, didn't go both ways. We stopped meeting for lunch; I'd catch her organizing after-work drinks and quickly shutting down the conversation when I entered the room. Other than the demise of our friendship, I enjoyed my new role. I think I was good at managing people, certainly better than managing myself.

I tried with Caris; I missed her and I wanted to do a good job of supporting her. I talked it through with Dylan most evenings, until he told me that he felt like he was married to her and not me. After that I decided we should clear the air; I invited Caris for dinner. We went to the mid-range Italian near the office and shared a bottle of wine; it was stilted but polite. I thought I had broken ground.

A couple of days later I was called to a meeting. Caris had accused me of bullying her. The dinner, she claimed, was used as an opportunity for mockery by lording my status as a mother over her. It was true I had talked about my children, but only because I had nothing else to talk about.

When whispers of redundancies circulated the office, I made clear I would be open to it. No one fought me. Dylan told me to do what made me happy, but I was choosing between a crappy situation at work and the crappy situation of being unemployed. In the end I decided to leave before I was pushed, like a teenage girl scrambling to be the dumper and not the dumped. On my last day, I worked late and left when the office was empty. I climbed into bed and stayed there for a week. Caris messaged me a month or so later to wish me well. I broke my laptop throwing it across the room.

Frank listened without much response. I felt a spike of panic that I had bored him, but then he tucked a piece of hair behind my ear and said, 'Will you make me a promise?' I nodded. 'Chase your own joy. You will only get hurt if you try and create it for someone else.' Tears sprang to my eyes and Frank wiped them away quickly without fuss, and then we danced again. I accepted his embrace when the music dictated I should; I allowed myself to lean in to him and stopped worrying about what it might mean. The whole evening had taken on an otherworldly quality; it was so removed from my everyday life, I sort of decided that it didn't count.

After an hour of dancing and drinking more of the greatest ever cocktail, I was happy but weary. Frank asked me if I was OK and although I replied I was fine, I had to think about it for a few seconds. He deposited me at the bar and disappeared for a few minutes. Whilst he was gone, I asked the barman his name.

'Patrick,' he said.

'I bet you've seen some stuff, Pat? Can I call you Pat?' I asked.

'You can call me whatever you like,' he said. 'I've seen everything.'

'I suppose you've seen Frank in here with a string of women.'

'No,' he said. 'Only you.' I felt a little explosion in my stomach and I berated myself for the involuntary reaction. I had no right to be excited but sensed that excitement might be the piece of the puzzle I was searching for. Frank returned and took hold of one of my hands.

'It's still cordoned off outside. There's rooms here; I've booked one for myself. You can come and rest for a while.' I didn't say yes but I didn't actually say no.

7

BELOW THE CLUB was a warren of suites, and Frank led me to a room at the end of a silent corridor. He opened the door with a small black electronic device and, as I entered, I was hit with the scent of freesias. The walls were pale grey and the floors covered in thick creamy carpets; I immediately removed my loafers to feel the softness. I was wiggling my toes into the floor when Frank removed his jacket, shoes and tie before settling on to the huge bed, and it struck me how quickly things can turn. The man who, for reasons unexplored, I had viewed as my protector all evening no longer made me feel safe. I felt anxious and angry – had this charming man been a wolf wearing Grandmother's expensive suit? I backed away. It was one thing to be next to each other on the dance floor, with witnesses and clothes on, but quite another to do so on a bed in the semi-darkness of a bedroom. I was so disappointed with Frank for falling this easily into a sad stereotype of a bloke, and with myself for getting swept up in all his shininess. Still, I didn't want to tell him I was angry. I didn't want to risk the negative repercussions of a rejection. I thought back to the cocktails and the cab ride, expenses that I had failed to understand were payments in advance. Surely as a marketing manager I could find the words to extrapolate myself without too much fallout. Frank reached for something on the bedside table. It was the remote control.

'I loved this one,' he said, after turning on the television. He watched for a few seconds and then let out that disarming laugh and that was it; no pressure, no words of seduction. I went over to the bed. It was so wide I had to crawl across it to sit next to him. The images on the screen looked familiar, but I couldn't place them and looked to Frank.

'*Adventures in Babysitting*,' he said.

'Oh yes!' I had forgotten about the film's existence, yet it was in the rotation of movies that I would watch through the long, hot summers of childhood. From the age of eleven, July meant being a surrogate mum to my brother Henry, eleven years my junior. Eddie was busy building his business and Mum wasn't there, even when she was. I made a big show of feeling encumbered by Henry's presence, but actually I adored having him around. I swear he was born smiling – they said it was wind but I knew differently. By some magic he grew up without the weight I always carried, and I wanted to protect him from that. We never got bored; we were so present. There weren't a million and one things to do so we invested in the few joys we had. We would build complicated Lego castles and chase squirrels on the common around the corner. When he got tired I would carry him on my hip like he was mine, and in many ways he was. In the afternoons I'd put in a video, always an adventure film, something that could carry me away from Essex for a couple of hours. Henry curled up next to me and quietly sucked on the first two fingers of his right hand.

I quoted a line at the same time as one of the characters. Frank looked at me, his face contorted in pleasure and surprise. 'Impressed?' I asked.

'Very,' he said, and paused just long enough to create tension. 'I thought you'd be too young to know this one.' I know many women are flattered by assessments like that, but I've been getting it my entire life and concluded that people often confuse height and age.

'Oh, I get it,' I said softly. 'You thought I was this young, impressionable ingénue that you could bring to this den of sin and corrupt.' Frank laughed.

'Perhaps I hoped you were, but it's good for the soul to be wrong. See, you challenge me without even trying.' It was this, the idea of being challenging and therefore, I concluded, complicated and intriguing, that had me completely hooked. Generally, I felt so uncomplicated – bill payer, ham sandwich maker, launderer. I wanted to be interesting and layered and Frank made me feel that way. We watched the rest of the film in silence, except for laughter when it was called for. I was aware that we reacted to exactly the same parts and also of his arm, pressed firmly against mine. As the credits rolled Frank sighed, a comfortable, satisfied sound that I accepted responsibility for evoking. He patted my forearm gently as he said, 'I don't think I've relaxed properly in years. Thanks for giving me this.' I placed my hand on top of his and told him he was welcome. He looked at my hand and then to my eyes and said, 'You are very cute.' It wasn't elegant but it was enough. I'm ashamed to say any emotional defences I had left fell away. I turned to the side and feigned annoyance.

'I'm a woman with my own home and a pension plan. I'm hardly cute.'

'We'll have to agree to disagree,' he said, shifting on to his side to take my face in his hand. I knew what was coming, of course I did, and I had enough time to stop it – to laugh, to turn away, to remember the promises I had made – but I didn't take the time. I let him run his thumb across my cheek, draw me towards him and kiss me.

Too soon he stopped. He pulled me on top of him and wrapped his arms around my back. 'That feels good.' He traced light circles down my spine. 'Sometimes I feel like I'm going to float away.' I paused because I wasn't sure if he was making a joke, and before I could respond I felt his body go slack as he gave in to sleep. I was tired but I stayed awake for what felt like hours; I wanted to have it committed to memory. I wanted to be able to bring to mind how it felt to be held by him whenever I needed it.

I eased the front door closed and took my shoes off in the hallway. Despite my efforts to remain undetected, my mother called out to me.

'What time do you call this?!' Then she cackled because she didn't care what time it was. She never had. As a teenager, if I came home from a party before midnight, she wouldn't hide her disappointment. I went to the living room where she sat on the sofa, blankets on the floor beside her and a half-empty bottle of pink gin on the coffee table. I fell into an armchair.

'Had a good time, Mum?' She wiped under her eyes.

'Hardly. The girls went to bed ridiculously early and Dylan disappeared after one drink, so on my own again.' She sang the last part, her personal jingle. I had been hearing it for a lifetime, her insistence that everyone would leave her and, to be fair, her fears weren't completely unfounded – a father and two husbands down, she was primed for abandonment. When I went to university, I phoned her daily to check she was coping; luckily, she's always had booze to keep her company. 'How about you? Any gossip?' Mum pushed her white-blonde hair from her face and her eyes glistened with anticipation.

'I went to a boring work event. Got stuck in town and spent a night on Betty's lumpy sofa bed.' Mum looked disappointed and I felt it. I wanted to tell her about my evening with Frank; denying it made it feel less real.

When I'd woken up that morning I was no longer in his arms, and what had felt cosy and sweet the night before seemed sordid. I'd always hated the expectations placed on mothers by society, but even I had to admit that pulling all-nighters with men they'd just met was something good mothers didn't do. I left Frank sleeping as I picked up my shoes and bag. I thought about leaving my number on the club's stationery but decided it was best to leave things as they were. I wish that was because I thought it wrong to maintain contact but, in truth, I didn't want to deal with how it would feel if he didn't get in touch. Mum would have loved to hear about my evening. She'd ask the right questions and make me describe Frank in forensic detail. She probably wouldn't judge me, and part of me thought I needed to be judged.

'How were the girls?'

'Chloe was a delight. She made me watch her perform this play she wrote. It was very dark, almost everyone died. Ruby was not a happy bunny. She barely looked up from her computer pad thingy. Seems to be hitting moody teens really early.' I pulled my feet up underneath me. I felt very tired.

'It's like she went to bed my little girl and woke up a full-blown diva. Tell me I wasn't that bad?'

Mum laughed. 'Darling, you were worse. I was living with a demon. A demon with spots all over her chin.'

'Thanks, Mum.'

'Aw.' She came and squidged herself next to me before pulling my head into her chest and squeezing it a little too hard. 'I'm trying to help. We all go through this. Welcome to motherhood.'

'Didn't I start that thirteen years ago?'

'Yes, but this is where the fun starts.' I groaned. 'Remember when you were in love with your geography teacher and you sent him that letter?' I pushed her away so I could look at her.

'Yes, but how do you know about that?'

'I read it in your diary.'

'For God's sake, Mum. That's such an invasion of privacy.' She forced my head back on to her chest.

'There are no secrets between a mother and her daughter.' I tried to push thoughts of Frank from my mind, in case there was any truth in what she said.

I left Mum watching a cookery programme and went to make coffee. Snapshots of the previous night kept working into my consciousness. It must have made me smile because, as I felt Dylan's arms reach round my waist, he whispered, 'Someone's happy.' I turned to face him and found myself caged between the counter and his chest. His face looked contented and sleepy. His proximity made me uncomfortable. I marvelled at how skilled he was at doing the right thing at exactly the wrong time.

'It's good to be home.'

'Long night?'

'Just unexpected.'

'Sometimes it's nice to have the odd surprise, eh?' I pecked him quickly, hoping it might lead to my release.

'No. I hate surprises. Don't ever get any ideas.' Dylan moved in closer to me.

'And there was me planning this huge shebang for your fortieth.'

'That's still years away.'

'That's how big the surprise is.' I hit him on the arm and it stung my hand a little. I had forgotten how solid he was.

'Piss off. I don't want anything.' He kissed my forehead.

'But you deserve it.' I felt my eyes sting and nuzzled my head into his shoulder to hide the excess emotion. He responded by picking me up and placing me on the counter so we were face to face. We kissed and it felt better than I remembered. He increased the pressure and I pulled away.

'Got to brush my teeth.' I pushed him back and eased on to the floor. 'When you leaving?' Dylan got two mugs from the cupboard and poured the coffee.

'I cancelled. I wanted to make sure you were OK.' I couldn't stop the tears then.

'You did?' I went and kissed his face, his stubble grazing my chin.

'Course I did, you sausage.' He wiped away my tears. 'So, Mickey's coming over here for lunch.' The spell was broken. I pushed him again, harder than I had planned, and he reached out to hold the worktop.

'And I suppose I'll have to cook for us all?'

'I'll do it if you like,' he said. Dylan opened another cupboard and, after surveying it for a few seconds, pulled out two tins of beans triumphantly. I closed my eyes and swallowed down my frustration.

'I'll do it,' I said.

'Thanks, babe.' He kissed me lightly on the nose before dumping sugar in his coffee.

'Any time,' I said, meaning all the time.

I took a bath. I used my body scrub and the posh moisturizer I had been saving for something, never sure what the something might be. I scraped my hair back from my face and committed to leaving the bathroom with a better attitude.

I cooked risotto because it needs constant supervision, giving me a reason to stare into a pan and become lost in my thoughts. I wanted to find a reason for the night we had, a lesson that would make me stronger. Without one I was just a selfish cow, a cheater, and not even a good one. I would have betrayed my husband for a few expensive drinks, a night of flirtation and a snog.

8

'D AD SAID TO ask if you wanted help.' Ruby walked past me and slumped on to one of the kitchen chairs.

'He did, did he? How kind of him.' I squeezed a garlic clove in the press, imagining only briefly that it was Dylan's head. 'Do you want to help?' I asked. Her top lip curled upwards.

'You either need help or you don't. Does it matter if the person wants to do it?' she asked.

'Yes, of course it does,' I said. I threw a chopping board on the counter. As it settled noisily, I turned to look at Ruby, who raised both her eyebrows – a new trick.

'That's really stupid.' I turned back and started to chop lettuce, slamming the cleaver down into the leaves.

'Watch your tone,' I said. Ruby didn't respond. 'Why wouldn't you want to help me? I'm your mother – look how much I do for you.' She sighed.

'I thought you told me to be my own person. Don't you want me to be a strong-minded woman or whatever.' It stung to hear my words parroted back at me.

'That's different,' I said quickly. 'I was talking about standing up for yourself at school or around men, not disrespecting your mother.' Ruby yawned effusively.

'You can't change the rules whenever you want,' she said. I put down the knife. I wanted to shout that I could. I could change the rules because I made them; as far as she should be concerned I *was* the rules. But before I could say anything, Mickey's face appeared round the doorframe.

'Hello, my little gingersnap,' he said.

'Hi, Mick.' The rest of him appeared, and he placed a bottle of Baileys and a bouquet of limp carnations on the already crowded worktop before giving me a messy kiss on the cheek. He glanced over at the hob.

'Rice pudding?'

'Risotto.'

'So, savoury rice pudding.'

'Sure,' I said. I turned off the gas and threw the lettuce into a bowl, before upending a bag of cherry tomatoes on top. 'Do you want a drink?'

'Got any beer?' I found one in the fridge and handed it to him. He took it and opened the bottle with his front teeth. Mickey ruffled Ruby's hair before joining her at the table. In response she giggled; had it been me she would have snarled.

'Grub's up!' I shouted. Mum, Dylan and Chloe filed in. Mickey stretched out his arm.

'Jacintha, you beauty, come sit by me.' Mum quickly followed his instruction.

'What are you doing with yourself, Michael?' she asked. Everyone turned to listen and left me to put out the plates and cutlery.

'Bit of this, bit of that – you know how I roll. I'm about to get into property.'

'How?' I said, taking the wobbly chair.

'You know – do things up and flip them.'

'Yeah, but how are you going to fund that?' I tried not

64

to sound too disbelieving. Mickey didn't seem perturbed by my question.

'I've got an investor,' he said, as he dished himself out some risotto. I took the pan and gave Chloe some food. As I started to do the same for Ruby, she grabbed the ladle from me.

'Where did you find them?'

'In Marbella. Amazing broad. We met in Linekers, got to talking. She's got some divorce money and wants to put it to good use.'

'Are you seeing her?' Dylan shot me a look, a request to stop or change direction. I wasn't sure what was offensive about my question, so I ignored him. 'You're in a relationship with your business partner.'

'Yeah, I guess. I mean, everyone wins.'

'Did you see the game yesterday?' asked Dylan. Mickey started to jabber enthusiastically about someone's left foot and I stood up to get wine. I wasn't sure why I was angry. The ease with which Mickey ricocheted from one disaster to another irked me, but I also was annoyed by this unknown woman, letting herself be seduced by a man and his unrealistic dreams. I felt like she was letting the side down.

'Can I get some of that?' asked Mum, looking at my glass.

'Didn't you have enough last night?'

'Hair of the dog,' she said. When I didn't move she got herself a glass, pouring until the liquid settled dangerously close to the brim. Dylan and Mickey started planning a trip to a Millwall home game. Knowing Dylan no longer followed the football, his enthusiasm for the outing felt like a betrayal. If I suggested a restaurant he'd tell me he liked my cooking; if I asked him to the cinema he'd outline all the channels included in our Virgin Media package.

When I confronted him on his choice to stay at home and create a permanent groove in the sofa, he joked that he was getting old – but at some point, it stopped feeling like a joke.

'Game's starting in half an hour,' said Mickey. 'If you girls don't mind us hogging the telly for a bit?'

'Why don't you do us your play after dinner, Chlo?' I said, carefully avoiding eye contact with him. Chloe's reply was obscured by a mouthful of rice.

'Don't speak with your mouth full, honey,' I said gently. She looked at me apologetically and swallowed.

'I'm changing some of it but I can do it in a bit.'

'That would be boss, darlin',' said Mickey, winking at her. I felt like telling him it was too soon to start his charm offensive on her. 'Did I tell you about when I was acting?' Mickey retold us the tale of his role (commonly referred to as 'extra') in a Guy Ritchie film. He waved his beer bottle around as he spoke. 'I told Brad at the end of the shoot, this is gonna be your year, son, and he married that Jennifer Aniston not long after. Course, they didn't last, but you can't blame a man for wanting an upgrade. Am I right, mate?' He winked at Dylan. It was my turn to shoot the warning look. Dylan smiled into his plate. 'Thanks for the grub, beauty,' Mickey said to me.

'Mum, you haven't eaten anything,' Chloe said.

'I'm not really hungry.'

'Bit of a heavy night?' Mickey wiggled his eyebrows suggestively. I stood up and loaded my unused plate in the dishwasher.

'I'm getting some air,' I said. I went out the front and stood on the doorstep, watching the neighbour's cat play with an earthworm. A cold breeze made my arms goose-pimple, but I didn't want to go back for my coat. I took a few deep breaths, which for some reason made me feel even more tense. Perhaps Frank was right and I needed to take up smoking. A man I recognized vaguely from somewhere, perhaps the school gates or the post office queue, nodded a greeting as he passed. I returned the gesture and felt sad. I was so suburban. My life was small and ordinary when it could have been so different.

I studied drama at university in Leeds and my aim was to end up on stage. I wasn't chasing fame or money, although I assumed those things would come; I simply wanted to be good at my craft and have others recognize that. I'd starred in a production at college and the effort resulted in the best six months of my life – collaborating, planning, the heady crescendo of performance. I loved being on the stage but more than that I adored the lifestyle – sitting with the cast, feeling part of something. It was then that I tried smoking, during late-night discussions fuelled by cheap supermarket wine; it seemed fitting.

During the first term of my degree I hoped to recreate that magic, and auditioned for a part in a play produced by the drama society. I managed to secure an inconsequential role and found that the theatre family I wanted to be a part of was seriously dysfunctional. Most conversations centred on how underused the individual initiating it felt they were. Our lead, a shrill Liverpudlian with an obvious eating disorder, would deride any scene she didn't feature in, leaving me self-conscious and sullen for the duration of the run. In the end I felt that getting through it was achievement enough; I might have had talent but I wasn't willing to endure the discomfort it would take to find out. I let the dream of glamour and curtain calls haunt me for a while, but then Dylan offered a new story – a happy family, a settled life, an easy one. I heard the door open behind me but couldn't compel myself to turn and see who it was; I knew it wouldn't be someone I wanted to see.

'Did you get lost on the way to the bins?' asked Dylan.

'I wasn't going to the bins.'

'I know,' he said softly. 'It was supposed to be a joke.'

'I'm not joking. I'm not taking the bin out again. I hate it. I hate how heavy it is. I hate that gross bin juice. I do enough. Can't someone else take out the bin?'

'I'll do it.' I looked at him then, so I could be sure he was listening.

'But will you? You say you will but will you actually do it? Not because I ask you but because it's full or it's bin day.'

'Yes.'

'Do you even know when bin day is?'

'Tuesday?' I wanted to weep.

'That was last year. They sent us a calendar. It's Monday now.'

'I'll take the bins out Monday. First thing. Don't worry about it, Nibs.' Nibs is what Dylan had called me for over a decade. It started as Munchkin – because of my size, I assume. That was shortened to Munch. One pre-menstrual day I complained that Munch was too aggressive, not feminine enough, and he converted it to Nibbles, which eventually settled as Nibs. In the early days he would call me that and I would feel a rush of intimacy, especially when it happened in public. Sometimes I would catch a confused look from an acquaintance and secretly revel in the sense that we were excluding them, not because I enjoyed their isolation but because it highlighted our togetherness. That afternoon on the steps of our home, it irritated me. It was such an obvious attempt to crawl into my good graces and dismiss my complaints. I would have to worry about it, because if I didn't no one else would.

'Why did you invite Mickey over?'

'Because I said I'd see him and I didn't want to let him down, and I didn't want to let you down either. It was a catch-22.'

'No, it wasn't really.'

'Honestly, babe, I was trying to do the right thing.'

'I know you were. It just wasn't a catch-22.' Dylan zipped up the hoodie he almost always wore on weekends. It was nearly threadbare, but no matter how many potential replacements I procured for him, he refused to part with it.

'Isn't a catch-22 just a shit situation?' he asked.

'Not really.'

'OK, it was a shit situation.' He smiled, and more lines than I remembered gathered around his eyes. I smiled back but without anything real behind it. He was simple. Not unintelligent – Dylan could probably build a space shuttle with a long weekend and a decent set of instructions, whereas I count on my fingers – but emotionally, he was simple. He didn't ask questions, he wasn't ashamed by his ignorance, he got by on a childlike level – I'm happy, I'm not so happy, I'm tired. At the end of a challenging day I didn't want to hash it out with him; I wanted to burp him and put him to bed.

Dylan hugged me and then used the closeness to steer me back into the house. Chloe ran up to us and announced that the afternoon performance of her show would begin in ten minutes. Her face radiated excitement and that made me feel guilty about my lack of commitment that day. Wasn't I hugely blessed to have all this love around me? To have so many who needed me? I decided my frustrations were down to a lack of rest, withdrawal from alcohol and shame, especially shame. I was making them responsible for pain that had been self-inflicted. My mother always excused her messes by claiming that it would be worse to live with regrets, but that morning made me think that a regret is far better than having something and then not being able to keep it.

I went to the bathroom and splashed water on my face. I gave myself three minutes to think about Frank, to remember how his words affected me, reached a part that had been asleep for what felt like a hundred years; to recall how strong he seemed and how much I enjoyed him taking control. I lingered on how it felt to pretend to be his new wife, and then I left the room and threw his book in with the recycling.

For the rest of the day I was an exceptional wife, mother, daughter and mate's missus. Chloe performed her play and it was indeed dark, so dark I vowed to address her television-viewing habits, but I smiled during the rare light-hearted moments and applauded wildly at the end. After the show I made everyone hot chocolates with the Baileys Mickey had brought for the grown-ups. That night I gave Dylan 'the signal' and did my best to stay present the entire time. As we fell asleep I curled against my husband's back and allowed him to grip my arm, even though it wasn't very comfortable. But in the early hours of the morning I crept downstairs to retrieve Frank's book and hide it under the sofa, just in case Dylan kept his promise about the bins and it was lost for ever.

9

O N MONDAY I TOOK Bettina's blazer to work. I told her I would take it to the crazy-expensive, super-speedy dry cleaner's in my lunch break. She took it from me and dismissed my assertions with a raise of her hand.

'I'm sure it couldn't have got that dirty in one night,' she said. I nodded mutely. 'How was it anyway?' I pretended to busy myself with the post.

'A bit of a let-down.'

'I did try and warn you. Don't worry – the pub was awful too. Marcus tried to get off with me.' I clapped a hand over my mouth. Bettina switched on her computer.

'I know,' she said. 'He was really going to town on the whole "no one will ever love me and my *Star Wars* figurines" diatribe and I felt for him, you know, in a stray-dog kind of way. Obviously I was too nice, because he mistook my kindness for flirtation and dived in. It was mortifying for all parties.'

Abruptly I questioned whether Frank had actually kissed me. I mean, we had kissed, but did I lean in and perhaps unconsciously offer myself to him, and had he been too gentlemanly to deny me? The possibility made the embarrassment I was still feeling pulsate. At the time I was sure things were mutual, but I questioned what I knew about sex in the modern world – technology had evolved, relationships were changing; perhaps flirtation had too. Or maybe it was simpler than that: perhaps we only see what we want to see?

'Go easy on him,' I said to Bettina. 'He's not that bad.'

'You snog him then!' she cried. She looked at me accusingly, oblivious to the stares we were garnering.

'I don't want to,' I hissed.

'Of course not, you've got your Diet-Coke-hunk husband. It's easy for you married-off lot to tell the rest of us to be happy with the dregs.'

'I'm not saying that, I'm just saying you should give him a break.' What I was saying was she should be grateful. To have someone desire you, even if they themselves aren't the most desirable, is a gift. Dylan liked me, he respected me, I think he even admired me – he'd stayed close to home most of his life, hadn't taken risks or sought adventure. I had travelled a bit, studied, and at twenty-two I thought I had experienced a lot – but desire? That urgent, aggressive pull? I didn't feel that from him; I wasn't sure I ever had. His love had always been of the consistent but muted kind.

'I'm trying to get a break. I don't have the reserves to take on anyone else's angst.' There was no joviality in her voice.

'Do we need a morning meeting?' I asked. She nodded and picked up her bag.

'Exes, meeting under the guise of friendship but he still wants to get in her pants.' Using the shield of my sunglasses I examined the couple closely. The guy, a tall thin redhead, was offering a tiny brunette woman half of his croissant. She shook her head and kept her eyes focused on her coffee.

'He screwed her over,' I added. Bettina narrowed her eyes in their direction.

'Think you're right.'

'What about them?' I pointed to a couple sitting under a tree, sharing a fruit salad.

'Third date,' she said firmly, 'too full of hope to care about grass stains.' Bettina and I had only worked together closely on one project, and when going over the details in the park one morning we'd found ourselves more interested in pontificating on the relationship statuses of the couples around us. From then on, despite having no cause to, we had regular morning meetings. I can't remember how they first came about, whether I had suggested it to her or she invited me, but we fell into a regular pattern of ducking out of the office for twenty minutes and putting our work personas to rest for a while. I was about to add my own commentary when I noticed that Bettina was no longer staring at the couple, but off into the distance.

'I wasn't trying to have a go at you about Marcus,' I said. 'I wanted to offer some perspective. He's harmless.'

'I know, there's absolutely nothing wrong with him. I mean, there's nothing right with him, but someone will want that. He's not my type and that's fine, but I'm scared my type don't want me.' I took off my glasses. I wanted to be sure that all my senses were working efficiently to take in the scene. Bettina, to me, represented the ultimate in womanhood – curves, confidence, career. The idea that she would have insecurities, let alone about her ability to attract a mate, was fascinating to me.

'I'm not sure there's such a thing as a type.' Even if there was, how could you trust yourself to know? I thought Dylan was my type before I saw him eating peanuts – first sucking them clean of salt and then crunching them in a rabbity fashion between his front teeth. 'Anyway, I thought you were seeing someone?' Bettina was always seeing someone. I'd assumed that the fact it never progressed to a fully fledged relationship was an active decision, made by her. Her flat was an oasis of femininity. The first time I went over for drinks, she served me hard-boiled quail eggs with a little pile of salt for dipping; we shared a bottle of champagne 'just because' and gossiped our way through several episodes of *Come Dine with Me* – who would want a man in the way of all that?

'I was – Ben. We saw each other on Saturday. He came over; I cooked for him! I cooked!' I nodded my head to let her know I appreciated the significance of this. 'That's what gets to me: I let him in.'

'What happened?'

'He ate my sea bass, my grandmother's recipe, and then he told me that he wanted to stop seeing me.'

'No! He ate it first?!'

'I know.'

'Why did he call it off?'

'He said he wants to have kids but not for a few years, and that will be too late for me.'

'The bastard,' I whispered. Bettina began to blink rapidly.

'It's OK – he offered me a consolation. I could keep sleeping with him until he found his younger model.'

'The prick!' I cried. Bettina's blinking had not been effective and I watched tears collect in her eyes.

'The worst thing is, I did sleep with him. I told myself I was saying goodbye, but I think I thought it might convince him to stay.'

'I'm so sorry, darling,' I said. I put my arm round her,

and she let me rest it there for a second or two before she shrugged me off.

'Don't be. It's my fault. I should have known better. It made the whole Marcus attack feel so much worse because I spent all weekend thinking that's what I'm gonna be left with.'

'Don't be ridiculous, you're gorgeous. You're bloody gorgeous.'

'Sometimes that's not enough. What if you only get one chance? Maybe I should have married Gianluca.' Bettina was engaged to Gianluca for a year in her twenties. They had gone as far as sending out invites when, to the horror of her fiancé and family, she backed out and went on their honeymoon to the Maldives alone. Bettina sometimes used her parallel existence as an Italian housewife as a punchline to jokes, but this time she wasn't laughing.

I told her, 'Everything happens for a reason, honey,' which isn't the same as saying she was wrong. Whatever future we create, we can never escape our past.

My past was David. He was blond, rakish, and did everything with a take-it-or-leave-it air, although I didn't know that on the night we met because he made it clear he wanted to take me. He was handsome and funny, but my favourite thing about him was the longing I saw in him that first evening. We met at a party, where he unabashedly followed me round the room and I pretended to hate it. It was the first term of my second year at university, and I was still smarting from the horror of the drama society disaster.

One of my housemates, Kathryn, was a fellow cast member, one who, despite the catastrophe of the play, was undeterred from her artistic pursuit. Despite this, or perhaps because of it, our friendship seemed based on an unspoken competitiveness. I always felt a need to demonstrate to her that I was cool enough, brave enough, just enough. One Friday I pitched what I thought was the perfect cosmopolitan night out, but nothing had gone as planned – the gig I got us on the guest list for turned out to be three middle-aged men playing in the upstairs room of a musty pub, and the cool bistro I booked seated us at a wobbly table wedged in next to the toilets. Waiting for the bus home, with Kathryn threatening to tell 'the girls' about how 'wank' our night had been, I pulled an ace out of my pocket. I remembered the location of a house party, and house parties were the official end of any night with potential to be the 'best night ever'. Better still, the hosts were a house share of engineers, which meant it would be heavy on the male contingent. We both agreed that the one thing that might resuscitate the evening was attention from men.

The word was out: bodies spilled into the garden and we had to fight to get into the smoke-filled kitchen where David was leaning against the fridge, as if waiting.

'Excuse me,' I said.

'You'll need to ask me more nicely than that,' he replied. His full lips curled into a sensual smile, and my focus on showing Kathryn a good time immediately began to wane.

For the next two hours I was always aware of where he was, and he was always in my eye line. When Kathryn, overwhelmed by the crowds and also by vodka jelly shots, asked to be taken home, I panicked. The party was yet to reach its peak and if I left, David was sure to be poached, but the attention he had shown me was so bewitching that I did something very out of character. I asked him to walk us home. He agreed and waited in our communal living room as I tucked Kathryn into her single bed. She hugged me round the neck. And slurred, 'He's so fit.' Her approval was like a shot of caffeine. When I went back to him I felt in control and it was like he sensed it, sitting up straighter on the couch and looking unsure for the first time. We didn't speak. I straddled him and we kissed. Despite the risk of intrusion, he started to take off my clothes.

That period was a time of many firsts and from his urgency and the way his hands were mapping my body, I could tell that this was the first time I was going to have sex. I told David this by saying, 'I've never done this before.' He froze as if cornered. 'It's OK,' I said, replacing his hands, which he had held up as if I were his arresting officer. He eased me from his lap and on to the seat next to him. The lust that he had been directing at me like a laser immediately evaporated and I spent another four years trying to get it back.

We didn't have sex that night. David accepted a cup of tea made with not-quite-turned milk and departed after some stilted small talk. Today I would view his actions as gallant, but at the time I could only see rejection. Months later, he told me that he had returned to the party and found a companion more suited to his needs. Although I had no claim to him at the time, it felt like a betrayal. I experienced his rejection all over again, like I was being slapped on top of bruises.

Remembering that hurt and seeing Bettina's pain made me think of Dylan and specifically what I had sort of, almost but not quite, done to him. He had never been anything but good to me and I had repaid him with treachery, for the sake of an ego boost. Bettina was amazing, one of the most amazing women I knew. She didn't need a man to show her that and neither did I. I took her hand.

'If he can't see how wonderful you are, it's his loss.'

'You wouldn't think I was wonderful if you saw me last

night, crying into a tiramisu and listening to Larry's *Late Evening Love Songs*.'

'Damn, girl,' I said in an American accent. 'The dessert I get, but late-evening love with Larry?' Bettina squeezed my hand and laughed.

'It's so tragic, it's my daily guilty pleasure. Usually it makes me feel better, but last night it hit home. I'm knackered today, I didn't even straighten my hair.' Bettina's glossy locks sat in beautiful waves around her shoulders.

'It's working for you. You wanna come over tonight? I'll keep you away from the radio.'

'Thank you, but no. Don't take this the wrong way, but I can't be around you and your beautiful family right now. I think I'm going to get really drunk, preferably alone.' She was right. Being part of something as special as what Dylan and I had *was* beautiful, and I would die for the girls even though, at times, I felt like killing them. I wasn't sure how I'd forgotten that.

I felt lighter as we returned to the office. Yes, I had steered off course for an evening, but we all have our down days. I let Bettina go ahead of me and called Dylan. It went to voicemail. I left a message telling him I would pick up something nice for dinner and for him to choose a new Netflix series. Sitting through ten hours of a war documentary – if that wasn't commitment, what was?

10

I WAS STILL HOLDING the phone to my ear as I walked into Carter. I hung up quickly and tried to embody the spirit of capability and productivity. He regarded me as he always did: with a puzzled expression; as if trying to place me.

'Any inspiration?' he asked.

'Yes. Yes, definitely. I mean, we're not working on anything right this minute but we've got a great idea in the pipeline.' Carter's forehead creased.

'We?'

'We. Bettina and me. You were asking about our meeting this morning?' Carter was silent for a few seconds; the clock in reception sounded incredibly loud.

'No. However, I look forward to hearing your plans. I was asking about Friday. Did you get any interesting leads?' I felt the internal warmth that signals the threat of blushing.

'Oh. Yes. Thanks for sending me over. It was really interesting.'

'Clients?' I thought about the woman in the ladybird dress.

'Probably not, unfortunately.' Carter rubbed his smooth, tanned chin.

'That's a shame. When you finish up with the Nature Tea launch, you'll be needing a project.' My throat felt dry and I had to make some effort to speak.

'Yes. I'll get on that,' I said. Carter nodded and walked past me. I rushed to my desk. I cleaned out my drawers, emptying old, softening gum and abandoned receipts into the wastepaper basket. I was hoping that I would uncover some artefact that would lead me to a new client; perhaps a business card from an individual I had dismissed or a fantastic idea scribbled absentmindedly on a scrap of note-paper. When my desk was clean I had nine pounds in loose change, half a dozen kirby grips and an unopened bottle of grey nail varnish. At a loss for anything else to do, I started to apply it. As I was finishing my second hand, Annie interrupted me.

'I thought you might want to get up to speed with the Emerge timeframes. I'll need you to work with me the week of the event, so it would be useful if you could di-arize your other projects around that.' When she stopped speaking, she let her eyes settle on my hands.

'I thought it was quite nice for the office.' I held my fin-gers towards her.

'Mmmm,' she said. I glanced at her nails. Manicured but polish-free. The nails of a woman ready to work.

'I could run through it with you now,' she said.

'You know, I've got something to finish off.'

'Mmmm,' she said again. I swore at her as she walked away. In my head, obviously – but violently. I've always been a hard worker. I had a paper round at twelve, even though the bag was almost as big as me and I took twice as long as the two older boys that also did my route. I felt so empowered when I could slip my earnings into my piggy bank and when I didn't have to ask my mum for money to go to town on a Saturday afternoon. I'd have a hot bath when I got home from the round and I enjoyed my aching muscles, seeing them as a badge of achievement. I still felt that way; I wanted to throw myself into something and feel the strain. I just needed someone to tell me what that thing should be. Then my phone rang. I picked it up quickly and immediately regretted it; taking my time might demonstrate a lack of availability created by demand.

I was considering this when he spoke, so it took some time to respond after he said, 'Hi, it's Frank.' I meant what I had concluded a few minutes earlier, that my family were a gift to be cherished. It felt genuine at the time, but in that moment I'm not sure I would have been able to identify Dylan in a line-up. Hang up the phone, I told myself, hang up and nothing bad can come of this.

Hang up, my conscience whispered, as I asked, 'How?'

He chuckled. 'My mother called me Francis and I never liked it.'

'I mean how did you get my number?' I hissed into the receiver. I glanced up at Bettina who was typing furiously, headphones in. 'I didn't give you my number,' I said in my normal voice.

'But you did. When you signed in.' I pulled forth a hazy memory of scribbling my details down when I arrived at the event. The thought of him sifting through the pages to find my number made my body vibrate.

'This is ridiculous,' I said. I meant it: the fact that I was so drawn to him when I knew so little about him.

But he said, 'Not really. I promised to introduce you to some clients.'

'You did. I guess after everything, I thought . . .'

'Everything?' Talking to him made me feel naked and he knew it. I could tell from his voice that he was enjoying

81

my discomfort, and that made me feel a prick of anger, which sadly one can feel simultaneously with longing.

'Thank you. I appreciate that. Can you email me the details.' I gave him my work address, which he repeated, still with the bemused tone in his voice. I hung up and congratulated myself on my maturity and professionalism. Perhaps I should have declined his help but I really needed something to offer to Carter. A great client would be the payoff – a career boost in exchange for one small sin. I could make that work; I would simply separate Frank, the man who had infiltrated my psyche and reignited my sexuality, from Frank, the useful work contact. Once I had allowed him to help me, I wouldn't think of him again. I tried not thinking of him for a couple of minutes and then I checked my email.

I repeated that pattern all day, pretending to listen to my colleagues talk about trends and spikes; mindlessly wandering through the internet looking for inspiration. But every conversation or article or cup of coffee or toilet break would lead my thoughts back to Frank. Even Annie couldn't penetrate my Frank fantasy. So when Bettina suggested the pub I said yes, because in some ways – although it pains me – I am my mother's child, and after a day of failing to do so I was sure that the only thing that would shut off my mind was alcohol.

'The thing about men is none of them, not a single one, knows what they want. Their mother told them what they wanted and now she's old or dead, they're looking for another one.' Two drinks in, Bettina had reached the anger stage of grief.

'That's not true,' said Marcus. 'I know what I want.' He looked at Bettina, his green eyes wistful.

'You think you know what you want because the patriarchy makes you think that all the little witterings in your brain are valid, but you don't truly know. How many guys have you met who are half-heartedly dating a woman, hit thirty and propose? Like someone yelled *freeze* and they had to tie the knot with whoever they were next to. It's bullshit.' Marcus rubbed his goatee.

'What's so wrong with that? People change – you might find the perfect person and in ten years' time they become a monster, or they're already with someone. It's not a bad idea to find someone OK and make it work. I mean, if you want to be with someone.'

'You don't know anything,' snapped Bettina, and he dropped his head.

'I think you're both right,' I offered, opening my arms as if I were royalty addressing my subjects. I grabbed Bettina's wrist. 'You seek truth.' I placed a hand on top of one of Marcus's. 'And you find beauty. In this world both are valid and also validating.' Bettina pulled her arm away and sneered at me. I didn't blame her; even I wasn't sure what I was going on about. Why could I not learn that just because a bartender suggests a double it isn't mandatory to have one? I turned to Marcus, who was beginning to go crimson. I lifted my hand, and watched his body relax and his standard colour return. 'I believe you know what you want.'

'Thanks,' he said.

'Why?' said Bettina, wine sloshing in her glass as she spoke. 'It's not like you could trust the words coming out of his mouth.' I looked for a lifeline.

'You've been with Chris for ages, haven't you, Dee. What are your thoughts?' Dee looked a little taken aback. As if she was at a show and hadn't expected audience participation.

'Er, Chris is a bit of a moron. Wouldn't know what he wanted if he was on fire and had to choose between a bucket of water and a parakeet.'

'Exactly!' shouted Bettina. She threw her arms up, splashing Marcus with Pinot Grigio in the process. Dee dabbed at his trouser leg with a tissue from her cardigan pocket.

'In fact, he won't know what he wants for his tea and will sit there till he starves, so I'd better be off.' Dee drained her shandy. 'See you later, troops.' As she left, Bettina finished what remained of her wine and stood up.

'I know I don't want to be running around after a man for the rest of my days. Who wants another drink?' I raised my hand and Marcus indicated his empty pint glass.

'She's gorgeous,' said Marcus, as we watched Bettina fight her way to the front of the bar. It sounded more like a prayer than a conversation starter, but I nodded enthusiastically.

'She's great! You're great! Everyone is in some way.' When I get drunk, I can be a bit overenthusiastic, but I do actually believe that we all have our individual gifts and, whilst those gifts might not be as obvious as, say, Jennifer Lawrence's gifts, someone will find them.

'I'm not sure you're right. I've pretty much consistently been told I'm not that great,' said Marcus. His voice held a quiver of sadness but he was smiling. Certainly that was part of his greatness – the way he kept smiling, even though, just looking at his grubby *Red Dwarf* T-shirt, you could tell that his life had been difficult. I felt intensely motherly towards him and wanted to give him a cuddle, so I did. He struggled a little, but eventually relented and allowed his head to rest on my shoulder.

'She's married,' I heard Bettina say. It was an accusation.

Marcus and I uncoupled and she placed our drinks in front of us.

'Thanks,' he whispered before starting on his lager, and I patted his head.

'Let's each tell the most tragic love story we've ever heard, preferably with a straight man's demise at the climax,' said Bettina.

'Um,' said Marcus, and glanced at me. He would never criticize her but we were both thinking that Betty had taken bitterness to professional levels.

'Oooooor,' I said, holding up a finger and noticing that I was slurring slightly. 'The most inspiring love story we have ever heard.' Marcus grinned. Bettina looked at the ceiling thoughtfully.

'I prefer my idea,' she said. 'So, this guy I worked with fell in love with this woman in the Netherlands. He was going to give up his whole life and move to a tiny little village in the mountains or something. He moved out of his flat and sold all his shit, and even had a leaving party before he flew out to stay with her. He lands, and it turns out she's at least ten years older than she made out and lives on a pig farm with her three kids.' Bettina drank deeply and allowed us to take in her words. 'The pathetic bit is that he tried to make it work. Stayed for three months.'

'Yeah,' I said, unable to find a positive spin for the woeful tale, 'that's pretty high on the tragedy meter.'

'What's your contribution?' Bettina asked Marcus. He cleared his throat.

'Well, I did know this guy who asked a girl out sixteen times. Finally, she said yes, but it was basically to stop him asking. They went on one date – he spent a fortune taking her to this play she wanted to see. At the end of the night, she told him he could have a selfie with her and asked if that would be enough for him to leave her alone.'

'Ouch,' I said.

'That was you, wasn't it?' asked Bettina. Marcus sighed and nodded. I gave him a sympathetic look as Bettina howled. Even though we had barely begun our drinks, he offered to return to the bar.

'Betty,' I said sternly, when we were alone.

'I'm giving him a break. I'm at the pub with him, aren't I? What's your story?'

I'd heard many dismal love stories over the years but always came back to one. 'My father left my mother when she had severe post-natal depression. Apparently, he wanted someone who could still do what she was good for. She never saw him again and neither have I.' It was my turn to receive a sympathetic look.

Then Bettina stuck her tongue out at me. 'I was just trying to have a wallow and you had to make it all serious.'

I laughed. 'You shouldn't be wallowing. I'm trying to tell you you've probably had a lucky escape.'

Bettina smiled; she had a smile that could stop traffic. 'You might be right. I'll have to move on to my other break-up technique then.'

'Which is?'

'Shots.'

I waved my hands in protest. 'I'm approaching forty. I don't do shots.'

'You do tonight.'

11

MARCUS RETURNED TO the table with drinks and Bettina immediately sent him back to the bar. The evening passed in a vodka-fuelled blur. We commandeered the jukebox; Bettina literally growled at anyone who tried to approach it. You got three songs for a pound, so we chose a song each for every coin. This resulted in a bizarre mash-up of nineties pop, punk and heartbreaking ballads. We were all supportive of each other's choices, singing along when memory permitted. It was the perfect way to end a Monday, and I had all but forgotten what I was supposed to be forgetting. I didn't even think about going home until I was weaving back to the table from my fifth toilet break, and found Bettina and Marcus kissing furiously. They were so focused on the task at mouth they didn't notice my return, so I picked up my things and left them to it.

I fell into a cab, feeling proud that I could remember my address. I think I had a little doze in the back, because before I knew it the car was flooded with light and I was being asked for the best part of twenty pounds.

'Did you go via Manchester?!' I admonished the driver, and he told me to enjoy my evening. I slammed the door in protest and tried to hide my struggle with the garden gate;

despite my ungraciousness, the driver waited until I was safely behind it to pull away.

After several attempts to get my key in the lock, I pushed the door open triumphantly. Slipping off my shoes, I recalled Marcus and Bettina's fervent groping, and giggled. I was shushing myself when I got the feeling that something was off, and not just my hand–eye coordination. I stood with my hands on my hips and examined the hallway – shoes scattered haphazardly; post piling up on the little side table; it all looked standard. And that was it. I could see how normal my home looked. The lights were on, every single one. That's when I heard the sobbing, high-pitched and erratic, still able to pierce a path straight to my heart. I walked slowly towards the kitchen, hoping to prepare myself for whatever I found there. Before I entered, I could see Ruby, her head on the table, long, skinny arms wrapped around it. Dylan stood against the counter silently, his face ashen.

'Hey, family,' I said tentatively, to no response. 'It's a bit late to be doing homework, Rubes.' I tried to catch Dylan's eye, but he would not or could not look away from our daughter. Even after I said his name he continued to stare at her, as if scared she was a vision and if he blinked she might disappear. I said his name more forcefully and he spoke, but not to me.

'Tell her. Tell your mother what you did.' I approached Ruby and, as I drew close, she raised her head. Her eyes were rimmed with red. A memory returned of Ruby at four; she needed surgery for a hernia. She was too young for us to explain general anaesthetic or surgery or hernias, so we told her she was going to the hospital for a nice long nap. When she was taken to theatre and a blue-gowned monster plunged a needle in her hand, she locked eyes with me. That evening she looked at me the same way – with pain, shock and also an accusation: that I had broken my promises. I had failed to keep her safe.

'Mum,' she whispered. I recognized it as an apology, and realized I hadn't heard her say the word for some time. I pulled her head to my body and the action unleashed a fresh batch of tears, which soaked through to my skin.

'Fine,' Dylan said, straightening up to his full height and folding his arms. When we first met and Dylan told me he used to be a doorman at a brazenly dodgy club, I didn't believe him. He had the size but was too gentle, definitely more teddy than bear. In that moment, I saw it. He could be intimidating; he seemed almost menacing. I felt protective of my little girl.

'Fine. I'll tell her.' Dylan took a step closer and Ruby pressed her face into me. 'I went to look at the bank statements today.'

'Did they take the water bill?' I asked.

'Not now, Alison!' Dylan roared. I felt Ruby's body tense and gripped her tighter. I was about to instruct my husband to calm down but he began speaking again, his words tumbling out on top of each other. 'There was an alert about downloads or uploads or whatever they are, and I clicked on it – I just wanted to stop it beeping – and it opens and there's a whole load of pictures. Pictures of Ruby, you know, selfies or whatever.' I tried to shrug but I was hampered by Ruby's unyielding embrace, so I shook my head. Ruby took selfies like other people drank water; they were part of her life force. 'Naked pictures, Alison!' Dylan shouted. I told him to be quiet then. I didn't think he had a right to his outrage; I'd told him we should check her phone each night but he'd talked me out of it. 'The girl needs her privacy,' he'd said with a little shake of his head, when I knew he meant that he couldn't be arsed.

'You'll wake Chloe and the neighbours,' I said, but as I was speaking I began to comprehend what he had said. I pulled Ruby off me and she fell limp, like a puppet. She folded over on to her knees, making a low moaning sound which was muffled by her pyjama-clad legs.

'What were you thinking?' I asked her. Although I knew. She was thinking she wanted to belong and to feel sought after and to be seen in a way that she probably didn't feel, and if she were another girl, someone else's daughter, I might have responded to that sympathetically. But she was mine. 'What on God's earth were you thinking?'

'She's not moving until she tells me who she's sent them to,' Dylan said.

Ruby started to speak but her legs obscured the words.

'Sit up, darling,' I said. 'Talk to us, please.' All I'd wanted was for her to talk to me. She sat up.

'I was in my bra,' she said mournfully.

'Barely,' muttered Dylan.

'This is serious,' I said. I noticed that I couldn't pronounce my S's properly and took a few breaths. Couldn't I have major parenting challenges in the morning, or at least sober? 'Ruby,' I said when I had composed myself. 'Once you've sent those pictures it's like a virus – you don't know where it can end up.'

'I know,' she said. 'I didn't send them. I promise. I wasn't going to send them to anyone.'

'Why did you take them then?' asked Dylan. 'You're a child. This is . . .' He covered his face with his hands. I saw Ruby wince. Even in her distress, I could tell she was miffed at being referred to as a child. It made me want to laugh; as children we think we have the answers, and then we reach adulthood and find only more questions.

'Go to your room,' I said. 'We'll deal with this tomorrow.' It sounded ridiculous even to me, like something a sitcom parent would say, but I needed to end it and return to the matter once at least some of the vodka had left my system. Ruby seized her opportunity, scurrying out of the kitchen and up the stairs before slamming her bedroom door closed. I reached out to Dylan but he didn't move, and my hand hung in the air uselessly.

'Do you really believe she didn't send them to anyone – is that very likely?' I sat in the chair Ruby had vacated and looked up at him.

'I don't know.'

'I was willing to keep her up all night.'

'I know, but she's got school, Dylan.'

'Like I'm gonna send her back there with the little perverts that have convinced her to do this.' I could feel my drunkenness converting to a hangover, a dull throb at the base of my skull.

'I think we both know that Ruby doesn't need anyone to convince her to do something.' Dylan looked at me as if he didn't recognize the person in front of him.

'Have some coffee. I'm going to bed,' he said before leaving. I stayed in the kitchen and forced myself to down a pint of tap water before following him. He was under the covers when I crept into our room; for a minute I thought he was asleep but as I climbed into bed in my underwear he spoke.

'Where have you been?'

'At the pub.'

'Clearly.'

'Don't do that.'

'I think I've got a right to ask why you're rocking home drunk on a Monday night.'

'It was an accident.'

'You sound like your mother.' I slapped him. Hard. It was an awkward blow, catching him half on his face and half on his neck. It was absurd, probably something my mother would do. Dylan barely reacted.

'Go to sleep, Alison,' he said. My throat began to ache.

'You should have just called me. I would have come straight back if I thought you needed me. I wanted a night out, that should be allowed.'

'Check your phone,' he said. I turned over and closed my eyes. My stomach rumbled angrily and I remembered I hadn't eaten, but for some reason getting up for food would have felt like losing a battle, so I continued to lie still until the room and the evening faded away.

It was just after five when thirst and daylight forced me from my bed. I crept downstairs and drank a glass of flat lemonade. I was grateful that I didn't feel as broken as I thought I would, and started to tidy up the kitchen. As I was wiping down the worktops I remembered my bag, abandoned in the hallway the night before. I sat at the bottom of the staircase and pulled out my phone. Seven missed calls and three messages from Dylan. I swore under my breath. Our little jukebox concert had obviously drowned out the sound of his calls. I had a lot of making up to do; Netflix wouldn't cut it. I compiled a list – dinner, foot rub, unlimited action movies – and that was as far as I got, because I saw a notification letting me know that I had a new email. I think I trembled as I opened it; my recollection is that I was shaking, although of course that could have been all the booze.

Hello Tiny Dancer,

I have an amazing client in mind for you. Pretty high profile and it could probably lead to making further connections. Shall we meet for dinner on Wednesday night to discuss? 7 p.m. at Eleanor's.

F.

Have you ever tried not to feel excited? It's an embarrassing process, like trying to withhold a sneeze. I squeezed my eyes closed and smiled to myself. He had given me a nickname. I knew I wasn't allowed to feel that way – that's what my wedding vows had amounted to: thou shalt not be excited by any other man – but vows and decisions are an active choice whilst feelings are uncontrollable. A hand on my shoulder made me jump and I let out a small shriek. I turned to see Chloe rubbing sleep from her eyes.

'Why are you awake, Mum?' she asked groggily.

'Why are you awake, silly?' I replied. She laughed.

'I don't know. My eyelids wouldn't stay closed.' I pinched her tummy; it was still gently rounded, even though the rest of her had become lean and angular.

'That was cheeky of them,' I said, and she scrunched her mouth into a pout before giggling. 'Since we have time, should I make pancakes?' Chloe's eyes opened wide.

'With Nutella?' she whispered.

'Why not.' My daughter squeezed past me and ran ahead to the kitchen. When I came in behind her, she was sitting in the chair where Ruby had been the night before. She swung her legs under the chair and twisted a lock of hair around a finger. A little girl, ready for breakfast; and that I wasn't ready to lose yet.

12

I'D FINISHED THE first stack when Dylan came down. He kissed me on the forehead, quick and dry like an uncle, before slipping a pod in the Nespresso machine. He could do that; erase any problems with a night of sleep. Whilst he didn't subscribe to the adage that one shouldn't go to bed on an argument, he tried his best not to wake up with one.

'You want bacon?' I asked him.

'No, that's OK.' He joined Chloe at the table.

'I don't mind,' I said, walking to the fridge.

'Then yes. Thanks, Nibs. I would love some.' That was my forgiveness. I should have been happy it was that easy but it left me frustrated. I wanted to tell Dylan to stick up for himself, that he deserved better, but I gave Chloe her pancakes and started on his bacon.

'Thanks, Mum,' she said, her mouth already full of food. Peeling the clammy strips of meat apart, I felt very domesticated. This, cooking a hearty breakfast for my family, was how I had envisioned being a wife would play out, and this part was as good as I had imagined. I hadn't factored in the rest of it, the other responsibilities that would push this one down my priority list.

After I'd served Dylan, he grabbed my hand. 'Maybe

I've bitten off more than I can chew living with three feisty women?' His mouth curled up on one side, a semi-smile that was both apology and absolution.

'You haven't,' I said, squeezing his fingers before letting go, 'but we have to work together. If we were more together on things, stuff like this wouldn't happen. We'd see it and we'd address it before it blows up in our faces.' I was saying it to convince myself as much as him.

'I know, I know,' said Dylan, which was not the same as committing to change. He stared hard at his fork, as though the answers he sought might be hidden between its tines. 'I was thinking I could expand the business, take on some drivers for commission. I could be home more then.' I poured another batch of batter into the pan and focused on the bubbles forming on the surface. I'd heard the expansion plan before; the first time I was excited, supportive. I imagined us doing it together, both being home for the kids. But the talk didn't go anywhere; whenever I suggested a definitive action, Dylan would become especially interested in peeling dry skin from his cuticles.

'Some extra money would be nice,' I said lightly. 'I could apply to do a four-day week.' Dylan chewed on some bacon rind thoughtfully.

'Are we poor?' Chloe piped up.

'No,' I said quickly. 'Why would you ask that?' She shrugged as she licked Nutella from a piece of pancake.

Ruby came in from the hall. She hovered in the doorway, already in her uniform. Her head was down but her fists were clenched. She was prepared for another assault. I put together another plate of pancakes and smothered them in syrup. As I held them out to her I asked, 'Is it over?' She nodded and took the plate. We ate our food together in silence. It was not comfortable but we were together in our discomfort. Dylan took the girls to school without further discussion and I felt quite triumphant. I had taken control of a sticky situation, the kind you advise fellow mums about in a knowing tone. I was even left with enough time to blow-dry my hair and get the kitchen in order. I looked behind me as I left for work and it was as if nothing had happened.

The sense of achievement didn't last long; at eleven I hit the hangover peak. What I had thought was a strong constitution and efficient processing was me still being pissed. Bettina had strategically decided to work from home, so I didn't have her to distract me from the pain. I did what any woman would do – overcompensated. I wrote half a dozen overdue blog posts for a chain of theme restaurants and, even though I was absolutely certain I would have to rewrite them, I rewarded myself with a latte when I finished. Before I took my first sip, Annie interrupted me to ask if I wanted to help her brainstorm campaign messages for Emerge.

'Of course, I'm brimming with ideas,' I said. In an attempt to distract from how odd that sounded, I threw her a thumbs up to convey my enthusiasm. I'm not sure it worked – if anything she looked scared – but I concluded that wasn't the worst thing. Fear is a short step from threatened, and if I could threaten Annie perhaps I could keep her away from my job.

'I've booked the blue meeting room,' she said. 'It's got the comfiest chairs.' I agreed although I hadn't noticed. I downed the rest of my coffee, eager for the caffeine to rouse my nervous system. When I got to the blue room Annie wasn't there, and a petite black woman was seated at the glass table.

'Sorry,' I said. 'Annie said she had booked this.' I felt a pulse of excitement that she might have made an error.

'Yeah, I'm here for the meeting,' said the woman. 'I'm Marie.' When she said her name I remembered her standing awkwardly at the front of a team catch-up some weeks ago, eyes trained on her shoes as Carter introduced her as a new intern. Today her head was held high, and earrings made of a string of tiny yellow pom-poms danced next to her neck as she spoke. She seemed very young a few months ago, and she still did, but now her youth spoke of potential and vitality rather than inexperience. She was blossoming as I withered. 'I'm assisting Annie with Emerge,' she added. So, my assistant now had an assistant. After Ruby learned to walk she developed a habit of making a break for it. We'd be ambling along, looking at dandelions, and she'd cut loose, sprinting across the park, careering down crowded pathways. I'd call her name and roll my eyes at laughing passers-by, but underneath I was terrified, convinced that this might be the day that I didn't catch up with her. As Marie watched the door for her new boss's arrival, I realized that Annie was off the reins.

I felt too low on resources to muster up even the tritest of small talk, so Marie and I sat in uncompanionable silence until Annie entered several minutes later. I'd never known her to be late. A few months before, there had been a bomb scare at Tower Bridge. London's public transport, messy at the best of times, was at a near standstill. I felt so smug when I arrived, sweaty and shaken, ready to share my commuter war stories, and there at her desk was Annie, her face a mask of concentration. The city's chaos had failed to ruffle a single feather on the wings powering her professional ascent. If Annie was late, she was making a point and the point was that she was in charge; the party didn't start till she got there. Annie gave us each a printout of the project outlines before sitting.

'See, so comfy. I told Carter about this chair company,' she said, and beamed at me. I didn't respond. The thought of riffing about office furniture with our ice-cold commander was unthinkable. I felt ambushed. It didn't seem considerate for her to usurp me without a heads up. She should have taken me out, sat me down and explained how she planned to expose me. I might have stepped aside graciously had she done so.

I certainly wouldn't have felt such a need to prove myself, and might not have blurted out, 'Teeth!' Both women stared at me. I noticed simultaneously that they were frowning and that neither had the furrows that run from my nose to my mouth. Marie even had a crop of acne glistening on her chin, a clear indicator of the fresh hormones flowing around her body. 'Let's lead with teeth!' I cried. Marie coughed. 'Teeth are the future?' I added with less fervour. Annie licked her lips.

'It's a bit obvious for a conference on orthodontistry. I'll get you up to speed on the messaging before we collate our ideas.' I should have backed down, but to do so would be to publicly acknowledge her as a leader, and I was paranoid that my pub antics could have made their way through the office grapevine. I wanted her to know I could match any pace she set.

'You might think that, that it's obvious, but often the obvious is . . . not so obvious. It's like no one would lead with teeth, so let's do it. Let's be . . .' Marie nodded slowly, as you do to a particularly elderly person. 'Let's be the teeth people.' Annie opened her mouth and I spoke quickly to curtail her objections. I think I believed that if I spoke long enough, if I gave them enough weak ideas, they could squeeze them together and make one good one. 'We could start with an image of teeth, you know, like that classic ad that had a photo of a . . . God, what was it? I know it. It's so famous. Anyway, it was just an image of this product because the product stood alone, and here the product is teeth and also—'

'Before you continue,' said Annie in a measured tone, 'I'll refresh us all on the client specifications.' She cleared her throat and read from the handout. 'No teeth. The industry is oversaturated with images of perfect smiles. So . . .' I wanted to evaporate or at least have a stroke, something big enough to distract from the previous minute. My phone rang, which would have to suffice.

'Sorry,' I said, 'it might be important.' I escaped to the hallway, resting my forehead on the cool paintwork before answering the number I didn't recognize.

'Stinkface!' came the greeting, after I offered a tentative hello.

'Henry,' I muttered, turning so I could lean back against the wall. 'Why are you calling me at work?' I knew why my younger brother was calling me on a Tuesday afternoon – because normal hours didn't apply to him. He had probably just woken up; I don't think he's ever owned a watch. Henry is a person for whom the term 'drifter' was invented. I haven't known him to have what could be classed as employment since . . . since ever. Which is why I knew if he was ringing me, he was calling to ask for money. 'What number is this?'

'Lost my phone, didn't I. Well, it was stolen by this chick, but that's a long story. Got this from a friend.' Henry had a lot of friends.

'I'm not giving you any money.'

'Sis. Sis, come on. Why do you assume I'm ringing to ask for something?'

'Because you're ringing to ask for something.'

'Well, I am. The pleasure of your company, for lunch today.'

'You're taking me to lunch?'

'Exactly.'

'When?'

'Now.'

I sighed. 'I can't just drop everything when you call.'

'Why?' said Henry, amusement in his voice. 'Whatcha doin'?' He treated working people like members of a quirky collective. I thought back to Annie and Marie – they were probably drafting the perfect anecdote to summarize my idiotic performance.

'I can fit you in if we meet right now.' I emphasized the last word.

'I'm already at Veggie Delight. It's on Curtain Road. See you when you get here.' Curtain Road was a ten-minute walk from the office, but getting Henry to move towards me would only result in untold delays. He'd meet a busker who would tell him about a squat in Dalston, and three days later I'd get a text apologizing and telling me about his new pet ferret. I rushed back to the meeting room and stuck my head around the doorframe.

'I'm afraid a client's moved a meeting forward. Send an email with what you need from me.' I tried to withdraw before Annie could question me, but of course her reflexes were as sharp as always.

'What client?' she sang.

Rather than saying, 'None of your business, you over-achieving little twot,' I replied, 'It's a secret.'

'A secret?' Annie shook her head, either with confusion or shock. And then she smiled evenly. The sort of smile that makes men on market stalls slip an extra apple into

100

your bag. 'OK. A secret.' She glanced at Marie, whose eyebrows flicked momentarily skywards.

'Yes. Confidentiality,' I said brusquely before walking away. I heard a high-pitched laugh follow me out of the office; it immediately took me back to leaving my first lesson the day after I had cut my own fringe aged twelve.

13

THE RESTAURANT WAS actually two roads away from the location Henry had specified, and locating it added another five minutes to my journey. I was sure I could feel my blood-sugar levels plummeting and felt panicked I wouldn't have time to get served. As I walked in, it became apparent that serving time wouldn't be required, because Veggie Delight was a buffet where for five pence less than a fiver you could eat as much as you desired. My brother was sitting at a table for four in the centre of the room, two steaming bowls in front of him. He stood up and kissed me on the cheek without finishing his mouthful.

'What a treat,' I said, looking past him to take in the peeling wallpaper. As I sat down, a profusely sweaty man in stained chef's whites placed a knife and fork wrapped in a paper napkin in front of me.

'Keep them,' he drawled.

'How sweet. A gift,' I said.

'No,' said Henry. 'You've got to keep hold of your cutlery between courses.'

'Yeah, I got that.' Henry pushed one of his bowls towards me.

'Here, don't get up,' he said. It looked like moulding

porridge; my stomach lurched in protest. I slid it back towards him and out of range of my nose.

'Don't be such a snob,' said Henry.

'You think a snob is someone who bathes, Hen.'

'When they use soap,' he said. He flashed me a grin, and I caught sight of the tooth he'd chipped falling out of a tree and never got fixed. In almost every memory I have of him as a child he has some part of his body plastered or bandaged. Mum would proclaim that she parented creatively, which was another way of saying she couldn't be bothered to set boundaries. It made Henry fearless, never willing to evaluate risk, whereas it terrified me and left me inclined to play safe. Henry put the fork in my hand and I dipped it tentatively into the goop. He pushed on my fingers so the tines sank deeper into the bowl. I pulled up a forkful, and Henry watched with what had become known in our family as his full-force grin, the same one he would use on me when I found him covered in my lipstick when he was five. I could never resist it. I closed my mouth around the fork, my mind skipping through several expressions of derision, but as the subtle, sweet yet spicy flavours danced on my tongue, I found myself unable to voice any. I closed my eyes to ward off other stimuli that might intrude upon the experience.

'Told you it was good,' said Henry. He pushed the bowl back to me and started on the other portion of goop. I was embarrassed that I had made assumptions about the food because of the non-existent service and casual regard for hygiene, but I assured myself it was a logical conclusion. This was not seeing a bloke in a hoodie believing he was going to rob me; this was seeing a bloke in a hoodie, waving a knife, shouting 'give me your money', and not being willing to take the risk that he would not. Some judgements protect us; they might not always be kind but they are necessary. Henry never made assumptions and I loved him for it, but it also drove me crazy, because when you fail to make judgements you let anyone in and accept everything. Worst of all, Henry never judged himself – not his ripped-beyond-a-fashion-statement jeans or his laissez-faire attitude to employment – which was why he never felt the need to make a change: there's no progress without shame.

'I did want to see you, obviously,' he said between mouthfuls, 'but I do also want some money.' I dropped my fork on the table. The noise drew the attention of the waiter/chef/manager, who stared at the utensil and then glared at me.

'Of course you do,' I said. 'Why do I ever think things will be different?' I barked the words; a spray of spittle landed on the table between us.

'What do you mean?' asked Henry. He tilted his head to the side, eyes wide, face receptive. I sort of wanted to throw something for him to fetch.

'You're who you are. You dance through life expecting everything to be OK because there's always someone waiting to put things right. Just because you're my brother and I'd like you to be different doesn't mean it's going to happen. People don't change, not at their core.'

'Does that mean you're always going to be grumpy?'

'I'm not grumpy, Hen, I'm exasperated.' Henry leaned back in his chair.

'You shouldn't be. You shouldn't let me dictate how you feel.'

'How can I help it when you're dragging me out of work, offering me this – OK, fine, delicious – gruel, under the pretext of sibling bonding, when you actually want to pump me for funds?'

'Not pump – request.'

'Fine, sweet brother, request away.' Henry wiped the

corners of his mouth with one of the scratchy serviettes and cleared his throat.

'I would like for you to consider gifting me a couple of hundred pounds for some of my essentials.'

'Which are?'

'Food, shelter and a very modest amount of marijuana.'

'No.'

'Well, thank you for your consideration. May I ask why?'

'Because you're an adult, you should be taking care of your own basic needs, and aren't you living with Dad?' By Dad I meant Eddie, Henry's father, whom he generously allowed me to claim too.

'We had a falling out. He didn't appreciate some of my acquaintances.'

'He's sick, Henry, you shouldn't be bringing stress to his door right now.' I felt a flush of regret then. What my step-father hadn't provided in chromosomes he more than made up for in affection. I understood from other people with absent parents that they felt a sense of loss, but I believed I was fortunate because I had a father who'd chosen me. Eddie always told me how lucky he was. A buy-one-get-one-free was what he said of his union with my mother. And even though they broke each other's hearts, he didn't allow it to diminish the care he offered to me. I made a silent promise to visit him. 'At least you're not asking him for money.' I took another mouthful of food. Henry burped.

'I did, but he didn't want to give me any.'

'Good. I don't want to either.'

'You never want to, but you do. You having money troubles?' I took some food from Henry's bowl. It was also delicious.

'It's not polite to ask people about their finances.'

'You're not people, you're family.'

105

'Family are people too, Henry.'

'We're only as sick as our secrets.' I did sort of want to unload.

'Things feel precarious at work. I think I've got a target on my back. I thought I'd be looking at a promotion by now and I'm worried about getting pushed out. I'm so paranoid after the redundancy.' I felt the rush of anxiety that had been visiting more and more frequently; it was accompanied by a fog descending on my brain and sharp stomach cramps.

'What you gonna do about it?'

'What can I do?'

'I don't know, do I? You're the woman who always has a plan.' I suppose to him it seemed like that. I was at university before he hit adolescence; saving for a house before he finished school; he got stoned at my wedding. To Henry I had everything in order.

'I don't know.'

He laughed. 'I don't believe that.' I wanted him to think of me as capable, someone he could still look up to, but also I needed to tell – it was ready to lurch from my mouth like a hiccup.

'I met this guy . . .' Henry nodded. 'On a night out.' He stopped nodding and regarded me intently. 'No, not like that. Well, kind of like that. Oh, shit. It was weird.' Henry grinned again.

'Weird I can do.' So, I told him. I told him almost everything. In fact, it spilled out of me. I explained how Carter had blindsided me and that I was feeling insecure and overwhelmed, and that Frank rescued me and it felt like I was in a movie or a dream. I told him about my bathroom encounter with the model; that her designer camisole was still in my laundry basket; and that we ended up held

106

hostage but that I had enjoyed being forced not to acknowledge my responsibilities. He looked amused and shocked and in awe at all the right places. Even though I was the older sibling, Henry had always been the one with the exciting stories.

'Very cool,' he said, which from Henry was high praise indeed. 'So, this guy says he can hook you up with someone to work with?'

'He did . . . but the thing is, we kissed.' I closed my eyes so that I couldn't see his reaction. 'And I don't think I can see him again now.' I opened my right eye first, still fearful of what it might show me. It seemed that Henry was trying not to laugh, although, as with everything in life, he wasn't trying very hard.

'This isn't funny,' I said, which made him lose control and openly convulse.

'It's a bit funny. Watching you freak out over a snog.'

'I'm married, Henry!'

'I know. I was there. Thousands of pounds on the driest chicken I've ever eaten.' I looked for something to throw at him, settling on his serviette, which floated down ineffectually between us.

'My marriage is important to me. My family. I don't know why but I made a stupid mistake.'

'You fancied someone. It happens; marriage doesn't cut off your desires.' I swallowed because I wanted to tell him it felt like so much more than that, and even though it was true to me that *would* be laughable.

'It should.'

'Well, that is very weird. I never knew that getting married would mean a castration.' I covered my eyes with my hands.

'I'm not about to start taking relationship advice from

you.' Henry had had a series of girlfriends that he met at festivals. The relationship was always over by the end of the summer.

'Career advice then,' he said with an impish smile. 'This guy sounds like he can help you out, which will help me out. So, you should get in touch with him.'

'I don't know—'

'Alison, you're gonna call him, not blow him.' I groaned. 'Be selfish for once. Feel better now? Thinking any differently about giving me some cash?'

'No, Henry.'

'OK,' he said, leaning forward as though it were a business meeting. 'You do this. You take this opportunity that has been put before you and if I'm wrong, if this guy can't help you out, I'll never ask you for money again.'

'Never?'

'For the rest of your natural life.' I held out my hand and he grasped it firmly.

'You're so gonna die before me,' I said, grabbing my fork. Henry nodded amiably, his mouth already full again.

I emailed Frank from my phone before I got back to the office and before I could change my mind. Then I switched off notifications and put the phone at the bottom of my bag; it felt like I had a great deal of self-restraint. As I walked back to my desk, I caught sight of Annie who waved gaily, probably to draw attention to my return time. 'Good meeting?' she mouthed.

'Yes, thank you,' I mimed, and it didn't feel like too much of a lie because I knew I had an ace in my handbag.

Dylan had a double lesson out of town, so I made the girls macaroni cheese – a family favourite – and bribed them to play Monopoly with me. I was consciously creating a connection, hoping it would hold me through the next day, when I knew I was to be tested. I wonder now if it's the case that you always know what you're going to do, and the only real choice is how long you wrestle with it.

'As long as you promise not to get all funny like Christmas,' said Chloe, after she had secured an extra pound for her pocket money.

'Your grandmother was cheating. And it's important that you know—'

'When you cheat you only cheat yourself,' the girls chorused.

'Yes. Good,' I said. I turned away to set up the pieces. I didn't want them to see that I was embarrassed to hear my own words and recognize how weak they sounded. Chloe and Ruby argued over the dog piece, so I confiscated it and then felt bad that I was always chiding or dictating to them. As they counted their money, I slipped into the kitchen and poured us some drinks.

'Let's make this a party,' I said, as I walked in with a tray holding three full champagne glasses. Chloe's eyes doubled in size as she took hers.

'It's grape, silly,' said Ruby, taking a sip of her own. 'Mum probably can't handle drinking today,' she muttered. I flashed her a look but she met my gaze squarely. What could I do? As much as I hated it, she was right.

'Get ready to be defeated,' I said, holding up my drink, and the girls giggled and bumped their glasses into mine. I played to win, even though Chloe was struggling with the rules and Ruby wasn't committed. I wanted to teach them to fight for what they wanted.

The three of us laughing together was like a tiny holiday from life. The girls asked me questions about all the places on the board, and even though I knew they were trying to distract me, I indulged them with stories of burning-hot curries in Whitechapel and dirty clubs off Tottenham Court Road. They listened so attentively. Through their eyes – although I knew how innocent they were – I felt glamorous. Despite my efforts, Chloe won. She did a very ungracious celebratory dance when I declared her the winner, and I gave her a big hug and told her that even victors had to brush their teeth and get ready for bed. She gave me a kiss and ran off upstairs. Her sister hesitated, but then leaned in for a quick peck before following. I stopped her before she walked away.

'I love you,' I said.

'Yeah,' she replied. I turned to watch her leave and saw Dylan standing in the doorway. He gave her a kiss as she passed.

'I didn't hear you come in,' I said.

'Things were too raucous,' he said, stepping into the room and taking in the scene. 'Getting pissed up?' He nodded to the glasses.

'Shloer,' I said. I walked over and kissed him. 'I'm sorry.'

'What for?'

'Everything.'

'It's OK. Want to say sorry again upstairs?' It wasn't quite flirtatious, definitely more of a joke, or at least said with enough ambiguity for me to take it as one if I chose to.

'Maybe. I need to clear up.' I collected the glasses and packed the game away. When I picked up the cushion Chloe had been sitting on, I uncovered a stack of brightly coloured bills.

14

I WANTED A FRESH look. That's what I said to Bettina when I persuaded her to cover yet another extended lunch break; that's what I said to Pedro, my stylist, as I begged him to squeeze in a last-minute appointment; that's what I said to myself.

'What 'appened,' said Pedro, eyeing me in the mirror, 'a break-up?'

'No, I fancied a change.'

'Don't we all, darling,' he said. He grabbed hold of my ponytail, I felt a tug and he presented it to me, a dry tuft of red. 'No going back now.'

Bettina removed her glasses as I approached my desk.

'What happened to you?!' she exclaimed.

'I told you. I wanted a new look.' I touched my fringe self-consciously. Pedro had cut my hair to just below my ears and added a sweeping fringe that I had hoped would be sexy but already feared would serve as an annoyance. 'We all make interesting choices,' I said, looking at her pointedly. We were yet to discuss her public make-out session with Marcus.

'Understood,' she said quickly, putting her glasses back on.

Annie squealed when she saw me. 'It's so chic!' she cried.

'Yeah,' I said. I felt a little bubble of pride form in my chest.

'You just need to get a few pieces that go with it and it will be a total makeover.' I looked down at my dress; a navy shift, chosen precisely because I thought it was chic.

'Thanks,' I said.

'Do you need me for anything? I've got a stack to do.'

Don't ask what, I coached myself before asking, 'What have you got on?' Annie wrinkled her nose. I'd noticed she often did this before saying something self-congratulatory, which was to say she did it a lot. I was very sure it wasn't a natural quirk; that someone, perhaps an admirer, had once told her it was cute and this had inspired her to incorporate it into her persona. I said a silent prayer that it would give her wrinkles.

'Well, there's Emerge, of course . . .'

'Of course.'

'And Carter has given me a new company to research and develop a pitch for. Heart Up? At least, that's what it's called now – not after I get my hands on it. It's kind of an online dating app for start-ups and investors. I guess Carter thought I'd be able to connect with the demographic.'

'Who knows what Carter's thinking,' I said. But I had an idea: he was thinking Annie's mind was fresh and malleable and mine was eroding by the day. 'No – if you're busy, I'll leave you to it,' I said.

'Oh no, I can definitely fit you in. Let me know what you need and I'll allocate some time.'

How very gracious of you, Annie, I thought, but I said, 'I'll be fine for the afternoon,' and when she didn't immediately leave, 'thank you.' Annie skipped away. OK – she didn't skip, but her gait was bouncy enough that her shiny blonde hair bobbed around her shoulders with each step.

When I sat down, Bettina was typing but shaking her head at the same time.

'Whatever,' I muttered, and blew my new fringe out of my eyes.

I don't know what I spent the afternoon doing; every act was an exercise in containment. I was so scared that if I involved myself too much in any conversation, my nerves or excitement would spill out involuntarily. I hung out in the storeroom, looking at old project files, and opened several folders on my desk to ward off impending small talk. It was unexpectedly hot and the office started to clear an hour before the end of the day, everyone claiming back those flexible hours that made up for the lower-than-market-standard pay. Bettina left with them, no mention of an after-work drink. I was pleased that I didn't have to explain I already had plans. By five it was just me and Carter remaining. I could see him in his cube on the phone and, whilst I couldn't hear what he was saying, I could tell from his posturing that he was being very direct. When he finished, he stood up and ran his fingers through his hair several times; unlike when I did this, it looked better afterwards. He scanned his office and, clearly failing to find what he was looking for, peered beyond the glass and directly at me. I waved. He walked towards me and I fought an urge to run.

'How are you getting on with identifying a new project?'

'I have something in the pipeline,' I said.

'What does that mean? Do things in the pipeline add to our turnover?' I didn't have an answer. 'Annie mentioned some issue with confidentiality.' He pressed his lips together as he waited for my answer.

'Yes. Well . . . The client doesn't want anyone to know they're shopping, I guess.'

113

'What client? I assume the confidentiality doesn't extend to me.'

'No, of course not. Sorry, I should have kept you in the loop. Let me find the name.' I could feel individual hairs clinging to my forehead. I shuffled the papers on my desk; Carter didn't move. 'You know, this is embarrassing but their name, it's unusual, it escapes me. I'll send you an email update ASAP.'

'I'd appreciate it,' said Carter. He eyed me for a few seconds before returning to his office and, even though I'd taken too many long lunches to have earned an early exit, I packed up my bag and left.

I had two hours to fill. Two hours after you've had kids feels like a long time. Fifteen years ago, I could lose two hours without even thinking about it. I would choose to doze after waking or sit in the sun with a fashion magazine. Those two hours were like a test. I walked aimlessly round Liverpool Street, wandering into shops, pretending to look at clothes whilst surreptitiously eyeing up the perky salesgirls. In one boutique I found myself staring at the woman behind the till. She drummed her nails against the counter between customers. She was dressed for a life she did not yet have – her shiny trousers appeared painted on and close to a metre of blonde hair extensions fell behind her.

'We have more in stock if we don't have your size,' said a voice, startling me. I turned to see that it belonged to a tall brunette. Her animated face radiated desire to help, and her brow glistened with evidence of recent effort. She held a stack of shirts over her arm, and her posture suggested that the load was causing a significant amount of discomfort. I could hear that at the counter the drumming had resumed. 'What size did you need?'

114

'Eight,' I said, because I wanted her to feel useful. I recognized the need to compensate for beauty with helpfulness. She scurried off and I stood awkwardly beside the occasion wear. I hadn't actually looked at the dress and so I held one up to see it properly. It was pink: a terrible colour for my complexion, and silk: a horrible material for my thighs. As I examined the seams I noticed the drumming had stopped, and I looked up to see the blonde staring at me and then at the dress and then back at me. She was sizing me up, and from her expression I concluded that I did not fit.

I left. I felt bad for bailing before my self-appointed helper returned. I could picture her unloading the shirts before searching through rails for a dress in my size; my guilt conjured an image of her standing on a stepladder and hauling heavy boxes. I could see her face as she came back to the floor triumphant, but then ashamed when she realized I had done a runner. I knew the blonde would take it all in.

I went to the restaurant half an hour early and, because I was alone, they demoted me to a seat at the bar. I felt on display and not in a good way, like a scarecrow in a field. I ordered a glass of white wine, even though I had sort of decided not to drink because drinking was what people did on dates, and this wasn't that. The barman asked me what variety I wanted and I told him that I didn't know. He recommended something he described as 'minerally' and I accepted. I checked the menu as he poured my drink and learned that what I wanted was something that cost less than ten pounds a glass.

'Waiting for a friend?' he asked, as he placed a small square serviette in front of me and the long-stemmed glass on top.

'A colleague,' I replied. He nodded and then walked a

115

few feet away to buff glasses – clearly not an interesting enough story to break up the tedium of his day. I read and reread the cocktail list; it featured a lot of herbs. My phone buzzed and immediately I thought it might be a message from Frank cancelling. I was simultaneously hurt and relieved, the same way I feel if I offer someone assistance and they refuse.

It wasn't Frank; it was Dylan. 'HAVE FUN!' it read, followed by that mocking winky-face emoji. Dylan had just started using emojis because I'd told him they were necessary – texts can't convey tone. At the time he said, 'Just assume I'm being nice.' But the next day he asked me to bring home bread and added a bright red heart. I closed my messages without replying because every response I started felt like a lie. I had sent him a text earlier in the day to say I was having dinner with a potential client; not quite a fib but not close enough to the truth.

I tapped on my news app, downloaded months ago but never once accessed. Waiting for Frank, I felt hyper-aware of my ignorance about current affairs. I was curious about the world around me; I had many concerns about what sort of future was being created for my children, but when I tried to take in the information it would swim around my mind, never settling. Over the years, I'd learned to hide my lack of knowledge by asking the opinions of others and then agreeing with whoever I was speaking to at the time, but from the little I knew of him, I understood that I wouldn't be able to hide from Frank. That was frightening but also seductive; if I couldn't hide it meant there would be no need to make the effort to do so. Frank was an air-conditioned bedroom in a heatwave, a place where I could drag off my clothes and flop on to the bed naked – sweaty and swollen but finally unrestricted.

I sipped my wine a little too quickly. I didn't savour any of the aromas, mineral or otherwise; I simply wanted to reach the place where your mind gives in, when your worries stop straining against the bear hug of alcohol and are carried away, panting and exhausted. The maître d' must have taken pity on me and handed me a menu to peruse. I read through it carefully, each descriptor a short story. Everything was muddled or enveloped. And it was expensive, undeniably so. At the bottom of the main courses there was a list of sides, none less than a fiver, and from my calculations it would take at least two of these to create something approaching a satisfying meal. I found myself struggling to find a way to justify the expense. I couldn't write it off as a client dinner and it was far too extravagant for a casual midweek meal – and it *was* to be casual, I had promised myself that. I decided to tell Frank that I only had time for drinks. I would have one more pound-a-sip glass of wine and return home to a pizza from my freezer.

I had decided this only moments before I felt his hand rest lightly between my shoulder blades and heard his baritone voice ask, 'Hungry?' And despite this I nodded eagerly, even before I had turned to see his face. When I did, I saw my response had pleased him and my stomach performed a cha cha.

15

FRANK LOOKED AWAY from me and across the room; seconds later the maître d' was before us. The world is made of two kinds of people: those that can gain the attention of restaurant staff and the rest of us. I can spend fifteen minutes waving and calling only to have dozens of waiters glide past me; sometimes I have to resort to grabbing a passing arm, startling the owner of the limb and furthering my sense of hopelessness. I felt like Frank could draw a server to him with a thought. His whole energy said 'you should want to make me happy'. I'm sure it was this that found us being led to a quiet booth near the back of the restaurant, two banquettes either side of a large table covered in thick, white linen. The glass panels creating the enclosure rose to the ceiling, making it feel like a room within a room. Both Frank and the maître d' gestured for me to sit, and I tried not to show that I was aware of them observing me as I wiggled gracelessly into the seat. I was right about not being able to hide from Frank.

'Not the easiest to access, but worth it,' he said, as he slid into his side effortlessly. Within the confines of the booth he felt dangerously close. I unfolded my napkin slowly to avoid his enquiring eyes. When I looked up he was still watching.

'Thanks for meeting me,' we both said simultaneously.

'Jinx,' I said. He held out his right hand, little finger extended towards me. 'What's that?' I asked.

'Aren't we supposed to lock fingers now?' he asked seriously.

'I think that means something else,' I said. He didn't move his hand away. I shook my head, hoping to convey that I was humouring him, when in fact the thought of touching him again, even in such a benign manner, made my mouth go dry. I wrapped my little finger around his and he responded with a firm, consistent pressure. It didn't hurt but it wasn't quite comfortable.

'What does this mean then?' he said. I looked past our hands and into his eyes.

'It's a promise,' I said.

'I like that,' he said.

'Are you ready for drinks?' said a voice beside us, and we both turned to look at the waitress before we let go.

'We'll have a bottle of the Malbec,' said Frank. The waitress nodded briskly and left without further comment. We sat in silence for a minute. I didn't know how or where to start. I felt like I should apologize, but for what I wasn't sure. I needed Frank to set the tone. Then he did.

'You've been on my mind,' he said.

And I responded, 'I'm married.'

'I know,' he said. I played with the edge of my napkin, smoothing and resmoothing it against my thighs. 'You have a ring.' I placed my hands face down on my lap and examined them. It was true I wore a ring on the fourth finger of my left hand, but it was an ornate band with a tiger's-eye stone and said student more than spouse. With funds stretched beyond our limits in the run-up to the wedding, Dylan and I found the ring in an antiques shop

119

in Camden. He promised to replace it when things were more settled. We never got around to it and I found that I didn't mind. I had grown fond of my quirky wedding band. 'It's not just that,' said Frank. 'I could tell you were holding back. And that's fine because—'

'Would you like to taste it?' the waitress asked. She held the bottle towards Frank and he moved his wine glass closer in reply. She carefully poured a mouthful of inky liquid. Frank lifted the glass and, though it was tall and bowl-like, it looked small in his hand. He closed his eyes as the wine touched his lips and breathed in the scent before placing it back down.

'Good, thank you,' he said. The waitress filled his glass. She paused to wipe the neck before she poured mine. I wanted to grab it from her and do it myself, or maybe swig straight from the bottle. As soon as she had retreated, I exhaled a breath I had been unaware I was holding.

'This is a favourite,' said Frank, picking up his drink.

'That's fine because . . .' I prompted.

'Ah yes,' he said. I thought I knew what he was going to say: that he didn't like me 'that way'. He wouldn't be the first. Even though hearing that would be for the best, would untangle the moral knots I had got myself into, I braced myself for the verbal blow. 'It's fine because I'm married too.' I wasn't ready for that. Even though I was sitting down I felt unsteady. And, also, I felt angry. Angry at myself, for not seeing the obvious – he didn't really like me; I was a box to be ticked on his list of mid-life-crisis clichés. I was angry with Frank because he purported to be so honest and authentic, all the while dancing, literally, around the truth. And I was angry on behalf of his wife, a woman I already despised for having a life that I had wondered, however briefly, whether I wanted for myself.

I should have hidden that anger; I had no right to berate him, but I believed that it no longer mattered how he saw me, so I had a mouthful of alcohol before asking, 'Anything else you failed to mention? Kids, dog?'

'One. A boy. Kid, that is.' When he said the word 'married' I had pictured someone young, undemanding; an accessory, not really a woman yet. Not a mother, someone who made up part of a family. 'Lionel. It's a family name. I call him Leo.'

'Fuck,' I said, and placed my face in my hands. I stayed there for several seconds, feeling the heat of my breath against my palms. I knew I looked strange but I thought I might look even odder crying.

'Are you ready for food?' I heard the waitress say. It was like she had a special gift for interrupting at terrible moments. I uncovered my face and she gazed at me. Her dramatically false lashes made her lids look heavy, exacerbating the bland expression that suggested she would rather be somewhere else. Well, that made two of us.

'We'll share the brisket,' said Frank. 'And can we also have some fondant potatoes and two portions of greens.'

'I won't eat a whole portion of greens,' I said when we were alone again.

'But you'll feel better with them on the table.' I didn't argue because he was right. I hated that he was right. He told me about a meal he had eaten earlier in the week, a business dinner at a Japanese restaurant I had read about online. He told me he let the client order and they chose the most exotic dish on the menu. 'When my chicken arrived, I could see him envying every mouthful. He spent so long chewing on his bat lungs or whatever he had selected, he could only nod in agreement to whatever I was suggesting.'

'Why didn't you tell me?' I asked. 'I mean, I'm not upset

but I do feel a bit stupid.' I was upset, very upset. More than I had any right to be.

'Don't feel stupid. I didn't say anything for the same reason you didn't.' We looked at each other. I noticed our breathing was in sync.

'Which is?'

'We wanted it to be real.' It was real. I knew it was real. I had the proof in my wash basket. If it wasn't real, why had he taken up residency in my head, and why did I feel so stupidly disappointed? I cleared my throat.

'It's not a problem,' I said. 'I had too much to drink. Got carried away. I really only wanted to meet to apologize, for imposing.'

'How long have you been doing that?'

'What? Apologizing?'

'Not being honest about how you feel.' He was very still. I laughed but he refused to free me from the awkwardness by joining me. When did I stop being honest about how I feel? It was probably a frigid Sunday afternoon, sitting by the shore at Southend-on-Sea with my mother. She had bought me a hot chocolate from a chintzy cafe; it was so thick there were mouthfuls that were chewable. She still smoked back then, and the acrid smell of her cigarette fought with the cocoa for my attention. Mum slipped her free hand around my shoulder and I snuggled against her, more for warmth than to return the affection.

'Just you and me. We don't need anyone else,' she whispered.

I paused because I thought maybe we did need someone else. Someone to stay up with Mum when she listened to sad music after I had gone to bed, or someone strong who could help me when sometimes I couldn't get her up in the morning. But I was worried that if I said this it would

mean no more Sunday visits to the beach or gloopy chocolate drinks, so I said, 'No.'

'How do I feel? If you're so sure I'm not being honest.'
Frank moved his wine, so that the path between us was
completely unobscured.

'Disappointed, a bit hurt. Intrigued. Excited, I would
guess, because that's how I feel.' If he doubted that my
emotions were aligned with his, he didn't show it.

'What are we doing?' I asked. He smiled. I shook my
head. 'No, no. Strike that from the record. This isn't a
romcom. This is my life and my family and my husband
and your wife. This is ridiculous.' I threw myself back
against the leather upholstery. He held his hands up.

'You're right. It's ridiculous. It's ridiculous how much
I like you.' He had stopped smiling. I could run, I thought. I
could slide clumsily out from the seat and flee. I was a kid
at the top of a slide trying to choose between the awkwardness of a retreat and the horror of the descent.

'I like things to be clear and upfront, and I want us to be
open about what we plan to do.' Something about how he
said these words made my face flush.

The world's least empathetic waitress interrupted us
with a plate at least a foot wide, loaded with fragrant rare
meat.

'I'll be back with your sides,' she said, as though it were
a threat. We sat in silence until she returned. As she tried
to find space for the bowls, I contemplated how I had
made everything so messy. Frank continued to look at me,
his deep-brown eyes revealing nothing of what he was
thinking.

He could be a spy, I thought, except what would a spy
want with a thirty-something, mid-level marketing manager and mother of two. I laughed out loud – at myself, at

my situation, and said to Frank, 'My plan is to eat.' He picked up his knife and fork, and we both started on the beef. It was almost effortless to eat. I had the thought that everything could be like that with Frank – easy and delicious.

16

'I LIKE YOUR HAIR like that,' Frank said. 'You have an elegant neck.' I had forgotten about my hair. I touched it and could tell that it had become flat. My first instinct was to comment on this, but instead I thanked him and asked how the book was going.

'Well, I think – it's almost impossible to tell. It's selling but I'm concerned that people aren't getting the core message.'

'Who cares, if they buy it?' I asked.

'I care,' said Frank.

'You can afford to care,' I said. The wine had gone to my tongue. Frank laughed.

'You're great,' he said with a chuckle. 'And right. And I'm grateful for that. I appreciate what I have. It wasn't always the case.'

'Go on,' I said. Frank told me that, growing up in West London, he wasn't special – far from it. He was born in the middle of seven siblings; his mother would often need two or three attempts to get his name correct when she addressed him. They ate out once a year, on holiday at a caravan site in Wales. He always had sausage and chips, even though they ate it all the time at home, because he was so fearful of being disappointed.

'I was chubby until I was about fifteen. Quiet too. I had a couple of friends, but if they weren't around I was happy to be alone and read my books,' said Frank. 'Then one day one of the most popular lads on the estate asked me to come and play pool after school. It was completely out of the blue; I figured he knew my older brother or something. We got round the corner and three of his friends were waiting to kick the shit out of me.' I gasped. I felt protective of this former version of Frank.

'Why?' I whispered.

'Why not?' said Frank. 'Because they could. Because I let them. Then I got home and my mum smacked me round the head for getting blood on my shirt.'

'I'm so sorry,' I said. I didn't have the best time at school. Some of the older girls tried to make life hard for me, and being trapped with an army of bored teenagers isn't always the most positive place for a skinny, ginger kid; but no blood was shed.

'Don't be. It made me. From that day I knew I had a choice about how people saw me and what I became. I decided that my kids weren't going to go to school with thugs or become one, and I wasn't going to let anyone get the best of me. I started reading personal-development books, began training and . . .' He shrugged then, a humble signifier of all he had become with this discipline.

'I've been trying to think of how I can get ahead at work, and all I need is to get my head kicked in.'

'Let's try something less grim. I do have a client for you. This wasn't an elaborate ruse to see you again . . . not entirely.'

'OK, well, thank you.'

'Do you want some more information?'

'I'm sure they're fine. Anyone's fine at this stage.'

'You have to want the best for yourself. You deserve it.'

Both Dylan and Frank seemed so sure of what I deserved, but life had already shown me that it doesn't play fair. When I was thirteen I had my one and only fight with Eddie. I went to a sleepover at my friend Frederica Hughes's house, except I didn't. We went to a party hosted by a boy who lived in the next town over. Frederica drank half a bottle of cider and fell asleep in a chrysanthemum bush. The buses had stopped running and I only had the earnings from my morning paper round in my pocket. After administering water and coffee, I knew I needed a reliable adult and I only knew one. I called Eddie and begged him to pick us up; twenty minutes later he arrived in his patched-up Skoda. Usually I would be embarrassed to be seen near it, but I flew into the passenger seat before remembering Frederica, and leading him back to the garden to get her. When he entered, teenagers fled like gazelles from a lion. Eddie scooped up Frederica and carried her out to the car, where he deposited her on the back seat and she lay face down on the pilling fabric. As we drove to her house, Eddie lectured me on underage drinking and lying and other daughterly sins. I responded minimally, which only made him deliver his words with more fervour, occasionally slamming his hand against the steering wheel to emphasize a point. Finally, as we turned into Frederica's road, he said, 'What were you thinking?'

'You don't get to tell me what to do,' I said. 'You left.'

'Your mother was being . . . unreasonable,' he said, his words now measured.

'Yeah well, you get what you deserve,' I retorted. He slammed on the brake, causing Frederica to roll from her perch and into the foot well.

'You're absolutely right,' he said, eyes facing the road. 'Get out.'

Eddie didn't deserve my mother's verbal assaults or my teenage angst, but he got it. What did I deserve? My reliable, loyal husband or Frank?

We finished our meal, sharing our histories between bites, steering clear of the most obvious aspect of our past and present. His stories weren't unique but the way he looked at them was. When he talked about his decision not to go to university, it wasn't with regret the way others did, the way Dylan did. He owned the decision as part of his journey.

'How did you get into what you're doing now – the writing and speaking?' I asked him, over coffees laced with liqueur.

'I'll tell you,' he said, 'if you stay open.' I put out my little finger and he gripped it with his own. 'OK,' he continued. 'One day I decided it was what I was going to do.' I nodded and waited for more, but he sipped his coffee.

'And then?' I asked.

'And then it all happened, but the decision was the making of it.'

'You make it sound so simple,' I said.

'It is and it isn't. They have a lovely terrace here. Would you like to have a nightcap?' I didn't say anything, but perhaps my face was giving take-me-anywhere vibes because he got up and held out his hand to help me. He left it resting lightly on my arm as he guided me up some stairs at the back of the room. I was anxious someone might think we were doing a bunk and stop us, but the staff all smiled politely and moved aside. Frank reminded me of a documentary Dylan and I watched on dog training. The host demonstrated how you had to convey, with your stance

128

and energy, that you were the alpha dog. Frank moved in a way that told the world he was the leader of the pack.

The stairs opened to a balcony. A man out there alone on his phone left as we entered, his face an apologetic frown. We must have looked like people who desired privacy, a couple. I wonder if it was this, seeing us through the stranger's eyes, that prompted Frank to kiss me. I resisted briefly, more because it felt unfamiliar than wrong, but then I was in it, like being trapped on a fairground ride, scared and excited and unable to get off until someone else stopped it. His head was bent but he still had to lift me to reach his mouth, and my feet had nearly cleared the ground. I thought to myself, I'm actually floating, and made myself laugh in his mouth. He placed me back to earth but kept his arms wrapped around me.

'Not my best review,' he said.

'I'm sorry,' I said. I shook my head and tried to regain my composure. 'This is so . . . I don't know what it is.'

'It's easy,' he said. He was right. I hadn't thought about homework or bills or Carter for an hour. 'You know what the biggest lie is? That things worth having aren't easy.' I let my head fall in to him. I wanted to set up camp there. 'Can we address this?' I looked up at him. 'How good I feel when you're around.' I put my head down and spoke into his shirt.

'Must we?'

'I think so,' he said.

'There's nothing we can do. You're married. I'm married.'

'There's things we can do. It's deciding whether we want to.' That wasn't true. Doing whatever you wanted meant being like my brother or my mum. Someone always has to be unhappy in life, and I'd accepted that it would probably be me. I stepped away from him.

129

'It's time I went home,' I said.

'This weekend,' he said back.

'No, now.'

'Give me this weekend. Two days, one night. I'm doing an event in Birmingham Saturday afternoon. Come with me.'

'I can't . . .'

'Tell him you have work.' It was the first time he had mentioned Dylan. He made him sound like a minor hurdle; I felt protective of him.

'It's not right.' He opened his suit jacket and pulled a packet of cigarettes from the inside pocket.

'You don't know that yet,' he said.

'I'm going,' I said, and walked towards the door, careful to leave plenty of space as I passed him. He didn't stop me, and I heard him light his cigarette and inhale as I pulled at the heavy metal. I ran down the stairs, stumbling at the bottom and drawing the attention of several diners. The light was starting to dim and I couldn't recall where the exit was. As I headed towards what I thought was the way out, the girl who had been serving us stopped me.

'Your bill?' she asked.

'God, yeah.' I could feel my cheeks burning. I rooted in my bag for my debit card. She took it from me before going to get the machine. When she returned, I tapped in the PIN without looking at the total.

'Where's the exit?' I asked. She pointed behind me and explained the route. 'Thanks,' I said before walking away, although I had already forgotten what she had said. My mind was consumed with two words: 'One night.'

I don't know how I went home that evening, kissed Dylan and dismissed his questions about the meeting; ironed the girls' uniforms and watched a film about two people waking up in each other's bodies. Externally, I was the perfect wife, or if I wasn't Dylan didn't seem to notice. I even initiated sex, not out of guilt but because I didn't want him to suspect anything was wrong.

'What's got into you?' asked Dylan as we both lay staring at the ceiling, so perhaps I had tried too hard.

17

I T WAS ALARMING how wrong it *didn't* feel, even though I forced myself to consider the irresponsibility of my actions at regular intervals. After having Chloe, the midwife advised me to exercise my battered pelvic floor whenever I went to the loo; I used the same system to try and strengthen my resolve. Whilst emptying my bladder I'd run through a list of horrifying potential outcomes – Dylan's anger; the girls' confusion; that Frank wouldn't want me after a weekend; that he would. My plan was misguided because it made me think about Frank, and thinking about him unleashed a soap opera's worth of emotions – anger at Dylan for not recognizing that I needed more, as well as frustration at myself for waiting so long to acknowledge that maybe I wanted it. Work, until now the bedrock of my anxiety, was a welcome distraction. Bettina had a date and wasn't prepared to let me get anything done until we had analysed every aspect of the limited information she had on the man. He didn't sound bad – he appeared to have both a legitimate profession and a full set of teeth. Generally, Bettina treated dating like a sport, possibly hunting, but she actually seemed nervous about this one – she was still living under the shadow of the one that came before.

'Does he look honest?' she asked, holding her phone towards me. It was a photo of him at the beach; he was holding a beer, and his face and arms were a worrying shade of pink.

'Definitely. Only an honest person would put that picture online.'

'He's a teacher,' she said.

'That's noble.'

'Hmmmm.' She examined the image again, her lips pursed in concentration. She looked especially beautiful when she was serious.

'Has anyone ever cheated on you?' I asked her. Bettina placed her phone next to her keyboard carefully.

'Not that I know of,' she said, 'but then I make it very clear that if I find evidence of indiscretion, and trust me I look for it, I will cut out their spleen with a rusty screwdriver.' I laughed and sounded like a faulty car horn.

'That's extreme.'

'No, it's the worst thing you can do to someone.'

'It's definitely up there. Where even is the spleen?'

'I meant the cheating,' clarified Bettina, as she clicked on her monitor.

'Not the worst, surely?' I noticed my right leg jiggling and crossed my left one over it. Bettina didn't answer and stared above my head. I followed her gaze to Annie, standing behind me.

'You have a visitor,' she said. 'In reception.' She seemed perturbed and I experienced a rush of fear. Frank didn't seem like the sort to spring an office-hours visit – too flashy and obvious – but he *had* made it clear that he wanted my attention. I paused in the hallway before walking down, gave myself a minute to steady my ragged breath. I'm ashamed to say it wasn't my rapidly loosening morals that alarmed me – I was scared that if he saw me in the real world, my everyday self in a humdrum office environment, whatever spell I had managed to weave would be broken. The foyer was empty apart from the receptionist and a slender woman wearing a close-fitting coral suit, perched on one of the modernist sofas. I started towards the door, thinking maybe Frank had gone for a smoke, and the woman called my name.

'Alison?'

'Yes,' I said. She approached, impressively quickly given the height of her spindly black heels, and extended a tanned hand. I took it, and a row of bangles on her arm jangled as we shook.

'I'm Anoushka Shuldeshov-Rollinson, but feel free to call me Nush.'

'Thanks. Great. I will.' She looked so happy. I felt awkward, not knowing why I was the source of it.

'Should we go in?' she asked, gesturing towards the office doors behind me.

'Sure,' I said. She didn't seem like a security risk. I led the way to a meeting room that no one ever booked because it was so near the toilets. She stood in the doorway, looking gleefully around the empty space.

'So, this is where the magic happens,' she said. She took a seat at the head of the table and pulled a compact out of her voluminous bag. 'Ugh,' she said, examining her face. 'I'm disgustingly pale. I look like I'm dead.' She was so bronzed her skin was in danger of clashing with her suit. If she was dead, I was decomposing. She closed her compact with a ready-for-action snap. For a few seconds she was still, her features a picture of contemplation. I took a seat as quietly as I could.

'Do we have bubbles?' she asked.

'I'm sorry?'

'Champs?' She looked at me, and I saw the confusion I felt reflected back at me. 'Don't we drink champagne? I thought you marketing people were all about the bubbles.'

'I . . . I think you're getting confused with *Absolutely Fabulous*.'

'What's that?'

'A TV show from the nineties, with Jennifer Saunders.' She frowned. 'Forget it. I think we might have some fizzy water somewhere.'

'Don't worry, I'm not thirsty. I'm on a juice cleanse, a whole-life detox actually. I've already had personal training this morning, and after that like a litre of green juice. My body is begging for mercy.' She slipped off her heels and swung both legs over one arm of the chair. Her toenails were also coral, and I wondered whether she changed them every day to match her outfit. Nush made a come-hither motion with her arms. 'Just throw me your ideas,' she said, and closed her eyes. When I didn't speak she opened them. Without warning, she laughed and clapped her hands together. 'He didn't tell you, did he?'

'Tell me what? And who?'

'Frank! He's so cheeky. Let's start again.' She placed her feet back on the floor and her palms flat on the table.

'I'm Nush. I'm pulling together an art show. The youngest, hippest artists from across Europe, basically my friends. I need to promote it and Frank said you're the best in the business.'

'He did, did he?'

'He's great, isn't he?' I examined her again. She appeared not to be wearing a top, or indeed underwear, under her jacket.

'Yep, he's certainly something. How do you guys know each other?'

'From around. OK, my project. I was thinking "Shining Lights" or "Under the Lights" but you can work on that. Will ten grand do for a start?' And with that, Anoushka Shuldeshov-Rollinson became my tropical-coloured saviour.

'Yes,' I said, 'I believe that would be a great start.'

Nush was working more with feelings than concrete ideas. She had a stack of family money and a sense that, either because or in spite of it, she wasn't taken seriously by those around her. I could tell from her demeanour and the way every conversation would spin off into a tale about a party, more often than not on a boat, that her lack of professional standing was not a consequence of her background. Basically, she was the high-end version of Henry. She wanted me to develop a brand for her event, but more than that she wanted me to rebrand her. I made some notes and told her that I would pull together a basic project outline. She looked weary but jubilant at the end of the meeting.

As I walked her out, Annie was loitering in reception. She thrust her hand towards Nush as we approached.

'Hi, I'm Annie. I work with Alison,' she said, without making eye contact with me.

'Yes, Annie assists me on a lot of projects,' I said. Nush let the hand hang between them and eventually Annie withdrew. Nush kissed my cheeks, leaving the scent of grapefruit in the air around me.

'Thanks for your time. I'll be in touch. Ciao,' she said.

'Rude,' said Annie when Nush was at a safe distance. It was the first time I had seen her unsettled. I certainly wasn't going to offer any reassurances.

'She's fine. Just particular.'

'Who is she?'

'Anoushka Shuldeshov-Rollinson,' I said, unable to contain a contented sigh after I spoke.

'Your confidential client? Carter told me she was foreign or something.'

'Yeah. Sort of. She's from here; her money isn't.' Annie's mouth fell open. I wanted to tell her to watch out for flies.

'Thanks for your notes from the Emerge meeting,' I told her. 'I have some thoughts for you. I'm not sure you're working with the best lead time.' I started back to my desk, without giving Annie the opportunity to fall in beside me. The staccato beat of her heels as she followed made my heart sing.

Of course, I had to get in touch to thank him. It would be rude not to. I was a liar and an adulterer but I wasn't impolite. His email footer included a mobile number and I texted a brief, professional thank you. One that left no room for a developed response. He messaged back immediately, chastising me for paying for dinner and then again with a string of numbers. A third message explained that the numbers were a booking for a first-class train ticket to Birmingham on Saturday morning. He wrote that he would see me at the station at midday or he would not. I didn't want to feel that because he had gifted me a new client I owed him, but I did owe him for something; for reconnecting me to a woman with a taste for excitement – the girl who backpacked through Asia and moved to the city with a single suitcase and an envelope stuffed with cash. I was grateful for that. That could have been enough. It should have been.

I stopped at a butcher's on the way home. I wanted to make a pie. The man behind the counter seemed frustrated with my lack of meat-related vocabulary. Mum rarely cooked for us when we were growing up. She said it wasn't an efficient use of her time; most of our meals were served on toast. We had a roast at my grandmother's on a Sunday, and that made up our weekly quota of veg. I was unable to answer his queries about cuts and kilos. With a queue of tutting customers expanding behind me, I pointed at some steaks and gulped back my surprise when he told me the cost.

I had them seasoned and ready to go when Dylan came in from his lesson. He kissed me on the head, right on the crown, and sat down heavily on one of the kitchen chairs.

'Perfect,' he sighed. 'What are we having with them, Nibs?'

'Chips,' I said.

'Homemade?'

'No.'

I cooked his meat how he liked it, so that juices flowed out with the first cut. He ate in silence. I didn't feel hungry; my stomach had been replaced with a concrete slab. I shovelled in oven chips without tasting them.

'I needed that,' he said when he was done. That was how Dylan had always been; with his belly full he was usually content. However, he didn't seem content, far from it.

'What's up?' I asked, and waited to be underwhelmed by the response. Last time I had seen that look on his face, he had misplaced his headphones. I knew I shielded him from a lot of our problems, or perhaps he placed me in their path.

'The college have stopped advertising me. They've got some corporate firm in now. It's half my customers.' It was silly – I should have been concerned for him, for us, but I was pleased. Dylan had inherited his business from an uncle who was retiring. Within a week of qualifying he was set up with a car and a string of new learners. Year after year he got referrals from the local college; that and word of mouth kept him afloat. He wasn't a hustler – he was always telling me not to fix things that weren't broken, but something doesn't have to stop working to warrant an upgrade. I had set him up with a website. He feigned interest for a while, but when I tried to log on a year later, a stark white page informed me the site was available for purchase. I thought perhaps he could do with some jeopardy in his life.

'Don't you have any other connections?' I asked. Although I was sure of the answer, I was being generous and giving him an opportunity to surprise me.

'No,' he said glumly.

'And they didn't give you any warning?' I imagined there were signs or even overt indicators that he wilfully ignored. Dylan pushed his plate away and leaned back in the chair. I winced as the back legs creaked.

'Maybe I'll retrain,' he said wistfully. 'Do plumbing like we talked about.' The only time I could recall us discussing that particular career path, we were at a wedding. It was my first outing after Ruby's birth and I was breathless: from worry about leaving her with my mother, and from ill-fitting Spanx. Dylan was tipsy. I was sober – trying to keep my breast milk clean. I had humoured him. I didn't consider that a talk.

'You'll work something out,' I said, patting his shoulder. He looked doubtful. 'I'll help.' I could tell this reassured him, and it irritated me. Of course I would be on hand to clean up the spill. 'Why don't you call Mickey and see if he wants to go for a pint?'

'You don't mind?'

'No, I sort of don't want to look at your face right now.'
He looked sad and I offered a parody of a laugh.

'I'll take a shower and then I'll call him,' Dylan said. He
was always showering. I remembered reading that it was a
sign of an affair, and for a week I'd tracked his hygiene
habits for evidence of this. Finding no common thread, I
sneaked a look at his phone one morning when he was
helping Chloe to look for her PE kit – he had never had a
PIN. There was no affair; just a man with a small house,
two children and a very high score on *Candy Crush*.

I went to Ruby's room. I could hear the electro guitar of
a pop song, so I pushed the door open without knocking.
Ruby was lying on her stomach on the bed, staring at her
tablet. She looked up at me briefly.

'Want some food?'

'No.'

'You need something.' She sat up and crossed her legs.
Even though I had bought her a new skirt at the start of
term, she was wearing an old one and it ended many inches
above the regulation knee length.

'Why would you ask me what I want and then dismiss
what I say?' I was impressed by her use of the word 'dismiss', but I couldn't tell her that when she was being so
surly. Why did she make it difficult to be nice to her?

'I'm just trying to look after you.' She snorted. Her
phone vibrated on her bedside table and she turned towards
its glowing face. What would she do, what could she do, if
I grabbed it and destroyed it in front of her?

'I've bought some nice steaks,' I tried.

'I don't eat meat,' she muttered.

'You ate chicken yesterday.' She responded with an
exaggerated sigh.

'I don't eat red meat.'

140

'Eat the chips then. Your dad's going out. Come and watch TV with me.'

'No.' I took a step into the room and she looked up sharply. Clearly, as her guilt about the photos had waned, so had any affection she felt towards me.

'Can you just make an effort!' I cried. She looked shocked for a moment, but it quickly gave way to calm. I knew she was enjoying the satisfaction experienced when you achieve something you weren't sure you could.

'I have homework,' she said smugly. I glanced around her room. The pink walls she had delighted in when she was eight were covered in photos of teenage faces smooshed together; there was a pile of clothes at the foot of the bed and a make-up counter worth of products scattered across her desk, but not a book in sight. I left without comment. As I headed back to the stairs, Dylan left the bathroom wrapped in a towel. I pressed myself against the wall to let him pass.

I made a cup of tea and posted myself in the living room. I heard Dylan pass up and down the stairs several times. He was looking for something, probably his jacket. I reached under the sofa where I had tucked Frank's book, rubbing some dust bunnies from the cover before opening it at random. I read a passage about the energy it takes to stand still: *it's a human drive to evolve*, it read, *we have to work hard not to change.* Dylan stuck his head into the room.

'There you are,' he said, as though you could lose a person in our home. 'I'm just going for one, and then I'll get Chloe from Elsie's. She's going to have dinner there and watch a film.' I had forgotten that Chloe was at her friend's house. It made sense that she would want to spend the evening pretending to be part of another family. I thought

141

that maybe I should offer to pick her up, let him spend more time with his friend, but Elsie's mother made me nervous; she was always watching very carefully and asking tricky questions like 'What are your plans for Christmas?' in the middle of spring. So, I simply said OK.

'My jacket!' said Dylan, walking past me to pick it up from the back of the armchair. 'All right, I'll see you in a bit.' Then he was gone. I didn't even tell him about my new client.

My Aunt Caitlin, Mum's older sister, believes in reincarnation and mediums and all that nonsense. Sometimes, when she and Mum were on speaking terms, Henry and I would stay with her at weekends, and she would fill us up with jam tarts and tales of the occult. She claimed that in her twenties she had an out-of-body experience. After one too many sherries she'd recount the sensation of floating above her friends at a party, watching them chat and smoke, completely unaware she was there. At her sixtieth, Uncle Hugh let slip that she had edited a tab of acid out of her story – a major plot point, I feel. Still, I thought of her then as I sat alone in the living room. I felt trapped outside my life and unsure I wanted to be let back in. I know it was this sensation that found me sipping a vodka before lunch that Saturday morning; racing away from the chaos of London on a fast train headed for Birmingham.

18

BIRMINGHAM NEW STREET looks like the inside of a
space station. Of course, I've never seen the inside of a
space station and I presume there isn't usually a coffee shop
in the centre, but the domed ceilings and glass doors gave it
an out-of-this-world air. It felt appropriate; I may as well
have been on another planet, one where virtue and mono-
gamy were not valued. Frank hadn't sent me any information
about where to find him. In my head I pictured a scene from
a wartime movie – exiting the train to find him couched in
steam and cigarette smoke on a deserted platform. Instead,
I was carried up an escalator with a throng of football fans
and families and spat out on to the main concourse, where
I stood clutching my overnight bag under the digital boards.
I could have called him, but I wanted to preserve the time
between hoping he was something and understanding that
he was not. I was chewing the inside of my mouth, and con-
templating popping into Marks & Spencer for another little
tin of vodka and orange, when a woman said my name. I
recognized her but not in a complete way.

'Frank told me to collect you,' she said and, hearing her
flat tone, I could immediately place where I had seen her
previously – sitting behind the table at Frank's launch, as
uninterested now as she was then.

'Where is he?' I asked, battling to sound calmer than I felt.

'He got held up at the event,' she said. 'He asked me to take you to the hotel.' This made me feel like serviced laundry, but I went with her. In a cab, I tried my best to make conversation.

'What's your name?'

'Jemima.' She looked in my direction rather than at me.

'How long have you been working for Frank?'

She shrugged, and when I continued to stare at her she exhaled before saying, 'Probably about a year. It's an internship really. I'm trying to get into project management.'

'Is he a good boss?' She looked at me directly then. Her eyes, already on the small side, narrowed to near obscurity.

Whatever she was looking for, I don't think she found it; she flashed the briefest of smiles and said, 'Of course.' The rest of the journey was silent, and thankfully it was short. So short we could have walked. Jemima paid with a ten-pound note, and told the driver to keep the change when he gruffly requested something smaller. Wordlessly, she led me to the hotel lobby where I hovered next to a miniature olive tree as she spoke to the receptionist. A minute later she returned and handed me a small plastic card.

'Room 702. He'll meet you up there.' I was floored. The execution of it was so brazen, so presumptuous. His belief that I would accept his assistant's involvement in our meeting and that I would happily trot up to a hotel room, with no knowledge of what I would find there – although that's exactly what I did.

The room was in fact a suite, with an area for sleeping and another for all the living one has to do whilst staying in a hotel. On a glass table in the centre of the space, a platter of seafood rested on ice. There was another of sliced fruit and a third of meats and cheese. A note written in small capital letters had been placed carefully beside them. It said 'MAKE YOURSELF AT HOME.' I breathed in the synthetic hotel-room smell and felt at ease for the first time that morning. I loved staying at hotels, even the most basic motorway-pit-stop variety, precisely because it is nothing like being at home. I could mess up the sheets and make soap rings in the bath, safe in the knowledge that someone else would have to deal with it. In the bathroom a glass shelf held a cluster of miniature, designer toiletries. I picked up a few to take back before remembering that this trip didn't exist. I was visiting an old university friend at her family home; I couldn't return with evidence to the contrary.

I took a shower, put on one of those huge, white bath-robes and blow-dried my hair, taking the time to get height at the roots and make sure that the ends curled under. I sat in front of the floor-to-ceiling windows to reapply my make-up. When finished, I examined my face for a while, and it occurred to me that when dealing with my reflection I focused on individual elements – the lashes being curled or the teeth to be flossed. I rarely thought about the impact of the whole. The woman I saw looked tired – not unattractive but not striking. You see her at the school gates and in line at Sainsbury's; you'd probably ask her where the nearest cashpoint was. I wasn't sure I knew her at all.

I stayed in the dressing gown and picked at the food. Eating calmed my nerves. I'd brought a dress as well as jeans and didn't know what would be appropriate. It felt like a mistake to allow Frank to let me arrive so unprepared. I unpacked my bag; the dress was crushed beyond recognition so I searched the room for an iron. Behind the cupboard doors I found a few items of clothing and a leather holdall tucked neatly in the corner. I shut the door again quickly, feeling stupidly ashamed. Even though Frank wasn't there, knowing that he had been, I felt like I was intruding. I finished the cheese. There was a knock on the door and I jumped and knotted my robe tighter. When no one entered, I approached it slowly. The knocking came again, louder and more insistent, and before I lost my nerve, I eased it open a few inches. A young, pale-faced man stood a few inches from the door. He was chewing on his lip nervously, and his waistcoat was far too big for his thin frame.

'Your champagne,' he said, holding up a bucket.

'Oh, right. Thank you,' I said. I took the bucket, balancing it awkwardly on my hip like a baby as I scrawled across the receipt. The boy paused for a few seconds before walking away, and it wasn't until he reached the end of the hallway that I realized he had been waiting for a tip. I felt embarrassed and then annoyed that Frank had put me in the position of feeling lost and alone and awkward. I poured myself a glass of champagne, drank it like water and served myself another. Frank was used to controlling the narrative and, emboldened by alcohol, I wanted to even the score. I went back to the cupboard, moving quickly to avoid having time to analyse my actions. His clothes told me nothing. I paused only briefly before kneeling on the ground and opening the holdall. There was some underwear – all black. A couple of books – both thick and imposing, the sort of thing I knew I would have neither the time nor the energy to read – a toilet bag and a leather-bound notebook. I opened it to the first page and a photograph fell out. Frank in sweats, holding a baby. The baby was very little, too small to have any defining features; nothing to signify that the wrinkled, jaundiced creature belonged to anyone yet. But the way Frank was looking at the child, the promise to protect imprinted on his face, made it clear the baby was his.

Another knock. I swallowed a scream. I heard the door open, and threw the notebook and photo back into the bag before shutting the cupboard door.

'Hello?' said Frank. He found me on the floor, legs out in front of me. I stretched my arms towards my feet.

'Hi,' I said casually. 'Still a bit stiff from the train.' He held out his hand and I reached to him. He pulled me up and used the momentum to draw me into an embrace. We kissed – firmly, decisively, as if we'd been kissing for years, but not for years because kisses after years of kisses are not like that. They don't hold the mystery; they don't have the urgency; they don't make you forget who or where you are. Frank sat on the little sofa and took off his tie. I told him I would get dressed but he asked me not to.

'I like you like that,' he said. 'I like knowing you're comfortable.'

'And nearly naked.'

'That too,' he said, his mouth forming half a smile. I sat next to him with my feet tucked up on the sofa and my knees pressing into his thigh. He put an arm around me and gave a tired groan.

'Hard day at the office?' I laughed, feeling the need to indicate that it was a joke. He rubbed my arm in response.

'I'm an introvert really. I like my work, but I find it draining being around all those people. I feel like they're all picking at me, wanting a piece of me, like little gnats.' I kissed his chest and then bit him quickly in the same spot. He grabbed me and pushed me back on the sofa.

I shrieked and struggled; I was aware that I was putting on a display.

'You don't know how good it is to come back to you and not an empty room,' he said. I watched him scanning my face, like he was trying to make a map of it. The tension was making my stomach cramp. I pushed him away from me.

'I'm sorry it was a tough day,' I said. 'Let me get you a drink.' He sat back on the sofa.

'You're wonderful,' he said, and I almost believed it. I went and got us two glasses of champagne.

'To small audiences,' he said before drinking. I raised my glass. He patted the space next to him and I scrambled to sit back down.

'You want to go out for a late lunch? I'm in the mood for some Thai.' I felt a bit light headed; I was barely wrapping my head around being together, let alone going out. 'You want to propose something else?' Frank asked when I didn't respond.

'No, it's just that . . .' It was that the cramping in my stomach had become fierce and urgent. What I thought was nerves had been a warning.

'It's just that . . .' I covered my mouth with my hands but vomit still spurted out from between my fingers. I ran to the glossy, white bathroom. I knew I didn't have enough time to open the toilet lid, and leaned over the bath and let myself release. I threw up everything I'd eaten; it felt like everything I'd *ever* eaten. I heard Frank come into the room and ask if I was OK, and desperately waved him away with one hand. I couldn't see if he had complied because I was still leaning over the tub, ready for another assault. Finally empty, I settled on the floor, weak and embarrassed. I wondered if it was a punishment, arranged

148

by the universe when I had been unable to make the right decisions by myself. I could hear Frank on the phone berating some poor hotel employee for their insurmountable ineptitude. I washed out the bath and took another shower.

I left the room sheepishly, head first, and when that proved to be tolerable, the rest of me. Frank was sitting on the edge of the bed. He looked like a man waiting to receive terrible news; his face was flooded with concern.

'Are you OK? I can't believe it. I won't be staying here again.'

'I'm fine. It might not have been the food – maybe I have flu or something. I hope I'm not contagious.'

'I don't care,' said Frank. He came to me and cupped my face; conscious that I hadn't brushed my teeth, I turned away.

'I need to lie down,' I said. I went to the bed, and as soon as I felt the cool surface of the sheets I knew it would take considerable force to get me up again. I lay on my back with my eyes closed, reminding myself that food poisoning was something I had lived through before. Frank lay down beside me and stroked my forehead. It immediately took me back to being a child, and Eddie tucking me into bed and making me cream of tomato soup when I was off school sick. There were times when I faked being ill, pressing my head against the radiator, just for the experience.

Frank whispered to me. I couldn't make out what he was saying but the sound was a comfort. It wasn't long before I was asleep. When I woke, the room was dark. I could still feel Frank beside me and I could hear the soft, shushing sound of crowd noises and the familiar hum of sports commentary from the television. Without all the

149

complication, it was just a bloke watching the game with his woman dozing next to him.

Frank shook my shoulder. I opened my eyes and saw him standing above me. He looked fresh – clean-shaven and already dressed in dark jeans and a white shirt. I panicked that in the unforgiving morning light he would realize the error of his ways, and pulled the covers over my head. If I looked half as bad as I felt, I knew I looked rough.

'You OK?' he asked. His voice was still brimming with worry; at home there was a twelve-hour limit on sympathy.

'I'm fine – just completely embarrassed,' I said.

'Don't be.' I felt him sit on the bed next to me. 'It's rare to be with someone when they're in such a vulnerable state. It makes me feel closer to you.' I poked my head out far enough to see if he was taking the piss. He smiled tentatively.

'You're a freak,' I said.

He laughed. 'You don't know the half of it.'

I want to, I thought.

'Do you think you'd be able to go for a walk?'

'Definitely, but can you give me fifteen minutes? I'll meet you in reception.'

'Yes, ma'am,' he said, kissing me on the forehead lightly before leaving.

As soon as I heard the door close, I jumped up and into action. I took the dress into the bathroom with me, so the steam from the shower could work on some of the creases. I blow-dried my hair again and slapped on a palmful of tinted moisturizer. Twenty minutes later, I was almost presentable.

In the foyer, I hung back and watched him for a moment.

150

He had an espresso, and seeing his hands manipulating the tiny, doll-like cup was so sexy, or maybe everything he did was sexy. I wasn't sure. As if he sensed me there, he turned. I stood up straighter and went to him. He took my hand and kissed my fingers. It was so intimate; I could feel my chest turning red.

'You want some breakfast?' he asked. I shook my head.

'Let's get out of here,' I said.

19

WE STROLLED THROUGH the city centre. I found Birmingham visually uninspiring but was taken by its
vibrancy, like an unattractive date who disappoints at first
but then wins you over with their charm. Unlike our surroundings, Frank was anything but disappointing. As
soon as we left the hotel, he took a firm hold of my hand
and gently steered me clear of high-street hazards as we
walked. At first the proximity made me paranoid – I had
visions in which we were seen by a friend on a work trip, or
a long-forgotten cousin – but after a few minutes I adjusted,
my fear extinguished by the joy that he was publicly claiming me. I watched as people clocked us. Frank's strong
features might seem harsh at first, but they hammered at
your brain until you relented and deemed him attractive.
When women passed, their mouths continued to move in
conversation but their eyes were trained on him. If, as an
afterthought, they glanced at me, their faces would crump-
le in bewilderment.

It had been the same when I was with David; wherever
we went, women gravitated towards him and I hated it. I
was constantly plagued by the fear that he would find
someone more appropriate, and more than once he did. He
was never bold enough to pick someone up when I was

with him but he would turn his body away, not much but enough to signal that he could be taken. That might have been why I was drawn to Dylan, who was handsome but without the energy that projects raw sexuality. When I met him, I no longer wanted that, but perhaps things had changed. Maybe I was bored of playing it safe. We walked without aim until we reached a canal-side cafe.

'Want to keep going?' Frank asked.

'Absolutely not,' I said. The air had eased my queasiness but I didn't want to push my luck.

'I like that you don't pretend,' he said.

'I like that you tell me what you like about me,' I replied. Frank squeezed my hand before letting go to pull out my chair.

'What else do you like about me?' I asked.

'Aren't we the curious one,' he said. He watched me for a few seconds before pulling out a cigarette and lighting it with heavy inhalations. I thought about dismissing what I had said, picking a new subject and allowing the sentiment to be hidden behind verbosity, but I took a gamble. If he was honest about liking my lack of pretence, he would appreciate my directness, and after our aborted night together we didn't have time for games.

'I'm not curious. I need to know. I'm risking a lot even being here.' Frank took another deep drag on the cigarette.

'Risks lead to reward.'

'No,' I said, pointing my finger at his face. 'Don't give me your guru shit. I need to know why. Why you've chosen me?' I hated sounding insecure; from what I could remember about dating, revealing your vulnerabilities was a massive blunder. But this wasn't dating, this was something else. 'I don't want to be a number on a list of your silly mistakes.' I felt my hand shaking, partly because I was weak and I needed to eat, but also because my body had sensed how important the moment was. Frank was still for a few seconds before he erupted in laughter.

'Stop! It's not funny!' I cried, but I couldn't help smiling. He stopped immediately, but I could tell he was holding in more and that started me off. 'Was I a bit dramatic?'

'A bit, but it's great. You're great. There's nothing silly about this and you're certainly not a mistake.' He stubbed out the cigarette and rubbed his chin. 'I haven't done this before.' I looked at the table. It was covered in wet rings left by the drinks of the previous occupants. 'I like the way you think about questions before you answer. I like when you're nervous or embarrassed and your bottom lip twitches. I like that you're open but you're not a pushover.'

'You don't know I'm not a pushover.'

'I know. I like you. I don't entirely understand why, and maybe that's what makes you so fascinating.' I looked at him.

'When you know you know,' I whispered.

'I take the piss out of people who say that,' he said. 'Or maybe I used to. Look, I understand if you don't want to see me again,' he continued. 'I won't be happy but I'll understand.' I desperately needed a drink, but the thought of having one made my stomach heave.

'I want to see you again but I don't know if I can handle . . .' I stopped speaking because the end of the sentence was too difficult to express. Frank reached across the table and interlocked his fingers with mine. We sat like that for a minute; twenty different questions raced through my mind.

'I want to get to know you,' Frank finally said. 'I know that might be asking for trouble but I think you're worth it.'

I did what I was good at and rebranded what I knew

was about to unfold. We were destined to do this; there was no choice. We were the right people meeting at the worst time; that might mean some pain and discomfort, but we would call them challenges and growth. Spending time together wasn't a choice but how we would go about it was. I think I convinced myself that an affair might actually help my marriage, that I would understand myself better; perhaps the guilt that was already an accompaniment for every other emotion would force me to treat Dylan and the girls with more patience and greater compassion. Looking back, I'm astounded by the deftness of my mental gymnastics.

Frank had another espresso and I drank a couple of mint teas. The tables around us emptied and refilled, and the waitress hovered impatiently and cleared our cups noisily, unable to hide her frustration at the loss of potential tips. We talked about our hopes for the future, the sort of world we wanted to help build for our children. Did I consider what it might be like to be together? Of course, every woman does. To assess a man as a mate is part of our basic biology. The world is always changing but that remains the same. And the more we talked, the more it felt like he would be a good fit for me; he'd bring out the best of me and quell the darker parts. I don't know what Frank was thinking, but I didn't want the morning to end.

Frank was staying another night but insisted on walking me to the station. The guard let him down on to the platform even though he didn't have a ticket. Our parting was like the movie scene I had imagined, only much more pensive. Frank stayed on the platform with his hands in his pockets as the train pulled away. I stared out of the window until I could no longer see him.

*

Dylan insisted on collecting me from Hackney Central, even though I told him I'd be fine walking. He arrived with both girls in tow.

'Welcome home,' he said as I put on my seatbelt. Chloe blew me kisses from the back seat. Ruby sat next to her in thundering silence.

'Hi, Rubes, good weekend?'

'It was, until Dad ruined it.' I pretended to look for something in my bag, a ruse to hide my smile. One weekend of solo parenting and Dylan had become the public enemy.

'I'm sure he didn't manage to ruin it entirely,' I said. I snuck a look at Dylan, but his eyes were fixed firmly on the road.

'I only wanted my friend to stay over. We were going to study together.' I leaned forward to catch Dylan's eyes. He seemed to be concentrating on the traffic lights.

'Well, it is a school night,' I said. With no communication from my husband, my only option was to provide a half-hearted cavalry.

'Yeah, but we aren't going to stay up late and we'll go in together. We'll motivate each other.' I glanced at Ruby in the rear-view mirror; her face was the picture of innocence. We'd had a chat about motivation a few weeks prior, and by 'chat' I mean that I had lectured and Ruby had rolled her eyes so violently I'd been concerned she'd do herself an injury. Perhaps despite her dismissiveness it was all gently sinking in.

'Right?' I looked at Dylan. We'd always encouraged the girls to have friends over. We strategized that it was better to keep them where we could see them. Well, I had strategized and he had agreed. 'I mean, that sounds OK . . . I guess . . .'

'See!' shouted Ruby. 'I told you she'd be fine with it.'

'Woah, woah, woah,' I said. I twisted round in the seat to look at her. I noticed that the skin around Ruby's eyes was swollen; the debate had clearly been going on for some time. 'Can someone break this down for me? Quietly. I have a headache.' I sat back in the seat properly and closed my eyes in preparation to analyse the problem – analyse, evaluate and sort it all out, as usual.

'I told you last week I wanted Dom to stay, and you both said it was fine and at the last minute you say no. You're always doing this to me.' I opened my eyes.

'Dom?' I turned towards Dylan and he nodded ruefully.

'Tell me that's short for Dominique.'

'What's the problem?' roared Ruby. 'He's my friend!'

'That's great,' I said in an angry whisper. 'I'm really glad you have so many friends.' I faced forward and said in a louder tone, 'But you can't have boys stay the night.'

'Why, though? That makes no sense! Eloise stays over all the time. What if we were lesbians?'

'But you're not, are you?'

'I don't know, yet. I might be.' I checked her in the mirror again. Her arms were folded, her face cold and obstinate. In fairness, she could be right.

'In that case, I suppose no one can stay over,' said Dylan.

'God!' shouted Ruby. Chloe covered her ears with her hands. 'You're actually trying to ruin my life! What do you think we're going to do? God! You two are gross.'

'He can't stay, it's not up for debate,' said Dylan, his voice edged with weariness.

'Listen to your dad,' I added.

'You literally don't understand anything,' Ruby muttered. 'You're never even here anyway, you're always working.'

'Ruby.' I paused to harness my irritation. 'I'm working

157

so you can have nice things, things like the phone you broke within five minutes of having. I'm working so you can have fun with your friends, friends who your father and I are pretty cool about letting you hang out with. No parent would let their teenage daughter have a male friend over to stay. We are not being unreasonable, so stop treating us like we are.'

'You're totally unreasonable. You're always unreasonable,' said Ruby. 'You're such a . . .' Her unfinished sentence hung menacingly in the air. This was the happy family life I was fretting so much about?

'Pull over,' I said. Dylan shot me a confused look.

'Are you OK?'

'Pull the car over,' I said. We were on the high street, a couple of minutes from home. I took off my seatbelt and got out of the car. I could hear my family calling me as I walked away but I refused to go back.

20

S HE TOOK SEVERAL minutes to answer the door, so I knew my mother was already well into her evening bottle of wine. She greeted me warmly but not too energetically, not with the exaggerated enthusiasm that would suggest it was too late for her to hold a conversation.

'What a wonderful surprise, darling.' Her breath was heavy in my ear as we embraced. I was surprised to find that it was still a comfort to be held by her. Only there in her arms did I realize that I was seeking the knowledge that I could be close to someone I had once thought of as a complete bitch.

Mum ushered me into her living room. Even though it was June, the heating was on and the room – a riot of knick-knacks and cushions – felt claustrophobic. Mum left and returned with a glass of red wine. My stomach wasn't ready for alcohol, but I reasoned it would be responsible to consume some of her stash.

'What's he done?' Mum asked, as she settled down with her own glass.

'He?'

'Your husband.' I pulled off my shoes and fell back against the sofa.

159

'Nothing – he's great. I mean, he's fine. It's Ruby. She's . . . she's doing my head in.'

'They tend to do that . . . daughters,' said Mum. Her wine glass didn't quite hide her grin as she lifted it to her mouth.

'Would it have been easier if I'd had boys?' I thought of all the messes Henry had dragged our parents into, parties that led to bitter confrontations with neighbours, yo-yoing back home after every failed attempt at adulthood.

'I reckon so,' said Mum. She leaned forward to top up her glass as she often did when needing to give something consideration. 'Henry ran me ragged but he was simpler, men are. If he had a problem he told me about it, not like you who would brood and sulk for days and days. Do you remember—'

'Fine, I wasn't always perfect,' I snapped, 'but we didn't have it the easiest in the early days.'

'No,' Mum said, 'and I was partly to blame for that. I knew the man who made you was no good, but I had to be the one to change him.' It was an odd kind of blame taking, only accepting responsibility for failing to recognize another's shortcomings.

'He wasn't around long enough to make that big a difference.' Mum laughed. When she stopped the silence was acute.

'No, he didn't help, but I never got better at making good choices.'

'Eddie's a good man. You had your problems but he's still there for you, for all of us.'

'Being a good man isn't always enough. Sometimes good is the last thing on the list.' There are many conversations that remain unspoken between a parent and a child.

160

You spend so long showing your child they can rely on you, and in order to do that you have to hide a lot of who you really are. Growing up, I had wished that my mother would make an effort to hide more; she would tell me about men she dated and subsequently how they let her down. She didn't have many girlfriends – she said they didn't trust her with their husbands and, were this to be true, I'm not sure I would blame them. In many ways I was an awkward substitute for friendship and a partner. Even still, despite her candidness, there were chapters of my mother's history that remained closed to me and that I wasn't necessarily ready to open.

'Do you think if you could have your time with Eddie again you would do it differently?' Mum waved her free hand about in front of her face.

'That's a pointless line of enquiry. You can't do things differently. You do the things you do because of who you are.' I knew that when I had been with Frank earlier, I hadn't felt like myself very much at all, and that it had been terrifying but pretty wonderful.

'Who are you?' I asked. I knew who she was to me – complex, troubled and a massive pain in the bum – but I genuinely wanted to know how she saw herself.

'The sort of woman who couldn't resist the lad that worked in Eastern Promise.' Despite my dodgy stomach, I drank the wine.

'What do you mean?'

'Well,' said Mum, and she shuffled towards me like we were schoolgirls sharing secrets on the playground. 'I couldn't resist him. I don't know why. I think it was his eyes, so sad . . . And, well, Eddie said he would forgive me but really, truly he never did, and I guess that cow from down the road was there to comfort him.'

'So, you're saying you cheated on Dad? With the guy from the curry place?' Mum roared with laughter.

'Don't you remember all the kormas we were getting?' When she saw that I hadn't found the comedy in this, she covered her mouth with her hand. 'Darling, darling, I'm sorry. It's in the past. Don't be angry.' I shifted away from her.

'You told me it was him. You made me think it was him.' Mum reached over and stroked my hair.

'Yes, but that was just me. What he did was so unlike him, that's what made it different.' I rubbed my eyes with the heels of my hands.

'Let me be clear. What you're saying is you're the sort of person who can't control yourself, and because of that you weren't in the wrong.'

Mum looked to the ceiling for a few seconds before saying, 'Well, yes. I suppose I am.' She slapped my thigh. 'Ancient history, my love. What will be will be. Let me see if I have any snacks.' I watched her make a wobbly exit, and tried to push away the thought that what was happening wasn't meant to be, it was down to who I was, who she had made me.

I woke in the corner of the bed with Dylan's body curled against mine, preventing escape. I lifted his arm from my waist as gently as I could, but he stirred.

'Come straight home from work,' he croaked. I busied myself in the bathroom as he and the girls got breakfast, and then hid in the bedroom until they were ready to leave the house. Dylan called, 'See you later, Nibs,' up the stairs.

At work, I busied myself with research for Nush's campaign. She had sent a series of emails with ideas clearly typed as she conceived them. Some simply consisted of one word such as 'Fun!' or 'Magical!' I found that the intense desire to avoid my own whirling questions was brilliant fuel for my productivity. Every time the weekend or the problems it raised threatened to invade my brain, I would complete another task. I worked through lunch and, when reception called late afternoon to say I had a package, my only thought was I hope that it's edible. It wasn't. On the glossy white desk was a bouquet of pink peonies, so fresh that drops of water still clung to their petals. There was no note but I knew they were from Frank. I rang him to say thank you.

'Let's meet on Friday,' he responded.

'I can't keep spending time away from . . . home.'

'Tell them you have a new client. It's true.'

I tried to ignore the low buzz of anxiety about how easily that had come to him. I could feel someone watching, and turned to see Annie's eyes swivel towards her monitor. 'Let's talk about it tomorrow. I'll call you.'

'Bye, Tiny Dancer.'

'Nice blooms,' said Bettina. 'They from your new client?'

'Yeah, have them. They'd look perfect in your flat.'

'Don't be stupid – you earned them. Do you wanna try and look happy about it? It's a good thing.'

'I've got a lot on my mind.'

'Should we go have a chat? And by chat I mean gin.'

'No, thanks. I'm on a roll.' I did want to talk, but I couldn't share the only thing I wanted to speak about. Also, I didn't want to leave the flowers behind and have Bettina question me about it. That's the problem with lying: it's never just one. I kept working on a plan that might somehow encompass all of Nush's whims. It was going to be a long day.

*

163

'Where are you?' asked Dylan. I wedged the phone receiver between my chin and shoulder, so that I could finish the email I was drafting to a company claiming to supply unicorns for events.

'Working,' I said. He was silent. I thought about filling it by asking about his day, but resisted – it would only drag out the conversation.

'I asked you to come straight home,' he said. He sounded wounded. It was unusual to hear him veer away from his comfortably affable state, and I experienced a wave of sympathy.

'I will as soon as I finish, babe.'

'Ah, sorry – my fault. I meant to say come home at six, when you're supposed to finish, I mean. I'm such a plonker.' I looked at the flowers on my desk.

'You're not a plonker. It's my fault. I should have thought about it. I'll leave now.'

'Don't worry, I'll pick you up. I'm taking you out.' I cringed. I recalled chastising him for not being fun or surprising me. What could be more surprising than taking me out on a date when it was the last thing I wanted to do?

'I'm not dressed for it.'

'I'm sure you look great. I'll be there in half an hour.'

When Dylan arrived, I was waiting downstairs. I didn't want to risk him seeing the flowers and asking questions or, which for some reason felt worse, seeing the flowers and asking nothing.

He had on his 'good' checked shirt, and had slicked his hair back the way he does when he's making an effort.

'Thanks for this,' I said as we pulled away.

'You look nice. I'm feeling a bit underdressed.'

'Don't worry about it. You're great.' I flipped down the

164

sunshade and saw myself in the little mirror. I looked pallid and drawn.

'Who's with the girls?' Dylan bit his lip.

'Don't say no one.' I don't know if I cared so much as I was looking for an excuse to go home. Dylan was paying a great deal of attention to the T-junction.

'Mickey's with them,' he said casually.

'Mickey!'

'It's OK, he's got that woman he's seeing with him.'

'That's great, there's a sociopath and a stranger in my home.' I sort of wanted to fight with him; I could feel the fury inching its way through my body.

'Mickey's not a sociopath, he's misunderstood, and yes she's a stranger, but she's got three kids so she's experienced.' My rage was immediately extinguished by mirth.

'Mickey's a stepfather!' I was barely able to get the words out.

'He's loving it. He's never had anyone who will believe the bullshit he comes out with.' This made me laugh even harder. Dylan never said anything bad about Mickey, and I knew he was offering the dig as a gift to me. A small betrayal for the greater good.

I decided to put on a bit of blush, so at first I didn't notice that Dylan had pulled into a complex near the docklands.

'Do we need petrol?' I asked, feeling myself getting preemptively annoyed at his cavalier attitude to refills.

'No,' he said brightly, pulling into an empty bay. 'We're here.' I looked around the deserted parking lot.

'We're where?'

Dylan pointed in front of us. I followed his arm to the entrance of Hollywood Bowl. I guess I didn't give a good enough display of enthusiasm.

'I've got it wrong,' said Dylan as we approached. Yes, obviously, I thought, but didn't respond.

'I was trying . . . I was thinking . . . Remember when we used to go to the bowling alley in Finsbury Park?' I did. 'We haven't been for years.'

'You're right,' I said. What I didn't say was that I thought the reason we hadn't been was because we had outgrown it, that when we started going out on dates again it would be to the theatre or jazz clubs, even though Dylan disliked both those things.

Dylan held the door open for me, and I was assaulted by the smell of warm grease and stale carpets. I could hear excited teenagers, and there was something about it that felt hopeful. I let Dylan talk to the bubbly Asian girl behind the counter. She told us which lane we were in, with reassurances that it was 'a good one', and rattled through the food offers in a bright, sing-song voice. Dylan thanked her and we started to walk away. 'Excuse me!' I heard her call towards our backs. I turned and pointed to myself, and she nodded.

'Sorry, you can't wear open toes. Really sorry. What size are you? I'll get you some shoes.'

'Four,' I said grudgingly. She disappeared to the back and returned with some tired-looking bowling shoes. I held them away from me as we walked to our lane. Dylan watched me put them on. I knew that I was frowning.

'Nice,' I said.

'You look sexy, babe,' he said.

'Yeah, the clown look is in this year.' Dylan put his arms round me.

'The sexy clown look. You can spray water in my face any time.'

'That was a good one,' I said. He grinned like an idiot. I moved away from him and picked up a ball.

'Are you ready to get beaten?' I asked. He wasn't. Dylan didn't hold back. There was no flirtatiously showing me how to hold the ball or weak throws to give me an advantage. Dylan treated me as an equal competitor, although clearly I was not. I was pleased he chose not to patronize me and did my best to be a worthy opponent; in the end I didn't lose by much.

We had a beer, sitting on sticky vinyl seats in the tired-looking bar area. It was flat and warm but still satisfying. 'I have to get back to the gym,' I said to Dylan, massaging an aching bicep.

'No, you don't. You look great.'

'It's not only about how I look. I want to do something for myself.' Dylan appeared puzzled.

'That sounds like a good idea, babe. Or we could go running together.'

'You run when I'm at work,' I said flatly.

'I can run at other times. The streets are always open.' I shook my head and fought back tears. I wasn't sure what I needed Dylan to acknowledge. He stroked the back of my hand with his thumb.

'I know things haven't been great the last couple of years. It's a blip, everyone has them. We'll get over it.'

'I don't care about everyone. I care about us,' I said.

'The best is yet to come, Nibs.' I wanted to ask him how he did that – accepted everything would work out fine, even when all the evidence pointed to the contrary. 'I'm having a good time,' he added. I felt bad that he could be happy with the little I was offering. 'This is nice. I think I've forgotten how to enjoy myself. Mickey said I should see a doctor, like a head one.' I disguised a snort of disbelief with a cough.

'I wouldn't take advice from Mickey.'

'He's sharper than you think,' said Dylan.

'Sharp as a mallet,' I muttered.

'What?' asked Dylan.

'Nothing.' I tipped the remainder of my beer into his pint. 'I'm sure his heart's in the right place.' Dylan picked up the glass and began swirling it in small circles.

'I keep having weird ideas,' he said, and I felt a rush of anticipation. 'Like we should sell the house.' My expectancy evolved into annoyance.

'That's not weird, that's the sort of thing people consider all the time. That's being a grown-up.'

'Maybe,' said Dylan. I took the drink from his hand and placed it on the table.

'Dylan, I think you're a bit bored.' For a few seconds he searched my face, like he was searching for something he had misplaced. Then he looked towards the group of kids playing in the lane we had vacated.

'Maybe. Probably . . . You know, I think the last time we went bowling together it resulted in Rubes.' I felt myself blushing. Ridiculous – the man had seen me crap myself during labour. He turned back to me; I shifted uncomfortably under his spotlight. 'Yeah, it was your birthday and we went to that Greek place, and then you didn't want the night to end so we decided to play a game to decide whether we went into town or home to bed. I won but you didn't seem bothered in the end.' It was the sort of silly, inconsequential detail I was always bemoaning him for not remembering. 'Do you want to go get a bite now?'

'I'm tired,' I said. 'Let's head back.'

'I love you,' he replied. I hit him on the shoulder and he lightly punched me back.

*

'Hey,' called Dylan as I shut the door behind us.

'In here,' shouted Mickey. In the living room, Mickey sat with a beer in one hand and the other slung round the shoulder of a woman. She looked her age, assuming that was late forties, but she had a youthful exuberance. She wore a green jersey lounge suit and her dark hair was cropped close to her head. Belying the rest of her low-maintenance appearance, her lips were painted a shocking pink.

'Ginger, this is Diane,' said Mickey.

'So nice to meet friends of Michael's,' she said as we sat down.

'Nice to finally meet a girlfriend of Mickey's,' I said. Dylan coughed. Diane was unfazed.

'Fiancée,' she said, thrusting her left hand towards me. I stood and leaned in. A sizeable diamond nestled between two rubies. It must have fallen off the back of a very nice lorry.

'Lovely,' I said, because it's what you say. Diane turned towards Mickey, who gave her two pecks on the mouth.

'You're so cool,' he said, and as much as Mickey means anything, I could tell he meant it. They were completely mismatched – she looked like an upstanding member of the community and he was part man, part wayward toddler – but in that moment I could see: you can't fight chemistry.

21

R UBY HAD A bunch of assessments coming up, and her anxiety made her much more receptive to care. Whilst it wasn't pleasant to see my child upset, it heartened me that the girl who made a performance of caring about nothing was concerned about her grades. When she came in from school, I made hot chocolate; heavy on the cocoa powder, exactly as she had it when she was small. The first time, she regarded me mistrustfully but drank it without comment, before disappearing to her room. From then on, I made her the drink at some point every evening, and it always earned me a few minutes of interaction. I did most of the talking but she let me. One night I told her how nervous I used to get before exams, and how I was so stressed about my English A level that I had to leave in the middle to throw up. Ruby seemed grateful, and for a few seconds I was a little less Mum and a bit more human. 'What did you do about it?' she asked. I tried to think of something poignant to say, something important that she could carry with her, but I couldn't so I went with the truth.

'The throwing up started a pregnancy rumour. It was pretty embarrassing but it made me realize that shit could always be worse.' Ruby giggled.

'Mum, you said shit!'

'I did. I do sometimes.'

'It's all right,' she said. 'I'll let you off.' I gave her a hug that night, which she allowed.

Free from having to dance around her moods, I found I had more headspace. I spent evenings with Chloe; I didn't consciously try not to be alone with Dylan. Chloe was planning to perform one of her one-woman shows at school assembly.

'Were you asked to do it?' I enquired.

'No,' she said. 'I asked Ms Khavari.' I suspected she was being set up. The woman I met on parents' evening didn't seem like the sort to be focused on fostering a child's dreams, or perhaps she didn't care that the other children might laugh at my girl. I told Chloe I would help her to revamp one of her pieces, and for three evenings in a row we did a careful rewrite. The result was more of a co-authored piece, but all parents give their children a leg up if they care.

My days I spent chained to my desk, doing my best to keep up with Nush's dizzying list of demands. Her main focus was securing a venue. Generally, a client would find their own and I'd simply help to make the space part of the marketing vision, but Nush seemed to want me involved in every aspect of the show and, for the money she was bringing to the table, I had to endure being a glorified PA. I didn't want to pass the tasks over to Annie and have her realize the gig was far from glamorous, or worse, give her enough access to steal another client.

Despite a backdrop of the promise of Frank, life seemed ordinary, and the truth was that ordinary was boring. As a child I was desperate to be normal, to be like the other girls with their symmetrical pigtails and triangular sandwiches.

I was never sure if Mum would be fun and affectionate or angry and distant; whether we would have money for school lunches or I would have to spin an elaborate tale to my teacher to justify another bounced cheque. I was so excited about becoming an adult and escaping all that inconsistency, but finding myself within a family like the ones I coveted, I longed for the unexpected. The only place I found it was in my daily phone call with a man who was not mine. We spoke throughout my lunch break. I would walk around the city, nibbling on a wrap, aware that I was smiling like a loon as we spoke. One evening I stood at the end of the garden, talking to him in whispers, under the pretext of watering the healthy, green lawn. Frank always asked me my thoughts about the day. The first time I tried to brush it off, but he insisted. He told me, 'I like how you see the world.' I told him about office politics and my secret theory that Carter spent his weekends clad in leather. He ended each call with the words, 'I can't wait to see you.' I felt the same. Frank was like a holiday on the horizon; knowing you have an escape approaching makes the days before so much lighter. I had forgotten the other truth about holidays – most of the time the expectation was far better than the reality.

One evening I crawled around the front of the house, pulling weeds out of cracks in the paving. I used my earbuds so it would look like I was listening to music, when in reality I was taking in Frank's pitch. 'Let's do Sunday. I'll drop you to work in the morning.'

'I feel like it's too soon,' I said.

'It's not soon enough – do you know how hard these days have been?' I did. It was an open wound not being near him, one that would weep and sting and need to be soothed with a text or a call. I wanted to touch him so

172

much that my palms actually itched, and I kept them in motion constantly in an attempt to relieve it. My home had never looked so clean; Bettina panicked when she saw my desk. She thought I was leaving and had neglected to tell her.

'Yes, I know, but seeing each other more might make it harder.' I said this firmly, as though I was a woman with restraint, the kind who could eat one biscuit and then twist the top of the packet closed. He knew better.

'I know you don't care if things are hard. You're strong. It's sexy. I'm not as tough as you. I need to see you. I need to spend the night with you.' How could I say no in the face of such open desire? It would have been impolite. 'Tell me you don't want me,' he said. I took off my gloves. In the distance I could hear children screaming, but I could tell they were cries of joy.

'I want you,' I said.

'Say it like you mean it,' he said in a low tone I hadn't heard before.

'I mean it. I want you.' I heard a sniff and jumped to my feet.

'Are my eyes red?' said Ruby.

'Oh God, I don't know. No redder than usual.'

'Fuck's sake,' she said angrily.

'Mind your language.'

'I'm gonna look like a rat at school tomorrow. Why does everyone keep cutting their grass?'

'It's mice that have pink eyes.'

'Way to miss the point, Mum. I don't want to look like any rodents. Especially not tomorrow.'

'Why not tomorrow?' She folded her arms.

'It doesn't matter,' she said, looking off down the road.

'So why bring it up?' I scooped up the weeds and threw

them in the bin, realizing too late it was the one for general and not garden waste.

'Whatever,' she said, and turned to walk back inside.

'I used to say that to your gran, you know,' I said to her disappearing back. 'You haven't invented adolescence!' I shouted as she climbed the stairs.

'You need a break.' I had forgotten Frank was there. I was mute with shame. I wasn't ready for him to meet the harassed-mum version of me. 'Let me give that to you.'

'OK, I'll work something out.'

'Thank you. I'll make it up to you soon.'

'Text me the details tomorrow.'

'I will,' said Frank. His tone was soft now he had secured the deal. 'Sounds like she's feisty. Like her mother,' he added before he was gone. I washed my hands at the kitchen sink. As I scrubbed earth from beneath my nails, I thought about Frank's words. Was Ruby like me? She certainly didn't have her father's temperament. And if he was right, if her combativeness was a burden I had given her, wasn't it my job to try and tame it? I dried my hands on my T-shirt and cut two thin slices of cucumber.

Ruby granted me entry to her room tentatively. She was sitting at her desk, which I was both surprised and delighted to see was covered with books.

'I brought you something.' I held up the cucumber.

'I'm not hungry.'

'It's not for eating, it's for your eyes.' She looked at me like I had finally lost the plot. 'Come and lie down.'

'I've got work,' she said tersely.

'You need a break.' Ruby closed her book and threw herself on her bed.

'Close your eyes,' I instructed. She complied without protest. I carefully placed one slice on each eye.

'It's cold,' she said accusingly.

'That's what helps. My mum taught me this. It helps soothe them.' Taught was a somewhat fraudulent claim. On a Sunday morning, my mother would lie on the sofa and disappear behind those cucumber slices after strict instructions for me to play 'silent games'.

'It does feel nice,' said Ruby. I felt a burst of exhilaration. I had managed to give her something and not have it mocked or rejected. It gave me the confidence to push my luck.

'Do you have an important assessment tomorrow?' I wondered if I should know. Should I have made her give me her timetable, so I could offer motivational messages? Her jaw tensed. I could sense her weighing up whether to let me in. Then she blew out a huff of air.

'OK,' she said. This weak signal of acceptance was all I needed to sit next to her on the bed. 'So, there's this boy . . .'

'Dom?' I asked.

'Yeah . . .' Ruby's mouth twitched. I parked the fact that this was the 'friend' she had been trying to convince me to allow in her room all night.

'And, you like him?' Ruby nodded so hard the cucumber slipped. I put my hand on her shoulder to still her, and placed them back on.

'I really do. He's not like the other boys. He's . . . I don't know. He's just really cool.'

'That's great, Rubes, as long as you know that you're too young to get into anything serious right now, and you've got a big year coming up and—'

'Yeah, I know, Mum.' She was silent again, and I wanted to smack myself for messing it up so quickly.

'Sorry. You like him. I get that.' Ruby sat up and the slices fell on to the duvet.

175

'I really do. I have since Year 7. He split up with his girl-friend yesterday and there's auditions for the drama club tomorrow. He's told me he's going to go, so I'm gonna try and join too!' Her cheeks were growing flushed. She must really like him; her excitement had superseded her disdain for me.

'I didn't know you were interested in drama! That's brilliant, Rubes.' It might be helpful to have her dramatics channelled elsewhere, and I was quite enamoured with the idea that my girls could continue my creative legacy.

'I don't care about the drama,' she said, 'but we'll spend all this time together and then he's blatantly going to ask me out.'

'Well, that is interesting,' I said carefully. 'Don't spend too much time thinking about it though, Rubes. Wait and see what tomorrow brings. I wouldn't want you to be dis-appointed . . .' She glared at me. Her eyes *were* a little red. I hadn't taken her to the GP for a hay-fever prescription that spring.

'Why would I be disappointed?' she said. In the words was a warning.

'No reason. Just if it doesn't go how you'd expect . . .' Ruby looked away.

'Great. Even my own mother doesn't think I'm good enough for him.' I put my hand on her leg, and she slowly but decisively moved it away.

'I do. Of course I do. He could be Robert Pattinson and I wouldn't think he was out of your league.' Ruby didn't turn back to me but gently shook her head. Obvi-ously, Robert was no longer du jour. I could practically taste her regret, caused by the misplaced belief that she could trust me with her secrets. 'I just want you to be pre-pared. And if I don't tell you, no one will.' I realized I'd heard those words before, from my mother's mouth. Without prompting she'd told me about sex, not just the mechanics of it but the mess and expectation. What I thought of her at the time was now displayed on my daughter's face. 'It will be fine, and your eyes look lovely. They always do.' She let out a bark of a laugh. 'I could put your hair in rags?'

When she was a kid, I would do this the night before she attended parties. I remember once hearing her say to a friend, 'No, I didn't go to the hairdresser. My mum did it.' She was so proud I belonged to her then.

'No,' she said. 'I have work to do.' She returned to her desk, her face a placid mask of dignity.

'I don't mind. You could read whilst I do it.'

'No,' she said harshly. 'You want me to be prepared, don't you?' I took my cue and left. Closing the door, I swore quietly and then again and again, a steady stream of fucks.

'You OK, babe?' Dylan called from the living room.

'Yeah,' I shouted back. 'Gonna lie down for a bit.'

'K!'

The bed was unmade; Dylan must have taken an afternoon nap. I felt helpless. Even when I was trying, it wasn't working; I would have to accept that the problem was me. I once watched a film about two babies inadvertently exchanged in a hospital ward. One, meek and bookish, was taken home by a raucous, extrovert family, and the other, wild and attention-seeking, by a quiet, academic pair. Though for a long time they didn't know the error had been made, they always sensed that something was wrong. I thought about another woman living in a home not far away, one who was patient and present and had grown up with a person who had taught her how to be a wife and mother. Of course, if she was supposed to be with my family where did that put me?

I pulled my phone out of my jeans pocket. No message from Frank. I searched 'rats eyes red'. The first result was an article on pet care. 'White rats usually have red eyes,' said the text below an image of one of the creatures. 'Fuck,' I said again.

22

FRANK MADE ME wait two days before he sent me the meeting point – the back of a restaurant in North London. Two waiters eyed me coolly as they smoked their break-time cigarettes. I smiled at one of them, and he elbowed his companion in the ribs before saying something in a foreign tongue. His friend responded with a snort of laughter. I clutched my huge handbag to my chest. If I'd paid more attention in school I might have understood what they were saying, or at least the language in which it was spoken. I could have shouted, 'I'm not an escort!' in Spanish or whatever.

Frank pulled up and rescued me. I scrambled into the passenger seat.

'You're late,' I chided.

'I'm sorry,' he said, and kissed me on the mouth. It's rare for a man to be able to apologize like that, without explanation and pontification. It requires a lot of self-possession. 'You look amazing,' he added. It was a cheap line, but it was great hearing it. Also, I believed he wouldn't have said it if he didn't mean it. I had spent a lot of time getting ready, done all the things I had been told to do by fashion magazines – I felt amazing.

'Where are we going?'

'A hotel in Gatwick.' I nodded. Our relationship wasn't taking us to the most exotic locations.

'I know, it's a bit of a cliché. I wish I could take you home with me.' And at that point the wish was enough. Frank drove in the way that he spoke – calm but assertive. He drove like he knew exactly where he was going; or maybe he did.

Despite my doubts about the location, I was impressed with the hotel. Small and chic with a spa attached. If we had to hole up in the suburban wilderness, this was the perfect hideout. I actually screamed when I entered the room, squealed like a child. A huge roll-top bath stood at the foot of the king-size bed.

'Frank, it's gorgeous,' I said, running my fingertips across the rim. 'I've always wanted to stay in a room with a bath.'

'You're gorgeous,' he said seriously.

'Let's christen it.' I turned on the taps.

Frank poured us drinks. I took off my clothes and sat in the tub as it filled. As I watched him undress, I considered how easy it was to be naked in front of him. Over the years with Dylan, what I'd worn to bed had become increasingly modest; a few more years and I'd be kissing him goodnight in an overcoat and boots. I dipped my head under the water, hoping to leave thoughts of home there. I'd told him I was going to an art show for research and would stay with Dee if it got late. I felt doubly wretched saying it, because I should have been going to art shows for research and I was coasting on Nush's ignorance. Dylan accepted the lie easily. He didn't even ask why the company's bookkeeper would be joining me for a research trip. It only proved how little he really listened, which on some dark, petty level may have been why I said it. Frank would have noticed; he noticed everything. I told him about a consultant who had visited the office for a day and, when he asked me about him the next week, I had no idea what he was talking about – he listened to me more than I listened to myself. I lifted my head and the room was empty. It was unsettling.

'Frank,' I said tentatively and then louder, more urgently, again.

'I'm in the bathroom!' came his voice from behind the door.

'Why are you in the bathroom when we're having a bath!' He came out with a towel round his waist. He kept his head down, eyes on the carpet at his feet.

'I'm, erm, I'm just waiting till I calm down.'

'What's wrong?' I stood up and grabbed a towel from a rail beside the tub. I didn't want him to tell me something awful whilst I was naked.

'You're not helping,' he said, his eyes now lifted to meet mine. He nodded towards the towel, and I understood it wasn't his mind that needed to settle. I laughed and dropped the towel, and then knelt back down in the bath and swooshed the water with my hands.

'I'll close my eyes,' I said, and covered my face with my hands. When I didn't hear him approach, I took them away. 'Get in, it's nothing I haven't seen before.' His face fell, and I didn't check but I'm pretty sure everything else did too. 'I'm sorry,' I said quickly.

'Don't be. There's no point denying our reality.' Which of course made me think about his wife, whom I had been doing a pretty decent job of denying. Frank crossed the room and sat on the bed. I got out and wrapped the towel under my arms. I climbed across the mattress to approach him from behind. As I put my arms around his shoulders, he tensed for a second before relenting. 'I'm really happy you're here,' he said, although he sounded incredibly sad.

'I'm glad to be here. I'm glad you brought me.' He pulled

my arms away and lay down on the bed. 'What did you tell her?' I said. He gave a meaty groan and I regretted inviting her to intrude on our afternoon.

'Nothing really. I didn't tell; she didn't ask. She's a sweet girl, but I don't know if she challenges me enough.' I congratulated myself on squashing the urge to ask exactly how old she was, but even without this knowledge she haunted me. For days after, I'd get pulled away without warning by the thought, does sweet equate to beautiful? 'In fact,' continued Frank, 'I know she doesn't challenge me. I knew it on our wedding day.' He sighed and I lay down beside him. 'We had this terrible, terrible DJ, Trevor I think he was called. He announced the first dance and it was this ridiculous love song she'd chosen, and everyone was standing in a circle staring at us and I thought, this probably isn't it. Do you know what I mean?'

I didn't. My wedding day was perfect. Until meeting Dylan I had been ambivalent about marriage, after watching my mother take an emotional hatchet to her own. He made the concept of matrimony feel logical; I managed to push aside all the stress of planning a wedding and focus on what I saw as the goal – becoming a team. I felt it *most* during our first dance. We swayed slowly to 'Ebony and Ivory' because it was silly and weird and so were we, but I wanted Frank to think that I understood him because that was the way he made me feel, so I lied a little and told him I knew exactly what he meant.

'I can't tell you how much I've wanted this,' he said. He didn't mean sex – he was talking about the foundation we had created – but I responded by kissing him, and he responded in turn by pulling me on top of him. The sex was good, the sort you brag about at brunch, but I knew I couldn't brag about it and the knowledge robbed me of my orgasm. I didn't feel completely free to enjoy what shouldn't be enjoyable, but I knew that in the future, if I could allow myself, we would be amazing together.

Afterwards, we lay naked on the bed, my head resting on his chest. 'I have someone I want you to meet,' Frank said. I sat up and ran my fingers through my hair. 'They're not here now.' I could hear him smiling at me.

'I know,' I said. I pulled the duvet up under my armpits. He stretched and gave a rich yawn.

'It's one of my oldest friends. We were at school together. He lives near here and I thought we could meet him for lunch.' It was so real. An actual person from his authentic life. Someone he had history with, which suggested he wanted to make history with me.

'Is that OK? Won't that complicate stuff?' Frank kissed me.

'Things are already very complicated.'

Frank drove us to a pub half an hour away, in the sort of nondescript place that reminded me of my hometown in Essex. Before she married Eddie, Mum would take me to pubs just like it on a Saturday. One comic and a packet of crisps had to last me for hours. She had a series of 'friends', portly men with red faces and suit jackets bunched awkwardly around their frames – Frank's mate Anthony looked like one of them. He stood as we approached and, if it weren't for his outstretched arms, I would never have guessed he had anything to do with my polished companion. As I watched them hug and exchange amiable banter, Anthony looked more like a benevolent uncle than a peer. Frank stepped back and pushed me forward, presenting me like a prize.

'This is Alison,' he said. Anthony pulled me in. His

embrace was almost overwhelming, but it was clear he wasn't letting go until I reciprocated. When I did, it felt better than I had expected.

'It's very good to meet you,' said Anthony as we sat down. 'I like you already.' He shouted over to the bar. 'Another bottle of red, Jan!' The landlady responded with a purse of her lips but moved into action. Anthony poured what was left of a bottle on the table into an empty glass in front of him. 'They look after me here,' he explained.

The men began an intense discussion about the sale of a house. It seemed that Anthony had an ex-wife refusing to vacate it. He spoke of her as if she were a leaky roof, merely an impediment in the sales process. I watched Anthony as he talked; a mole on his right cheek bobbed as his mouth moved. Frank nodded empathetically and offered up the name of a good lawyer; I wondered if he knew him in a personal or professional capacity. The wine arrived, and I thanked Jan and poured myself a glass.

'Sorry, Alison,' said Anthony. 'Boy talk.'

'You're hardly boys,' I countered. Anthony delivered a honking laugh, one so abrasive it made me commit to not saying anything that might provoke it again.

'Well observed,' he said when the noise had concluded. 'We've known each other since we were kids. I'm still a kid,' he patted his stomach, 'a big kid, but Frank here – he's all grown up.' Frank didn't respond, not even the flicker of an eyelid. 'Who are you though, Alison? Tell me everything.' I shook my head rapidly. He laughed again and I winced. 'She's shy!' The two men exchanged a look, but I couldn't tell what it communicated.

'It's not that . . .' It's that I was no longer sure of the answer to that question.

'OK, tell me this. Do you like boats?'

23

IT WAS EASIER being dropped off at work. I decided if we did it again, that's what I would do – and I already knew we would do it again. I appreciated having a buffer between Frank's world and home life. When the two were next to each other, it was too easy to compare them and find Dylan and the girls lacking. I didn't want to do that. I didn't want to think my husband wasn't good enough. He was good enough for someone, but I was starting to think it wasn't me. Bettina was so fired up about her afternoon with the teacher, she barely noticed my noncommittal anecdotes about my weekend.

'He brought me a book,' she purred, 'which you know I appreciated more than flowers or chocolates. Most guys wouldn't be brave enough to do that. They'd fear judgement over their choice – which they should.'

'I got you a book.' Marcus's voice floated out from under Bettina's desk, where he was connecting her new monitor. 'In the Secret Santa last year. I know it's meant to be a secret . . .' It wasn't a secret; Marcus had spent weeks negotiating, campaigning and finally paying for her name in the draw. Bettina looked to the ceiling, and then shrugged as if she had been asked to remember what she had for lunch last Wednesday.

'It was a collection of Dostoevsky's short stories. I mean, you couldn't get any more perfect. I'm getting a herbal tea if anyone wants one.'

Marcus appeared from under the desk and threw himself into Bettina's chair. 'I'm never gonna get her,' he said.

I don't think it was a question but I answered. 'Women are not for getting,' I said.

He looked appropriately apologetic and I felt a flash of warmth for him.

'What was the book?' I asked.

'Love letters,' he said, 'from famous men to the women they loved, I guess.' I placed my hands on the desk, and leaned forward in an effort to create at least the illusion of privacy.

'Marcus,' I said. 'Stop trying so hard.' He stroked his goatee thoughtfully.

'OK,' he said. 'How do I do that?' I shook my head. 'Oh, oh, I get it,' he said.

'Move,' said Bettina forcefully. He jumped up quickly and then, catching himself, wandered slowly away from the desk.

'Yeah, I was going anyway,' he said in a languid tone. Bettina examined the chair before sitting. Marcus gave her one last wistful look before scurrying away.

'I don't think this monitor's any better than the last one,' she said. 'Anyway, Tristan. He finally asked me to the wedding! That's an official thing, right? He wouldn't ask me if we weren't official?' I opened my email to see if Frank had sent anything, but there was only a string of updates from Annie.

'Have you spoken about exclusivity? I wouldn't assume anything unless you have.'

'Really? I guess I didn't think people did that. It seems a bit "back of the school bus", actually asking someone to be your girlfriend.'

'I agree it would be fab if we could rely on men to get all the subtext, but you and I both know they're not that nuanced.'

'Hmmm,' said Bettina. Her extension began to cry for attention, but she ignored it. 'I think he might be.'

'I hope so, but don't count on it. I don't want to see you hurt again.' My words broke her from a hypnotic trance.

'You're right,' she said. 'The deal's not done till it's done.' She picked up her phone and began responding to the caller in clipped monosyllables. I felt hungry. It was guilt. I raided the break room and found a bag of spongy pretzels. I didn't want to be that cynical friend bursting bubbles and debunking the fairy tale; if anything, that was Bettina's job. I was meant to be the optimistic sidekick in the romantic comedy of life, but it pained me to hear Bettina falling for someone in such an uncomplicated way. I wanted to tell her this, but I resented the disapproval I knew she would unleash in her trademark, uncensored manner. The carbs seemed to quell my crabbiness, and I committed to presenting a better friend face. What was the point of a mate if they didn't help to prop up your fantasies? I was scraping the crumbs from the bottom of the packet when Carter strode into the room. He had on a suit with an open-necked shirt, which I took to be his version of casual.

'How's everything going?' he asked as he made himself a coffee.

'Yes, good.'

'Annie says Emerge is going well.' She would, I thought. Under the guise of good communication, Annie would narrate her every action through painstakingly tedious email updates.

'So I hear,' I said.

187

'You did a good job with her,' said Carter thoughtfully. I spluttered, emitting a small spray of pretzel dust. 'She's jumped in feet first, extremely enthusiastic.'

'Sometimes a little too enthusiastic,' I said. I made sure I gave him a small smile, one ready to advance or retreat depending on his response.

'Can you be too enthusiastic?' he asked, and it withdrew.

'No, probably not,' I said.

'And this art project seems very promising. You've been quiet about the progress.'

'You know me,' I said brightly. 'I like to share the results and not the process.' Carter took a sip of his coffee. Even the way he lifted the cup to his mouth was elegant.

'That's the thing,' he said. 'I'm not sure I do – know you, that is. I think we should schedule a meeting. Lunch maybe?' I couldn't decide whether to be pleased or terrified. 'What have you got on today?'

'I'm meeting Nush – I mean the client – today.' Nush had sent me a text the previous evening, actually very early that morning, insisting we meet. I had pictured her bright nails clacking on the screen as she tried to process her definitely exaggerated, possibly drug-induced crisis. At the time I was only irritated that her ineffective efforts at adulting were interrupting my sleep. Standing there awkwardly with bits of pretzel wedged in between my back teeth, I was grateful.

'OK, another time,' he said.

Nush's message had said that she would be around Islington. I called her on my way out and the line went straight to voicemail. I assumed she was on the phone; Nush was a woman who required an audience at all times. I headed to Angel, an area I had always loved. The first time I found myself there in my twenties, I thought I'd landed on the set of a Richard Curtis film; everyone was so cheerful and stylish. I promised myself that in a few years, when successful in whatever path I chose, I would live there. That was before I knew that Angel, like one of its supernatural namesakes, was in an inaccessible realm – those people weren't just cheerful and stylish, they were probably very rich. I had boxed up the dream of Angel, along with so many others; I had accepted adulthood as an accumulation of dying dreams. That morning, sitting on a bench outside the tube station, I felt differently. Had my dream died or had I suffocated it with conventionality? When I tried Nush again, she answered.

'Yes?' she asked.

'Where do you want to meet?'

'When?' I gripped the seat of the bench with my free hand.

'Today,' I said slowly. I paused, and when she didn't take the opportunity to attempt an apology, I continued. 'You sent me a frankly hysterical-sounding text very early this morning, proposing we meet. Is everything OK with the show?'

'Oh yeah, don't worry, it's fine,' she said.

'I wasn't worrying until you messaged me, strongly indicating I should worry.'

'I'm getting another call, one second.'

'No!' I barked. 'Nush, I already have two children – I don't have the headspace for another. If you want to be a professional you have to behave, well, professionally. Honestly, this project is really interesting but if your plan is to piss about with your dad's money, I can't be a part of it.' I felt a lump develop in my throat; perhaps my body was doing whatever it could to stop me speaking.

In the silence, I started to draft my resignation letter to

Carter, but then Nush said, 'You're right. I'm sorry. I know I shouldn't drink tequila. I'm on my way to Sainte-Marine. Taking a few days to get my head together. I'll call you when I'm back. Not before!' She giggled. I told her to have a good time but not too good a time. She promised she wouldn't, in a sing-song voice. I remembered Frank telling me that he knew I wasn't a pushover. I thought he knew me better than I knew myself. I sent him a voice note saying thank you, nothing more. I believed we needed so few words. Reluctant to return to the office and the threat of Carter's attention, I decided to use the precious time I had gained to complete a long-overdue task. I caught the bus and went to visit my dad.

He looked surprised when he saw me at the door, and his expression solidified the feeling that I had been away too long. 'You're not busy, are you?' I asked when he hesitated to invite me in.

'No, no. Doing some filing.' I followed him to the living room, where the contents of the recycling bin were strewn across his coffee table. I tried to help him put them back in the plastic crate that usually lived outside his front door but he shooed me away, and I settled on to the sofa and watched him methodically place each item back into the box.

Eddie insisted on making the tea, even though it took him four times longer than it would have taken me. I flitted through the television channels, trying to seem occupied so he wouldn't feel like he was being judged. The living room was neat and orderly, and the small kitchen attached to it the same. I thought about the time and effort it would have taken to maintain it and marvelled at his commitment. He brought me the tea and I stood up to take it.

'Biscuit?' he asked. I said yes without thinking, and watched him take the long journey back across the room.

He was wearing plaid trousers, loose because of his weight loss. As I watched them flapping around his wizened form, I almost regretted my decision to visit. Finally, he re-emerged with a packet of rich tea. I accepted them and nibbled on one, even though it was soggy. He smiled as I ate the snack, and I thought that maybe all the effort he made wasn't commitment but necessity. He kept up with his chores and pressed those trousers, despite what it must cost him, to help maintain the belief that everything was going to be OK.

'Have you seen Henry?' I asked. I hadn't heard from him, which wasn't unexpected. I had sent him a message to let him know I had gained a new client and thus relieved myself of the role of human cashpoint for the foreseeable future, to which he sent me a thumbs-up emoji.

'He came by a couple of days ago. Brought a new girl. He met her on a bus, apparently, and she's the one. How about that for luck?' I laughed.

'What's she like?'

'Like the others.'

'It's a shame he won't settle down. I think it could chill him out a bit.'

'I believe that's what he's afraid of.' Eddie chuckled at his own joke, and the laugh turned into a cough. The act appeared to consume his whole body.

'Can I get you something?' I asked. Although what, I didn't know. Some new lungs perhaps? Eddie shook his hand towards me to indicate that no, there was nothing I could do. Once he had composed himself, he took a sloppy sip of tea.

'He's tempted by shiny things. Like your mother in that way.' Even though I was the first to berate Mum's flightiness, I was offended on her behalf.

'It's not always a bad thing to go after what you want,' I said. I put the rich teas on the coffee table.

'No, it's a good thing, if you know what you want,' Eddie said.

'Come on. She's made her fair share of mistakes but she's got a few things right.'

'Two,' said Eddie, reaching out to touch my hand. 'Well, one and a half. However, I wasn't talking about your mum. I meant me.' Eddie stared at the television screen as he spoke. 'I had everything and I kept chasing more – more work, a bigger house. I refused to see what was in front of me.'

'That's not true,' I said, although I didn't know that to be the case. I simply wasn't sure I wanted to hear it.

'It is. Take it from a dying man.' I moved towards him, not sure what I would do but instinctively wanting to make him stop. He held up a hand and I froze obediently. 'Your mother made me so angry. I thought that her carrying on meant she didn't love me. I wanted her to be different when it was her, the way that she is, who I fell in love with. I didn't see what I had with her, with us. It's the thing I regret most.'

'That's not right, Dad. Trust me, you're being hard on yourself.' He looked at me.

'Maybe, but maybe I was too easy on myself before.' I remembered trying to steal time with him when I was a kid; I'd offer to accompany him on any errand. People would always comment on how alike we were. We'd be in a shop and the woman behind the till would proclaim I was a 'chip off the old block'. He would never correct them. I thought at the time he was trying to preserve my dignity, but later I decided he might have believed it to be true. And that morning I took his words as a message. The message being – I know you because part of you is me, and that part won't want to leave with regrets.

192

24

I HAD BOOKED THE morning off to be a better mother and attend Chloe's assembly. As the parent with flexible hours, such activities had always been Dylan's domain, and as much as he claimed to dislike social gatherings, I noticed he was on first-name terms with several of the mothers waiting in the hall. On the odd occasions I took the girls to school, I felt like those women were looking down on me from their four-by-fours and side-eyeing my high-street leggings, but Dylan seemed right at home as we sat amongst them on the tiny school chairs. 'Hey, Jen! Hey, Kerry!' he said to a muscular, ash-blonde woman and a curvaceous brunette in the seats in front of us.

'Hi, Dylan,' they chorused, twisting round in their seats to face him fully.

'Did you get in touch with that Facebook group I was telling you about?' asked the blonde.

'Yeah, thanks for that,' he said. 'Already got a couple of leads. And I've done the spreadsheet so I can start doing the referral thing we chatted about.' I was watching his mouth move but I still couldn't believe the words coming out were his. 'Oh. This is my wife, Alison.' He said this quickly; it was an afterthought. I saw the women exchange a glance before muttering hello. I wondered what assumptions they had already made about me and whether I had proven them right.

'Nice to meet you,' I said. They both nodded.

'Drop me a message if you need any help with the mail-out,' the blonde said to Dylan.

'Thanks, I will.' The women turned away and I nudged him.

'All right, babe?' he asked.

I made a face that I hoped would translate as, 'Why would you ask this random woman for help when you live with someone who works in marketing?' It wasn't effective.

Dylan mouthed, 'What?'

'Nothing, the show's starting,' I whispered. Thirty or so children shuffled on to the stage and treated us to an earnest rendition of Katy Perry's 'Firework'. The show, as always, comprised a series of individual skits or talents interspersed with group renditions of pop songs featuring uplifting messages. The children, all on the precipice of acute self-awareness, performed with gusto, and although it wasn't quite cute, it was charming. Following the opening number there was a dance performed by a group of girls; it involved more booty shaking than I was comfortable with, but they were very tight. Afterwards a lad demonstrated his talent for kick-ups which, to be fair, was really impressive.

Then, it was Chloe's turn. Dylan raised his phone to shoulder height. It was against school policy to take videos, so he was trying to film without looking at the screen. I could tell it was going to be a terrible shot. I'd been to many school performances over the years, but I still felt a rush of adrenaline when Chloe stepped to the front of the stage. She was wearing one of my summer dresses, hitched up somewhat unsuccessfully with one of Dylan's belts. She looked somewhere beyond the audience, her brown eyes wide, and for a few agonizing seconds I thought she was going to cry, but it seems she was setting the scene because when she began the piece, her voice was clear and strong.

'Long ago in a place like this, but different because there were no cars or shops and stuff like that, there was an evil queen who stole the beauty of young women.' The plot was heavily borrowed from *Snow White and the Huntsman*, which we had watched at least sixteen times. During our rehearsals I had tried to introduce the concept of plagiarism, which Chloe had dismissed because 'everybody copies', and I couldn't really argue against that. Chloe gave a fabulously camp performance as the ageing queen desperately fighting to retain her youth. She clawed at her face in front of an imaginary mirror, convulsing with theatrical sobs at the appearance of new wrinkles. It was funny because it was true. The final scene was the slaughter of the queen by an unseen army. Chloe staged this by repeatedly breaking the fourth wall to explain what was happening. After several minutes of battle she fell to her knees. She then clutched her throat before dropping to the floor with a thud that implied there might be bruising. Assuming this was the end, the audience cheered. Buoyed by their reaction, Chloe rose again and staggered around the stage – she looked more drunk than fatally wounded, but I couldn't deny she was committed. When she fell again and lay on the stage open-eyed and quivering, I stood and led the applause before there could be another resurrection. In my peripheral vision I saw one of Dylan's friends turn, but I kept my head high. As the clapping faded, Chloe rose and gave a deep bow before joining her classmates for a Journey number.

After the show, I made Dylan wait by the car with me.

The dark-haired woman sashayed past with her daughter, a 50 per cent copy of her. 'See you at the fete,' she said to Dylan. 'Please bring your lemon slices.' He leaned back against the passenger-side window.

'Sure thing,' he said.

'What's she talking about?' I demanded, as she wiggled out of sight.

'At Easter there was this bake thing. I took in my lemon slices.' Dylan kept his eyes trained on the school doors. I prodded him in the arm.

'You don't have any lemon slices.'

'Technically they were Morrisons lemon slices that I knocked about a bit. Chloe forgot to tell us about it.' I stepped in front of him.

'You lied.' Dylan pulled me towards him. I put my hands on his chest to keep some distance.

'Yes, and I'd do it again. They think they're so perfect.' He lied and he sorted something out. It was new information.

'Here's my superstar,' said Dylan. I spun around to see Chloe flying towards us. She was still in my dress and held bunches of it in her hands as she ran.

'Brava, gorgeous girl,' I said as she threw herself at me. 'Although that wasn't exactly what we rehearsed.'

'I know,' Chloe said joyously. She had my colouring but her father's quality of completely missing subtext.

'Hello,' said a warm, quiet voice from behind me. I peeled Chloe away and looked up. It took me a second to recognize Ms Khavari with her hair down and her glasses absent. She looked less stern than at our previous parents'-evening encounters. It occurred to me that her presentation as a harsh but fair educator was a performance, that everything is a bit of a performance.

'I wanted to say well done,' she said to Chloe. Chloe

196

appeared to grow an inch. 'She said you helped her a lot,' she continued, addressing me, 'so that goes for you too.' Silly as it seems, the compliment landed. 'Woodrow Class are very proud of all your effort, Chloe,' she said. I could tell she was being genuine and I felt a rush of gratitude. She wanted to foster my little girl's passion – dark and chaotic as it was. It didn't matter that the performance was dreadful; it had heart. Ms Khavari said goodbye and I watched her walk to her car – a black Mini convertible.

'You want to get ice cream?' I asked Chloe.

'Really?'

'I think it's what all the great actors do after a performance.' She cheered.

In the car, Dylan reached across and put his hand on my thigh. It felt strange, foreign. I squeezed it before moving away.

'I want Ruby to come,' said Chloe from the back. Her resilience astonished me. Ruby continuously rejected her and yet she kept seeking her out. The trait would either be her greatest strength or her undoing.

'I don't know,' I said carefully. 'She has work. I'll call her.'

'Don't call her, she'll say no. Let's go and get her.' She was right. Underneath the innocence and boundless excitement there was a canniness that made me proud.

Dylan pulled up outside the house and stopped the engine.

'I'll go!' shouted Chloe.

'No, you stay,' I said, unsnapping my belt. I didn't want Ruby to stick a pin in Chloe's full-to-bursting bubble. I could hear Ruby's music from the front door, softer than her usual choice but still with that tinny, synthetic bassline. I played classical music to my belly when she was inside me. I don't even like classical music – fat lot of good it did. I knocked at her door and she didn't respond. I knocked again harder, pausing between blows to make each bang distinct. The music stopped.

'Yeah,' she said. She sounded tired or reluctant or maybe resentful, full of malice that I had forced her to waste a whole syllable on me.

'Can I come in?' I asked. Silence. I decided I could go in because I owned the door. Ruby was face down on her bed. I squeezed in beside her and patted her back tentatively, like she was an animal I didn't know and couldn't trust not to bite.

'You tired?' I asked. She had been staying up too late. Sometimes in the night when I was going for my between-sleep-cycles pee, I'd hear shouty, high-pitched American accents emanating from her room. One morning, when she refused to be roused, I threatened to turn the wifi off overnight. She told me the Kardashians helped her sleep. I retorted that they would give me nightmares, and I could tell she nearly laughed. Ruby shifted awkwardly and sat on her pillow, her legs drawn in front of her like a shield. Her left eye twitched, a vestige from childhood that signalled she was about to cry.

'I feel so sad,' she stuttered. She spoke as if she were claiming the feeling.

'What about, honey – is it the drama club?'

'No, that's done with.' Her life moved so quickly; how could I be expected to keep up? 'It's nothing and it's everything,' she said. 'That's what makes it feel so bad.'

For a few seconds I felt the heat of anger fill my chest. I felt like shouting, 'Look at you! You have everything!' I wanted to tell her she could have a mother who flirted with her teachers and forgot to collect her from school. I felt like

198

saying, 'I'll give you something to feel sad about.' And that thought seemed so silly and meaningless and parodically parental that the anger dissipated. I saw the first tear – a huge, singular drop – work its way steadily down the right side of her face. When she first started school she would wake me in the night with complaints of stomach pain, and she looked just the same back then. I touched her lightly. She jolted and wiped her face with her palm. Of course she could have everything and feel sad – I knew that.

'You know what I think might help?' She shook her head. 'Ice cream.'

'That's so stupid,' she said, but I heard the beginnings of a smile.

'So stupid it just might work.'

Dylan told the girls they could have anything they wanted: 'No holes barred.' I cringed but didn't correct him. The girls piled every topping available on to their sundaes. Ruby admitted that the results weren't that palatable, but Chloe announced that it had been the 'best day ever'. If that were the case I was sort of annoyed that I'd spent all that money taking them to Disneyland, but mostly it made me really happy. Ruby listened patiently as Chloe recounted her performance. Dylan did a re-enactment of the audience's reaction to her many deaths. He was taking the mickey out of her, but we all knew that was the way he showed his love.

When we were side by side at the sinks in the toilet, Ruby said to me, 'It was stupid but it did kind of work.'

As we walked back to the car, I felt my phone quivering in my pocket. Before he could speak, I said, 'I can't do this.'

'Alison,' he started, and I cut him off, certain that whatever he said would send me back to the brink.

'I'm sorry.' I stopped the call. I paused before catching up with Dylan and the girls. He swung Chloe over his shoulder; Ruby clapped her hands in delight as her sister shrieked. I realized the truly frightening thought was that they might be fine without me.

25

'YOU'VE GOT TO help me with your dad before I kill him,' said Mum. She was calling Eddie 'Dad' to manipulate me into going over, and infuriatingly it worked. I had spent two days making up for my sketchy work hours and too-frequent breaks for text sessions with Frank, but I still had a pile of unread emails blinking at me menacingly.

'Can you give me an hour?'

'As soon as you can spare some time for your family.' She hung up without saying goodbye.

'Fuck,' I whispered. Annie appeared at my desk, her tragedy sensor immediately alerting her to crisis.

'Everything all right?' she chirruped.

'Great, but I have to leave early,' I told her begrudgingly.

'Client?' If I said yes, she'd ask which one. She'd want the details and I wouldn't have them.

'Family emergency,' I said, in a 'don't probe' tone.

'I'm sorry,' she said. 'Let me know if there's anything I can get on with whilst you're out.' Her face was a composite of responsibility and concern but I detected something in her voice, a slight inflection that if I had to guess I would identify as glee.

*

I let myself into Eddie's flat with the key he'd given me 'for emergencies'. He and my mother and brother were in the living room. It looked like a scene from a Pinter play. Eddie sat in an armchair, wearing a shirt and boxers, his greying head in his hands; my mother stood across the room, one hand on her hip, the other holding a glass of dark liquid; and between them my brother lay on the sofa.

'Why am I here?' They all became animated when I spoke. Eddie shouted at my mother and waved his hands frenetically; Mum was shouting at me but I couldn't make out the words above Eddie. I could only see Henry's mouth moving, but I could tell he was greeting me jovially.

'Stop!' I shouted, and they did. 'Mum, why am I here when Henry's here already?' Mum gestured towards my brother, now sitting up and picking at the toenails of his right foot. Her expression asked me if I was crazy. 'Fine,' I said. 'Dad, what happened?' Eddie sighed; for a heart-stopping second, I thought he might cry.

'I was going to work,' he said slowly, carefully, as though trying to convince himself.

'You don't work any more, Eddie!' cried Mum. Now it was Eddie's turn to shout 'stop'. He covered his ears and shook his head.

'Mum, sit down.' She hesitated. 'Sit.' She finished her drink and placed the glass on the mantelpiece before taking a seat next to Henry. 'Someone, start.' They all began to speak at once. I raised my hands and they stopped. 'Dad, start. Slowly.'

'I was just going to work,' he said. I waited for more; he had no more to give.

'Mum,' I said.

'This idiot—'

'Mum.'

'Eddie decided, despite his debilitating condition and the fact he's been retired for years, that he wanted to rejoin the workforce.'

'OK,' I said. I glanced at Eddie to gauge his reaction as she spoke. He was looking away from me, towards the kitchen or something beyond it.

'So, he drags himself and his oxygen tank and some kitchen scissors, and starts pruning next door's garden.'

'I don't understand, Dad – you were a sales rep.'

'He did gardening when he finished school. You're missing the point. He went into someone else's garden and started . . . started bloody gardening.'

'I don't understand – that sounds helpful.'

'That's what I said,' said Henry, nudging Mum. If I was on the same page as Henry, I had missed several paragraphs.

'It might have been helpful if he had been asked, and it might have been helpful if he wasn't standing in a stranger's front garden in his underpants.'

'Jesus,' I said. I looked at Eddie. He lowered his head.

'The neighbour's husband thought he was getting his kicks, not that he could, and they've called the police. The guy is built like a brick shithouse. If I hadn't come over he'd have knocked him out cold.' Eddie muttered something. 'What was that?' snapped Mum.

'They're not married,' he said.

'Yep, that's the important bit.'

'What did the police say?'

'They haven't come. I said I would take him home and they told me someone would call round.'

'And they haven't yet. So, it's not that serious. Don't worry, Dad, they have more important things to deal with.'

I knelt down next to him. He didn't respond. I put my hand over one of his and he eased it away.

'I just wanted to feel useful,' he said quietly.

I'd left my jacket at the office, and as I stood on the station platform waiting for a train back to central London, I could feel my skin goosepimpling. I crossed my arms over my chest and rubbed them with my hands. The man next to me peered in my direction over his glasses.

'Well that was a good summer,' he said, followed by a confident chuckle. I ignored him. I heard the rustle of a newspaper, and when I glanced back he seemed engrossed in the text, but I noticed his face had turned crimson. I felt bad; he was trying to inject some warmth into a cold, stale morning and I had denied him that. I caught his eye and offered a smile, but he shook the paper haughtily and turned his body away. How quickly men turn when they are denied. Who teaches them it is their right to receive attention and validation whenever they demand it? As a train approached, he folded his paper and offered it to a woman behind him. She took it and smiled gratefully. As the train doors closed, I watched her place the paper on a bench behind her, and understood that the ones who teach them that are women.

I let the first tube go past. It was rammed, and I wanted a seat and space to think. The next one wasn't much better, but if I waited any longer I would give Annie cause to comment. As the door opened, my phone rang and it was him. I let people jostle me as they pushed their way on, and as the carriages pulled away, I answered.

'I can't talk now. I'm going to be late.' I checked the digital display. 'I'm already late.'

'Don't go. Come here.' I should have hung up. I wanted to but I didn't.

'Where's here?'

'My house.' And how could I say no when he was asking me in?

He lived in a posh bit of North London nestled between two crap ones. He opened the door in jeans and a thinning, purple T-shirt. This was him off-duty. I felt like I was catching him unawares, even though he knew I was coming. The house was pretty; it had a glossy red door and a well-kept front garden. I couldn't help but compare it to my own scrap of concrete and weeds. He opened the door just enough that I could slip in. I felt like an intruder. The hallway was wide and clear; the walls were painted a soft mint green, a colour that even a man as stylish as Frank wouldn't have picked. On the left-hand side was a white chest of drawers; I imagined it was filled with useful things. On top was a cut-glass vase overflowing with pink peonies.

'I'm sorry I cut you off like that. It seemed like the best thing to do. All I can see is this getting really messy, for everyone.' He stepped towards me. I moved away until my back met the door. Frank came closer. I felt trapped but not by him, by myself. He put his hand up to my face.

'I want things to be messy,' he said. He kissed me and I couldn't remember why I hadn't wanted to come. We had sex in the hallway, like they do in films. When I watched those scenes I thought, but where has she put her feet? And why don't they topple over? But you manage. For a minute I worried he would get tired holding me up, but then I forgot myself – it was that forgetting that kept me coming back to him.

Afterwards he led the way upstairs. I left my dress in the hall and followed. He took me to a bedroom. It was too anonymous to be theirs but I still looked for clues. A stack of interiors magazines in a rack in the corner, a box of tissues next to the bed – she was thoughtful. Frank left me alone and I got under the sheets. They smelled amazing; it was probably just fabric conditioner, but every time I moved the air was filled with a floral scent. Frank returned with two glasses of orange juice. He handed one to me before getting in beside me.

'Thank you,' I said. The first swig made me cough.

'It's a screwdriver. I thought we both might need it.'

'Give a girl a clue.'

'And I want you to speak freely.'

'I will. I always do.' He turned towards me and pushed my hair back from my face.

'Good. Never stop.' He slipped his arm round my shoulder and his proximity made me fret about my bra, which was once white but had turned grey after too many machine washes. I looked at the waxed wood floors. The woman who maintained them probably hand-washed her bras.

'What's she like? Really,' I asked.

Frank held the bridge of his nose between his forefinger and thumb. 'Will it help to know?'

I pulled the duvet up over my chest. 'I don't know.'

Frank made small circles on my arm with his fingers. 'All you need to understand is I don't think I love her any more. When you told me you wanted to end things it really brought that home.'

'Oh, Jesus,' I said.

'I'm not on my own in this, am I? Tell me it was a nightmare for you too.' He didn't seem nervous that I would say otherwise, but I reassured him that being disconnected was torture for me too.

'But it's hard being with you as well. I don't like doing this behind everyone's back. I hate being in her house.' I felt his body grow tense beside me.

'Are you saying you want to be out in the open? Make things official?' I realized that without being able to see him, I wasn't sure of how I should answer.

'Is that what you want?' I asked. I thought about living in his space, not the physical space but the realm of being comforted and adored, and I thought maybe I wanted it, whatever the cost. Frank kissed my shoulder. 'I don't know if I can, you know, live with Dylan and see you as well. It's not fair on him or us.'

'Dylan,' said Frank, rolling the word around his mouth like a new flavour.

We had sex again. Was it just about sex? I had asked myself so many times. And if the answer was yes, was that all bad? Sex was better with Frank because I was better. I felt younger, lither when I was with him; he made me feel more like me or perhaps, more accurately, he amplified a part of me that I liked.

We were still entwined when he said, 'I've been thinking about leaving her. Even before the baby, I was looking at places. I didn't want to say anything because I didn't want you to feel under pressure.' I couldn't remember the last time someone tried to relieve me of pressure, and now that he had, I was more than happy to take it on.

'You need to chase your own happiness,' I told him. He pulled me on to his lap.

'Are you quoting me?' I buried my face into his shoulder. 'Are you quoting me?' he said again, his voice mocking but loving and still sexy.

'When were you going to leave?' I whispered.

'Soon, maybe the next couple of months. But, listen – I don't want you to worry that this is about you.' But I wasn't worried; I was elated.

'Mrs Meecham?' I had almost not answered my phone; withheld numbers usually mean young men with northern accents asking me about a mythical accident I have recently had. Frank and I had napped together, nestled into the afternoon as if we had all the time in the world; I wasn't eager to disturb that, but paranoia was a constant companion, and I accepted the call in case not doing so initiated a chain of events that led to our discovery. As it turned out, it might have. 'Mrs Meecham, I'm glad I got you.'

'It's Ms Meecham,' I said.

'Yes, Mrs Meecham. I'm calling from school. I'm afraid to say we have a bit of an issue here. Is it possible you could come and collect Ruby?'

'Is she sick?'

'No, she's fine. We just have an issue, and we need you to come and collect her.'

'If she's not sick, what's going on? Is she OK?' Frank started to rub my back and I shrugged him away. I wasn't ready for those two parts of my life to coexist.

'I think it would be better if we discuss it when you come down.'

'I'll be there in . . .' I faltered, unsure how long it would take me to get there from where I was, scared that highlighting the distance might reveal something. 'I'll be there as soon as I can.' I got out of bed, scanning the room frantically for my belongings. 'Fuck, where's my dress!'

'By the front door,' said Frank. 'Is everything OK?'

'No, it's not OK. Nothing's OK. I think something's

wrong with Ruby.' He sat on the stairs and watched me dress in the hallway. I was too agitated to feel embarrassed, but I did take a second to think about how different I felt when the dress was coming off – despite how they're created, kids take the sex out of everything.

The receptionist asked me to write my name in a visitors' book, and although she had been nothing but amiable, I detested her for keeping me from my child. I scrawled my name on the page and handed it back to her. She gave me a visitor's pass in exchange.

'Have a seat and I'll take you to the head's office.'

'I know the way,' I said.

'It's policy,' she simpered. I couldn't sit; I paced tiny circles on the russet carpet. I could hear her answering the phone and giving laboured directions to the school.

'Look for the huge building full of kids,' I muttered. She turned and gave me that infuriating 'one second' finger signal. I watched her end the call and organize herself at evolutionary pace. Finally, she left her little Perspex-windowed box and walked out to where I stood.

'Follow me, Mrs Meecham,' she said. We wandered the hallways. It was suspiciously quiet, like they had drugged the children or gagged them. The receptionist stopped before we reached the room and let me take the last few steps alone. I peered in through a small glass window; it had never occurred to me before how much high school was like prison. Ruby sat in her uniform, head down. I couldn't see her face, but I could tell by her posture she'd been crying or was about to. The headmaster, Mr Kindeace, a middle-aged man who always looked as though he was on his way to a Spandau Ballet tribute band audition, was sitting in a chair opposite her. His shiny suit trousers bunched awkwardly as he crossed his legs. I pushed open the door and Ruby looked up at me. She had two wonky black streaks running down her face, which meant I had to add wearing make-up to school to her list of crimes.

There was an empty chair next to her. As I sat, she shuffled away from me. I reached towards her and when she didn't move, I took hold of her hand. When she was young and had stolen biscuits or broken the washing machine trying to clean one of her toys, I would hold her hands as she confessed. 'Whatever you say can't make me love you any less,' I would assure her.

'Thanks for coming so quickly,' said Mr Kindeace.

'Of course, no problem.' The windows were open but I felt hot.

'I'm afraid Ruby hasn't been making the best use of her time here.' I looked to my daughter, who shook her head quickly.

'Ruby used false details to befriend her form tutor Ms Davison on social media. Following that, she found some, um, provocative pictures and distributed them amongst the student body. With annotations.'

'Right . . .' I had heard all the words but was struggling to understand what they meant in that specific order. I tried shuffling the sentence round in my head. I felt Ruby's hand go limp in mine.

'Perhaps if I showed you . . . I'm loath to add to Ms Davison's humiliation, but I think it's the only way you'll understand.' He reached behind him to his desk, picked up a tablet and poked around on it for a few seconds. Ruby and I sat in heavy silence as he swiped and prodded. 'Ah, OK, here it is.' He passed me the device. On the screen was a photo of a young, buxom woman wearing a scant pink bikini. A crudely drawn arrow ran from her breasts to the word 'saggy' and another from her bum to the word 'flat'. I knew I was opening and closing my mouth like a deranged goldfish but I had no words.

'We think it's best if Ruby takes the rest of today and tomorrow off. We'll have a discussion before she returns.'

'Yes, of course.' I stood up. 'I'm sorry. So very sorry.' I left without checking that Ruby was behind me.

As I passed reception, the woman at reception stood and called out, 'Excuse me!' She added more gently, 'We need your pass.' I ripped it from my lapel and threw it down on the desk. 'Thank you,' she said, 'it's for security reasons.'

'Because you do such a good job of protecting children,' I spat. She maintained her smile but blinked several times.

'Come on, Mum,' Ruby whispered. I let her pull me into the car park but shook myself free as soon as we were outside. I looked at the sky for inspiration; it was an edgeless field of blue.

'How could you be so disrespectful?' I asked. I had viewed my teachers as deities. The thought of handing in homework late would have been enough to send me head-first into a shame spiral. One, Miss Gibbs, had been so kind and so reassuring that I had asked to stay with her for the summer. I had interpreted the encouraging comments at the end of my rambling essays, and the lengthy chats that she would let run well into break time, as far more than they were. At the end of my first year of high school, I gave her a silver chain on which dangled a trinket in the shape of a stack of books. It took all my birthday and Christmas money to buy. On the card I presented with it, I wrote how grateful I was for her lessons and offered my services to her for the holidays – cleaning up, helping with marking, walking her little dog Oscar, of whom I had heard so much over the year. She returned the chain. She told me that my success in English was gift enough for her. She asked me a lot of questions about my mum, about when we got up and what we ate. I left her classroom, my belly heavy with a feeling I didn't recognize. I dropped the chain down a drain outside the technology block and said little more than 'here' to Miss Gibbs again.

'It was a joke,' said Ruby with a sniff. We caught the train home in silence. Every time I attempted to speak, the words 'Why would you do this to me?' bubbled up in my throat. I can't bear those parents who see their children as an extension of themselves and push them to be what they could never be, but at that moment, I felt more than ever that the dark-haired child beside me was representative of who I was. And that meant part of who I was wasn't good at all.

As my key was in the door, Ruby touched my back. I hesitated but did not look at her.

'Can we not tell Dad,' she said. I withdrew my key and turned to her.

'How can we not tell him? Don't you think he'll notice when you're hanging round the house all day?'

'Can we just tell him something else?'

'Like what?' I folded my arms. 'You're the one who's full of bright ideas.'

'I'm really sorry,' she said. 'I don't know why I did it. I wanted Dom to like me. It was so stupid. I like Ms Davison. She's really nice and funny. He promised he wouldn't show anyone. Honestly, she was never meant to find out.'

'Do you think that makes it OK?'

'No ... I just. I thought she put it up there in the first place and ... Dad won't get it. He'll freak out.' I let us in without giving her a response. We filed into the living room, where Dylan was watching unattractive people screaming at each other on the TV.

'What are my beautiful girls doing home so early?' he said.

'Ruby got sent home,' I said. 'She's not going in tomorrow either.' His expression lurched from contentment to agitation. He leaned forward and placed his elbows on his knees, bracing himself for whatever was to come. Ruby shuffled towards me. I felt her arm resting against mine and weakened. In retrospect, it was pitiful how eager I was to share something with her again.

'Too many lates. This new head is taking attendance very seriously.'

'Wow,' said Dylan. His face scrunched in contemplation. For a second I thought he was going to call me out on the lie. 'That's tough. I'm sorry, darling, I probably had something to do with that.' Ruby exhaled audibly.

'It's OK,' she said. 'I've got a project to do.' She ran upstairs without so much as a glance at me.

'Come give me a cuddle,' said Dylan, holding his arm out. I sat on his lap. Lies upon lies. It was becoming so easy.

26

'HOW WAS SAINT Mary?'

'Sainte-Marine, and it was divine,' said Nush with a sigh. 'Just what I needed. I went with Cal and Eleanor – they're such a riot.' Nush often did this thing where she spoke about people as if I should know who they were. At first, I thought perhaps they were people of significance – she is well connected – but it turned out she had a strange, childlike habit of assuming others possessed the same knowledge she did.

'We'll have two champagnes, please,' said Nush to a passing waiter. 'We should start as we mean to go on.' She smiled at me. Her teeth looked impossibly white next to her even more tanned skin.

'Not if we actually want to get any work done.'

'It will unlock our creativity.' Nush examined her face in the back of a spoon. Clearly finding her reflection to her satisfaction, she blew herself a kiss before replacing the cutlery on the table.

'For you, maybe. In my experience it does the opposite.'

'You're so right,' said Nush, nodding solemnly. 'I'm not supposed to drink anyway. My sponsor says it might lower my ability to resist the rest of the stuff.' She waved a hand about in front of her, suggesting that 'the rest of the stuff' was everyday trivialities that everyone deals with. 'I'm going to stick to day drinking; you don't often get offered blow at breakfast.' She giggled. My face felt itchy.

'You had a cocaine problem?' Nush pursed her ample lips as she considered this for a few seconds.

'Mostly – and a bit of smack. It got me into quite a lot of trouble.' She smiled as she looked into the distance, as if recounting youthful high jinks. 'Yeah, it started small – a weekend thing, a holiday thing, a mid-week pick-up – but it got out of hand. I owed a lot of money to some not very nice people. My dad cut me off. I ended up dancing for a spell.' I felt incredibly sad – you could give your child everything and it still might not be enough. 'That's how I met Frank actually.' The waiter brought the drinks and I decided to risk the damage to my creativity.

'Sorry? You met Frank when you were stripping?'

'Yeah. I mean, not actually at the club. He wasn't a client. His friend owned the place. I met him at a drinks thing and he got me to change my whole outlook.'

'He does that,' I murmured.

'He's pretty special. Have you met his wife?'

'No.' I meant, 'No, don't tell me.' I didn't want the hazy shape I had of her to become solid.

'She's amazing. She totally took me under her wing. You know, if my husband brought home some strung-out stripper, I'd be livid.' So would I. Anyone would be, but maybe with Frank you would hide that because he makes everything seem OK.

'That was kind of her,' I said.

'They're great. He's like my uncle. He's better than my uncle because my uncle is into some pretty shady shit. And now he's brought me to you!' She opened her hands, ready to receive me as the gift that I was.

'Yes, he did. So, let's get on, shall we? What's on the agenda?'

'I thought we'd go over the details, and then after breakfast I'll take you to visit one of my artists. Ooh, artists! It sounds so official!' She clapped her hands, finished her drink in two gulps, and called out to the waiter to order another.

We arrived at a studio on a back street in Hoxton more than a little tipsy. There was no buzzer, so Nush beat at the heavy wooden door with her fist. 'Charlie!' she shouted. 'Charlie darling, we're here.' Eventually, the door creaked open and a short, anaemic-looking man with thick-rimmed glasses and a serious expression opened the door.

'Yeah, Nush,' he said. More of an observation than a greeting.

'Hi, darling. This is my marketing manager, Alison.' Charlie nodded and walked back into the darkness. It took a minute for my eyes to adjust to the gloom. The space was largely empty. A few tables of odds and ends were scattered about, and a sink with a makeshift tea station sat in the corner.

'Want a coffee?' said Charlie. It didn't feel like a genuine offer and I refused.

'Got anything stronger?' asked Nush.

'I might have some scotch,' he said in the same flat tone. He went to the sink and crouched down to rifle through the cupboard underneath. I walked up to one of the tables; it held a stack of books, a few empty beer cans and dozens of crumpled bus tickets. I picked up one of the books. It was called *Cowboy Dreams* and the image on the front made explicit what the cowboys were dreaming about.

'Don't touch the art!' came a shout from behind me. I looked for the owner of the voice before realizing that it belonged to Charlie. I was both flustered and impressed. I dropped the book on the table and held my hands up. He scurried over, his sandals making frantic shuffling sounds on the dusty floor. He pushed me aside to replace the book where it had been, stepping back to survey it before making a small adjustment.

'I'm sorry, I didn't realize—' Charlie glowered at me. I dropped my hands and swallowed my words.

'Isn't it fabulous,' said Nush. She sauntered over and placed herself between Charlie and me. 'Why don't you give us a tour?' Charlie stepped in front of me. He was not much taller and probably lighter, but he squared up as if preparing for an attack.

'I'd love to understand the work,' I said softly, lowering my head. Seemingly pleased that I had offered him the appropriate amount of deference, he cleared his throat and began.

'This is *Route Twenty-Five Library*,' he said of the books and detritus. 'The objects were all found on the twenty-five bus route. It's an evolving piece.' I nodded. Nush tipped her head to the side.

'It's so evocative,' she purred. He led us to a second table. There was some make-up, a few cigarettes, a set of keys and a pair of knickers that were definitely not new.

'This one I call *Fallen Angels*. I ask women in clubs to give me something.' I looked at Charlie again. His shirt was stained with ketchup or blood, and his fingertips were yellowed. I was impressed that he had been able to play to his strengths – he'd turned being a creep in a club into art. 'This is what I'm currently working on,' he said. His voice rose an octave as his excitement grew. We followed him to one of the far corners of the room. Alone on a table was a hi-top trainer, lying on its side.

'Oooh,' said Nush solemnly. I tried to meet her eye but she was staring at the footwear with what appeared to be great reverence.

'Is that shit?' I said – out loud, I realized too late. Nush and Charlie both stared at me, their faces veiled in shock.

'I mean, on the shoe. Is that shit.' Nush looked aghast. Charlie leaned in and examined the 'piece'.

'I don't know. The not knowing is part of it.' I took a step back.

'And people pay for this?' Charlie's head whipped round to look at me. 'And people are buying?' I said, using all the muscles in my face to smile.

'I have a few investors,' Charlie said coyly. His shirt, grubby as it was, looked to be of good quality, and renting a space of this size in London wouldn't be cheap. The realization that I had gone about everything in completely the wrong way hit me like a bucket of gunge in a cheap kids' game-show. I'd been trying to work hard and play the game of life by the rules, and here was this little punk building a career out of shit.

'You're a rule breaker,' I said to Charlie. He gave me a 'you got me' smile. His teeth suggested he also bypassed the rule of six-monthly dentist visits. 'We need to make the attendees of the event feel the same.'

Nush looked perturbed. 'It's all got to be above board. Dad would kill me. I mean, he might actually kill me. We can have a little sniff at the after-party but everything else has to be completely kosher.' It was my turn to look perturbed. Nush looked confused, or more confused than usual. 'What?' she said.

'Everything, and I mean everything,' I looked pointedly at Nush, 'will be legal. I mean, we make the event seem like it's underground. As if they're breaking the rules by attending. We'll keep the location under wraps until the last minute; the copy will allude to nefarious goings-on. We'll make it feel naughty – doesn't everyone want to be naughty?'

'Yes!' shouted Nush. 'I could get some of my old friends from the club to come and dance.' She was practically panting with excitement.

'That's not a bad idea.' I got out my phone and made some notes.

'Charlie, rather than revealing whole pieces in the marketing, we could select individual objects.'

'I feel that,' said Charlie.

'This is going to be sick!' cried Nush. 'Dig out that scotch.' Charlie sloped back towards the sink.

'Sick is good, right?' Nush laughed and nodded. 'Do we still do high fives?'

'No, babe.'

I stopped by home on the way back to the office. I could hear music from the living room and assumed Dylan had left the television on. It's astonishing how quickly someone else's action, or more often inaction, can slice through a positive mood. I went to turn it off, at the same time considering whether it was too patronizing to leave a note about it. I was so distracted by the thought that when I saw Ruby sprawled on the couch, I greeted her casually. It took another step for a sense of unease to set in; another to add bewilderment to the mix; by the third my head was empty of anything but outrage.

'Are you taking the—' I stopped, exhaled, and rolled my shoulders backwards to try and relieve some tension. 'Are you kidding me?' Ruby didn't move from her position stretched across the length of the sofa. She had dragged her hair into a haphazard ponytail and was still wearing her emoji-print pyjamas, but I noticed that both her finger- and toenails had been painted a fresh shade of electric blue.

'You can say "piss", you know. I've heard the word before.' I crouched down, balancing on the balls of my feet and resting my bum on my heels. Instantly, my knees began to throb, but I stuck it out in order to meet her at her level. I did the same when she was a toddler, falling to my knees so that we could be at eye level when I chastised her, showing her respect in the hope that it would be repaid.

'Good to know,' I said. 'Here's some other words you may have heard before – grounded, indefinitely.' Ruby rolled over so she was face down on the sofa cushions. She started to speak, and although I couldn't make out the words the indignant tone was clear.

'I can't hear what you're saying.' Ruby turned her head to the side but away from me.

'What am I supposed to do all day?'

'Read, study, think about what you've done,' I said rapidly. She plunged her face back into the cushions. I stood up and my knees popped loudly.

I rang Carter as I made myself coffee. He was agreeable when I told him I was working from home. He didn't actually say as much, but didn't express displeasure, which was as close as it gets with him. His lunch suggestion had failed to materialize. I'd been having far fewer interactions with him and I liked it that way. Nush's money kept him at bay. I parked myself in the kitchen with my laptop and my thoughts.

Dylan seemed troubled to find me there when he came home. After greeting me, he hovered seemingly aimlessly in the kitchen. I wondered, not for the first time, what he did all day. How exactly he filled the hours and still managed to leave so much for me to do. Finally he said, 'You don't have to be here, I've only got a couple of lessons.' I wondered what I was getting in the way of him doing.

'I found her laid up on the sofa having quite the holiday when I came in.' He chuckled. It was the stifled laugh every parent gives when their child is behaving badly but they can't help but find it endearing. 'It's not funny!' I slammed my laptop closed. 'She needs to think about what she's done.' Dylan pulled an exaggerated expression of shock before breaking into an easy smile. It was broad enough that I could see the gap on the right side near the back. I remember clocking it when we first met. I made a note of the space each time we saw each other, not wanting to ask him about it and make him uncomfortable. The night he asked me to move in with him, instead of saying yes, I said, 'What happened to your tooth?' We were in bed. He held me closer. I was anxious that it was because he was about to disclose a violent past.

'Rhubarb and custard,' he replied. 'The sweets. Those hard ones?' I stroked his head.

'I know the ones,' I said.

'So, you wanna live with this toothless codger?'

'Yes,' I said, because it was true.

Dylan sat next to me at the table. He leaned towards me and lowered his voice. 'Do you not think it's a bit extreme? I mean, I don't think I got to school on time ever. I didn't do too badly.' That smile again. I had forgotten we were talking about two different things – he was reacting to his daughter having a few tardies and I was responding to the possibility she was amoral.

'She has to learn to respect rules. It might not seem like a big deal, but it's important to the school, and she has to know that she can't just do what she wants when she wants.' Dylan considered this for a moment.

'Whatever you think,' he said. And although he was agreeing with me, I was annoyed. I wanted to tell him to argue, if he wanted to argue; I wanted him to question my logic and drag the real story out of me, and if that wasn't an option, I wanted him to leave.

'I've got a lot to get on with.' Dylan nodded obediently and gave me a kiss on the cheek. 'Thanks,' I said as he stepped into the hallway. I waited until I heard him climb the stairs before opening my computer again. There was a new email from Frank, the latest in a chain arranging a weekend away on his friend Anthony's boat. I had resisted initially, but then he wrote that 'sea air is the perfect thing for clearing your head' and I wanted in. I didn't see Ruby for the rest of the day; if she ate or relieved herself, she did it when I was out of earshot. Dylan took up her place on the sofa for the afternoon. When he collected Chloe they returned with fish and chips, which they ate out of their laps in front of the television. It was like I wasn't even there.

27

PACKING WAS AN issue. What do you wear on a boat? It's the sort of thing I'd ask Dylan. He'd make a naff joke about galoshes. I told him I was going to Italy with Bettina. Where, I claimed, we were staying at her family's holiday home. I should have said we were going on a boat; the more details that were changed, the more there was to remember. I nearly cancelled the entire thing when he offered to drop my bag to Betty's after work. It was too close. In the end he got a last-minute booking and apologized for letting *me* down.

I dragged my suitcase behind me the entire commute to work. It bruised my calves and chafed my hand and I felt like I deserved it. Bettina watched as I tried to force it under my desk.

'Minibreak?' she said.

'Yeah, something like that.'

'Where's he taking you?' I fumbled and the case fell to the floor with a thump. Bettina tutted, walked round and gave me a little shove out of the way. She smoothly turned the case on its side and slid it under the desk. 'Did he plan something or did you have to do it all yourself?' She rolled her eyes playfully. It was then I realized that the 'he' she was referring to was Dylan.

'Yeah,' I said. Not really answering the question.

'What you doing? Bit of spa? Bit of food?' I made a non-committal noise. Bettina returned to her desk.

'I think me and Tristan are heading towards minibreak territory. He keeps talking about events in the future, you know? Like he's planning a holiday next year and he hasn't officially invited me, but he talks about it like I'm there.' She looked all flushed. I loved seeing her bathed in the bright glow of the early days, and I also felt jealous that I couldn't tell her why I was feeling the same. 'Tell me where you're going. I want to get ideas.'

'Um . . .' I played with a pile of paperclips on my desk. 'Well, we're going to stay in Bristol, see a gig of some sort. Just mooch about. Mum's staying with the girls.'

'Sounds good. Have you seen the hotel?' said Bettina.

'No.'

'A surprise. There's life in the old dog yet. I don't think Tristan's the surprise type. He plans his pants and socks for the week.'

'I'm sorry,' I said. 'I've been really busy with Nush and we haven't had a proper catch-up in ages. Do you want to go for a coffee this afternoon?'

'I can't. Carter's busting my arse with new business pitches. Fancy a drink later?' I indicated the case.

'We're leaving straight after work. Maybe Monday?'

'What's happening Monday?' said Annie from behind me. Bettina started typing rapidly.

'Nothing,' I said lightly.

'Oh,' said Annie, matching my tone. 'I thought you might be meeting Nush.' She was wearing a blue pleated skirt and sleeveless white shirt. It was office appropriate but still cute and feminine. Annie would know what to wear on a boat.

224

'I have nothing scheduled.' I turned towards my computer screen to signal the close of the conversation.

'Only she called you several times yesterday,' Annie said. 'I tried to help but I don't know much about the project.' I turned back to her slowly. When I didn't respond immediately, Annie's mouth twitched but the rest of her remained composed.

'Why didn't you let me know she called?' I asked. My jaw was tight and the words emerged unevenly.

'You said you didn't want to be disturbed.' I did. And darling Annie always followed my instructions so carefully.

'Thank you, Annie,' I said. She pushed aside a stack of paperwork on my desk and perched herself daintily next to my keyboard.

'Frantic clients are part of the job, I suppose. If you want me to be back-up, you know, for the client management . . .' I gave Annie a look that told her I was well aware her goal was to manage my clients right out of my portfolio. She coloured and slipped back to the floor. I pretended to read emails as I listened to her click away.

'Monday,' said Bettina. 'She's second on the agenda.'

My day was taken up with placating Nush. When she hadn't been able to get hold of me, she had panicked and contacted another agency. It took several phone calls to reassure her I was still the best fit.

'Why didn't you ring my mobile?' I reprimanded softly.

'I haven't saved your number in my phone.' I rubbed a throbbing artery in my temple.

'Well, do that as soon as we finish this call.' I took several deep breaths. 'Frank sent you to me for a reason. I know what it means to want a fresh start.'

'I know. I know,' said Nush. 'People have let me down before and I think I have . . . um . . .'

225

'Abandonment issues?'

'No, that's not the one.'

'Commitment phobia?'

'No. No. It will come to me.'

'When it does, call me. On my mobile.' I placed the phone back in its nook and it rang immediately.

'ADD!' exclaimed Nush.

'Great, Nush. Thanks. My mobile.'

Bettina walked out with me.

'It's so nice tonight. You sure Dylan doesn't want a pint before you set off?' Aunt Caitlin, the one who believes in spirits, has tinnitus. As obsessed with ghosts as she was, the thing that really haunted her was a constant ringing in her head. She would say it was like a car alarm going off in the night. If she's distracted she can ignore it; when she thinks about it, it drowns out everything else. I don't know why I told Dylan I was going to be with Bettina but the error bounced round my brain, ramming everything else aside. I hadn't had to hide anything in so long, not a stray fart or a pair of period pants. I was monstrously out of practice. Right then it occurred to me that at some point they would meet, at a birthday or impromptu barbecue, and devoid of any other connection he would ask about the trip. Bettina wouldn't laugh it off politely, that wasn't her way. She would probe until every detail had been excavated, like decay from a tooth.

I tried to concentrate but still couldn't take in what she was saying. '... I hope it stays like this ...' We stopped in front of the building. Frank was due to pick me up at six-thirty – 'SHARP' he added, with a winky-face emoji. I was so taken with the idea of him carrying me away from it all that I didn't assess the potential dangers of meeting outside the office. '... We're going to Hyde Park. I want to go on one of those boats. Is that too cutesy?' A car horn startled me. I looked around but couldn't see Frank's car.

'I'm in a rush,' I told Bettina. I gave her a quick hug, hoping to convey the warmth I was aware my voice had not held. Her mouth closed; I knew she had been mid-sentence and that I should ask her to repeat it, but I couldn't. I let my fingers linger on her silk blouse. I hoped she would understand that it meant I was sorry and that I wasn't a bad friend, I was just bad at being good. I lugged my case up the street and my phone started to ring, but I didn't want Bettina to see me stop, so I kept walking to the first turn and then ducked into the doorway of a closed shop. It was Frank.

'Why are you running away from me?' he asked.

'I'm round the corner,' I said.

'Yeah, I saw you bolting. Why are we whispering?'

'I'm not whispering,' I said, although I had unconsciously lowered my voice.

'I'm coming,' he said. He pulled up seconds later, honking the horn and rattling my already shattered nerves. I threw the suitcase in the back, and bolted round the front of the car to climb into the passenger seat.

'Very dramatic,' Frank said. 'Is this that thing women are always talking about – keeping me on my toes?'

'Just go,' I urged. 'I didn't want Bettina to see us.'

'You could have said I was an Uber or something.'

'Go!' I shrieked. I was feeling genuine, primal, will-I-be-eaten-by-a-lion fear. I didn't understand it, why the thought of revealing myself to Bettina was so terrifying.

I noticed Frank didn't check his mirrors before he pulled

227

away. He was sure of his safety, or maybe he didn't care. I, on the other hand, didn't relax until we were beyond the city and the road signs sold the promise of escape.

'All aboard,' called Anthony from the deck. He had on frayed denim shorts, a polo shirt and a captain's cap. The hat only made me feel less confident about his role as leader. I watched Frank pass our bags across from the dock and eyed the plank of wood serving as an entryway warily. Midi pencil skirts were not boat wear. Frank traversed the plank deftly before reaching towards me. I'd have to take several steps by myself before I could touch him. It was an exercise in trust. When you're looking for the right answers, everything feels symbolic – if he caught me, what we were doing was OK, and if he didn't, I might drown. As I stepped on to the wood, the boat moved.

'Did I do that?' I asked. Anthony laughed and slapped his thighs. Spittle gathered at the corner of his mouth. I suspected he might be a little drunk.

'You'll get your sea legs in no time, darling.' I retreated back to the shore and took off my heels. The second time I tried, I knew what to expect. I held my breath and moved forward. The first few steps were steady, but for the last few I was overconfident and veered to the left. Frank grabbed me by the arm and I half stepped, half fell on to the deck. 'All aboard!' shouted Anthony. He pulled me into an embrace. His scent confirmed my suspicion – a confusing mix of spirits, aftershave and enthusiasm.

'Thank you for having me. I'm not sure I dressed appropriately.' I used the opportunity of gesturing to my outfit to step away from him.

'You can borrow something of mine,' said a voice behind me. A woman's head popped up from inside the cabin. Her harshly bleached hair was pulled back into a bun, highlighting the unnatural tightness of her face.

'Come down. Get a drink. The boys can launch.' That didn't sound like something I wanted to do, so I squeezed Frank's hand before joining her below deck. The woman wasn't much taller than me, but what she lacked in size, she made up for in presence. Everything about her was brash, from her voice to her floral-print muumuu.

'I'm Margie,' she said. 'Let me get you a drink.' The boat had a perfectly formed miniature kitchen. She pulled an open bottle of champagne from a tiny fridge and poured me a glass.

'Alison,' I said. 'Thank you.'

'I know,' she said. 'I know everything!' This kind of bold, patently untrue statement would normally aggravate me, but it was such a relief not to have to hide. 'I'll give you the tour.' She pointed to the front of the boat. 'Bedroom.' She pointed behind me. 'Bedroom, bathroom. No number twos in the port.'

'No port poos. Got it.' She smiled and did an odd little dance on the spot.

'I'm so pleased you're here. We're going to have such a fun time. Sonya never wants to come.' She clapped her hand over her mouth. 'Oh, I'm so sorry.' So, her name was Sonya. I tried to stop myself imagining what a Sonya might be like – how she would speak, what sort of underwear she might wear.

'No, I'm sorry if we've put you in an awkward position,' I said.

'Not. At. All. It's maritime laws on here,' she said. She laughed at her own joke. Or at least, I assumed that's what she was doing. Her face and body shook violently, but in contrast to her the rest of the time, she made no noise.

Whilst she wasn't offensive, I didn't feel completely comfortable in her presence. If I found myself next to her at a dinner party, I might subtly switch seats. But she was the only person I could speak openly to about Frank. She was my new best friend.

'Your boat is lovely. Thanks for inviting me. You know, it's difficult being together.'

'Are you happy though?' It's the question that had escaped me the whole time. I was so fixated on the right and the wrong of it, what was for the best and how to manage the inevitable fallout, that I'd missed the key to any choice I'd made. Did it make me happy? And at that point he did.

'Yes,' I said.

'That's all that matters then. Forget all the other stuff. I'm Tony's third wife, and the second was none too happy about my appearance on the scene. Anyway, that's in the past. She loves me now. People do, they can't help themselves.' She gave a sympathetic shrug. 'You can't be expected to get everything right first try.' The boat moved and I grabbed for the counter, slopping my drink on my skirt in the process.

'Shit,' I said, at the same time as Margie screamed, 'Ships ahoy!' For seasoned sailors, these guys were still very excited by all the lingo. 'Oh dear,' she said, looking at the patch on my crotch. 'Do you want to borrow something?' I looked at Margie's muumuu and thought, when in Rome, put on a toga.

28

AFTER I HAD acclimatized to the floor moving and an unexpected sense of claustrophobia, it was peaceful being out at sea. The air or the water, or the distance from anything I had to take responsibility for, was very relaxing. I'd been focused on comparing my life at home with the possibility of life with Frank, but it was all my life. I could be part of this and the girls could be part of it with me. Chloe would love it on the boat. It would completely align with her sense of drama, and she would write a play about being a pirate. Ruby would declare it totally Instaworthy. And Dylan would be fine, because he was a good man and a great father and in time he'd understand. The sound of the motor must have masked his approach, because I didn't hear Frank before I felt him move in behind me and cradle me in his arms and legs.

'You good?' he asked.

'I'm great.'

'Was worried you might feel sick.'

'Shut up!' I slapped his arm and he squeezed me closer.

'I'm so, so glad you've come,' he whispered. I closed my eyes. I wanted to keep the moment. I concentrated on the pressure of him against my back, and the warmth of his arms, and the contrast of this with the wet wind stroking my skin.

'I was thinking about what it would be like to bring the girls out here,' I said. Saying it made me nervous. I didn't want to deny my children but I also didn't particularly want to draw attention to how confused our situation was.

'That would be great,' he said. 'Every childhood should be filled with opportunities.' I definitely think the word 'love' is thrown out too readily. At the end of phone calls; in testimonials about Frappuccinos – but that was the moment I realized that I loved him. Scared the feeling would fall out of my mouth, I stood. I shuffled to the bow of the boat, Margie's spare muumuu billowing like another sail.

'I'm the king of the world!' I shouted into the distance.

'Oh, darling,' Margie called back from the deck. 'Everyone does that.'

I offered to make dinner. The captain and his mate were far too merry. The main ingredient available was alcohol, but I managed to cobble together a pasta dish with a tomato and vodka sauce. I had become used to the motion of the boat, keeping my feet apart and engaging my core as I diced garlic. It astonished me how quickly we adapt. The rest of the crew cheered when I passed the steaming pan up to the deck.

'A proper little wifey,' said Anthony, with an exaggerated wink to Frank.

'Eat up,' I said, returning to the cabin for kitchenware. When I returned, Anthony was eating pasta straight from the pan with his fingers. I smacked the back of his hand as he reached in for more.

'Have I been naughty?' he said, and Margie did her weird seizure-laugh.

'No, you've been great. I had no idea how much I needed to get away.' Frank kissed my shoulder and served me some food.

'She's been working with Nush,' he said, as he served himself and then Margie.

'Oh Jesus, is she still knocking around? She used to work for me,' Anthony explained.

'Oh,' I said through a mouthful of food. So, he was the strip-club owner.

'She's hard work but she's got a heart of gold underneath the messiness.'

'Yeah,' I said sadly. 'She seems a bit lost. I really hope this show she's planning comes together.'

'I'll offer any help I can. If you need venues or anything,' said Anthony. Despite his words running into each other, he sounded sort of professional. I conceded that he might have more dimensions than the lovable buffoon he generally presented as. My body hummed with excitement. I wasn't necessarily confident about the types of venues he could provide, but I loved that we were sitting over dinner chatting about someone in common; that he spoke about a future, with me in it, so casually. 'She still pretending to be clean?' he asked. I wasn't sure if offering an opinion amounted to breaking client confidentiality, so focused on evenly coating a piece of pasta in sauce. Anthony took this as concurrence. 'She needs to slow down if she doesn't want a hole straight through her head. We all do a bit of blow now and then, but she's turned it from a hobby into a full-time occupation.'

I do not do a bit of blow, not now, not then, not ever. I've taken non-prescription drugs twice. Once with David – we were at a club; I told him I wasn't feeling well. It was true; his blatant flirting was making me ill. He handed me something. I assumed it was a painkiller but it turned out to be ecstasy. I was livid when he told me the next morning, whilst snorting with laughter into the tea I had made him. I was used to the betrayal and angrier that it had worked. After the pill, the evening felt so much easier – interactions were effortless and I felt inexplicably close to David, and everyone else for that matter. But it had all been a chemically induced farce.

The second time, I was attending one of Henry's festivals to watch him play the bongos in a ska-influenced folk band. I ate a cannabis-laced brownie, mainly to alleviate my boredom. I then inhaled two falafel wraps and slept for the first time that weekend. Despite both experiences providing much-needed escapism, I wanted a life that I didn't need to escape from. I was always fearful that my mother had passed on her addictive personality, and although I got away with it with booze, I wasn't prepared to take too many chances. I also wasn't prepared to spend my life with someone who would expose the girls to anything more than a hangover.

I watched for a few seconds as Frank reacted, or failed to react, to what Anthony had said, and it was like my lungs were shrinking. Each second that he chewed and nodded, breathing became more difficult. It was the first time I had considered that I might be wrong about him; that I might not really know him and that as quickly as I had found him, he could be lost. Eventually, I said I was feeling a bit dizzy and would turn in early and read. Frank didn't stop me, but watched with a puzzled expression as I climbed down the ladder. In our cabin I crawled on to the bed. The ceiling was only a foot or so from my face. It felt like a coffin. Because we had such a strong connection, I had assumed that everything he was would be in alignment with what I wanted. It couldn't be possible otherwise.

I lay listening to the sound of the water lapping against the boat and Anthony's laugh floating in through the port-hole. After an hour or so it was silent. I rearranged my limbs in an effort to feign sleep, but it was a pointless per-formance, because after Anthony and Margie crashed into the cabin, Frank didn't follow. When the silence started to become unnerving, I dragged myself out of the sleep space and went back up to the deck. Frank was looking back towards the shore, a blurry shadow in the distance.

'Hi,' I said quietly. He turned and smiled. A smile that said nothing other than he was pleased to see me.

'Did you sleep?' I shook my head. 'Was Anthony a bit much? He can be an acquired taste but he's loyal to a fault.' I thought of the ex-wife he was eager to evict.

'It's not Anthony. Not really. Well, sort of it's Anthony . . .'

'You can tell me,' said Frank. 'You can tell me any-thing.' I stood next to him, close but not touching.

'Drugs are not my thing, and if that's what you wanna do that's cool, but it's not for me.' What I didn't add was, 'Therefore you're not for me.'

'No. No, of course not.' He removed his shirt. And then his shoes, trousers and socks. Then, with a pause that I suspected was for effect rather than hesitation, he removed his underwear. He held my gaze, challenging me to main-tain eye contact. 'I get my highs elsewhere,' he said. He took two strides and bombed into the English Channel. I covered my mouth with both hands to stop a scream flying out. Frank disappeared beneath the water and the seconds seemed to stretch to minutes. We hadn't had a safety brief-ing; I could hear the captain's snores; I really couldn't be involved in a tragic accident during a holiday I wasn't sup-posed to be on. As I was scanning the deck for anything buoyant, Frank emerged a couple of feet from the boat. He spat a stream of water in my direction, like a cherub on a fountain.

'What you waiting for?' he shouted.

'Shhh! You'll wake the others.'

'It's not even that cold.'

'I can't.'

'You will though.' I glanced back to the cabin. No movement from below. Before I could talk myself out of it, I took off the muumuu and my underwear.

'Amazing,' said Frank, and it gave me the burst of adrenaline I needed to jump. It was so quiet under the water. Briefly, I felt sad I couldn't stay there. But then the instinct for continuity took over, or whatever it is that keeps us eating and working and having sex when so much of life is overwhelming. I kicked my legs to the surface. Frank swam over and I wrapped myself around him.

'You could have just answered the question.'

'Where's the fun in that?'

'You know, I wasn't even supposed to go to your event. Do you think everything happens for a reason?'

'No. It's all just random chaos, babe.' I liked feeling adventurous. I liked him calling me 'babe'. I'll never deny that I liked it.

29

R UBY WAS INVITED back to school. She wrote a letter of apology to Ms Davison and was quietly moved to another form. Her new tutor, Mrs Case, was approaching retirement – little danger of another social media scandal. I made her give me the password to every one of her accounts, promising I wouldn't use them unless she gave me cause to. We had a long discussion about the trust-building process. Ruby failed to see how my suggestion of helping out around the house had any correlation to rebuilding my confidence that she could be safe online. The discussion devolved into an argument, and again to an unrestrained screaming match. I didn't even say goodnight to her, and remorse kept me awake until the early hours of the morning. On Ruby's first day back, I ironed her shirt and skirt and offered to French braid her hair. She refused, as I had known she would, but I wanted her to believe I was willing. From the living-room window, I watched my daughter's ponytail bob as she disappeared down the road, and said a silent apology for all the occasions she had begged me to braid her hair before school and I told her I didn't have the time. If I could do it again I would make the time, I would steal it.

When I arrived at work, Nush was in reception. She was

also openly crying. I could see damp patches on the front of her white T-shirt from the door. Marcus was sitting next to her, holding a box of tissues.

'Alison,' she whimpered when she saw me. I think she intended to summon me but I felt like backing away. I inhaled, pushed my hair back from my face, and accessed my inner 'work mode'.

'Marcus, thanks for your help. I can take it from here,' I said firmly. Marcus handed Nush another tissue and kept his eyes on her as he stood. 'She'll be fine, Marcus. I'll give you a call if I need you. Don't wait for that call.' He hung his head and sloped off. 'Nush,' I said. 'You cannot turn up like this. It's not professional.' Nush crumpled and uncrumpled the tissue in her hand.

'I know, but I have no one else to turn to.' I tried not to dwell on how dismal that was.

'What's happened? Has someone died?' I had the idiotic thought that Frank might be hurt. Crashed his car or fallen into an empty elevator shaft. And no one would have told me, because why would they?

'I feel like I'm dying,' said Nush plainly, as though the statement was reasonable.

'I don't want to dismiss your feelings, but you are young, you are beautiful and you're about to create something fantastic. Whatever this is, it can be solved.' I took the tissue from her fidgeting hands. 'We'll solve it.' Nush searched my face, perhaps for evidence that I could come good on this assertion.

'I broke up with my boyfriend.' I felt a bit affronted. We had spent all that time together and yet Nush hadn't mentioned a romance. My expression must have matched my emotion because Nush said, 'I'm sorry I didn't tell you. He's a little bit famous and we wanted to keep it under wraps.'

'Who?' I asked. And why wasn't he helping us to promote the gallery, I questioned silently.

'Tino McMillan,' Nush sighed. He wasn't a little bit famous. He was gossip-site-sidebar famous. I mean, I knew who he was for a start. I also knew he had a not-a-little-bit-famous girlfriend – a British soap actress who had gone through puberty in my living room. Which explained why he was holding back on the promotion front.

'I'm sorry to hear that,' I said. I was. I remember the week after graduation, when David dumped me for the third and final time, it felt like my vital organs were about to fall out of my body. 'It does sound like maybe he wasn't in it for the long haul anyway.'

'What makes you say that!' snapped Nush.

'Nothing. I'm sorry. I just thought . . . Doesn't he have a girlfriend?' Nush sniffed noisily and I gave her back the tissue, which she immediately set about crumpling and uncrumpling again.

'It was over between them. Their agents basically insisted they stay together. And now they've made me stop seeing him. For the publicity, you know?' I didn't.

'It sounds suspect,' I said delicately. 'If he wanted to be with you he would be taking steps to make that happen.'

'Maybe, maybe not. I don't care. I don't care about anything.' But she had to care, because if she didn't care I could kiss goodbye to my contract, the only thing keeping Carter and Annie and the bank manager at bay. It was fine for Nush to become apathetic – she had youth on her side – but not when my work life was in her hands.

'The best thing for you to do is have him see you being successful.' Nush glanced at me suspiciously. I nodded as if I had all the answers. 'If he sees you go to shit right now, he'll think he has all the power, but if he sees you thriving he might understand what a fool he's been to have lost this.'

'Oh, Alison,' she said. 'Have you thought about micro-blading your brows? It would give so much more definition to your face.'

'No,' I said. 'Nush, the art show?' She sighed.

'You're right. I can't let him undo all the good work I've done. I need to go *Lemonade* on his arse. That's Beyoncé.'

'I know.' I didn't know. Nush looked over my shoulder and towards the window. Something she saw there in the empty street made her well up again. 'Nush, you've got twenty-four hours. Eat crap, listen to sad songs, and then let's make this happen!' I gave her a couple of firm pats on the knee.

'You're totally right. Who the fuck does he think he is?' I shook my head, although I was pretty sure he knew he was a rock star. 'I'll have a self-care day, get a massage and a colonic, and then I'll show him who he's fucking with, the fuckbag.'

'Great stuff. Get to it.' Nush stood up, wedged her tiny crocodile-skin bag under her arm, and marched out on to the street. I sank back into the sofa to allow my body to recover from the near miss, and examined my eyebrows with my compact before heading upstairs.

Annie could have tried harder. She might have lowered her head and spoken in a slower, more careful way. I've seen her do it. When Dee's thirteen-year-old cat died of pancreatic cancer, she organized a collection and gave a speech that, if I believed she had a heart, I would have accepted as heartfelt. But ten minutes after I had packed off Nush and fallen into something of a groove with my admin, Annie appeared by my chair to tell me that Dylan had left an urgent message. She was not emoting sympathy; she

240

looked relieved to have ticked one of her many boxes for the day. I thanked her because it was the grown-up thing to do and I was the grown-up. With this came responsibilities and emergencies and urgent calls – she would learn that in time.

I called Dylan and asked him why he was ringing the office when there was a direct route to me via my mobile.

'It's Ruby. There's been an incident at school,' he said. He was panting. 'I tried your mobile but it wouldn't connect.'

'I was on the tube. Leave a message. What's happened? Is she hurt?' My mouth went dry. An image of the pony-tail, no longer bouncing, flashed through my mind.

'She got in a fight. Something about Snapchat.' I only recognized my fear as it was replaced by irritation.

'You don't need to call me because Ruby's had a falling out with one of her friends. Have you not noticed how fast her rotation is?' Ruby had so many best friends that I'd stopped keeping track of their names. If I found one in my kitchen I would refer to them as 'dear'. It was one of the rare times I felt like a proper mum.

'Not a falling out,' said Dylan. I could tell from the way the volume of his voice rose and fell that he was distracted, perhaps looking around for someone. I imagined it being one of those smug school mums, Lycra'd up and ready for the gym and brunch.

'What's going on, Dylan?' I snapped.

'A fight. An actual fight. Hair pulling, scratching, the works. It was vicious, Al. And there were other kids filming it. We both need to be here.' Now terror and rage jostled around my body, competing for top billing. I left, walked out without shutting down my computer. I didn't tell any-one; I didn't prepare my excuses. I retraced my steps, and went straight back down to the tube platform I had emerged from not an hour before. As a kid I had believed that if I retraced my steps, I might turn back time. One afternoon, I was home alone whilst Mum was out with one of her friends. He collected her in a huge silver car, but I didn't see his face because she'd told me to stay out of sight until they were gone. She'd left me a stack of sandwiches and an orange Club bar. I was methodically nibbling the chocolate from the biscuit when there was a knock at the door. Standing on the mat was an old man, or at least he seemed old to me at the time. He was probably only in his fifties – or forties with some tough times thrown in. He asked me if my mother was home, and when I confirmed she wasn't, he told me he was there to value her jewellery. I remembered my legs burning when we didn't have the fare for the bus, and the school trip I spent in the office because Mum 'forgot' to pay for my place. She hadn't said it explicitly, but I knew we needed more money and thought she'd be pleased I had found a way to get some. The man waited as I ran upstairs to fetch the big crimson box where she kept all her rings and bracelets. He peered inside before closing it with an authoritative snap.

'Looks good. I have to nip back to the shop and work out the figure, and I'll let you know how much I can give you.' I offered to give him our number, which I had recently memorized, but he told me there was no need and was off down the path. I don't know how long he was gone before I panicked; I didn't yet wear a watch. I'd watched two episodes of *Danger Mouse* and looked at all my comics before the sick, heavy feeling came over me. I went upstairs, got back into my pyjamas and pulled the blanket up to my neck. I thought if I tried hard enough I could undo the day, and go back to waking up in the morning. It worked. I didn't even know Mum was home until she woke me up the next morning; she didn't mention the box. When we moved in with Eddie a few years later, she accused a delivery guy of stealing it. I suppose my emotional evolution had been stunted, because when I climbed the escalator back to the daylight, instead of heading for school, I turned towards home. I shut the door behind me and the house felt exactly as it had before I left that morning. My phone rang.

'I'm at home, Dylan. I can't. I can't look at that smug git's face again.'

'We're on our way,' he said.

I didn't know where to put myself. I sat in the armchair but it felt too foreboding, like a villain from a crappy movie. The sofa was too relaxed; the kitchen too formal. In the end I stood by the window, watching the street. A woman walked by wearing a toddler on her back. He was chatting away merrily but his mother had a scowl on her face. I wanted to tell her that whatever was troubling her wasn't that bad, it couldn't be.

I heard a car door slam and I knew it was them. I could feel Dylan's anger radiating down the road. I went to the kitchen and then back to the living room. When they entered the house, I was moving again and in the hallway. I had no idea why I was so nervous. Ruby and I stared at each other like cornered animals, neither sure if we were the hunter or hunted.

30

RUBY'S PONYTAIL HAD fallen, or been dragged, to the nape of her neck. The right side of her face was pink and swollen, and the shirt I'd pressed that morning had a rip along the seam of the left sleeve. I wanted to take a picture. Ruby was always so conscientious about capturing her various looks; why not stick a filter on this one? With the caption 'ASBO Chic'. The thought of doing this made me smile.

'It's not funny!' she shouted. 'She came at me out of nowhere! And because Kindeace has it in for me, because he totally fancies Ms Davison by the way, I'm the one that's gonna get in trouble.' Dylan stayed behind her, staring at his trainers. I assumed he had exhausted his anger.

'Ruby,' I said, and I was ready to offer her comfort, but as I spoke she folded her arms, already defensive and emotionally primed to reject whatever I might say. I dragged my palms up and down my face and then pressed them together. 'Ruby. I do not care. I do not care whose fault it was. I do not care who Mr Kindeace may or may not fancy. I only care that my daughter, who I have gone to great pains to teach the difference between wrong and right, keeps making such incredibly stupid decisions, and I'm starting to wonder how many more she's made that I don't know about. Anything else you want to share? Any warrants for your arrest? Are you the leader of an international drug cartel?' I shrugged. 'You may as well tell me now, because the one thing you have right is that you're in big trouble.' Ruby's lip began to tremble and I felt horrible but also relieved. She darted towards the stairs.

'Wait,' I said. She stopped. I went to the kitchen and returned with a packet of frozen peas. 'For your face.' She choked out a sob and thundered up the stairs without taking it. 'Shit,' I said. 'What did the school say?' Dylan hadn't moved; he still held the car keys in his hand. I started to go to him, but he looked up and something in his face made me stay at a distance.

'You let me sit in front of that man and look like a complete and utter prick,' he said. His voice had none of its usual bounce, no emotion – they sounded like words read from an autocue. 'You lied to me about why Ruby was excluded . . . for days.'

'I—'

'You don't trust me to parent our daughter with you. You have to make the decisions for everyone.' He returned to examining his shoes. 'I'm just the driver,' he said finally.

'I'm sorry,' I said, because I was, about a lot of things, but especially about making him feel stupid because he wasn't. I was the one who thought trying to keep a secret with a teenage girl was a good idea. 'I really am.'

'I'm going to have a shower.' He disappeared up the stairs. I pictured them both up there, the same wounded expression on their faces; disappointment reflected in their identical blue eyes. I put the peas on the radiator and left.

*

I told Frank to meet me on the steps of St Mary's church. If anyone at home asked, I could tell them I had to go back to work, but I was sure no one would. A woman walked towards me, and I knew from her frequent glances in my direction that she was wondering if I needed to be saved. She paused before starting her ascent and I accidentally caught her eye.

'Hello,' she said as she trundled over. She had tight, roller-set hair and, despite the warm weather, wore a thick woollen skirt. She looked like I wished my mother would. 'Are you here for prayers?' she asked.

'No,' I said. 'No, thank you. I'm meeting someone.'

'Perhaps they'd like to come too, your friend.'

'I very much doubt it.'

'You'd both be very welcome,' she said. I could tell she was warming up to her role as senior salesperson for the Lord. I felt weary and bad for wasting her time. I was beyond saving.

'We're having an affair, so I don't know about that.' Her mouth fell open. I didn't blame her – I was shocked too. It was the first time I'd said it to anyone. It felt like I had popped a zit; I was disgusted with myself but oddly satisfied. She didn't speak for several seconds.

'Well,' said the woman, before turning away and shakily climbing the steps. I twisted my body and watched her pull open the door, and when I turned back he was there. I fell into his arms. He patted my back and made shushing noises as I cried into his shirt. Even through my pain I noticed how amazing he smelled.

'My car's round the corner,' he said after a minute or so. I let him guide me there. He opened the passenger door for me and walked away. I felt dizzy. I thought he was leaving me. You would think I'd be used to it. As a child, my mum was constantly dropping me off at neighbours' and friends' houses. Once I went to sleep in my own bed and woke up head to tail with a school friend. Of course, I hadn't known that at first, and thought maybe I had died in the night and that heaven meant being wrapped in a thick, fluffy duvet. When I understood what had happened, I was angry and ashamed. I ignored Mum for a week when she came back. She always came back, but it didn't make it hurt any less. Frank returned too, with two takeaway cups in a holder. He got into the driver's seat and handed me one. I tasted it: hot chocolate.

'It's July!' I said, laughing for what felt like the first time in a century.

'I wanted to make you smile,' he said.

'You did. You do.'

Frank took the lid from his drink and blew on it.

'Did you see that woman back there at the church? I told her we were having an affair.'

He nodded thoughtfully. 'I don't think she's going to tell anyone.'

'That's what this is though.'

Frank put his cup into the holder without drinking. 'I don't like that,' he said. 'That's not what's going on here.'

My arms began to tingle, a signal my body was gearing up for a fight. He was dismissing my reality and it felt like he was erasing me. 'You can't ignore something just because you don't like it.'

He shifted in his seat and angled his body towards mine. 'You're right,' he said softly, and the sparks of anger popped and fizzled into nothing.

'I'm sorry,' I said. A heaviness settled on my chest, the kind that I knew could only be lifted by a good cry. But I didn't want to cry; I already felt that I had shown too much – too much sadness, too much weakness – and it was another disappointment. It wasn't that I didn't want Frank to see that side of me, but that I had hoped with him, it wouldn't exist. He stroked my hair.

'It's home really,' I said. 'Yet another catastrophe with Ruby. I don't know where I went wrong. I've tried with her; I swear I've done nothing but try. What more can I do?'

'You will never know. You need to focus on what you can control.' That was easy for him to say – he didn't have an adversary living under his roof. I knew his son wasn't in school yet; he was still small and malleable. You don't realize it at the time, but parenting is easier when you can pick them up and put them down exactly where you want them. I didn't question Frank; looking back, I think I needed him to be right, because if he was wrong maybe what we were doing was too, and I couldn't create room for that. 'Look, this might not be the best time to say this, but I found a place. A mate came through – I was going to tell you tomorrow. It's small, but it's central and it's available, and you sound like you might need some space . . .' I did cry then, tears of excitement and relief and also fear.

'I don't know.' I had wanted Frank to be a place of escape, but I wasn't sure I was ready to break out. He took my hot chocolate from me and grabbed both of my hands in his.

'I'm going on Monday. You don't have to think of it as leaving; think of it as gaining some time.' I pulled my hands back.

'Monday – but that's so soon, there's too much to do.' My mind flitted through a list of things I had to get done – fill the freezer, regrout the bath, sort out my teenage daughter.

'Take control. Do something for yourself and sort the

rest out later. You have to show them that things need to change. I'll help you deal with everything.' It was so alluring, more than the idea of fancy trips and crazy sex, the idea that there would be someone, someone capable, that I could hand my problems to and say, 'Hold this whilst I have a shower.' I was so tired of trying to have it all. Having it all also meant having all the maintenance. I only wanted some of it – the good bits.

31

Frank dropped me off a couple of blocks from the house. Before I got out he kissed me on the mouth, a kiss full of both the best and the worst intentions. 'You can do this,' he said, and rather than buoying me it made me worry that I had gained yet another person to let down. The house was quiet. I found Dylan on our bed, so deep into a crossword he didn't seem to notice me come in.

'Is she OK?' Dylan folded the corner of the page, and placed his book and pen on the bedside table.

'She's taking some time. She's in her room.' He didn't ask where I had been.

'Did she talk to you?' I thought he might ask me to sit with him, but he took the pillow from my side and placed it behind his back.

'A bit. This girl, apparently she's been messaging Ruby for weeks. Nasty stuff. It's no excuse but—'

'Clearly you think it is.'

'Not an excuse but—'

'Dylan, we taught her better.'

'Is that right? Because . . .' He stopped; his mouth became a hard line.

'What? What, Dylan?'

'We taught her not to lie too, but you still told her it was OK to lie to me.'

'It wasn't. It isn't. I don't know, she was scared and I didn't want to . . .' It was my turn to stop because I couldn't say what I knew, that I didn't want to let him in.

'I was angry about the photos but we sorted it out. I feel like you're punishing me or something.' I think maybe he was right. I was punishing him for not being enough to stop me from making choices that scared me; I was punishing him for not being able to save me from myself.

'I know I messed up. I was trying to do the right thing.' Dylan picked up his crossword book.

'We all are, Alison.' You could go to him, said a voice in my head. You could change things, you could stop things, you could try. But I didn't trust that voice because I didn't trust myself.

'I'm going to talk to her,' I said. Dylan didn't offer any encouragement. 'I'm going to sort this out,' I said, and he grunted.

I could only see the bottom half of my daughter; the rest was obscured by her wardrobe door. I could hear her rummaging around the bottom of it. Since she stopped letting me in to tidy up, it had started to resemble a jumble sale.

'Ruby, can we chat?' She crawled out and sat amongst a sea of clothes on the floor.

'I can't talk now. Have you seen my holdall?' I picked my way towards her.

'Rubes, we have to—'

'No, we don't,' she snarled. 'You can't actually make me. Anyway, it hurts to talk.' I sat in the sea with her.

'It does look sore. You should really ice it.' She shook her head. She wanted us to see her pain. 'Dad says this girl has been messaging you.'

251

'Yeah.'

'Saying nasty things.'

'Yeah.' I inched closer to her.

'Like what?'

'Like calling me a sket.' Ruby tried to say this dismissively but her voice cracked on the last syllable.

'What does that mean? It doesn't sound all that bad.'

'Like a slag,' she said. 'Like a ho.' She swallowed audibly.

'Because of Dom?' Ruby was on her knees; she pushed her chin forward and her shoulders back.

'What?' she asked. She sounded low and mean.

'Did something happen with Dom?' I pressed. 'I won't be angry but I'm worried about you.' She punched the wardrobe door; I reeled back, fearful the next blow would be for me.

'So basically, *you're* calling me a slag.'

'No, don't be silly—'

'I'm not silly. I'm not stupid. You think I don't know anything but I do. I know what you think of me. I know you wish you never had me.' She picked up a sequin-covered trainer and lobbed it at the wall.

'Ruby, Ruby, don't be . . . Ruby, no. Why would you think that?' I tried to hold her but she batted me away and returned to the wardrobe.

'I'm going to Nan's,' she informed me from its depths.

'No, you can't go. We need to talk about this.' Ruby straightened up.

'I don't want to talk!' she screamed towards the ceiling. Then she held her cheek with both hands and began to sob.

I heard Dylan's rushed footsteps and then his sharp intake of breath. His 'What's going on?' felt accusatory.

I could see it might look like I had hit her and that denying it would only make it worse.

'What's going on?' he said again, and what I thought was, I'm losing everything.

'We're fine,' I said. 'She's upset.'

'Ruby?' he asked, as though inclined not to believe me.

'I want to stay at Nan's,' she whimpered.

'That's probably a good idea,' Dylan said. I moved to Ruby's bed so I could see the both of them.

'It's ridiculous, Dylan. She can't leave—'

'Dad, she thinks you're stupid too.'

I threw up my hands. 'Nobody's stupid. I don't like that word.'

Ruby scowled at me. 'Just because you don't like something doesn't mean it's not true.'

'Get your stuff,' said Dylan. 'I'll run you round.' I stood up.

'No,' I said. 'No you won't, because I'm going.' Neither of them intervened as I packed a bag. When I emerged from the bedroom, Dylan was in the hallway.

'It will be better tomorrow,' he said, and kissed my cheek as if thanking me for removing myself.

'Can you get away tonight?' I asked, reaching for his comfort for the second time that day. A few minutes later, Frank sent me the name of a central London hotel where he had booked a room under 'Meecham'.

Once again, I was alone in a suite waiting for Frank, but this time there was no uncertainty. I knew he would come and I knew he would help to make things right. He didn't arrive until after ten, full of warmth and apologies. I realized it didn't matter if someone let you down; it was how they responded to the failing that counted.

'What's going on with you?' he asked, after making us both a drink and sitting with me on the king-size bed. 'You've got needy,' he added, giving me a playful nudge.

'I'm sorry,' I said. I felt mournful; I had allowed us to become infected.

'I don't mind,' he said as he stroked my neck. 'I kind of like it. It's good to feel needed.' I knew he was right and understood why things at home felt so wrong. They didn't need me – they needed their laundry and their dinner and the bills paid and the plans made, but they didn't need *me*. Those tasks could be performed by anyone.

'I think I do need to get out,' I told him. 'I think I want to stay with you at the apartment for a while.'

'It doesn't have to be permanent,' he said. 'But this situation needs some distance.' I thought about us being able to spend whole days together, collaborate on trivial tasks such as unloading the dishwasher.

'My mum and dad, well, my stepdad, split up and I never felt like I lost him.' When they first separated, Eddie still came for dinner every evening; often he cooked it too. 'But to not see the girls every day . . . Ruby went on a school trip to France but she wanted to come home early. Aside from that . . .'

'We always think about loss; we should focus on how much there is to gain.' I pulled Frank down on the bed and curled my back against his front. I could feel his breath warm on my scalp.

'The girls know something's wrong, or they can feel it if they don't. I care for him, I really do, but I'm not sure how much I like him.' I felt a bit bad saying it aloud but also unburdened.

'When the respect has gone, everything else follows.'

That was it: I didn't respect Dylan and he'd had long enough to earn it.

'He's a nice guy,' I said. I think I wanted Frank to push, to tell me to make the decision I had already made.

'If nice is enough, stay,' said Frank. 'If you want more . . .'

'I do,' I told him. 'I want more of everything – more time, more money, more . . .' You, was what I was thinking. I wanted all of him, I no longer wanted to share.

'I'm ready to move on. If you know you are too, say the word.'

'The word,' I whispered. Frank put his arm around my waist, and even though it felt heavy and a bit restrictive, I let myself go to sleep.

In the morning, he was up before me and when I woke, he was in a chair reading *The Times*. 'I have to go,' he said, 'but I thought we could have breakfast.' His hair was still wet from the shower. He passed me a tray of pastries and fruit.

'I must have been really asleep,' I said. He sat on top of the covers next to me and took a large bite of an almond croissant.

'Can I have coffee?' I asked, batting my lashes. He went to get me a cup.

'So, this is what it will be like, you'll be having me do your bidding,' he said as he handed it to me. It had been so long since I'd felt that kind of pleasure, I wasn't sure what to do with the feeling.

'So, you're definitely going?' I asked, in case it had been a dream.

'I have to.'

'And you're around next week?'

'Nothing whatsoever in the diary.'

'I'm scared.'

'I know.'

'I don't know what I'm doing.'

'You do.' We kissed. 'Will you be late for work?' he asked.

'I'll tell them I had a meeting,' I said.

'See – you've got everything worked out.' He smiled and fed me a strawberry. 'I was just reading a piece about bees. Did you know it's only the females that can sting?'

'I didn't,' I said, and I loved that I didn't, that he always had something to teach me.

'I was thinking I'd include something about them in one of my talks.' He put his hands behind his head. 'Something about how we see it as an attack, when really it's defence. It's protective; it's instinctual.'

'Sounds good,' I said, although every word he spoke did.

'You could help me write it, next week. After . . . when you have time. I'd really appreciate your help.'

'I'm sure you don't need my help.' He made me feel shy; unlike with Dylan, where I could be sure of what he needed, I didn't yet see myself as valuable to Frank.

'I want it though,' he said. 'You're helping me now, just by being here and looking so beautiful.' I kissed him again.

'Do you have to go?' I asked.

'I could maybe spare a bit of time,' he said. It pains me to recall how we were because I'm not sure I'll feel that way again – you can't spend a lifetime communicating in clichés. But in that moment I thought maybe we could; I convinced myself that we'd stop the everyday from creeping in. Love was a firewall protecting me from boredom and doubt, but also keeping logic at bay.

32

'WHAT ARE YOU wearing?' I asked her. Mum looked down, like she needed to check. She had on white jeans and a sunshine-yellow vest. 'I thought you said we were going to work out?'

'Work *it*. It's a day rave.' Mum had called me the previous evening, insisting we needed some bonding time. I found myself eager for her company; perhaps as a means to escape the frigid atmosphere at home, but also because her perpetual chaos, maddening as it was, made me feel more balanced. She told me to meet her outside the working men's club. I'd protested and tried to pitch lattes and cake for our morning of connection. She made a gagging sound.

'Jesus. Why can't you crochet or play bridge like normal mothers?'

'You said you wanted to spend time with me. This is how I spend my time. Anyway, does anyone actually know how to play bridge?'

'Plenty of people do. People your age.'

'You're only as young as the man that you feel,' she said, as she readjusted her bra straps to pull her breasts higher.

'I don't want to know anything about anyone who's feeling you.'

'You don't wither up and die inside because time has

257

robbed you of a bit of youth, you know.' She sounded upset and I felt ashamed, although I'd never admit it to her. 'Well, you do wither a bit,' she added wryly. 'Dry as bone these days.' If she was someone else's mother I would think she was fun and quirky – certainly that's what my friends said about her – but it's easy to want what you don't have, when you're watching the glossy trailer and you don't really know what you're in for.

Mum paid for both of us, which instantly made me suspicious; she was always looking for opportunities to be treated by her daughter. I think she thought I was meant to be making up for the treats I had as a kid, but they were few and far between, and consisted of shopping trips or theatre visits to see wildly inappropriate plays about sex and death. Even back then, my treats were hers. The room was dark and a trestle table had been set up to one side as a makeshift bar. The tall, skinny guy manning it was wearing a fluorescent-green string vest and matching headband.

'We've got coconut water and aloe juice and plain old tap water,' he announced as we approached.

'I'll have aloe, please,' said Mum. He handed her a bottle.

'Yeah, me too,' I said. Mum opened hers and threw back a third of it. 'Come on,' she urged. 'It's good for you.'

'Since when do you do what's good for you?' Mum ignored the dig and gestured for me to drink up.

'It's about balance. Have the good and you can indulge in the not so good.' I opened the bottle; even in the dim light I could make out stringy bits floating in the murky liquid. I let my brain override my body to take a sip, and then chastised my brain for its folly.

'Mum, this tastes like swamp.' Mum rolled her eyes.

'You're full of crap. When was the last time you had swamp water?'

'I've never had swamp water. I wouldn't drink swamp water. That's the point.' Mum let her head loll backwards.

'Please,' she sighed, 'let go a little.' Without introduction, a song with a heavy bassline started. Mum began to shake her hips from side to side, almost in time. 'Chill out,' she shouted above the din, and it occurred to me that instructing someone to chill out produces exactly the opposite effect. She wiggled towards the centre of the room where a small group of people were dancing. Everyone seemed to have checked their inhibitions in at the cloakroom – limbs were flying everywhere. I weighed up how much damage I would do to our already injured relationship if I snuck out and did the latte bonding alone.

'Hey, girl,' said the barman, interrupting my thoughts. 'Sorry,' he said, whatever he saw in my expression making him repentant. 'I inherited a lot of misogynistic vocabulary from my father.'

'It's OK,' I said.

'What?!' he shouted.

'It's OK,' I yelled.

'That your mum?' He nodded towards the dance floor. My mother was doing knee raises, thrusting her chest out with each lift of a leg. I nodded. He handed me a glow stick. I was unsure if it was celebratory or in commiseration, but it seemed rude to leave after this generosity. I carried it to the edge of the growing group and shuffled tentatively to the music – one long song, the same unrepentant beat accompanied by a variety of electro-based melodies. Everyone continued to dance around me, each person lost in their own experience. For all her talk of bonding, Mum didn't pay any attention to what I was doing. After a few minutes, it became clear to me that I would feel less out of place if I committed to the weirdness. I tried to remember the times I went clubbing in my twenties, to recreate the sense of abandonment that comes with youth. I moved my body in an unselfconscious, unplanned way. It felt good, better than I remembered, because I wasn't worrying about whether a man was admiring me or what how I moved said about me as a person. I don't know how long we danced for – I didn't ask, I didn't care. It occurred to me that not caring was a lot of fun, and so in a funny way I had bonded with my mother.

'How was it for you?' said Mum when we were outside afterwards. I lifted my fringe and dabbed at my forehead with my sleeve.

'Good,' I conceded. 'Felt like a bit of an idiot but, I don't know, alive maybe?' Mum cheered and held her hand up until I relented and gave her a high five.

'I'm so glad, because I need to tell you your dad's got dementia.' For a minute I thought she meant my real dad – bio-dad, the seed provider – and I wondered why she had chosen this time to tell me about him. There had always been questions I knew she had the answers to, but I thought she would start with the colour of his eyes or something. 'When the police visited about the gardening, peeping-Tom thing, they suggested we go to his doctor.' I realized she was speaking about Eddie, and I felt disappointed before I remembered to be upset. 'He's been especially annoying recently . . .' Mum rambled. 'I thought it was just old age, and it is old age in a way. You know Grandma Gladys wasn't his real mum, and his dad died when he was little, so he had no idea if it was in his genes.'

'No, I didn't know that Grandma Gladys wasn't his real mum, no one ever told me. You never really tell me anything.' I was angry, the kind of intense but unfocused rage I felt throughout my childhood.

'I'm telling you now, aren't I, Eddie's not well and he needs more help than I can give him.'

'It's not a good time, Mum.'

'Why, what's going on?' I didn't trust that she wanted to know in order to offer me support; she was assessing how much my problems would impinge upon my usefulness.

'It doesn't matter. What do you need?'

'I was thinking we could do a schedule, to check up on him.' My mother knew nothing of schedules; I think it might have been the first time I'd heard her speak the word. 'I'm heading over there now – come with me and we can tell him what we're planning.'

'I can't. I've got an appointment,' I said. 'But tell him I'll see him soon.' I kissed her on the cheek and walked towards the tube.

'When's soon?' said Mum, trotting along beside me. 'Tomorrow? I thought maybe you could take Sundays.' I stopped, looking again at her in her outfit, inappropriate for anything.

'I've got a lot on. Let's talk early next week.' By that time everything could be different.

When I met with the estate agent Tim, a nephew of one of Frank's clients, I felt like a fool shaking his hand. There was me in my sweaty leggings and there was him, at least a decade younger, in his slick office with his suit and tie. It made me speak in an unnatural, pinched voice that I hoped would convey assuredness.

'We'll walk,' he said. 'It's not far.' As we made our way through the litter-strewn pavements, it became clear that my attire was well suited to my new neighbourhood. It was what I imagined many people think of when they speak of London – dirty, loud and very crowded. In the same city as my compact family home, but a world away.

'They've nearly finished work on the tube station,' said Tim. 'It's up and coming. In a few years it will be the new Shoreditch.'

'Meaning it's currently the old Shoreditch,' I said.

'You're getting in at the right time,' he offered.

'I think that only works for buying. I don't know that I'll be here that long.' I swerved to avoid what was left of a kebab on the pavement.

'It's a twelve-month lease but we can put in a break clause,' said Tim. I assume he thought that would be reassuring. We reached a gated block and Tim pressed some buttons on a keypad. It took some effort for him to open the door. 'Just needs some oil,' he said as it groaned open. We stepped into a small courtyard; a child's bike and an armchair had been abandoned in one corner. 'As you see, it's very safe,' said Tim. I wondered what we needed to be kept safe from. A woman stood in the doorway of one of the ground-floor flats having an expletive-laced conversation on her phone. I threw her a friendly new-neighbour smile and she frowned. I couldn't tell if it was aimed at me or the lucky person she was speaking to. 'The lift is broken but the exercise is good,' said Tim, as he led the way up a dark stairwell. Why did they always smell of urine? Surely being in the stairwell meant you were close to home?

I wanted Frank with me; he would make it an occasion, or at least less of a nightmare. He told me he couldn't get away – Sonya's uncle had died and they were going to visit the family. He wouldn't hear of delaying the move. He told me there would never be a good time but we both agreed it was better that he go away with her for the weekend, to avoid arousing suspicion. It meant he wasn't available to text or speak to me, and without his contact I felt adrift. It shocked me how quickly I had got used to the security he gave me. 'Here we are,' said Tim. He was placing the key into the door at the end of the third-floor walkway. The windows were so smeared and cloudy I couldn't see what was hidden behind them, but pressed against one was a row of terracotta pots, remnants from a time when the place had been offered some love.

We had to step over a pile of mail to get in. The air smelled rotten. Tim saw me react. 'It needs some airing,' he said, unable to upsell the stench. 'The living room,' he said, striding to the end of the hall. The room was filled with furniture for a home twice its size – a huge suedette sofa flanked by chintzy side tables; a glass dining-room table, nearly invisible under piles of newspapers and yellowing bills. 'It's getting cleared out this afternoon,' said Tim, 'but you get the idea. And check out the view.' He held back the heavy velvet curtain; the window revealed a burnt-out pub. 'No noise from next door any more, and if you look behind it . . .' Between the high-rises I could just make out Canary Wharf.

'Nice,' I said. Satisfied with my response, Tim let the curtain fall.

'Shall we see the rest?' he asked.

'You know, I'm fine,' I said. 'We're taking it. I just wanted a quick look.' I retreated to the hallway and out through the open front door. When I got to the stairwell I started to race. The woman was still standing in her doorway and watched me suspiciously as I sped to the exit. I tried to pull the gate open but it wouldn't budge. I gripped the handle with both hands and threw my weight backwards; my shoulder jarred as it rattled but didn't give. I tried again, this time grunting with the effort.

'You have to press here,' said Tim from behind me. Leaving a respectful distance, he reached his arm past me and pressed a blue button on the left-hand wall. I heard a click and the gate sprang open. On the pavement, Tim handed me the key. 'Frank sorted the deposit and stuff, so come whenever you're ready. Like I say, it will be clear by the end of today.'

'Thank you,' I said, clutching the keys until their sharp edges dug into my palm.

'Excited?' asked Tim.

'I will be,' I said.

When Dylan and I first visited our house, it was the fourteenth property we had seen together. Our list of wants had grown smaller and smaller with each viewing, and by the time we arrived at Mayview Road it consisted of something with a roof that we could afford. The agent was much like Tim; they must make them in a factory somewhere. He was doing a lot of work to mentally prep us – promises of good structure and talk of planning permissions. He needn't have bothered – as soon as he pushed open the door, I knew I wanted it. It wasn't big, it wasn't modern, and in many ways it was no different from the thirteen properties we had seen before it, but I knew it was home. As the agent blathered on about original features, Dylan had slipped his arm around my waist and whispered, 'There's space for a pram in this hall.' He was joking and also not joking, as was his way, broaching things lightly, giving me plenty of space to back away from it. I didn't though; I smiled at him because at the time he felt like home too.

The rest of the weekend, I was almost overpowered by the knowledge that it was our last – our last as we were. I moved more slowly and chose each word carefully. I was so consumed with paranoia I believed that the wrong phrase or syntax would alert them. I think they were aware of something. Dylan had softened; he made the corny joke about his morning client being a maniac behind the wheel. After a couple of days ensconced in her room, Ruby had started to use the common areas again. She and her sister curled up on the sofa together and watched a marathon of a show called *Ex on the Beach*. It didn't look appropriate but I was glad they were spending time together. I sat there for a while, but I found myself staring at them and not at the TV. I couldn't stop looking at the scar on Chloe's forehead, from back when she fell off her bike the first time she tried to ride without stabilizers, and that one strand of Ruby's hair that grows in another direction to the rest. I was sickened by the thought that my actions could mean I wouldn't see every moment, wouldn't be there for all the next changes and new scars. When people say they stay together for the kids, they don't mean to protect them or to provide them with stability; they mean to see them, whenever they need to. I was sad, not because of all the hurt I would cause them, but because I wanted them to have everything, and they wouldn't, because to get what you want, you always have to give something up.

33

08:10. MOVE DAY. I'd been calling it 'moving-on day' in the conversations I'd had with Bettina in my head. I got the suitcase out from under the bed. We only had one big suit-case; when we went away as a family we'd share. In a hurried call, Frank had explained when he was leaving and asked me to join him the same day. He said I should bring what I would need for a week; we would sort out the rest later. Usually I'm great at packing – I utilize every cor-ner and fill every shoe with a pair of socks – but I couldn't order my mind, let alone my underwear, and threw items in indiscriminately until the case was full.

08:35. I dragged the case to the living room, and left it by the door as I sat on the sofa to wait. I entertained a thousand different visions in which Dylan returned home early and I had to explain what I was doing. In some I con-tinued the deception and he carried my bag outside, helping me to leave. In others I confessed.

08:45. I wrote Dylan a note, an apology. I tried to explain what had happened even though I wasn't sure myself.

09:05. I heaved my case into the back of the people car-rier. The driver eyed me in the wing mirror and muttered something about an old back injury. In the rear of the car

I read the address from my phone even though I knew it by heart. I didn't want room for mistakes. I talked too much to the driver, but he didn't seem to mind. He told me about his three sons and his daughter. He was worried about the girl; she wasn't paying attention in school. I lied and told him it would get easier.

09:27. I arrived at my new home. It was bigger than I remembered. My footsteps echoed. I learned that part-furnished meant the suedette sofa, two grubby mattresses, and a chest of drawers with one functioning drawer.

09:30. I found some Jif Lemon and an old sponge under the sink. I scrubbed every surface. When I was done the sponge was black.

10:53. I didn't want to call Frank. He might be with her. He wouldn't leave her until she was OK or at least calm. I decided to give them some time. I owed her that.

10:55. I regretted not bringing food or bedclothes; I thought maybe Frank would. I pictured his wife holding on to his belt loops as he tried to walk out of the glossy red door. I didn't know what she looked like, so I pictured her as Carol Vorderman.

11:05. My phone rang; it was Dylan. I didn't pick up. He rang again. I turned it off.

11:30. I walked to the high street. A street market took up most of the pavement, pedestrians bumping into each other like ants in the remaining space. I was walking too slowly; the other occupants jostled and overtook me. Vendors shouted from their posts but I couldn't make out the words.

11:47. I bought a set of bedsheets, some fruit and a bunch of wilting lilies. The weight of them made me feel lighter. I felt like I was building our home.

12:05. I dragged the sofa to the other side of the lounge,

which made the room look smaller. I tried to push it back but it felt heavier and I broke a nail. I filed the nail with the jagged edge of a tooth. I abandoned the sofa in the centre of the room. Then I sat on it and cried.

12:28. I ate most of the fruit.

12:51. I started to panic about Frank not calling and then remembered my phone was off. I switched it back on and the alerts startled me. Three voicemails from Dylan. I listened to him say my name before deleting them all.

14:15. I decided to go to his house. I thought perhaps she was in denial and wouldn't let him leave. Maybe she was refusing to accept I was real. I thought I should go and be there for him because we were a team now.

14:30. I stood outside the tube station but couldn't go in. When a man in skinny jeans handed me a fifty-pence piece I knew I had to move. I walked until I came to a supermarket – a Sainsbury's – the same one I used at home. I walked up and down the aisles, all of them, even the one with dog food. Nothing seemed right. At the drinks aisle, I was paralysed again. What do you get for an occasion that's both a celebration and a death? I chose a Shiraz.

16:05. Back at the flat, I left the door open to try and release the chemical citrus smell that still lingered. Also, I didn't want to be shut in there alone. From where I had dragged the sofa, I could see the front door. I sat and stared at the building opposite. I thought about how to greet Frank; it would be disrespectful to be too happy. We would have a cuddle; we might have a cry. The day would be about endings and we'd begin again tomorrow.

17:10. I had six unread messages from Dylan. The last one was displayed on my home screen. It read, 'WHY?' I called Frank; I had to call him. The call went to voicemail. He told me to leave a message in a breezy, confident tone.

I tried again. When I heard the silence that indicated I was being diverted, I hung up and redialled. I tried a third time. No rings – straight to voicemail.

18:21. Two people were arguing along the hall – a man and a woman. The woman told the man how useless he was. She was screaming with rage but still listed his failings methodically. I remembered doing the same, storing my misgivings and releasing them when offered the right trigger. The man began by defending himself but quickly fell back on petty insults. He spent some time describing the way her stomach hung over the waistband of her jeans. I moved quietly to the door and closed it.

19:48. I decided to sleep – sleep would make the time pass faster. I thought that maybe when I woke Frank would be there. He'd apologize; we'd comfort each other and start our new lives. I turned over one of the mattresses; the stains were worse on the other side. I covered them with the new sheet, and pushed what might have caused them to the very back of my mind. My body resisted sleep. I thought back to when I first met Frank, journeying through our relationship, how sweet the stolen moments had been. It was like a lullaby.

21:20. When I woke the house felt emptier than before. The neighbours were quiet and I sort of missed them. The wine had a cork and I didn't have a corkscrew.

22:35. My alerts kept chiming. I looked only to check if they were from Frank, but none were. I didn't read the messages from Dylan; I knew what they would say. I knew him. The neighbours started up again. I couldn't make out the words but I could hear the rage and sense the resentment. Then I heard crockery breaking and wondered if I should intervene – ask if she needed help or call the police. I decided that if I could still hear them in ten minutes

I would go out. After eight minutes there was silence; the silence was scarier.

22:47. I sat in the dark room holding my phone as the battery died.

00:56. I understood. He wasn't coming.

34

I WOKE UP WITH no recollection of falling asleep; confused as to where I was. As I became familiar with my surroundings, the disorientation remained. My stomach ached angrily; I knew it was hunger but it felt like an internal representation of my anguish. I went to the kitchen for water. The grubby glass looked out on to a row of balconies. A man stepped out on to one from the flat opposite mine; he wore briefs and a ripped Guns N' Roses T-shirt. He stretched and then wiggled a finger in his ear, completely oblivious to the world outside his balcony – I wanted to be him. He raised his arms above his head and yawned, his blank expression uninterpretable. I couldn't stop watching; something about his ease was mesmerizing.

My phone was dead, and I sat on the floor beside it to wait for enough charge to make a call. As soon as it came to life, I quickly tapped out his name. I needed to speak to the only person who wouldn't criticize me.

'Please come. I can't be by myself,' I said when he answered.

'Sure, sis, you at home?'

'No. Sort of. I'll send you the address.' Tears fell on to the screen as I typed; I wasn't sure I would ever stop crying. I called Frank again, even though I knew he wouldn't pick up. As I listened to the phone ring over and over with no interruption, it gave me no satisfaction to be proved right. I sent him a series of messages – in the first I told him never to call me again and in the last I begged him to get in touch. I lay on the mattress and tried to pinpoint where I had gone wrong, what it was about me that I had failed to keep hidden long enough. In a sad way, it was understandable – I ruined good things, it was only a matter of time.

There was a knock at the door and I sat up. For one beautiful second, I thought it could be Frank. It was a brief but wonderful moment, and when it was gone the sadness that returned felt heavier; it took all I had to walk to the door.

'Nice digs,' said Henry. He was wearing a tie-dye T-shirt and a beanie and holding a frozen pizza; it was such a comforting sight. I fell into his arms and cried. The snotty, untamed tears left me feeling weak. Henry supported me to the sofa. 'Minimalist. I like it,' he said, looking round the room. He waved the pizza in my direction. 'Let me put this on and you can tell me about the relocation.'

'I don't want to eat,' I said. My stomach did feel empty but I knew food wouldn't fill it.

'It's stuffed crust,' said Henry, before disappearing to the kitchen. He returned with the wine and took a swig before handing it to me.

'How did you open this?' I asked, sipping tentatively.

'Little trick with my key. See, I come through when it's really necessary.'

'Thank you, Hen.'

'Any time. Wanna tell me why you're hiding out on the wrong side of town? Have you done something dodgy, is this like a police safe house?' He couldn't help looking excited.

'Henry, it's not a game. I've fucked up, I've seriously fucked up.' I felt like crying again but my eyes remained dry. Henry patted my arm. In other circumstances I would laugh at how uncomfortable he looked. Maybe he wasn't the best emergency contact but he was all I had. 'I've left Dylan.' Henry's eyes widened. 'I know, it was a shock to him too.'

'You've been a bit miserable the last few years, I mean more miserable than usual, but I thought that was just you.'

'No, there've been problems – nothing huge but it hasn't been right . . . I think.'

'He cheated?'

'I did.' Henry looked a little impressed, and beneath my sorrow something stirred, a small spark of satisfaction that I had managed to surprise him. 'But it didn't really feel like cheating. I mean, I know it was but it felt like maybe I'd met the right guy at the wrong time.'

'Who was this guy?'

'His name is Frank. Frank Molony.' Henry pulled a face.

'What does that mean?' I demanded.

'Nothing, it . . . well, it kinda sounds like a fake name.' It kind of did, and for all I knew it was. It was the name on his books, but authors use false names all the time. Only when it was too late did I consider how little I knew about him.

'What's so special about him?' asked Henry.

'Everything and nothing, really. I mean, he's impressive. He has a great career and stuff, but it wasn't that part I was attracted to.'

'You must have been a bit attracted to it.'

'Well, of course it wasn't a bad thing, but I mean that wasn't why I . . . why I wanted to be with him.'

'Not even a little?' He poked me in the arm.

'That hurt,' I scolded.

'Good, you know you're still alive.'

'Barely,' I whispered. 'I honestly do love him . . . did? It really wasn't about what he had.'

'OK.' Henry nodded slowly. 'I know you're not like that.'

'It really wasn't,' I said again, because I doubted myself.

Henry served the pizza on the cardboard box it came in. He had found a mug somewhere and allowed me to use it for the wine. He let me talk without interruption, and even though I was full of questions he didn't ask any more. When I had exhausted myself, he slapped his thighs.

'Now we sort everything out,' said Henry. I felt far from convinced. It was usually my job to sort everything out and I didn't have a clue where to start. 'Give me your phone,' he demanded.

'It's in the bedroom.' He moved quickly – I'm not sure I'd seen him move with purpose before. Even as a small child he navigated the world in an indifferent, dreamy manner. His energy made me feel anxious. He handed me the phone.

'Unlock it,' he said.

I wordlessly followed his direction.

'Right.' He had an officious tone I'd never heard from him. 'Who's your boss?'

'What? You can't tell Carter this!'

'Carter, thanks.' He busied himself on the screen, and when satisfied lifted it to his ear.

'Please, no,' I begged. Henry shook his head, briefly placing a finger on his lips to silence me.

'In case you hadn't noticed, you're supposed to be at work today. Hi ... Yes ... No it's not Alison, I'm calling on her behalf ... I'm her husband ... Yes, thank you, you too. Alison won't be coming in today. It's unlikely she'll be in this week actually ... She has a very extreme case of endometriosis and complications mean she will need a lot of rest ... Yes, she's had a lot of treatment and sadly the only thing she can do is ride it out ... Yes, I will. Thanks for understanding.' Henry ended the call with a flourish.

'I'm impressed,' I said. 'What the hell do you know about endometriosis?'

'Not a frickin' thing, but it sounds good, right? I used to use it when I worked in that bar. Now – furniture.' He sized up the empty room.

'Oh, no,' I said. 'Frank might bring some.' Henry crouched down beside me.

'You know he's not coming, sis?'

'He couldn't come yesterday but—'

'He's not coming.'

'You don't know that. He—'

'I know.' I knew too. It's why I felt empty, like my soul had fled and I'd woken up a ghost.

'I can't stay here.'

'Where else are you going to stay?' I lay down and stared at the yellowing paint on the ceiling. I wasn't emotionally prepared for logic; trust now to be the time for Henry to start employing it.

'I can't afford it,' I said, although it felt like the least of my problems. Henry passed back my phone.

'Landlord,' he said. I complied.

'Call the agent. He's called Tim,' I whispered as I handed it back. Henry rose and began to pace as he listened to the rings.

'Hello,' he said, after what felt like hours. 'Is this Tim?' His voice was louder than usual, strong and consistent in tone. You could believe he was a person in control of his life and not someone wearing a hat with flip-flops. 'Yes, there's been something of a crisis I'm afraid . . . No, no the flat is fine. Very nice place. A hot commodity . . . No, no, sadly Frank has been sectioned.' I was suddenly awake. I moved towards him but Henry held out his palm. 'There was an incident with a tin opener in Budgens . . . I'm afraid I can't share the details . . . Yes, it's unlikely they'll be able to fulfil the contract. There's a lot of organizing to do . . . I understand, but I wanted to come to an arrangement with you. Clearly if it was back on the market it would be snapped up.' That part wasn't a lie. Grotty as it was, the place would be claimed by some eager young professionals in a heartbeat – we had all come to accept so little. Henry was silent for a couple of seconds before saying, 'So grateful for your help.' He threw me my phone. 'He'll keep the deposit and you've got it for a month.'

'Henry! Frank knows his uncle. Why did you tell him that?'

'He won't find out. He won't even speak to them. If there's one thing I know about, it's running away from a situation.' I knew that was what he was doing, but the thought of Frank – confident, capable Frank – fleeing from me, made me wonder how horrendous I was.

'Frank paid the deposit,' I said. The words sounded hard to believe; it was only a few days ago he wanted to take care of me.

'He owes you.'

Henry and I went to get food. I told him I didn't want to leave the house but he insisted. He said he was afraid to leave me alone, but I think he wanted my purse. It helped to move;

seeing people going about their everyday business was a gentle reminder that the earth was still turning. Henry wouldn't let me buy any more alcohol; he told me half a bottle of wine was probably enough for one morning.

'You need to stay clear headed, in case he calls,' he told me as we walked back with the bags.

'Do you think he will?' My heart forgot to beat for a second.

'Nah,' he replied.

Henry helped me push the sofa back to the corner of the room and made us breaded chicken and oven chips. I used to make it for us when we were kids. We ate with our fingers on the sofa.

'How's it going with the girl you're seeing?' I asked.

'I finished it,' he said, as he picked up an escaped breadcrumb with his last bite of chicken. I started to sob. I felt so much pain for this woman I didn't know. I knew she would be questioning herself and that, even though it meant nothing to Henry, she might be changed irrevocably. The crying exhausted me and I slept again.

The sound of the doorbell woke me up. I opened my eyes to find Henry standing over me.

'I called back-up,' he said. 'I have to go to work.'

'You don't work,' I said, my voice stiff from sleep.

'Yeah, I do – delivery for the veggie place. I have to, I don't have my big sister to bail me out any more.'

'I don't need a babysitter,' I whispered. Henry didn't respond. He squatted down next to me and let his lips brush my cheek. Henry had to leave to meet his commitments and he had come through for me when I needed him. It was like waking up in a parallel universe.

'I don't know much but I know that this dude, whoever he is, is a complete and utter arsehole, and that you will fix this – you always do.' I closed my eyes because I felt like crying again and I didn't think my tear ducts could take any more. I opened them when I heard Henry speaking to the person at the door, and closed them again as she walked into the room. She was the last person I wanted to see.

'Alison.'

'Mum.'

'I brought vodka.'

'I love you.'

She didn't just bring vodka; she also had tonic, lime wedges and cut-glass tumblers. Mum might be an alcoholic but she's a classy one. She sat down on the sofa and poured two drinks. Henry, she explained, had given her the blurb on what had unfolded; she surprised me by not seeming surprised. She was angry.

'You stupid, stupid girl. What were you thinking?' My head started throbbing so badly I was sure I could hear it. The rant Mum delivered wasn't making it through. '. . . everything. You have everything and you've chucked it all away to live in this piss hole. What even is this place? It's like some sort of drug den . . .' Then I couldn't hear anything because she was right, and when my mother is right, something is very wrong. I pulled my knees up into my body and wrapped my arms around my head. I wanted to be small, so small it might feel like I wasn't there. When I felt her arms around me it was awkward, but still comforting. Mum patted my shoulder before letting go to reach down for the drinks. She encouraged me to start mine before saying, 'Tell me about him.' She was not the audience I imagined processing the details of my affair to, but she was the right one. She didn't judge me, she couldn't. I told her about my plan. How I had secretly imagined that over the summer we could develop our relationship and rebuild our families; we would create something elaborate and unconventional but still beautiful.

'He came out of nowhere, really. The whole time I've been with Dylan, I've never been attracted to anyone else.'

'Well, that's a lie.'

'It's not!' I felt panicked. Did I no longer know the truth? 'I promise it came out of nowhere.' Mum looked unconvinced; I guess my promises didn't mean much.

'Where did you meet him?'

'At work.' She nodded; the story was as she expected. Her nonchalant response was like finding out the diamonds I had been wearing were glass. 'He made me see . . . made me think that there was something else out there for me.' Mum patted my hand.

'That's what they do.'

'But maybe there is? Mum, please don't take this the wrong way, but all I wanted was something different from what we had. I wanted my kids to live in the same house all their life. I wanted them to eat hot dinners in the evening, every evening. I didn't want them to have to worry about me or about anything. I think I got so focused on that, I forgot about myself. Is that stupid?' Mum reached over and ran her hand down my face.

'They fuck you up,' she said softly. 'You need to speak to Dylan, darling.'

'I don't know what to say.' Mum sighed. It was so heavy it couldn't only be for me.

'Why did you trust this man, Ally?'

'I had no reason not to. He seemed trustworthy. He has such lovely forearms.' Mum shook her head.

'He has a penis, darling. He's not to be trusted.' An animalistic noise escaped me, the sound of hurt and grief and humiliation. 'Too soon?' I nodded. 'You need to see Dylan,' she said. She waited, confirming my attention was focused before continuing. 'Go whilst the girls are still in school.'

'I can't.'

'You have to.'

'But I can't. I don't know if I—'

'What are you going to do, hide in here for the rest of your life? Try that and it will be a short one.'

'What am I supposed to say?'

'The truth.'

'I fell in love, or I'd gone crazy.' Perhaps they are the same thing. My mind caught on a memory of a homeless guy who sometimes sat on a bench opposite the office. I didn't acknowledge him for my first year in the job; maybe I was too distracted, but more likely I didn't want to be tainted by association. I was eager to present an image of success and fearful of anything or anyone that might damage what I knew to be a fragile position. The second summer I was slightly less fearful. I'd found my feet, found Bettina, and one afternoon I offered the man a cheese-and-coleslaw sandwich. He declined it politely, and I remember feeling embarrassed that I had assumed he would need anything from me. It was because he had surprised me that I examined him closely for the first time. His suit was worn and dirty but fitted him perfectly; it had clearly cost someone a good chunk of money at one time.

'I'm waiting for my brother,' he said. 'He works in the factory but he's undercover. He works for the government.' I think I looked shocked or scared or a combination of the two, because he said, 'Don't worry, he's one of the good ones. I shouldn't tell you that but you have a nice face.' I heard him whistling as I walked away. I felt incredibly sad, and not because he was alone or unloved or that he was clearly very mad, but because he was clearly very mad and had no idea that was the case. I drank my vodka.

'OK, let's not go with the truth,' Mum said, in an uncharacteristically instructional tone. 'Tell him you made a mistake and you realize he's the best thing that ever happened to you, and you're very, very sorry.' She poured some more vodka into my unfinished drink. 'For courage. He'll take you back. What other option does he have?' I'd always seen myself as the parent in my relationship with my mum. She was the one who would get caught up in the fun or lost in fantasy, and I had to be the person to hold on to her sleeve and keep her anchored to the ground; yet here she was urging me to retrace my steps. I could tell she was sincere in wanting to alert me to what she saw as my folly, and the horror of this was enough to spur me into action.

35

I STOOD OUTSIDE WEIGHING up whether I should use the key. I thought it might seem confrontational to enter without knocking, but ringing the bell would seem cold. My decisions had made even the smallest actions feel impossible. I was still debating how to enter when the door opened. It was Mickey. He didn't greet me or indicate that I should come in. I only knew him to be unnaturally animated, and Mickey's stillness in that moment made me uneasy. I was at the part in the movie when you know something terrible, something loud and violent, is about to occur. Mickey held a tea towel, an old one I used for dusting. He dried his hands carefully before saying, 'He's resting.'

'I need to talk to him,' I said. Mickey didn't move. He tucked the tea towel into his back pocket.

'He didn't sleep. I think it would be better if you came back later. Can you at least do that for him?' This was when the guilt took over. Mickey, a man whose moral compass couldn't find north, was judging me. It was more than I could take.

'Dylan!' I shouted. I didn't care about waking him. I'd done so much damage; waking him up would be a rain shower following an earthquake. Mickey shook his head and whispered something about respect, as if he had any understanding of that. I pushed past him and raced down the hall. I thought he might pull me back, bar me from entering my own home. I felt a rush of energy; I was ready to fight if necessary. I had my head down as I flew up the stairs, and didn't see Dylan until he caught me by the shoulders. He was barely awake; certainly he had been conscious less than five minutes. I could tell by the fact that his eyes weren't quite focused. We all stood in silence, waiting to hear the first thing he would say.

'I need coffee.'

We filed into the kitchen. As I sat in one of the chairs, I recalled the day we found them in an independent shop in Islington. We were only meant to be there for ideas. The plan was to gather up inspiration and take it to Wembley, where we could get the same in Ikea at a price we could almost afford. I remember stroking the smooth resin, noting how well the quirky duck-egg blue colour would match the kitchen tiles and knowing we would never get the same. As I had predicted, we didn't find anything in the flat-pack theme park on the outskirts of London, and we sat on empty crates until a week later, when a man arrived with a delivery slip for me to sign. I stood in stunned silence as my chairs were carried through the house. They were even more beautiful than I remembered; I don't think I had allowed myself to see how lovely they really were. 'How? When? Why?' I stuttered. Dylan didn't answer my questions but his shy smile told me the answer to the last one – to make me happy.

Now, as I watched my husband move around the room to make the coffee, he wasn't smiling. I felt a stab of anxiety that I might never see it again. I was transfixed by the careful way he poured milk into the cups and the time he took to ensure the sugar was level before tipping it from the spoon. It was like I was watching him for the first time. Mickey stood sentry, leaning against the counter with his arms folded.

Dylan made me a drink without asking and hundreds of memories rushed back. I thought of the second time we spent the night together. We woke in his house, a grubby terrace he shared with Mickey and a small, skittish guy called Pete. Dylan got out of bed and sheepishly pulled on his pants. He rubbed his head and averted his eyes as he asked, 'You want coffee?'

'I'll always want coffee,' I had answered.

Dylan sat in the seat opposite mine; he wrapped his hands round the mug. I waited for him to blow on it but he didn't.

'I'm sorry,' I said. I wondered how many times I would have to say it before it felt like enough.

'I know,' said Dylan. He didn't, how could he? Even at the worst of times he was assuming the best. 'Is it worth asking what happened? What I did?' I reached towards him, but thought better of it and left my hand on the table.

'You didn't do anything, Dylan. I promise this isn't about you.' He nodded. I knew it was a gesture to quieten me rather than one of agreement.

'Course you didn't, mate,' said Mickey.

'Could you just let us talk, Mickey?' I was begging. I was appealing to a side of him that I wasn't sure existed. I had never really liked Mickey. He was coarse and immature and I worried that he might lead Dylan into something untoward, but I loved him because he cared for Dylan so much. On many occasions I wondered why my husband kept him around, but now I understood it was because no quality was as valuable as loyalty.

'Talk about what, love?' said Mickey. 'This rat you've been creeping around with? Where is he? Bloody coward.'

'Please, Mickey,' I said again.

'It's OK. Leave us for a while,' said Dylan. Mickey bristled.

'Are you sure, mate?'

'Yeah.' Dylan looked at me as he said this, and I was suddenly unsure I wanted Mickey to go. All the sadness and hurt I saw in him, I didn't want to be alone with it. Mickey threw the tea towel on the counter.

'I'll be back to check on my casserole,' he said. He shot me a warning look before walking away, but it was unnecessary; there was no more hurt I could cause.

'Babe—' I said. He interrupted.

'You don't get to call me that. Not any more.' I felt the tears warm on my cheeks and I was surprised there were any left in me. Dylan didn't move. I had treated him as if he was weak, but he was stronger than I knew.

'You can ask me anything,' I said.

'Why didn't you answer my calls?'

'I didn't know what to say.'

'And now?'

'I still don't. Apart from I'm sorry.' Dylan took a sip of his drink. I knew it was still too hot, must have burned his mouth, but he didn't show it. I had never allowed myself to imagine how he would react when he found out but I assumed there would be anger, screamed accusations, maybe objects thrown. The cold, stoic man before me was worse than I imagined. He placed the mug back on the table, and twisted it round until the handle was facing towards me and I could no longer see the words 'World's Best Dad' on the side.

'Do I know him?' he asked.

'What? No!' His cheeks filled with air, which he released slowly and evenly.

'That's something. The thought of it being someone I've seen . . . spoken to. I thought it was that Carter.'

'Carter! For God's sake, no.'

'So, who is he?'

'Dylan, it doesn't matter. I mean, he isn't the point, not really. I'm tired. I'm so tired all the time and I feel lonely in my own home and I'm pissed off every day. I don't like who I am when I'm with . . . when I'm here.' I reached towards him again and he swiped the mug in the act of pulling away. Coffee slopped on to the table. Dylan stood up. 'Leave it,' I said. I felt so tired. I knew if I put my head on the table I would sleep, deeply and for a long time. Dylan raised a finger, like he did when he admonished the girls when they were little.

'No. You do not get to tell me what to do.' He moved to the sink and picked up a cloth hanging over the taps. He wiped up the spill carefully, and then folded the cloth and placed it on the counter. 'It's not unreasonable,' he said when he sat down. 'You're at work all the time. Everything is about work.'

'No, Dylan. That was real.'

'But the rest of it wasn't. Me and the girls, that was all make-believe.'

'That's not what I'm saying.'

'What are you saying?' He clasped his hands together, like he was waiting for his yearly appraisal. I put my head in my hands and prayed for inspiration. Why hadn't I planned in advance what I would say? I looked up at him.

'When we met, I was a different person.' I didn't see any understanding in his expression, and why would I? I had changed but he hadn't, not really. He had remained the same; through the kids and the challenges he was always just Dylan. 'I don't know if this is what I need any more.'

'What you need?' I started to respond but he repeated the words, a hard edge creeping into his voice. 'What you need? You're fine. The girls are fine. You don't need anything. It's about what you want. This wasn't what I planned. I had dreams, you know . . .' That surprised me, but I believed him.

'Why didn't you talk to me? We could have worked on them together.'

'You mean you could have told me what to do.' And in that moment, I saw another Dylan – a Dylan who wasn't only someone's husband or someone's father. 'It doesn't matter now, I guess.' I didn't know the answer to that. 'You should go,' he said.

'I want to wait for the girls. We should explain to them together.'

'No, I don't want to upset them. We'll say you're on another work trip.' I thought I heard a stress on 'another' but I might have imagined it. It seemed I was good at that.

'Please, Dylan.' A cough came from behind me. Mickey walked in and pulled open the oven door; a meaty aroma filled the room. He bent down to peer inside and, despite the heat, didn't stop examining it until I pushed back my chair and stood up.

'Can we speak tomorrow?' I asked Dylan. He nodded.

'Bye, Mickey,' I said as I left the room.

'Alison,' he replied curtly.

36

I WANDERED AROUND THE neighbourhood, noticing details I had long ago filtered out. The front gardens that had been cultivated with so much care over many years, and the dilapidated cafe, owned by Carmel who made a fresh Victoria sponge every morning. I hated Frank in that moment. He had distracted me from what I had and made me think I needed something else. I found myself at a bus stop and boarded the first one that arrived. The driver barely made eye contact as I presented my debit card. It felt like there was something repellent about me, a thing I had tried to push down for years that had finally risen to the surface, oozing out of me – thick and putrid. I sat in a seat near the back and watched the scenes of London roll by. I felt safe on that bus, but I was aware the whole time that at some point I would have to get off. I'd been taking London buses alone since I was a small child. A sudden house move had Mum and me living several miles from my primary school. Not wanting to leave my friends, I begged her to let me stay, but it meant a solo bus trip home on the days that she worked. Often I would ride the route several times; I'd chat to the driver as he smoked and waited for the timetable to catch up with him. There was an old lady who would get on at the Tesco and give me an extra-strong mint.

I didn't like the taste but I enjoyed the experience – so minty they felt hot, or maybe it was the part when she pressed it into my hand, closing my fist tight around the sweet to make sure it was secure; probably that. The bus, with its strangers, was more homely than my empty house, where I knew the key would have grown cold under the doormat and I'd have only slightly manic children's TV presenters to keep me company. They made me anxious; they still did when the girls were small. Something about their perpetual joy was unnerving. I imagined that when the cameras were off they would sink to the floor like deflated balloons. I rode the buses until we moved in with Eddie. Even though I was timid and monosyllabic around him at first, I liked that he gave me someone to come back to. Occasionally, I would sit in the hall and listen to the tapping of his keyboard from his home office next to the kitchen. I felt like I belonged to someone, which was why I felt so betrayed when he left. I understood it was the same with Frank, and I wanted to tell him that. I didn't call him. I knew he wouldn't pick up and I believed I was owed more. Seeing Dylan and facing up to the shock and discomfort of what I had done – Frank needed to do that too. I got off the bus.

I'd never thought about a doorbell being refined before. Frank's was – clear, not too high-pitched – in stark contrast to mine, which had been left on 'Jingle Bells' since Christmas 2014. Everything was so still I could hear the rustle of the leaves; somehow I knew he wasn't there. I was nearly at the gate when I heard the door open. I turned slowly, giving myself time to prepare, and there she was. Taller than me – most people are – but not by much. Her dark hair was in a long braid over one shoulder. On the other rested the head of a child.

'He's not here,' she said, and then, with a small sigh of resignation, 'Let me put this one down.' She went back inside and I followed. 'I take it you know where the kitchen is?' She didn't wait for me to respond before taking the stairs. I thought leaving me alone in the hallway was careless; I could have been there to do her harm, more than I already had. Perhaps she was too trusting; maybe she no longer cared. I walked through to the kitchen, purposefully looking ahead and not at the spot where we had made love. Not that it had been that, not unless love can be made independently. The kitchen was light and modern. I didn't sit down; I knew I hadn't been invited. I could hear her talking to the baby in a comforting, melodic way. Then nothing, and I didn't know she was there until she offered me a drink. She didn't walk, she glided – quickly, almost silently. I hadn't responded to the question, but she still pulled out two mugs and brewed us each a strong cup of tea. The sort of woman who knew what was needed in every situation. She placed one cup on the island in front of a high stool and took the one opposite. I sat where she had quietly instructed and, for the second time that day, I was face to face with my conscience.

'I'm—'

She had been drinking but stopped to shake her head. 'No,' she said. 'Don't say sorry. It will mean nothing.' She wasn't angry, or at least she didn't project that. She was calm and also very sad. The sadness filled the room and my lungs and made it difficult to speak.

'OK.' I was hurt, even though I had no right to be. I had always taken a dim view of people who blamed the mistress – not her relationship, not her responsibility – but in that room I accepted my blame because, yes, this woman was a stranger, but it didn't mean I owed her nothing. People need to earn the right to be treated like shit.

'Are you OK?' she asked. I still wonder where she found the compassion to ask. I think she felt a sense of responsibility. He was her husband; she was accountable. We do this. Make our partners' deeds our own.

'I *am* sorry,' I said. The mask of kindness lifted then and I caught a glimmer of something else. I thought it was contempt but now I think it may have been boredom. Her face wasn't easily readable and her features distracted me from the task. A wide mouth, huge dark eyes and a delicate nose, as if she had handpicked the features from different faces – each beautiful but not meant to be together. 'Do you know everything?' I wanted to understand how much she hated me. She shrugged wearily. She wasn't all that forgiving – I just wasn't particularly significant to her. I was simply a tool through which her husband revealed his flaws.

'Has he done this before?' But I knew the answer. The amount of callousness he had shown me took practice. You had to be entirely comfortable with disregarding someone to do it so easily.

'We've had our problems,' she said – a politician's answer. I had no time for euphemisms.

'How many times?' Her look told me that I was crossing a line and she was right, but I had crossed so many, I could see no reason to stop. It became important to me to know how insignificant I was. I wanted the facts to validate the pain I was in.

'Fine,' she said. There was a bowl of fruit on the table. She picked a couple of shrivelled grapes from the bunch and walked over to a bin in the corner. When she waved her hand, it opened and she let the fruit fall. 'When we met he was married,' she said as she sat down. 'I was over here doing a master's. I'm from Brazil.' I heard it then, the otherness in her voice – another layer, her own story. 'I was so homesick, and the weather! You think the weather thing is a joke until you live through it. I hadn't packed properly and I didn't have enough money for a decent coat, and one day I was shivering in the rain and Frank came over and gave me his. When I returned it, he took me for dinner.' I wish I had asked more questions about her, or at least examined why I didn't want to know more. I think I knew that I would have learned what I did that day – that Frank likes to rescue people and our relationship had not been about me at all. 'I did pressure him to marry me. I needed a visa and I wanted the commitment. That's why I've been so forgiving, I believe.' The women who stay are stupid, that's what I always thought – stupid, weak or both – but this woman wasn't stupid; she spoke carefully and articulately. And she looked me in the eye and accepted my presence with grace. She certainly wasn't weak. I was the weak one, the one who had thrown everything away because someone had shown me a little attention.

'Is that when it started, when you were married?' I remember telling everyone that marriage wouldn't change anything, but it did. It was like securing your seatbelt on a plane; you know that if it crashes you'll be obliterated, and some metal and a bit of nylon won't prevent that, but it still feels better. I guess for some people that belt seems like bondage. She shrugged again. At first I thought she was being dismissive but then recognized the gesture as acceptance. She knew that every person, and so by default every relationship, has flaws, and this was the one she had been assigned. I felt angry for her and myself.

'You don't have to put up with this,' I said. 'He has money, you can leave him.' In that moment she was my ally. I didn't know her at all really, but we were bonded in such an intimate, private way that I was genuinely invested in her wellbeing. 'I could help, be a witness or something.' She laughed. It was quiet and pretty but very genuine.

'You don't need to be involved any more.' She saw what I was doing before I did, trying to remain involved where I was no longer wanted. What did I think, that this was some madcap chick flick and we would launch a revenge plan that would play out to a sassy soundtrack? 'In fact, why are you here?'

What could I say? I wanted to see him; as much as I hated him, I wanted him to make me feel the way he had. Instead I said, 'I wanted to make sure you were aware.'

She picked up my untouched tea and poured it down the sink. 'Thank you,' she said. 'You've done that. I've got to see to the baby now.' The baby was silent. It was my cue to leave.

'How old is he?' I asked.

'Seven months,' she said. Like any mother, she couldn't resist sharing, even with the enemy.

'He's very cute,' I said.

'He's my world. I would do anything to protect him.' Anything. Endure embarrassment and betrayal, accept less than she was worth. I stood, thanked her for the tea. She followed close behind me to the door; she wanted to be sure I was gone. Before I left, I asked her – I had to.

'Will you tell him I was here?'

'No,' she said – not harshly. Unlike her husband, she was letting me down gently.

'He's not answering my calls,' I admitted.

293

'He won't,' she said. 'He's not here. He's gone.' That's how quickly something can be over.

I was hungry. The morning drinking had ushered in an afternoon hangover. I found a kebab shop where the owner was setting up for the evening. I asked him what he could offer me and he pulled a greying burger from the glass case in front of him. As I waited for it to cook, its edges curling on the dirty grill, I thought about what Frank might be eating and where. I missed hearing about his day and telling him about mine. I felt bewildered and broken and, even though he was the cause of it, he was the only person I wanted to talk it through with. That thought alone made me want to scream or smash something; everything I had felt for Frank was stuck inside me with nowhere to go. The guy in the kebab shop offered me salad and sauces but I declined. I didn't think I deserved it. I sat on a bench to eat. The grease coated my fingers and fell on to my jeans but I didn't care. I wasn't sure what I cared about any more; certainly not Dorothy Perkins denim.

37

A N AFFAIR GIVES you practice at being sneaky. Sonya
said Frank was gone and I needed to know where.
The next day I started sleuthing. During a phone call to
Nush, under the guise of touching base, I quizzed her on
her previous life as an exotic dancer. Never one to turn
down an opportunity to talk about herself, Nush gladly
told me about her turn around the pole. She said it was the
only job she'd had where the girls were nice to each other –
someone was always on hand to give you a tampon or
some talcum powder (she didn't clarify what the talcum
powder was for). She told me she had to leave because it
had started to make her dislike men; she began to understand the way they viewed women, and themselves, and
what she came to know was pretty dark. I think I did a
good job of sounding interested in Nush's feminist awaken-
ing, but all I wanted was the name.

'The Bang Bang,' she said wistfully. 'Why, do you want
to go?'

'Maybe. I'll call you later.' From the website the place
looked decent – upmarket, inviting even. Of course, pictures lie. I wasn't interested in spending an evening there;
it was simply a step towards finding Frank. There was a
number on the website and, after four attempts, the line

was answered by a woman who managed to sound both hurried and bored.

'Bang Bang, more bang for your buck.'

'Can I speak to Anthony, please?'

'Who?'

'Anthony.' She sighed.

'Wrong number.'

'It's definitely the right place, he's the owner.'

'Oh, Tony. The pervy one.'

'That's the one.'

'Yeah, he doesn't really come in.' Silence. When I reached him, I would tell Anthony to invest in some customer-service training.

'Do you think you could help me contact him?' More silence. 'Maybe you could find a number . . .'

'Connie!' There was some fumbling with the phone and a bit of whispering before another voice came on the line. 'Zero, seven, seven—' she barked.

'Stop, wait!' I dug around in my bag and, failing to find a pen, retrieved an eyeliner pencil from my make-up case. 'OK, one more time.' She reeled off the numbers in between smacks of gum chewing, and I scratched them on to my arm. 'Thanks.'

'No problem. When you speak to him, tell him he owes me a call.'

I still had no food or drink in the flat, so I took myself to a local Starbucks for the next part of the plan. I ordered an espresso even though I prefer milky drinks; the bitterness, the no-bullshit of a pure shot of coffee seemed appropriate. Anthony answered immediately. He was not a man to be flustered by an unknown number.

'Hello, darling,' he said after I greeted him.

'It's Alison.'

296

'Alison who, my sweet?'

'Frank's Alison.' I wanted to see if he corrected me. How far my disownment had spread.

'Oh yes, poppet. How are you?' His tone had shifted from predatory to paternal.

'Good, great actually. Busy though, trying to get this show sorted.'

'Ah, yes. I said I'd help with venues, didn't I?'

'Yes,' I said gratefully. I hadn't planned what excuse I would use for calling him; I was no Josephine Baker.

'Well, what capacity are you looking at?'

'Oh.' I scanned the cafe for inspiration but there was none to be found. 'I'm not sure yet.'

'Seat-of-your-pants kind of girl.'

'Hmm.' It really was a marvel how he managed to make everything sound slightly rude. 'I'm pretty open to spaces. Did you go to Frank's last book launch? That was a great event.'

'No, no. I was away, I think. Has he given you the contact?'

'No, he's erm . . . He's . . .'

'Oh yeah, he's off to Berlin, isn't he? Berlin is fantastic, isn't it? A hedonist's dream.'

'That's right.' So, I knew where he was and that I was so repulsive he had to flee the country to escape me. I chose not to ask Anthony any more details, deciding he probably wouldn't tell me and might alert Frank to my enquiries. Also, I didn't want him to know the truth. I wanted to suspend disbelief for a little more time, even with all the evidence of the illusion.

Frank had Twitter, Facebook and Instagram. All were business focused. Shots of his books or him looking earnest during talks. I had looked before, hidden under my covers and pored over the images when we couldn't be together. Exploring them again, I could see they told me nothing – they represented the glossy shell that Frank offered the world. I found her amongst his followers; her pictures showed a vibrant, popular woman. She appeared comfortable with herself and like someone who appreciated every facet of life. Jemima's photos did not represent the taciturn girl I'd encountered as Frank's assistant. I had to set up an Instagram account to message her. I used my phone screensaver – an image of Chloe and me at the skate park – as my profile picture, so she would know I wasn't a scammer. I sent her my number and asked her to call. It shouldn't have surprised me that she did so within a few minutes. She was of the generation that viewed phones not as an accessory but as an extension of themselves.

'He mugged you off?' she asked when I picked up. I didn't understand her words but I could read the sentiment. She knew that I had been disposed of – dumped, chucked, broken up with. Whatever the name, something violent and callous had occurred. I chose not to answer her question and instead asked where he was.

'Gone. Berlin.'

'Do you know why? I mean, what he's doing?'

'I don't really care,' she said, in a way that suggested it was true. 'You shouldn't either.'

'Why not?' I asked, and the fear was immediate. Was I one of several women? Had they been laughing about me together? It was very possible this young woman knew more about my relationship than me.

'Aw,' she said. 'He's not worth it.' She sounded softer then – sympathetic, the voice female friends use amongst themselves when they're not too embarrassed to sound nurturing. 'I get it. I reckon I can still hack his diary if you

298

like. I'm not working for him any more, so fuck it.' Course she got it; she was probably in the middle of her own heartbreak. She was at the age when these things were supposed to happen, when you were young enough to bounce back and the lessons you learned could inform the future you had ahead of you. I drank another coffee as I waited for her intel, but I knew the jittery feeling in my chest wasn't from the caffeine. Jemima called me back with a succinct brief; she would have been a good assistant in some respects. Frank was in Berlin for two weeks to provide one-to-one corporate coaching. He was being paid big bucks to improve people's lives and had gone out of his way to make sure I wouldn't find him.

Next door to the coffee shop was a pizza restaurant, the kind that is dim even in daylight, and although the burger from the day before was still parked awkwardly in my gut, I went in. A sign at the entrance commanded that I wait for someone to seat me, and standing next to the podium I felt acutely alone. After several minutes I called out to a waiter who was arranging cutlery into little pots.

'Do you need a table?' he asked as he approached.

'That's why I'm waiting here.' I pointed to the sign.

'Right.' He surveyed the empty room with a great deal of purpose. 'What about there by the window?' I shook my head. He gave an exaggerated frown. 'One of those days. I've got what you need.' He started to cross the room and I had nothing to do other than follow. We stopped in a corner, heavily saturated with smells and sounds from the kitchen. 'I think it's a booth day,' said the waiter. I sat on one of the benches, the plastic covering groaning as I settled on it. 'Have you eaten here before?'

'No.'

"K. Plates and forks are over there, buffet is over there,

pay at the till. It's £6.99 at lunchtime.' As he spoke, he gestured like an air steward highlighting the emergency exits.

'Do you have a drinks menu?'

'There's a drinks machine by the plates.'

'Do you have a wine list?' He glanced towards the kitchen before sitting down opposite me.

'No wine, no alcohol at all. The owner's Muslim, or so he says. Personally, I think he's pretending, to appeal to the local market, but then again I'm a sucker for a conspiracy theory. If you're looking to feel out of it, go for the stuffed-crust mighty meaty. So much MSG, you'll be flying.'

'Thanks, I will,' I said, but I didn't move. The lad seemed happy about the brief distraction from the monotony of arranging cutlery. He removed his red cap, allowing a heap of dark curls to escape.

He rested his chin in his hands before saying, 'Don't take this the wrong way, but I'm training to be a psychic and you have a lot of negative energy hanging around you. Like here . . .' He pointed to a space to the left of me. 'And all up in here.' He waved his hand in front of my face. I shifted away from him, although fully aware that any negative energy would be coming with me.

'Can you train to be a psychic?' I asked. 'I thought you either had it or you didn't.'

'Of course,' he said. 'You can train to be anything – the mind is amazing. And I'm learning under Eliza McCreadie. She's one of the best. I moved to London to work with her. Well, that's not actually true – I moved to London coz my mum kicked me out, you know? I guess she couldn't handle how fabulous I am. I kinda knew this guy who lived in Tottenham – well, I thought I did, but it turns out I totally didn't and he was into pretending to be a baby, you know, nappies and shit, like literally shit, and I was like, you do you, boo, but I'm not ready to be a parent. Then I met Eliza. She was eating scrambled eggs in Polo at like three in the morning, and she sort of took me under her wing.' I wanted to hug him; he wasn't that much older than Ruby, and he genuinely believed that his diabolical circumstances were chapters of a lifelong adventure. And then I felt like crying because I wanted to be able to do the same. 'Babe, babe, let me make you a plate.' He replaced his cap and darted off towards the buffet table. I watched him load up potato skins and chicken wings, and marvelled at his willingness to show me kindness when I had offered nothing in return. Frank made me see that a stranger could alter the course of your life, but a trainee psychic helped me to understand that it's up to you to rewrite your story. I slipped out, leaving a twenty on the table; I knew what I wanted my story to be and also how it could lead me back to Frank.

As I headed to the tube, I glanced at a woman walking alongside me. I felt a wave of pity but then realized the woman was my reflection. Ignoring the steady foot traffic, I studied myself in the window of a bank. If this was how I presented myself to the world, it was no wonder he left me.

I went into Cos, a shop I had never entered because I thought it too grown-up for me. Obviously, I was an adult with the debts and stretch marks to prove it, but I had never achieved the sense of accomplishment I assumed came with being a proper grown-up lady; the mannequins in Cos looked like they knew what they were doing and how to get things done. I found a raw-silk blazer and matching trousers in my size; I didn't recognize what I saw in the changing-room mirror. Perhaps I had got it wrong. Maybe you didn't acquire the clothes after you had learned how to navigate life successfully; perhaps the clothes came first. That's what I was hoping for. After paying, I asked the woman at the counter if I could go back to the changing room and put the suit on.

'Of course,' she said. 'Big day?' The biggest.

When I walked into the office, Bettina stood and clapped.

'I knew this time would come,' she said as I reached my desk.

'I'll take it as a compliment.'

'You should, because it is one. You look amazing. I thought you were sick.'

'Thank you.' From Bettina it meant something. I appreciated being around someone who meant what they said. 'I'm fine. I'm glad I caught you. I want to take you for a drink tonight.' Bettina held the hem of my blazer and rubbed the material between her thumb and forefinger.

'I'm certainly not going to argue with that.'

'It can be a celebration.'

'Of what?' She put her hands on her hips. 'You're already married, and you're not stupid enough to have got yourself up the duff again. You're not leaving me, are you? You can't. Shit, this is why the bullshit illness and the fancy get-up.'

'No.' I grabbed her forearms. 'I promise I'm not leaving. In fact, I want to spend a lot more time together. I want to ask you to work with me on the art show, on a lot of other projects going forward. I want us to form a kind of division.'

'Why?'

'Because I'm good and you're amazing, and because I

don't want us to get stuck and then become disposable.' Bettina squinted at me.

'Are you sure you're OK, Alison? You have this wild look in your eyes.'

'I'm fine. I will be fine. I know what I've got to do.' Bettina pulled away from me; she looked a little afraid. 'I'm fine. I promise. Wait for me, I won't be long.'

'Where are you going?'

'To give the performance of my life.'

Carter did an actual double take.

'Alison?' he asked, as if he doubted it was me.

I wanted to say, 'It's just a suit – underneath it all I'm the same,' but instead I said, 'I want to try something different.'

'I'm listening,' said Carter, and he was. He was leaning forward, his energy completely focused.

'Anoushka doesn't want an event, she wants a career, and I think we can be the people to launch it. Rather than doing a one-off show, I want to help her do a series of showcases highlighting up-and-coming artists. We'll create a team around her and provide a full package of communications and marketing support. We'll be making art accessible to a whole new generation, and introducing new artists to the world on a much larger scale.' My palms were sweating. I wiped them on my new trousers.

'To the world?' Carter coughed, but I could see the smile it was trying to conceal. Part of me wanted to retreat, the part that felt she was wobbling away on a life raft, constantly waiting for the sea to overturn her. But another part of me was willing to plough forward, the part of me that didn't care how much she lost because so much had already been taken away from her. Frank gave me that.

'To the world. The first show will be a presentation of

the work of the artist Charlie X. The real stage will be social media, but the actual event will take place in ten days in Berlin.' Carter rubbed the back of his neck. He did this when he was thinking; he had never done it much when talking to me.

'That sounds like a lot to pull off in such a short timescale.'

'I can do it, but I'll need a team.'

'I can't spare people at such short notice.'

'I'll take Bettina and I've already sourced a freelancer.' He looked surprised by my forthrightness and I was a little surprised too.

'And you're OK?'

'I'm fine. I'm great.'

'But your husband said . . .'

'It comes and goes, and now it's gone.' Carter returned to his laptop.

'OK, look, get me a brief tonight and I'll sign off. I'm impressed with your ambition, Alison.' I stood up and smoothed down my blazer.

'I always say go big or go home,' I said. Although I never say that and I no longer had a home to go to.

38

BETTINA WAS SILENT for the longest time. I waited; I was growing better at that. Eventually she took another mouthful of wine, then said, 'You want me to help you launch this project in Berlin?'

'Exactly.'

'But why? It's not what I do. I mean, I write tags and blurbs and websites. I don't launch anything; I don't think I have the outfit for it.'

'We'll go shopping. In Berlin. I know you can do more than you're giving right now. If we were men, this wouldn't seem crazy. We'd simply be taking our rightful place in the world. Look at Tom, when did he start?'

'Five minutes ago,' said Bettina with a generous eye roll.

'And now he's running a department. That's not because he's good.'

'He's all right,' Bettina conceded.

'Exactly. All right. When you have a penis you can get away with being all right, as long as at the same time you shout about how bloody amazing you are. But you don't shout, even though you're amazing.'

'And you're amazing, honey.'

'I know.' I didn't know this at all, but I was giving the hard sell and it felt important to be able to fake it. I had meant the advice I offered to Nush after her break-up; the best course of action was to make your ex see you as successful. I didn't know then about the footnote explaining that you secretly hoped it would make him want you again. I didn't have doubts about what I was doing; I didn't consider that following Frank across Europe might cause him to see me as an unhinged, rabbit-boiling psychopath, and I didn't consider the ethics of pulling my friend into my dysfunction. I think that's what an affair can do: with all that time living in an altered reality, you no longer feel the need to observe the rules of civil society. Of course, Bettina said yes because she trusted me, and when you trust someone and they unleash that level of enthusiasm on you, why would you question their motives?

I called Nush; she told me she was having drinks in The Ned. I instructed her to sit tight until I arrived and, knowing that even this instruction might prove too complicated, I raced across town. After several minutes wandering round the same block, I found the door. The entrance was discreet and plain; you wouldn't notice it if you weren't looking. Clearly, they didn't want riff-raff wandering in for a pint or pee. I could feel the events of the day catching up with me. The base of my spine had started to call out for attention and little white blobs appeared to be floating in front of my eyes, but Nush was the last hurdle so I knew I had to push on. Behind the door I was bombarded with unfamiliar sounds – live piano music, crystal glasses chiming against each other, the rolling laughter of rich, contented people. Nush had said 'The Ned' as if it was her friendly local, yet the main bar hosted more people than I had at my wedding.

'Alison!' she called from somewhere within the crowd. She was standing on a banquette, beckoning me with two hands. As I approached, she fell back down to her seat, wobbling dangerously on landing. She was held steady by two young men on either side of her; two women sat across from them. It reminded me of my twenties – long evenings spent planning and dreaming over cheap bottles of wine. The place was palatial but in essence it *was* Nush's local.

'Darling,' said Nush. 'This is Bryce.' She indicated the man on her left, a lanky guy with a scraggy beard.

'Hey,' he drawled. I nodded a greeting. Nush introduced the rest of the group and I let the flurry of names wash over me. I needed to focus. They weren't interested in me anyway; probably I wasn't young or beautiful enough. Even in my new suit, I guess I didn't look powerful enough. I didn't care.

'Ladies, gentlemen,' I said, working my face into a smile that I could feel wouldn't look genuine. 'Could you give Nush and me some time?' They all turned to her, awaiting instruction like primary-school children.

'It's cool,' said Nush, 'I'll catch up with you at the club.' They dutifully tipped back the last of their drinks and gathered their belongings. Entering a scenario where Nush was the person in charge helped me to push aside any doubts about what I was engineering. I admit they were there – a little voice, low but insistent, that I should be spending the time with my children; my conscience tap, tap, tapping me on the shoulder. I spoke loudly and clearly to drown it out.

'Sorry to ambush you, but we need to speak about the show.'

'Am I in trouble?' Her eyes became wide and warned of tears.

'No, far from it.' Rather than looking relieved, Nush seemed perplexed. At least she was aware that it would be unrealistic for me to be impressed with her performance to date. 'I don't think I've ever made clear how expansive I think your idea is. I've been thinking about it and I believe we've underestimated the scale of the potential.' Nush winced; to her, potential meant work and not opportunity. 'Rather than executing one show, which is just one chance to make an impact, we need to do a series. It will increase the amount of exposure you and each artist gets.'

Nush pouted. Her eyes danced over to the bar. She was growing bored, not only with me but with the whole project. I couldn't really blame her. Why bother working when you could have a man look after you? I had failed her; used her as a cash cow when I could have been showing her how important it is for a woman to follow her passions and build something for herself. 'There's a couple of great angles to this. Firstly, we get to move it forward really speedily, get things going immediately. You can prove yourself to the industry, to the world, but if things don't pan out, we haven't lost too much.' I knew the last part would clinch it – everyone loves an escape route. Nush opened and closed her mouth a few times, without speaking. I could tell she was trying to configure the right words to let me down with. I was not going to allow it. 'Nush, can I tell you what I'm worried about?' She tipped her head, which I took as a yes. 'If we don't press ahead with this now, right now, we'll lose momentum, and then your father will have invested all this money and . . .' I left her to finish the sentence herself. I was sure she would come up with something far scarier than I could imagine. I didn't know if there would be any consequence; it was cruel of me to suggest there would be, but life is cruel. I kept talking. I did the same with the girls when they were young, ensuring they wouldn't have time to analyse my words before more came; ensuring the speech was delivered with so much energy and warmth that they would absorb this and not question the message. When I ran out of steam, Nush tipped her head in the other direction.

'I'm not sure. I mean, organizing this internationally sounds like a lot.' I wanted to scream. She picked this moment to be thoughtful and cautious?

'It won't be because I'm going to pull a team together.'

'A whole team? Won't that cost more?'

'We can fit it all into the existing budget.' Which was true because the budget was ludicrous.

'A team,' said Nush. 'OK. What do you need from me?' I wanted to laugh that this was what had clinched it. A team made her feel important; maybe it's what we're all looking for, and everything would be easier if we could admit it. I told her I would take care of the logistics, but she needed to brief Charlie and get a list of what he required sent to me by the morning. 'I'm seeing him in a bit,' she said. 'I'll get dates he's available in the next two weeks and then meet him tomorrow for deets.'

'Great. Remember, as soon as possible – let's get moving. I'll send venue details in the next couple of days.'

'Fab. Ooh it's happening! I'm excited.' It felt like we were working together for the first time since we met.

I went back to the flat; it took a while. I had to keep stopping to remind myself where I was going. When I got back, I wanted to do nothing other than fall face first into a massive glass of wine, but I had one more call to make.

'I have a job for you.'

'What kind of job? Because you know I don't fix stuff. My experience is mainly in breaking shit. Remember when I blew up the microwave.'

'A real job, Henry. Effort in exchange for money.'

'I'm listening . . .'

'I was really impressed with you yesterday. How you got things sorted.'

'I'm sorry, can you say that again?'

'I was impressed with you. You stepped up to the plate.'

'That first bit. One more time.'

'Henry, don't ruin this.'

'OK. I'll be your glorified PA or whatever it is. My rate is fifty an hour.'

'You'll get a grand for the whole project.'

'Deal.'

I lay back on the mattress. I could feel the suit crumpling beneath me, but I couldn't summon the will to take it off. Alone in the dark, I had misgivings about whether I could pull it off; whether Frank had taken too much from me. But I found it was helpful to have a purpose.

In the morning, when I woke at dawn, I redirected the repetitive cycle of turbulent thoughts into action. Nush had come through and sent me a few dates and Charlie's contact details by text at four in the morning. Knowing nothing about Berlin and even less about setting up an art show, I was able to secure a venue. I was amazed by how much you can do when fuelled by spite. I set Henry up with a Gmail address and then sent him the details of the venue, asking him to find flights and a hotel for the whole team. I hadn't had a team since my last job. I hadn't realized it, but I had avoided the situation because the last experience had ended so painfully. There was a line in Frank's book: *You can try and hide from fear but it will find you.* I was stepping into the light.

I called Charlie and invited myself to his studio. He grunted down the line that he would accept my presence. I put several coats of concealer under my eyes, hoping MAC could offer me the impression of alertness. When I arrived, Charlie was on all fours examining a large map on the floor. His focus was totally channelled into his work. I might not have appreciated his art but I respected the energy that went into it, and perhaps that was what made it successful. I knelt down beside him. He barely reacted to my presence; he sat back on his knees, so we were side by side as if worshipping together.

'Hi,' I said. In response, he ran his hand up and down the back of his neck.

'Do you think this is a bit too literal?' I looked at the map. It was ripped around the edges and looked damp in places. Dotted about it were images of penises, all different shapes, sizes and states of arousal.

'Um, I'm gonna say it depends on what you're trying to say?'

'It's not obvious?' I shook my head and tried to look more apologetic than amused.

'I found the porn in Soho. Abandoned in an alley. I guess people don't bother with literature that much any more. I found the map in Finchley bus station – well, stole it. So, the cocks represent places I've had sex, but only the throwaway experiences.' I leaned in to examine the work. An incredibly long thin member was stuck on Wood Green library.

'Now you've explained it, I guess it is a bit . . . um, literal.' Charlie pulled the map from the floor and tore it to pieces. I gasped. Not that I thought it was worthy of much else, but his ability to react and move on was strangely thrilling. I stood up. 'You're on board with Berlin.'

'Absolutely,' he said. 'Very fitting with my style. Who do you have shipping the art?'

I realized I had a lot to learn in a very short amount of time.

39

'I HAVEN'T COME TO talk,' I told Dylan. 'We will, but I understand that now isn't the time.' I delivered this from outside the house. Dylan had opened the door but not completely, just enough to wedge his body into the gap.

'I told them you were on a trip, remember,' he whispered. I nodded because I understood the instinct to conceal the truth, but it irritated me that he couldn't see how it would do more harm in the long run.

'I am going on a trip actually, but before I leave, I need to see my girls. And explain what's going on, so they don't try and fill in the gaps or think it's about them.'

'Isn't it?' said Dylan. 'Isn't it a bit about them?' He knew me, and maybe I had dismissed and disregarded him precisely because of this, because he understood the parts of me that I wanted to pretend weren't real. I moved towards him, he remained unnaturally still. I reached up to his shoulder and pulled him towards me. He didn't respond but didn't resist as I pressed my lips against his. There was nothing right about the moment – in fact it was completely inappropriate – but I'd suddenly realized that I could not remember the last time we had kissed, and knew I might never have the opportunity again.

'Dylan, I'm so sorry.' Such a silly word. I was embarrassed by it, how small and weak it sounded. When I stepped back, Dylan let his head sink to his chest, like he had grown tired of holding it up.

'Is that Mum?!' Chloe's voice rang out from the hallway, excitement causing her pitch to rise an octave. Something else I had forgotten: how overt the love of a child is, especially when they are young and have not learned to hide it. When they were babies, I would leave the room for a few seconds and return to squeals of delight. Dylan stepped back and let me into the hallway. Chloe bounced on the spot and declared that she needed to show me a 'cerfiticate' she got for spelling. I didn't correct her; I hoped in that moment that no one ever would and she could preserve a tiny piece of childhood for ever. I gave her a hug and told her I was proud.

'Get your sister and tell her to come to the living room.'

Dylan and I waited on chairs in opposite corners of the room. The place was a mess. A small pile of pizza boxes lay next to my feet and half the glasses we owned were dotted around the room. I cleared my throat and stopped my eyes from settling in any one place. I wasn't in a position to judge. Chloe bounded in; Ruby trailed behind her. Ruby seemed older, even more beautiful. I had looked away and she'd scrambled up the rungs of the ladder to womanhood. 'Sit down, girls,' I said. Chloe complied and, after a pause to demonstrate she was making the decision for herself, Ruby did the same. I left space for Dylan to speak; he folded his arms and leaned back into his seat. I was on my own. 'Girls, I'm not going to be around for a while. Your dad's told you I'm going to be away working for a bit.' Ruby glanced at Dylan and they exchanged a look I couldn't decipher. 'After that, I'll be back and we'll plan something nice together. Maybe go away for a couple of weeks, but your dad and I . . .' A memory forced its way into my consciousness. The three of them had sat in exactly the same way when I told them about the redundancy. I remember reminding myself to keep it together and reassuring them that everything would be OK, even though I didn't believe it to be true. Every member of a family has a role to play and there are no understudies. I had to be strong; it was my part. 'Your dad and I have some things we need to sort out. Things might be a bit muddled for a while. I'm not going to stay here, just for a little bit. But we still love you both, very much. Very, very much.' Chloe looked from me to her father a few times, and when neither of us added anything further she smiled sweetly and threw herself on me.

'As long as you come back and live here and you can come to my summer festival,' she said into my neck.

I pushed her away gently so that we were face to face as I said, 'That's the thing, sweet pea. I might not move back here. But I will definitely, absolutely come to your festival.' Chloe sucked on her bottom lip for a few seconds.

'I guess across the road is OK,' she said. 'Can I go on the tablet?'

'Sure,' I said, and she ran off.

I turned to Ruby. Her head was down, and at first I thought she was laughing but then the laughs began to take on a hissing sound preceded by great gulps of air, and I understood that she was having a panic attack. I rubbed her back, and when she calmed I pulled her to me, and even though we were nearly the same size she climbed on to my lap and sobbed and sobbed.

*

314

Eddie taught me to ride a bike. He took me to the park three weekends in a row. I was timid at first, conscious that I was learning too late and afraid that he would grow impatient with me. He didn't. By the third weekend, I could ride the length of the main path, Eddie close behind shouting words of encouragement.

'I did it!' I shouted when we reached the gate. We didn't hug much, but I was overcome with exhilaration and wrapped my arms around him.

'You did it,' said Eddie, dabbing at his forehead with a hanky. 'Do you want to try again without me holding on?'

Working on the art show, I felt the way I had that day. All the time I'd thought I'd been working hard, but I'd had other people holding me up. In the past, I would canvass opinions and replicate the work of others; now I had a deadline, and that meant decisions that I made quickly and without second-guessing myself. I made the decision to work from home, telling Carter it would help me avoid distractions. The lumpy sofa became my desk and the flat my temporary office. We would have two days in Berlin before the show, enough time to prepare and hopefully enough to find Frank.

I met Henry, Bettina and Nush in a local bar to finalize things a few days before we left. Henry was there early and, when he saw me, he pulled out a laptop.

'Where'd you get that?'

'It's Dad's – he doesn't use it.'

'How's he doing?'

'It's kind of hard to tell. He's not been doing much but I don't think it's the brain stuff, I think he's depressed. I mean, that's brain stuff but, yunno, different brain stuff.' I made a note on my mental to-do list to visit him as soon as we were back. Bettina interrupted my thoughts.

'Why are we meeting in the hood?' she asked, brushing off her seat before sitting down.

Henry started to speak but I talked over him. 'I met with an artist close to here. Possible choice for the second event. Let's get this one in the bag though,' I said, shooting him a threatening look.

'Yes, let's. I've got so many ideas. I didn't really sleep last night – I look a state.' She looked radiant. 'And this must be Henry.' She extended her hand. 'I've heard a lot about you – none of it was very good.' Henry had enough manners to look bashful.

'I'm sure my sister has exaggerated,' he said.

'I hope so,' Bettina said firmly, 'because we've got work to do and there's no time for games.' Henry nodded obediently. 'But first, let's have a drink.' We shared a bottle of red. Henry and Bettina had an unexpected rapport; he was happy to tolerate the schoolmarm tone she took with him and diligently recorded all the ideas she threw out. I knew the evening should have been enjoyable, but for some reason I felt like I was a spectator, watching it unfold.

40

Henry with his battered backpack; Nush with her monogrammed trunk; Bettina with her matching brown leather bags; and me with the big suitcase that carried my life. We were a team, maybe one on the brink of relegation, but united. Doing my best to avert disaster from the offset, I'd fibbed to Nush about the departure time and had everyone meet me an hour early.

I took the lead, steering us all through security. It felt not unlike going away with Dylan and the girls. Bettina, never a morning person, was giving Ruby a run for her money in surliness; Nush was as excitable as Chloe; and Henry exactly like Dylan at airports – lost. We hadn't been on holiday for a couple of years; the redundancy and my sense of unease at work had made me cautious about spending money. When I'd got my promotion and didn't yet know how doomed it was, I celebrated by booking us a holiday, forgetting that a holiday for a mother isn't really a holiday. There were the weeks of research and then days of getting everyone organized and then sorting out the practicalities of getting to the airport. By the time we arrived at Gatwick, I wanted to leave them all behind and have my holiday at home alone. I told Dylan I was going to buy sunscreen, and then read the backs of the bottles in

Boots until they called our plane. This time I sat with my makeshift family at the gate.

At Schönefeld, Henry gave the driver the name of the hotel, and twenty minutes later we arrived at the sleek, modern building.

'I approve,' I said, as I took a bottle of still water from a basket on the reception desk.

'It was the best for our budget,' said Henry.

'Well done,' I said. He looked down at the chequered floor bashfully, then distributed the keys; we were all on the same corridor.

'Let's freshen up and then have our first planning meeting at four. Why don't you guys get something to eat and I'll check in on the venue.'

'Is there a gym?' asked Nush.

'Yeah,' said Henry. 'It's open till ten.'

'I'm off then,' said Nush. She was starting to impress me. I began to think that underneath the lashes and histrionics was a focused and disciplined woman. 'That's where the fit guys will be,' she added.

'Do you want me to come with you?' Bettina asked me.

'No, thanks. Why don't you and Henry eat and get started on reconfirming the guest list. I won't be long.'

'Great,' said Bettina. 'This is so exciting, Alison. Call me if you need anything, but if not we'll see you in the bar at four?'

'Brilliant. And don't worry, I'll be fine.' As I walked away, I heard Bettina telling Henry about the website. It had been a black screen with the word 'Rebel' in white until she launched it the night before. It was great to hear her so animated and know that I was responsible for it, but I wasn't excited – I was uneasy, because from the moment we landed in Germany my thoughts had turned to Frank.

I left my bag with the concierge, and grabbed a taxi to a hotel that was in the same chain as the one we'd stayed at in Birmingham. I figured I could see him, have our confrontation, and continue with the preparation for the show unburdened and clear headed. The reception was decorated with the same fixtures as its Brummie sibling, and it felt like stepping back. I entertained the possibility that if he was there, we could also step back to how we felt.

The receptionist didn't share my dream; she refused to tell me if Frank was staying. She said, 'It's against the rules, I'm afraid,' although she was young and elegant and exuded confidence, and I didn't believe she was afraid of anything.

'I understand, but he's my partner and he's forgotten something important, something he really needs.' She looked behind me, where a party of middle-aged men were waiting impatiently.

'Why don't you call him?' She was right. I envied the fact that she was comfortable with that and had no desire to please. 'Would you mind moving aside?' She gestured to her right and I followed her cue. After days and late nights of frantic planning, the tiredness I had been keeping at bay took hold. I rested my arms on the counter and tried to align my thoughts. To come this far and fail was unthinkable. I didn't want to move until I had a plan because not having a plan would feel like giving up. The men checking in bombarded the receptionist with questions. She seemed much happier to assist them than she had me. Their quips and queries were incessant and jarring.

'How far are the clubs?'

'What you doing tonight?'

'You gonna have a fry-up or that continental crap?'

And then from the back, 'Where can we watch the

game?' And it occurred to me that these were men, men who liked to watch other men chase a small spherical object – as was Frank. I waited until they'd checked in, pretending to scan my phone as they made their arrangements and handed their luggage to the concierge, then I followed. I didn't do it covertly. I trailed behind them like I was a younger sibling forced to accompany her elders, but they didn't seem to notice. They led me to a bar, populated almost entirely with men. The men were a variety of shades and shapes, some glowing with the sheen of boyhood, others dulled by the years, but all holding a glass of amber liquid and staring at a wall-sized screen on which the game, the game that needed no name, was being projected. I looked for some time, examined them all; none was Frank. I tugged the sleeve of the man next to me. His eyes didn't leave the screen. The days when I could compete with eleven men were long gone.

'Is this the only place showing the game?' I asked. I thought about the things that Frank might desire. 'Somewhere quieter, where I could get food?' The man looked at me then.

'This match?' he confirmed. I guess he didn't understand why I would want to look for what I already had. I didn't let his doubt disarm me; a seed of an idea had been planted and grown into an oak. I was sure that Frank was somewhere in the city watching that match, and he didn't yet know it but he was waiting for me. I would find him, and from that he would remember that I understood him, and would no longer be afraid of whatever had scared him shitless. I was sure of it. The man said that there was another bar down the road. He didn't know the name but he was sure there was food. I thanked him and he snorted in reply.

Outside, it had started to darken and the air was heavy with promised rain. There was something mysterious about the city, dark corners and doorways looking to hold secrets. I'd like to blame Berlin and its mystery for keeping me on my ridiculous quest. When I reached the end of the road and found nothing but apartment buildings, I walked to the next; that corner was home to a metro station and it occurred to me that I had been had. I was furious – that I had trusted another man and yet another man had let me down. My anger fuelled me. I no longer wanted to just find Frank, I wanted to find him and unleash hell. I wanted him to feel the force of my hurt through my words; I wanted him to know that my life was not a game that he could toss away when the levels got too complicated. I would tell him that women, all women, including his wife, should be honoured and adored, and that if he couldn't offer that he didn't deserve anyone. I wanted to tell him he was a total penis and that his actual penis was not much to write home about, and I wanted to tell him loudly and in public because I wanted to share some of the humiliation I had been living with.

I found another bar. It was small and dusty, not at all the sort of place I would associate with Frank, but then did I really know him enough to say? The television sat above the bar, and the picture was so pixelated it was hard to tell what was showing from the entrance. I moved closer and the barman spoke sharply in German.

'I'm sorry, I'm English,' I said. He shook his head and served an older man sitting at the end of the bar. After giving his order, he turned to me.

'Pay no mind to Bart. He had a fight with his wife tonight.' His voice was friendly and lived-in, every word sounding as if it concealed a laugh. 'Here, I get you a beer.'

'No, no thank you. I'm looking for someone.'

'Ah, yes,' he said, and his eyes sparkled. 'Tell me. Maybe I know them.' I could hear he was hungry for distraction. The barman set down a pint and pushed the glass across the bar in my direction.

'It's fine,' I said, backing away.

'No. Sit. I'm Albert.' I was tired and thirsty and so sober, more sober than I had ever felt, and the thought of blurring the edges was very tempting. I climbed on to the stool next to him. He chuckled as he watched me take several mouthfuls of beer. 'See, you need drink. Who has got away from you?' I knew it was unintentional but the words were crushing; even this stranger knew that someone needed to run from me. 'It must be a lover,' said Albert when I didn't respond. 'A man, I assume.'

'He . . . I thought he loved me,' I said. I looked into Albert's eyes, dark blue with yellowing whites; they looked like they might have seen enough to understand. He placed a hand over mine. His skin was leathery and cracked but still soft.

'If a man doesn't want to be found, he won't be,' he said. 'You must not cry.' I wiped my face with my sleeve, unaware I was.

'It's fine. I'm tired,' I told him. I was – tired of so many things. The balls of my feet hurt, my phone had run out of battery, and my heart felt so broken I could barely understand how blood kept pumping around my body. I asked him where I could find my hotel. After some discussion with the surly bartender, he informed me that I was on the right road but warned that the road was very, very long. I thanked him for the drink and his wisdom and left.

The road *was* long. Parts were lined with bars and restaurants; much more of it was dim and desolate. I should have felt afraid but I had nothing left to lose. Despite what

Albert had said, I kept looking. I slowed down to peer into every bar window and scan each hotel reception. Age didn't mean that he knew what was true. I was the oldest I had ever been and less sure of myself then ever.

At the hotel, Bettina was in the lobby. She had her legs crossed in front of her and a laptop balanced on top of them. Her hair was tied back in a bun and her long, pale neck was exposed as she leaned forward to examine the screen. She looked comfortable and capable and beautiful; I didn't really want to speak to her. But as I watched she looked up, and I felt unable to walk away.

'What happened to you?' she asked, as I sat next to her on the sofa. 'I've been calling and calling.'

'It's dead,' I said, and threw my mobile on to the hard-wood floor.

'Is everything OK with the venue?' The venue could have burned to the ground for all I cared. I nodded. 'The balcony is usable, right?' I scanned the room for someone who could bring me alcohol.

'Do they come over or do I have to go to the bar?'

'The balcony?'

I sat back in the sofa; it was so big that my feet dangled off the edge. I used one foot and then the other to push my shoes off, and let my head fall back so that all I could see was the sparkling chandeliers.

'I don't know.'

'You don't know? The art's arriving in the morning. We don't have insurance – if one of Charlie's wacky installations falls through the ceiling, we're fucked.'

'Yes. I mean, I know it is, but no.'

'Can you mean something that makes sense?' It became too much, all of it. I felt groggy and confused. Like when you wake up from a dream in which you're running and running but not sure if you're heading towards something or being chased.

'I didn't go.' Bettina placed her laptop on the table in front of us.

'Why?'

'I didn't have time.'

'Then what the hell have you been doing? If you were planning to bunk off and go sightseeing, you should at least have taken me with you.'

'I wasn't sightseeing. I was trying . . . I needed . . .' Bettina reached out for me, and the action made tears come again.

'Jesus, you're stressed. There's so much buzz about the show, you don't need to worry. It will be great. Let me get you up to speed.' I was backed into a corner and all I had left was honesty.

'Bettina, I need to tell you something.'

'Well, that sounds ominous.' I considered retracting the statement, but she noticed my hesitation and squeezed my thigh. 'I'm joking, don't worry. You can tell me anything.' She said this so solemnly that I thought maybe she could be imagining far worse than what had happened; that maybe in my own mind I had inflated it all. After the briefest of pauses, I began with the book launch.

'That was ages ago,' she said, after I tried to recount the night Frank and I met.

'Not really, it's gone so quickly.'

'It was. It was before I met Tristan.'

'I guess so.'

'Why didn't you say anything?'

'It caught me off guard. I didn't know what was happening, and then he took me for dinner and I thought that would be it, but—'

'Did you sleep with him?!' In her question was all the judgement I had feared.

'Yes, but please listen, it wasn't sex. I got caught up in something bigger than me, do you know what I mean?' Her face told me that she didn't. 'Please. Please, Bettina, let me explain.'

I told her everything – about the boat, the break-up and the wife, and finally why I'd chosen Berlin for our joint endeavour. Bettina sat silently, open mouthed and blinking. When I'd finished she shook her head.

'You're here for a man?'

'I mean, sort of, not really. I'm here for the show but also for closure.' She moved to the edge of the sofa. I could no longer see her expression but what I imagined wasn't good.

'Basically, we're *all* here because of some random man. You've taken me away from my work and my life so you can chase a dude.'

'No. No. Try to understand. He took my life from me.' She moved enough that I could see her profile – naturally thick lashes, full lips, and a small bump on her nose that she always tried to hide in photos.

'No, Alison,' she said, 'you handed it to him. And then you bring me on, claim you want to work together, and you're doing it for a man?' I could hear her anger gaining momentum with each word. 'Which is bad enough, but made far worse by the fact that you already have one!'

'No,' I whispered, 'I wanted to do it, work with you I mean, I always have. I genuinely think you're brilliant, but also . . . I needed a way to get close to him. I wanted him to see me as successful.'

'Successful? Successful as what? A crazy person? For God's sake, what does that even mean?'

'I don't know, making things happen, being in control . . .' Yet I felt completely untethered.

'What do you need to make happen? You have everything. Lovely house, *husband*, kids.'

'Yes, yes.' How could I explain that I *did* have everything but something was still missing? 'But Betty, I didn't feel—'

'Fuck feelings. You're so ungrateful. You had it all and you risked that for a man. And you already have a man – a good one!' I couldn't hide my frustration. I needed her to see how entangled everything was.

I pulled at her arm as I said, 'You don't know Dylan. You see the tiniest bit of our life. It's not that easy, Bettina. You don't trick some bloke into marrying you and then all your problems are gone. Like poof, the ring is on and I'm happily ever after.' Bettina looked like I had slapped her, or maybe like she wanted to slap me. 'I mean, I met someone, someone else. I was in love when I married Dylan, but then I met Frank and thought maybe I'd found the one.' She shook her head so fast her bun started to slide down from its perch.

'Jesus, Alison, you're not twelve. There's no such thing as the one. If there was, surely you wouldn't have to go through all this for him?'

'He isn't taking my calls and I wanted to be here on my own terms. You know? I didn't want him to think I was chasing him.'

'But you are!' she shouted. The lobby went silent, and I waited until the low murmurs of conversation restarted before I spoke again.

'It's not like that, you don't understand.'

'How could I? No one wants to marry me.'

'That's not what I mean.'

'You know, I always thought you were pitying me or

326

patronizing me. When I would talk to you about being single or how fucking tedious the search is, I could detect this sadness, which made me feel like shit but I accepted it because, really, it is quite sad. But what you've done is so much more pathetic.' I shuffled to the edge of the sofa, to address her face to face.

'I don't get why you're so angry. Yes, I've fucked up, but I really wasn't using you or anybody. You know I want the show to be a success.'

'I don't know anything because you don't tell me.' She slammed her laptop closed. 'I had other work I could be doing. I thought you wanted to start something with me, and you were trying to start something with a bloke.'

'I did want to work with you. I do.'

'Why would I believe you? You've been lying to me this whole time.'

'I wasn't lying, Bettina. Yes, I kept some parts of my life private, but to be fair we're colleagues – it's not healthy to share everything.'

'We're colleagues, right. Got it.' She slurped loudly from a glass of wine resting on the table.

'You want another?'

'Nope, wouldn't be right to get drunk with a colleague.'

'I didn't mean it like that. I mean, we're friends of course, but friends who work together.'

'Yes. Colleagues.'

'Betty—'

'I broke up with Tristan. He didn't want me to come here. It meant missing his sister's wedding. He told me I would have to choose. And I didn't tell you because I didn't want to stress you out. Because generally I pretty much tell you everything.'

327

'Not everything . . .'

'Everything. When my diaphragm got stuck, who did I call?'

'I know, Betty, but this was different. This was about my family and—'

'I wouldn't understand.' She nodded and finished the last of her drink. 'Everything's ready for the show. Marcus has scheduled all the media to go out. I'm gonna head back to London. I don't want to get behind on my work.'

'Bettina, you're taking this—'

She stood up and tucked her computer under her arm. 'Night, Alison. Best of luck with whatever it is you think you want to achieve.'

41

M Y ALARM RANG. I had set it to birdsong; I thought
bringing nature into the room would make waking
up feel less violent, but opening my eyes was no less dis-
tressing than it was every morning. I was miserable; I
wanted to shoot those birds. I stared at the ceiling, trying
to untangle the actual events of the day before from my
frantic, fretful dreams. Mostly the nightmare was real. I
pushed my fingers into my mouth, pleased to find my teeth
in place. My room phone rang.

'Yeah?' I croaked into the receiver.

'Wake up,' said Henry. 'I know how much you love
your mornings so I'm sending you breakfast. I've convinced the cute chick on reception to let us use one of
their meeting rooms as a base today. Meet us downstairs
in forty-five.' I pulled my body off the mattress; muscles
I didn't know I had ached. When I opened the curtains
and let the day in, the city stretched out beyond what I
could see and I digested how insane my mission had been.
My time with Frank had felt so magical that I somehow
believed that my need to see him would overpower reality. There was a knock at the door; it was time to let
reality in.

In the meeting room Nush was curled up in the only

comfortable seat, a high-backed wing chair in the corner. She had a throw wrapped round her and a pair of over-sized sunglasses obscuring most of her face. Henry was at the table slamming the keys of his laptop.

'What happened to Bettina?' he asked before I could sit down. 'She sent me an email in the middle of the night saying she was off the project.'

'Yeah, something came up,' I replied. 'Can I get a coffee?' Henry ignored my request. He pushed his scraggly fringe back from his head, revealing a streak of grey that had developed in his dark locks.

'Mate, that's not on. If anyone knows about bailing it's me, and this is a bad time to bail. She was running the ticketing system and I can't make any sense of it.'

'Give it here and go get me a coffee.' Henry pushed the screen towards me and left the room, muttering something about incompetency. The open window displayed a mish-mash of numbers and names; I had no idea whether what I was looking at was good or bad, and not enough energy to begin to work it out. 'Nush, you must have heard from your contacts. How many people have you got coming?' Nush let out a low moan. 'Nush?'

'I don't know!' she shrieked, pulling the throw over her head. 'Stop nagging me.'

'This isn't nagging, Nush. If you don't get your act together, you will understand what nagging is. You will feel the full force of me at peak nagging, and believe me I could get a master's degree in nagging. You will not survive it.' Nush pulled her glasses down to peer at me. The previous night's eye make-up had melted and spread into the appearance of two black eyes. 'Get out your phone. Check Instagram, see how many people are liking your stuff or whatever. Give me numbers.' It seemed to be taking a lot more effort than normal to breathe. I had been so focused on finding Frank that I'd missed the fact that if the event failed, Carter would lose all faith in me; Nush, or rather her daddy, would stop paying me, and the house of cards I had spent twenty years meticulously building would topple down.

The door flew open and the promise of caffeine momentarily lifted my spirits, but it was Charlie who burst into the room and he wasn't holding a latte.

'The venue are being completely unreasonable about *Picnic*. They're saying it's indecent.' He began pacing the length of the room in the manner of a very important man considering an equally important decision, but with a black vest revealing his pale, spindly arms he looked more like a toddler gearing up for a tantrum. '*Picnic* is the cornerstone of the collection,' he cried. 'If you don't get *Picnic*, you don't get me!' *Picnic* was a collection of found condoms; Charlie had foraged them from parks and woodland areas in and around London. Art is subjective but it was objectively gross.

'Charlie, leave *Picnic* for a more aligned audience. You have so many other . . . wonderful pieces. If anything, I wonder if it would detract from all that.' I made an effort to appear as though I really was in that very second wondering, when in fact I was silently screaming.

'Take it out!' Charlie banged a fist on the table. 'You can't just take it out. The project needs to be viewed as a whole. It's a journey.' A journey through your depraved mind, I thought. Henry rushed in, also coffeeless. Things felt very bleak.

'The drinks have arrived here,' he said breathlessly.

'They haven't. Do you see a coffee in front of me?' I said with the last of my patience.

'No, the drinks for the show, they turned up at reception. I must have given them the wrong address or something.'

'What are you going to do about *Picnic*?' demanded Charlie.

'Can you excuse me for a minute,' I muttered. I went to the women's bathroom and sat on the closed lid of one of the toilets. It was a trick I tried to use when the girls were young and I needed some time to myself. As it had then, it failed, and within a minute Nush was calling my name.

'Are you in here? We need you.' I held my breath and the room fell silent. I exhaled prematurely, alerting her to my presence. Three heavy thumps shook the stall. I wriggled out of my navy linen trousers, pushing them down to my ankles in case she peeked through the gap at the bottom of the door. 'Charlie's freaking out and he's blaming me, and people are saying that they haven't got ticket confirmation and I can't deal with this. I had about three minutes' sleep last night.'

'Anoushka, this is your show. You have to take some responsibility.' She sniffed.

'I hired you to take responsibility. You work for me.' I listened to her heels tapping on the tiles as she walked away. I considered it, but knew that hiding in the toilet for two days was not a viable option. He picked up on the second ring.

'Carter,' I said. 'I'm sorry.' There was no time for elaboration. 'I may be in over my head.'

'Why's that?' he asked, and I sensed a hint of distraction or amusement.

'Things aren't going to plan. Bettina, um, she's had to . . .' I bit down on my lower lip to compose myself. 'Bettina's gone and I don't understand the booking system. Honestly, I don't understand any of the systems we use really.' Carter was silent. I imagined him slipping off his glasses and holding the bridge of his nose, exhausted by my existence. 'Carter?' I whispered.

'Do you want to know something, Alison?' I said yes because what could he say about me that I hadn't already said to myself? I was a fraud, I was a liar, and I always bit off more than I could chew. 'Alison, no one really knows how those systems work. That's how they make money. If we knew, we probably wouldn't buy them.' Relief flooded out of me with a snort. 'Leave it with me,' he said. 'I'll get back to you shortly.' I clutched my phone tightly, my trousers still round my ankles; a small voice in my head berated me for asking a man to save me, but a louder one told me I might be beyond help. Even though I was waiting, I wasn't ready and when the phone rang, I jumped and fumbled with the slider before gushing a hurried hello.

'Carter said you needed an extra body.' Annie, her delight bouncing down the line. 'Email me some details. I can be there by late afternoon.' What could I say but yes?

I left the toilets, not quite determined but something approaching it. I was tired of losing people and things, and I wasn't willing to let the art project go. I had the sense that something good could come from Frank and me – the show would be the child that made a failed relationship worthy and, ultimately, I couldn't let Annie see me fall apart. In the meeting room Nush was snoring softly in the wing chair, the throw pulled up to her chin. Henry, hunched over the laptop, whispered, 'I think I'm getting somewhere with this.' I stood beside him and watched as he pulled names and numbers across the screen. I kissed the top of his head; he smelled a bit like sawdust.

'Thanks for sticking with it, bro.' He gave a shy smile. 'My colleague Annie's coming to replace Bettina. I'll go and finish setting up the venue and you keep going with this. Where's Charlie?'

'Not a clue.' We exchanged a look we used to in childhood, when Mum was reaching for another drink. I rang Charlie's room before combing the bar and gym. As I searched, I began to strategize – would anyone notice if the artist wasn't present? How feasible would it be to have Henry stand in as Charlie X? I couldn't spend any more time searching for a man in Berlin. I decided it was best to get to the gallery and arrange the pieces myself; if the artist had a problem with that, he would have to channel it into his next creation. For the next two days, I was in charge.

Outside, Charlie was crouched next to a large terracotta pot, a hand-rolled cigarette burning between his fingers; several discarded butts were scattered at his feet.

'Charlie? Charlie, are you crying?' He stood and threw the cigarette down with the others.

'No.' But his blotchy face said otherwise.

'I'm heading to the venue, are you ready to go?' I started towards the road.

'What's the point?' I turned slowly, to give me time to take several inhalations.

'Because we have an event starting in about thirty hours, and it's pretty much centred around you.' Charlie leaned back on to the wall behind him. I clasped my hands together to stop myself from dragging him away from it.

'My dad's an actuary, senior partner,' he said. 'Do you know what that means?'

'Not really. I mean, I have a vague idea. I can picture the type of person—'

'It means he makes a shitload of money, which means that nothing I ever do will ever be good enough. He's made that abundantly clear.' He dropped his head as though it was heavy with his thoughts. I joined him against the wall, addressing the space in front of me so I wouldn't seem too confrontational.

'Charlie, you won't know this because you're not a parent, but it's nothing like they say it is. Everyone thinks you get this tiny creature and you love it and it's as simple as that, but it's not, because nothing's simple. Yes, you love them, but sometimes you resent them for depriving you of the dreams you had or envy them for living out their own.' Charlie gave an incredulous grunt.

'Really?'

'Really,' I said. And at the time I thought I was only saying it to comfort him, but later I realized it was true. That I resented Ruby for having everything I had wanted when I was growing up, and was jealous that she used her voice to speak out against the little she had to complain about. 'I bet he wishes he had all your creativity, I bet actuarying doesn't give him much of an outlet. I bet he wears jazzy socks.' Charlie laughed, and it was light and relaxed.

'He does, lime green – they're rank.'

'See. I'm right. He wants a bit of what you have, but he only has socks. Don't let his failings become your own.' Charlie stood upright and squared his shoulders.

'Let's put on a show,' he said. I could tell he wasn't completely convinced, but he was getting there.

The venue was an old school building, converted into meeting rooms. We'd hired the entire space, and I was more than a little intimidated as Charlie and I stood in the centre of the hall, engulfed by its potential. The venue staff were young and smiley and seemed ready to help, but their English faltered and their presence was scarce when there was any real work to be done. Charlie and I set up between the two of us. He let me know in short, terse sentences how he wanted the art positioned or that I had inadvertently placed a piece upside down. And he listened carefully, hands on hips and jaw set, as I explained the importance of giving the attendees space to move and congregate. I felt harried, and sweat had glued my shirt to my back, but we were collaborating and that made me feel a lot less alone.

When the main room was finished we went upstairs to the balcony, where Charlie had decided he wanted to display *Picnic*. He had to force the door so hard that he fell forward as it opened, into an area that was definitely not as functional as advertised. Abandoned paperwork was piled around the room and the remaining floor space covered with dust so thick it looked like carpeting. Charlie swore and moved towards one of the first stack of papers. As he did, the floorboards creaked menacingly.

'Get out, Charlie!'

He let out an anguished cry before shouting, 'Everything's fucked!' The noise disturbed a pigeon that had been concealed somewhere in the rafters; it flew haphazardly above our heads before crashing into a window and plummeting to the floor, to turn in jerky circles.

'Come on,' I said. 'I'll sort it.' He followed me to reception, where two of the staff members were engaged in a conversation too animated to be about work.

'I need to speak with someone about the balcony.' The pair, a young man with a bleached-blond crew cut and a girl with visible tattoos and large black-rimmed glasses, stopped talking and stared at me blankly. 'The balcony, it seems unsafe and it's very dirty.'

'Dirty,' said the boy with a smile, and then disappeared into a small office behind the desk. Charlie and I waited in heavy silence. The girl didn't move from her position, her inked arms hanging limply by her sides. 'Dirty,' the boy said again, as he re-emerged clutching a wooden broom. Charlie slammed his forehead on to the desk, and the sound of the impact echoed around the space. The girl looked alarmed but the boy maintained his satisfied smile.

'No . . .' I cleared my throat. 'I don't want to clean it, I want it to be usable now, as stated in our contract.'

'You don't want it clean?' asked the boy. Charlie, who had not removed his face from the counter, began to bounce his head rhythmically on the wood.

'No, I want it clean but I don't want to do it, I want it to be done.' My pitch rose as I felt things start to slip out of control yet again. A stern female voice came from behind me; I didn't understand the German but the commanding tone was universal.

The boy's smile drooped and he whispered a halting, 'I'm sorry.'

'Finally,' I said. 'Someone in charge.'

'I don't know about that,' said Annie, as she slipped in between Charlie and me. I flip-flopped between awe and annoyance as she conversed with the boy, but by the time she had finished I had landed on acceptance. 'Jasper and his colleague will stay tonight to help with the event and clean up, and he'll speak to the owner about a partial refund. Henry's nearly finished the ticketing system and then he'll head over with Nush; in the meantime, Charlie, please introduce me to your art.'

From the moment Annie arrived, Charlie softened and became completely malleable. I'm sure her looks helped – it would be difficult for any red-blooded man not to submit to those charms – but it wasn't just that: she knew exactly what to say and how to say it. She convinced him to save the condom piece for his next show. 'I like to save something for later,' she said, just suggestively enough to remain professional. She cajoled the venue staff like a benevolent dictator, and under her watchful eye they began to resemble useful members of society. When Annie asked me what food I wanted her to order, I realized I was famished.

'I could literally eat anything,' I said. 'And thank you.'

'It's no problem.' She pulled her hair back from her face and secured a ponytail with a band she had on her wrist. It was one of those ones that looks like an old-style phone cord; I was always finding them between the sofa cushions.

'Annie. Thanks for everything – for coming and, well, just being you.' Annie did her nose wrinkle.

'Well, I can't be anyone else, can I?'

'No,' I told her, 'you really can't.'

Henry arrived triumphant from taming the ticketing system, and spent the rest of the day emailing Berlin's movers and shakers with the location; even Nush stayed sober long enough to post some intriguing set-up pictures on her numerous social media accounts. At the very end of the day Annie, Henry, Nush and I squeezed on to one of the hotel-lobby sofas and toasted our efforts with a bottle of champagne. I was proud of them and myself. I'd achieved something that felt like it could be spectacular, and for the first time I didn't feel like I was faking.

The show *was* spectacular. Charlie flicked an internal switch and overnight transformed himself from a doubt-ridden wannabe to a bona fide artist. Annie had Henry man the door with her, and even when things got backed up they flirted the crowd into submission. Line after line of people shuffled into the hall to gawp in wonder at Charlie's imaginings; they were delighted to have the man himself explaining the deep symbolism behind used gum. I tried to stay in the shadows; I wanted to watch it unfold, witness all those people enjoying what I had created, and all the time I never gave up hope that one of those people would be him.

'We did it!' screamed Nush, as she caught me carrying discarded champagne flutes to the kitchen. She didn't wait for me to put them down before pulling me to her.

'Ooh, we're nearly the same height,' she breathed into my hair.

'It's the shoes,' I muttered. She held me at arm's length and examined my feet.

'You mean business,' she said.

'I do, Nush, I really do. I want to make this big.' Now it was done, I found I did. A few months previously I would never have known you could start something with one intention and end with another entirely. 'This all started with your vision, Nush.'

'I know!' she squealed; I don't think either of us really believed we would get there. 'I'm going to find Charlie. I want him to give a little speech. You too.'

'Course, I'll be out in a minute. Need to . . .' I nodded towards the glasses in my hands.

'Sure,' said Nush. She grabbed one of the flutes, still half full of booze, and took it with her as she headed back into the throng. I carried the rest to the kitchen and stacked them in the industrial dishwasher. Afterwards, I used the counter for balance as I kicked off the shoes. They were ridiculous and a sharp pain had been tormenting my left sole all evening. I lifted my foot to rub it and watched a ladder race up the length of my inside leg. I tried to readjust my tights and only succeeded in widening the hole. As I grappled with my hosiery a loud, crisp clap startled me. I looked up and he clapped again. I kept hold of the counter to steady myself as he walked towards me, continuing his slow-motion applause. Frank stopped within touching distance.

'What a performance,' he said. 'Was this all for me?'

42

H E SMILED, BUT it wasn't a smile to be shared. 'Dramatic as always.' He didn't say this the way he had in the past, laughing with me at my quirkiness and whimsy. His words were heavy and their weight left bruises. What left me even more tender was that I still wanted him to hold me. If he'd opened his arms and let me in, if I was given permission to put my cheek to his chest, I would have forgiven everything. 'You can't approach my family.' When I had fantasized about the moment, I had never imagined he would say that, and after all he had done, it was me who felt ashamed.

'I didn't know where you were,' I stammered. Each word an apology. 'Why did you go?' He grimaced. I wanted to know what he was feeling – disappointment? Disapproval? 'I sat her down and confessed everything – it was the right thing to do.' I thought of my note to Dylan; is it possible to do right when you're so deep in the wrong?

'She forgave me but said that if I saw you again, she would take my boy back to Brazil. I can't sacrifice him for you, you understand that?' I would never have expected him to. There were things that could be done – regular flights, school holidays – and we would have dealt with it together. There are always options, even if you don't like them all.

341

'But you're seeing me now.'

'For the last time.'

'But you don't love her,' I whispered.

'We're married; I have love for her.' I glanced at the door, afraid that someone would walk in to witness the scene of my greatest humiliation.

'You said you knew at the wedding,' I insisted. Hopeful, still hopeful, that something I could say would take him back to where we'd been.

'Did I?' He seemed weary. 'I don't know any more. I do love her, it's a sort of love . . .'

'Not like you love me?' There. The question I should have asked long ago but didn't think I needed to.

'You're very special,' he said. 'I mean that.'

'So why didn't you come? Why not at least say goodbye? Why run?' I could hear the desperation in my voice and did nothing to try and curtail it.

'Yes, the timing wasn't great. I accept that, but I thought it best to have distance from the situation.' His hand went to his pocket; I could see him toying with his lighter. 'Fucking hell, she made it completely clear I couldn't have any contact with you.' I wasn't sure what to believe. The woman who made tea and calmly requested I stop destroying her life didn't seem like the type to make demands, but then again, I probably didn't seem like the type to lie and cheat. 'It looks good, the event. You did well.' Him saying that, him seeing it, didn't feel as good as I had anticipated. The feeling I used to have, that he was never bored with me and would always want more of me, was gone. I knew I was on borrowed time.

'Your son is only a baby.' I remembered how I was in the first months, aching and vulnerable.

'People don't talk about how fatherhood affects men.

That was probably part of it, if I'm honest.' Frank's brow furrowed as he formulated his theory.

'*Are* you honest? That's what I've been asking myself over and over again. Were you lying to me about everything? It can't all have been in my head.' His left cheek twitched as he tried to conceal the truth yet again and pretend that he didn't want to laugh.

'You know, I didn't realize how vulnerable you were at first,' he said. He moved forward but stopped short of touching me. He removed his hand from his pocket and displayed his palms. 'And then you had so much happening with work and your kids, and I wanted to be there for you.' He spoke in a careful manner, like he was delivering one of his speeches and I, as the grateful audience, was expected to lap it up. No more. No way.

'You are so full of shit! I don't know how I didn't see it.' He did laugh then, although he didn't convince me that he thought what I'd said was funny.

'You saw what you wanted to see. You wanted to leave your husband so you constructed a . . . a story, and now you're angry I'm not playing my part.'

'This wasn't a story!' He stepped away from me and retrieved his cigarettes from the inside of his jacket. I was losing him again. 'It wasn't about leaving, it was about starting something.' I jabbed a finger towards him. 'I've got all the messages you sent me. I have evidence of the things you said.'

His jaw stiffened. 'I thought maybe we could meet and have something to eat and put this to bed, but I can see that can't happen. This has to be it, Alison. You were having problems, I wanted to be there for you, but we let things cross the line. I'm sorry about that.'

'Sorry,' I said. 'Sorry? Sorry!' He backed away. 'You're

a liar, you're nothing but a liar.' He shook his head, not in defence of himself but with pity for me. 'You lied and lied.'

'Goodbye, Alison,' he said, before placing the cigarette between his lips.

'No!' I shouted. 'You don't walk away from me!' But he did.

'Alison?' said Annie softly. It was so soon after he'd left that I knew she must have heard some of what had occurred, but I couldn't bring myself to care. 'They're asking for you out there,' she said. When I didn't respond, she came towards me slowly and placed her hand under my chin to lift my face. 'Are you OK? Can you speak?' The event had been a success; I would soon discover it was the start of something big for me, but at that point I couldn't see it. I didn't believe in silver linings; there was no cosmic plan. Some things were just shit. Annie waited patiently for me to respond.

'It's all lies,' I said.

I could smell myself. It's not often that occurs. Sometimes you're aware that it's likely you might smell; that enough time has elapsed that it would certainly be beneficial to wash. But to be able to smell yourself and have that scent repulse you – that is very rare. I smelled unloved. I had been on the mattress for two days, my suitcase from Berlin still open on the floor next to me. I sent a few messages to say I was taking a couple of days to recover from the trip, and then let my phone die. I wanted to see my girls, I ached to hold them, but I didn't think I could present this version of myself. Those times when I was a kid and Mum would leave for days, I assumed it was a choice motivated by selfishness, but perhaps she was hiding – from who she was and who she couldn't be for me.

I smacked my hand against the multipack of crisps beside me; the packet crackled but there was no more crunch. I lay back down, confused as to what my next move should be. Having spent the last week making all the decisions, I couldn't do it any more. I wouldn't have responded to the thump at the door, but I thought it might be Henry with carbohydrates. It wasn't. Carter looked me up and down as one would a pet with mange: kindness tinged with disgust.

'One of your, um, neighbours let me in,' he explained. I led him to the living room.

'I'm sorry I can't offer you a drink or anything.'

'No, that's fine,' he said. Carter opened his suit jacket before sitting gingerly on the sofa. 'I'll wait for you to get ready.' I looked down at myself. I had on faded flannel maternity pyjama bottoms and a stretched, stained vest top. I returned to the bedroom and changed into my Cos suit, figuring if I was going to get fired, I might as well wear my best outfit.

'How did you know I was here?'

'I asked your contractor; his details were on file.'

'Henry?'

'Yes, that's the one. There's been a lot of contact following the show.'

'Yes?' My head swam with hypothetical complaints.

'Yes. It seems it was very successful.' Not everything is as it seems, I thought.

'I wanted to check in with you, see when you would be ready to come back. It would be good to ride the wave.' I always thought 'ready' was a simple concept but it required a great deal of reflection – the ability to accurately predict what was to come and competently assess whether you had the resources to withstand it. I wasn't even ready to decide if I was ready. Carter made an awkward motion, his hand jerking forward as he moved the rest of his body away from me. I thought perhaps he was in pain; it seemed in line with my run of misfortune for him to have a heart attack and die on the threadbare floor. However, he stayed upright and breathing, and simply patted his extended hand very lightly on my shoulder. His attempt to offer support when it was so unnatural to him made me feel immensely grateful. 'Come back,' he said. I could tell he wasn't particularly committed to the request, but it was enough. He wanted me, wanted me enough to navigate the grimy streets of East London and to sit in my squalid living room and uncomfortably pat my arm. It wasn't much but it was more than I could have hoped for.

'I need one more day,' I told him. He stood up without comment and rebuttoned his jacket. I grabbed his hand and he stared down at my fingers in horror. 'Thank you. For coming and for giving me a chance.' Carter wriggled free. He removed his glasses and cleaned the already sparkling lenses with a little grey cloth he drew from his blazer pocket.

As he worked in tiny circles around the glass he said, 'I didn't give you anything. You created the opportunity.' He replaced his specs. I noticed that he looked better with them – they gave his face structure; without them he had a certain vulnerability that was distracting, like a reverse Clark Kent. I wondered how long he had worn glasses, whether he had been teased in the playground as a result of his sub-par vision. Of course, he hadn't come into existence completely intimidating and incredibly stylish; he had had his own journey, one that had probably involved hardships and betrayals, and he had overcome those the way I was beginning to hope I could move past my own.

'I'll see you tomorrow,' I said. I felt the urge to salute but resisted it.

43

WHEN CARTER LEFT, I sat on the floor with my laptop and tried to make my mental to-do list physical. It was long. There were items that had been languishing in the crevices of my mind for years – take Chloe to the theatre, clean out the cupboard under the stairs, find peace of mind. I knew I couldn't let myself feel overwhelmed or wait to be rescued from it all. I had no choice but to deal with each thing one by one. I started with the last thing I had itemized – visit Dad.

It was Mum who answered the door.

'You're finally here,' she said. I chose not to defend myself. What I had to give would have to be enough. 'He's in the living room.' She had a defeated air. I went through, guarding myself against what I might find. The scene looked the same as the last time I was there: Dad in his smart trousers, craning towards daytime television, like time moved differently for him and me; perhaps it did. When he saw me, he rose from his chair without comment and shuffled to the kitchen. Moments later, I heard his ancient kettle struggle to life. Mum and I settled on the sofa. She was very still and seemed sober; it was unnerving.

'He looks fine,' I whispered.

'He's not,' she said. 'See if he comes back with tea or

gravy or worse.' I couldn't imagine what could be worse than gravy in a mug.

'Is everything sorted with what's-his-name?' she said in a low tone. I couldn't be sure which 'his' she was referencing, but if sorted meant over then the answer was yes to both. I said yes, and she looked relieved. I grabbed her hand, comforted by the fact that, however hapless she was, some maternal instinct had seeped through. 'You'll be able to come on Sundays then?' I understood that the instinct wasn't maternal but self-preservation, and for once I didn't resent her for it because I knew what it meant to get lost in your own needs.

'Dad?' I called. There was no response. I left Mum on the sofa and walked quietly to the kitchen. Eddie was wiping down the counter top. He looked the same as always but I felt nervous – something about the way he was moving the cloth, pushing it repeatedly along the grouting where the Formica met the tiles, was unnatural. 'I think the water's boiled.' Without comment, he pressed the switch on the kettle and it gurgled back into action. 'Dad, are you eating? Is Mum coming to see you every day?'

'Yes, yes,' he said. I recognized the way he said it, hoping the swiftness of the words would make up for the conviction they lacked. I pulled open his fridge; inside, a cucumber sat in a puddle of its own juice and the milk was crowned with a disc of yellowing curd. I dumped the whole bottle in the bin, flinching as I heard the plastic thud on the bottom of the bagless surface.

'Was it gravy?' called Mum. I went back through to the hallway without acknowledging her. The door to the spare room was shut, as it always was, and I eased it open. Although it was stale with lack of use, the double bed was neatly made with navy-blue sheets, and there was a pile of clean towels on a folding chair in the corner.

'Dad!' I shouted as I returned to the living room. He came to the doorway of the kitchen and waited unsteadily. 'Can I move in for a while? Dylan and I have been having problems and I need somewhere to stay.' I didn't say that he also needed me and that being there might be a start in repaying him for rescuing me from my childhood, but I could tell from his posture, the way his shoulders settled and he relaxed his head against the frame, that he knew this – some things don't have to be said out loud.

I borrowed Eddie's car, so I could move in immediately. I wanted to be out of the flat both physically and emotionally. I drove back and packed up the suitcase, and when I left I posted the keys through the letterbox.

On the way back to Eddie's, I took a detour to Islington and pulled in across the road from Bettina's flat. Her curtains were open and I could see shadows from her designer candles flickering on the cream walls. I called the radio show, and had to listen to twenty minutes of anniversary messages and Phil Collins before a comforting voice told me I was 'on the air with *Late Evening Love Songs*'.

'Oh, thanks,' I said, looking back to the window. I hoped she was listening.

'What's your message and name your song,' said Larry.

'This is Alison. I don't want a love song really, well, not that sort of love, but I really do love the person I'm playing this for. She's someone who's always there for me; sees the best parts of me and accepts the not-so-good bits but expects better – that's a kind of love. And it's the kind of love we sometimes take for granted, and we don't say it enough or sometimes ever, because we're scared or we're stupid or we've been conditioned or whatever—'

'You know it's a four-hour show,' said Larry.

'Yes, sorry. I want to play this song for Bettina, Betty, because we haven't known each other that long and we don't tell each other everything, but we're there for each other every day and I want her to know how much that means to me. And I'm parked outside her house, so if she can forgive me, I'd love to see her, but I totally get if she doesn't want to.'

'Your song?'

'Yes. Sorry. Can I have "You Can Call Me Al".'

'Coming right up.'

I turned off the radio, and when I looked back outside, Bettina was standing in the window, and I could tell by the way her body was shaking that she was laughing. I got out of the car and threw my hands up in defeat. She stepped away from the glass and reappeared a minute later downstairs. I felt shy as she came over and braced myself for whatever snarky observation she would throw at me, but it didn't come. Instead, she pulled my head into her neck and squeezed.

'I love you too, you complete doughnut. When you're a single girl about town, having a good female friend is massively important. You mean a lot to me, lady, and that . . .' She separated from me to ensure I could see the sincerity in her face. 'That was the most romantic thing anyone has ever done for me.'

'Yeah, it was my *Say Anything* moment.'

'Say what?'

I groaned. 'Have you seen any films?'

Bettina flipped her hair over her shoulder. 'Do you want to come up and have some food? I've got leftover risotto.'

'I can't. I'm moving. In with my dad.' I held my hand up

to delay the expression of shock on her face. 'I need to get back.'

'OK, yeah, but what happened with the man?'

'You don't want to know.'

'That's where you're wrong. I really do want to know. I want to know everything. Immediately.'

'I need to get back,' I said again, but then I stayed for another half-hour, not noticing as the temperature dropped and the lights dimmed in the homes around us. It was like the end of an amazing date, but without all the questions about whether they're good enough or if you can really trust them, because I knew she was and that I could. When I tried to explain how Frank had beguiled me, she didn't interject the way I had anticipated she would.

'I'm sorry I went off so hard in Berlin,' she said. 'I mean, I was angry with you but I was angry with myself too, because I get it. I get the need to be seen in a certain way, by certain people, and I was so mad you didn't tell me because clearly you were going to get hurt, and I would have made you stop.'

'I know, and that's why I didn't tell you.'

'And now, what's happening with Nush and the shows?'

I stole another hug. 'A lot – I think, I hope. But I'll explain everything tomorrow. Breakfast meeting?'

'Definitely,' she said. 'I'll make up an agenda.' Bettina watched from the pavement as I belted up and pulled away. It was exhilarating to have another item crossed off my list. I knew I had many more stops to make on the way to putting my life back together, but only one more for that night.

The road was busy; everyone was home. I had to park some distance from the house. Even though I knew the path well, I trod carefully – writing to the council about

351

the lighting had been on my list. I only thought about my appearance when my finger was on the bell, but I talked myself out of backing off. I reasoned he had seen me looking worse – ravaged by flu, contorted with labour pains. He'd seen it all and still chosen me again and again. He took a while to come to the door, always did. I used to think this sluggishness was a tool to dodge responsibility, have me deal with the peddlers and campaigners and save his emotional energy, but clearly it was just his way. He didn't hide his confusion; Dylan had always been happy to have his feelings available for the world to see.

'The girls are in bed,' he said. He didn't seem angry. I would have been angry if I were him.

'I know, I'll come back. I wanted to ask you something.' I wanted to ask so many things, but I started with this. 'Do you think we could all go bowling tomorrow night?'

'Yeah, Nibs,' he replied. 'I mean, we can try.'

44

DYLAN READJUSTED HIS watch strap. Most of those watching wouldn't register it, but I knew it meant he was agitated. I felt the energy of the crowd shift, people closing conversations and turning in their chairs. All eyes on Dylan: something that before our own wedding he had described as his 'personal hell', but perhaps after what I put him through, he had reassessed that. Reading from a piece of paper, Dylan started.

'For those of you who don't know me, I'm Dylan, and it is an honour and privilege to be speaking to you all today. It's also torture, which those of you who know Mickey will know is exactly why he asked me to do it.' Everyone laughed, because it was funny but also because it was honest and open, just like him. 'No offence, mate, but I genuinely never thought I'd see this day. It's nothing short of a miracle that you've found someone who will put up with you, let alone a woman as wonderful as Diane.' There was a collective 'Awwww'; tears streamed down Mickey's face. 'I'm not going to tell any embarrassing stories about you because, frankly, there are too many to choose from, and you've all heard about the time he got arrested with his hand stuck in a letterbox in Derby, right?' I had, many times, but when, after much encouragement from the audience, Dylan told it again, I enjoyed it more than I ever had. In the past, it only reminded me of being left to host Chloe's birthday party when Dylan rushed off to save his friend. Hearing it again, I could see how loving he was, and how reliable he is, and how easy it is to believe that someone's actions are about you.

When he had finished speaking, Dylan accepted his applause graciously and then slipped out as waiters swooped in with chocolate fondants. I watched him leave through the French doors, open to let the autumn breeze in, leaving his dessert to deflate as it cooled.

'Are you girls OK?' I asked. Chloe and Ruby offered chocolatey affirmations, so I left our table and traced the path I had seen him take. In the manicured gardens, I watched cigarette smoke curling out from behind an arch of white roses and followed the trail. Standing at the end was Dylan. 'Since when have you smoked?' I asked. He took another inhalation before putting out the rest on top of a bin.

'Since I was about fourteen, but then I gave up . . . when I met you. So, I guess this is my rebellion.' I sat on a stone bench in front of the arch and indicated for him to join me.

'I didn't ask you to do that,' I said. He loosened his tie before sitting next to me.

'I wanted to. Thanks for bringing the girls.'

'I wouldn't miss it. I needed to see it with my own eyes.' Dylan tutted but when I peeked at him, he was smiling.

'Leave him alone, it's his wedding day.' I traced a figure of eight in the gravel with the toe of my shoe.

'Does it bring back memories?'

'Of course.'

'I'm sorry.' Dylan touched my knee, long enough to still me but not long enough.

'Don't be. It was a great day. How's your dad doing?'

'He's fine. As fine as he can be.' Eddie went to a residential facility a few weeks after I moved in with him. He had become so scared and confused; I could see how much he had to battle each day. I was terrified of telling him, of him thinking I had let him down, but he seemed relieved when I gave him the brochure, reassured he wouldn't be a burden. His savings and the sale of his flat would pay the expenses, and I chipped in for extras. I wanted him to have the best, and for the first time I could afford it.

Nush's father met with me a week after the show. He was extremely impressed with the success of the event, and by success he meant that Nush had turned up at all. He helped her set up an entertainment company, 'Rebel Arts'. Nush recruited me as COO and I invited Bettina to come with me. She describes herself as my right- and left-hand woman, and that's pretty accurate. Henry freelances for us sometimes, when he's not touring with his neo-soul punk band, and very, very occasionally Nush shows up to the office in Angel. Although I didn't ask, Annie let me know she wasn't ready to leave Pepperpot – she didn't feel she had 'made her mark' – and, whilst Carter wasn't pleased by my departure, he wished me luck and I think he meant it. In the business, everyone comes to me with their questions, but it doesn't feel overwhelming because I've learned that no one has the answers; it's about helping people to find their own.

I rented a place equidistant from Bettina's flat and Dylan and the girls. Chloe and Ruby come to stay every weekend. In a sad way we seemed able to arrange our lives more easily – I could focus on setting up the business in the week, and Dylan scheduled back-to-back lessons all weekend. I struggled not seeing the girls every day, but the loss amplified my appreciation – I think everyone should be given the opportunity to miss the people they care about. And I miss Dylan, I miss him the way you miss a belonging left on public transport – an urgent grip of panic, a flurry of self-flagellation, but underneath it the hope that you can make it right. Bowling became a bi-weekly trip and for two hours, we are a unit; it's astonishing how much I revel in it and all the things I'd failed to cherish for so long. When things fell apart, I wasn't sure what I felt about Dylan, but I knew immediately that I wanted what I thought I never had – a family. I had believed the lie that good things don't come easily, and Dylan came so readily I couldn't trust it. Once the company had been established and the hurt from Frank had dulled and I examined Dylan from the distance of my silent flat, I could see only what was good about him. Every now and then, I'll drink too much and send a message asking if he wants to talk, and he will message back that he isn't quite ready.

'We'll go soon,' I said. 'Let me say goodbye, in case I don't get to speak to you.' He stood and held his arms open, and when I wrapped mine around his waist, it felt like home. He patted my shoulder and pulled away.

'When you back from New York?'

'Ten days.'

'Want me to drop the girls off?'

'No, I'll come and get them.'

'Thanks.' It seemed like he was going to say more, but then he started back to the hall. I wanted to call him back but stood and watched him go. If there was more to say, there was time, and I was willing to wait.

Acknowledgements

Thank you all at Transworld, especially Francesca and Sally for being such wonderful mothers to my book.

Thanks to the writers and readers, especially Nels, Naz, Ben, Rebecca, Geraldine, Emma and Katie for our water-cooler chats.

Big thanks to my family and chosen family, especially Martin for keeping me fed, Gemma for speed-reading and Adele for 24/7 tech support.

Born and raised in London and now living in Brighton with her five-year-old son, Charlene Allcott works part-time with young people in a residential care home. She writes a parenting blog at http://www.moderate mum.co.uk/. *More Than a Mum* is her second novel, her first, *The Single Mum's Wish List*, is also published by Corgi.

THE Single Mum's WISH LIST

Charlene Allcott

Martha Ross dreams of being a singer but – for now – she's working in a call centre. She's also separating from her husband and moving back in with her parents as a single mum, toddler in tow.

Life might have thrown her a few lemons . . . but Martha's going to make a gin and tonic. It's not too late to become the woman she's always wanted to be.

Soon she realizes that in order to find lasting love and fulfilment, she needs to find herself first. But her attempts at reinvention – from writing a definitive wish list of everything she wants in a new man, to half-marathons and meditation retreats – tend to go awry in the most surprising of ways.

'One of the freshest, funniest, most exciting new voices I've read for a long time'
JANE FALLON

'Fresh and funny and REAL . . . Martha really spoke to me. She will steal everyone's heart!'
VERONICA HENRY

'Beautifully written and emotionally intelligent. I rooted for Martha from the start.'
DAILY MAIL